PENGUIN BOOKS

The Raven on the Water

'Taylor is a major talent' *Time Out*

'The most underrated crime writer in Britain today'
Val McDermid

'The master of small lives write large' Frances Fyfield

'An excellent writer' *The Times*

'Andrew Taylor is a master storyteller' *Daily Telegraph*

'A sophisticated writer with a high de⸺ ⸺erary
expertise' *New Y⸺*

'As Andrew Taylor ⸺ ⸺ill

'Like Hitc⸺ ⸺d gothic
events ⸺ normality'
T⸺ ⸺upplement

'What's rare and admirable in Taylor's fiction is his painterly
and poetic skill in transforming the humdrum into something
emblematic and important' *Literary Review*

By the same author

Caroline Minuscule

Waiting for the End of the World

Our Fathers' Lies

An Old School Tie

Freelance Death

The Second Midnight

Blacklist

Blood Relation

Toyshop

The Barred Window

The Sleeping Policeman

Odd Man Out

An Air that Kills

The Mortal Sickness

The Lover of the Grave

The Judgement of Strangers

The Suffocating Night

Where Roses Fade

The Office of the Dead

Death's Own Door

The American Boy

Call the Dying

A Stain on the Silence

The Raven
on the Water

ANDREW TAYLOR

PENGUIN BOOKS

PENGUIN BOOKS

Published by the Penguin Group
Penguin Books Ltd, 80 Strand, London WC2R ORL, England
Penguin Group (USA) Inc., 375 Hudson Street, New York, New York 10014, USA
Penguin Group (Canada), 90 Eglinton Avenue East, Suite 700, Toronto, Ontario, Canada M4P 2Y3
(a division of Pearson Penguin Canada Inc.)
Penguin Ireland, 25 St Stephen's Green, Dublin 2, Ireland
(a division of Penguin Books Ltd)
Penguin Group (Australia), 250 Camberwell Road, Camberwell, Victoria 3124, Australia
(a division of Pearson Australia Group Pty Ltd)
Penguin Books India Pvt Ltd, 11 Community Centre, Panchsheel Park, New Delhi – 110 017, India
Penguin Group (NZ), 67 Apollo Drive, Rosedale, North Shore 0632, New Zealand
(a division of Pearson New Zealand Ltd)
Penguin Books (South Africa) (Pty) Ltd, 24 Sturdee Avenue, Rosebank, Johannesburg 2196, South Africa

Penguin Books Ltd, Registered Offices: 80 Strand, London WC2R ORL, England

www.penguin.com

Published by HarperCollins 1991
Published in Penguin Books 2007

1

Set in 11.75/14 pt Monotype Garamond
Typeset by Rowland Phototypesetting Ltd, Bury St Edmunds, Suffolk
Printed in England by Clays Ltd, St Ives plc

ISBN: 978-0-141-02765-4

For Philip

One

She knew what she wanted to do was wrong.

Not really wrong. Not a sin. Not the sort of thing she would have to confess to Father Molland at St Clement's on Wednesday afternoon. After Mr Coleby's visit, she needed the relief it would give her.

John had asked her not to go up to the loft. But he hadn't forbidden her.

'Please, Lucasta,' he'd said. 'Just for me.'

'I'm not an invalid.'

'Yes, I know, dearest. But it's a heavy ladder, and you'd have to lug it all the way upstairs.'

'I'd be very careful.'

'You might slip off the stepladder. Lifting the hatch is rather tricky even for me.' He ran his finger down the nape of her neck. 'And then you'd have to haul yourself into the loft. Once you get there, it's a mine-field. It hasn't even got a proper floor. You could trap a foot between the joists or something.'

'But it's such a mess,' she said. 'I'd like to sort things out before baby arrives.'

He knelt down beside her chair. His face was only inches away from hers. His concern warmed her.

'The nesting instinct?' he said. 'But seriously – if you had an accident when I was at school, you might lie there for hours. It's not as if people are popping in and out of the house all day.'

No, this was their home; they didn't want strangers to disturb them at 29 Champney Road. That was the way it would always be. For ever and ever. Amen.

All right, dear John didn't like her going up to the loft especially when he was out of the house. She would never disobey him; she had promised. But he hadn't actually made it an order. In any case, when they had talked about it, the circumstances had been different. At the time she had had Peter in her tummy and a fall could have had serious consequences for both herself and the unborn baby.

John was very late this evening. It had been dark for hours. In termtime he worked all the hours God gave. The school didn't appreciate his dedication. She wished he would come home. She wished he had been here when that unpleasant Mr Coleby had called. Dealing with people like Mr Coleby was a man's job. John would have known exactly what to say to him.

Mr Coleby was clever. He always came when John was at school. She had been expecting Hubert Molland with the parish magazine, which was why she had answered the door.

Mr Coleby was standing right on the step. His big brown car was parked beneath the streetlamp on the road. As she opened the door, he leaned forwards. She stepped back. Too late, she realized her mistake. He was in the house. Flecks of rain sparkled on the shoulders of his navy-blue overcoat.

Mr Coleby had a loud Fen voice with broad vowels that grated on her ears. She was afraid that he would wake Peter if she talked to him in the hall. She re-treated to the sitting room. He followed. He was a big man with a square red face. The room was small and so was she; Mr Coleby was out of scale. He took up too much space, like a baby cuckoo in someone else's nest.

'Well, Mrs Redburn,' he said. 'I wondered if you'd reconsidered your position.'

She shook her head. She sat down to conceal the fact that she was trembling.

Mr Coleby sighed. 'It would be nice to get something settled by Christmas.'

Lucasta stared at the pile of library books on the table. 'There's nothing to settle.'

'Now, be reasonable.'

'Your reasons,' she said. 'Not mine.'

'You won't get a better offer.'

'Sorry. Not interested.'

He moved to the bay window, parted the curtains and looked out on Champney Road.

'It's a funny area, isn't it?' he said. 'I reckon you'd be happier somewhere like Locksley Gardens or Ivanhoe Drive.'

'I'm quite happy here, thank you,' Lucasta said.

However, she understood what he meant. Hubert Molland had said as much the other day. Champney Road was on the east side of Plumford. Here were the factories, the council estates and – just a few yards beyond the Redburns' back garden – the railway. Most of John's colleagues lived to the west of the town centre in a suburb where the professional classes clustered in a grid of tree-lined streets with names taken from the works of Sir Walter Scott.

'Not much of a house, either. Don't you find it dark?

A bit depressing? Needs a lot of work done to it. Anyone can see that.'

She shrugged. Money was tight, especially since Peter's arrival. She didn't think the house was dark. True, it faced north, but you got used to that. Number 29 was their home.

'You're quite isolated, too. Not even a telephone.' Mr Coleby peered into the darkness on either side of the streetlamp. 'Big hedge in front – needs a trim, that does. A blank wall the height of a house on your right. Can't say I'd like to live next to a bakery. And on the other side you've got all those trees on the strip of wasteland. My wasteland now. You must find it quite worrying.' He turned, slowly, and stared at her. 'Seeing as you're on your own for so much of the time.'

The little room filled with menace. It hung like a haze and obscured the outlines of the furniture. Mr Coleby was a huge shadow. His face dissolved. Only his eyes were as crisply defined as before: cold, clear and blue.

If only John were here. Lucasta touched her breast. It was full of milk. The knowledge steadied her. Peter was still feeding from her, and would continue to do so for months. She had to be strong.

The haze cleared.

'I'm afraid you're wasting your time, Mr Coleby.'

'Am I?' He raised his eyebrows. 'Why don't you have another little think about it? It's a big decision – I know that. You got to look at all the angles.'

'The decision's already –'

'Like, for example, what happens if you have an accident when you're alone in the house? Or if there's

4

a fire in the night? Or if some of the local yobbos come round in search of beer money or a bit of fun?'

Deliver me from evil, she thought. For Thine is the kingdom, the power and the glory.

'You're threatening me.'

'Me?' He chuckled. 'That's a good one. Just trying to help, Mrs Redburn, that's all. You know me. Anyway, I mustn't keep you. Don't bother – I can find my own way out. I'll be in touch.'

Mr Coleby's footsteps echoed in the uncarpeted hall. She hoped that they wouldn't wake Peter. She heard him open and close the front door. The latch on the front gate clicked. She went to the window. A moment later the big brown car pulled away from the kerb.

Lucasta went into the hall. She was tempted to bolt the door. But if she did that John wouldn't be able to let himself in with his key. She never used the bolts when John was out. *Hurry home, John.*

She listened at the bottom of the stairs. All was quiet, which was a blessing. Peter had only just begun to go through the night without demanding a feed. Unbroken nights were such a luxury. In the evenings she and John had time to be together.

Gradually the trembling stopped. She tiptoed upstairs and listened outside the door of Peter's room. She didn't dare go in: he was such a light sleeper, and he seemed to know by instinct when his mother was in the same room. She glanced upwards, at the hatch that led to the loft. The temptation was so strong it made her feel breathless.

John wouldn't mind if she went into the loft. He would understand. She would tell him about Mr

Coleby's visit and her going to the loft as soon as he came in.

She crept downstairs, through the kitchen and out into the little back garden. It was much darker on this side of the house. Behind the garden were several acres of rough pasture, which Mr Coleby had bought at the same time as he bought the strip of wasteland that linked the pasture to Champney Road. The railway ran in a cutting along the far boundary of the fields. You couldn't see the trains but you could hear them.

The stepladder was strapped to the outside wall beneath the kitchen window. John had built a little shelter for it; he was so clever with his hands. She undid the straps and carried the ladder into the house. Mindful of what John had said, she stopped to rest – once in the hall, twice on the stairs and once on the landing.

She set up the ladder beneath the hatch. Practice had made perfect: she hardly made a sound. Peter slept on.

Rung by rung, she crept up the ladder. Two-thirds of the way up, she paused to get her breath back before lifting the heavy hatch and sliding it away from the opening. A shower of gritty dust pattered on her face. Try as she might, it was impossible to keep the loft as clean as she would have liked. She climbed higher and at last managed the difficult transition from the top of the ladder to the edge of the hatch frame. She glanced down at the landing and the dizziness swept up to meet her.

'Serves you right, my girl,' she whispered. 'You know you've got no head for heights.'

Lucasta reached through the darkness for the light switch. The loft sprang to life. She sighed with relief.

The loft ran the length of the house from front to back, and it was lit by two unshaded forty-watt bulbs. Down the centre was a narrow gangway; she had placed boards across the joists to make movement easier. On either side of the gangway were neat piles of trunks, cases, cardboard boxes and tea chests – even a bed, propped on its side and wrapped in polythene. Everything was as she had left it. Everything was in apple-pie order.

For a moment she stood listening. Peter was still asleep. She walked slowly down the gangway, her eyes lingering on the treasures she passed. She paused twice. First she lifted the lid of a trunk plastered with the labels of railway companies. The smell of mothballs rose to greet her. She stroked the lapel of one of John's old suits, a Prince of Wales check that he had bought before they even met. She shut the trunk and moved on to a large cardboard box. She eased off the lid. Inside, buried in acid-free tissue paper, was her wedding dress. She closed her eyes and let her fingers burrow through the tissue paper until she felt the lace of the collar.

One day, God willing, she and John might have a daughter; one day their daughter would want to get married. Carefully she replaced the tissue paper and the lid of the box.

Her excitement grew steadily higher. On the left, near the end of the gangway, was a blue suitcase resting on top of a tea chest. John kept the photographs here. Before their marriage he had made quite a hobby of photography. Some photographs were in albums, others in envelopes and folders, and everything was neatly labelled. John was a scientist by training and inclination;

he had a passion for order. It was one of the many characteristics they shared.

She stared at the contents. Spoiled for choice, she thought, like a kid in a sweetshop. She glanced at the framed print of John at the Salpertons' wedding, which was lying on top. John had been best man; he looked so beautiful in morning dress, far more handsome than the groom.

Tonight, because of Mr Coleby's visit and because John was so late, she deserved a treat. She would compare the snaps they'd taken of Peter on the lawn in the summer with the photographs of John as a baby. She delighted in finding resemblances between father and son.

'My two men,' she crooned.

She lifted out the Salperton photograph. Underneath was a team photograph – a schoolboy cricket eleven with John the second from the right in the back row. As she lifted it out, she realized that the backing was beginning to come away from the heavy cream cardboard of the mount. Perhaps the loft was too damp to store photographs. She would have to mention it to John. She examined the edge of the mount. All it needed was a little glue. She would do it this evening. John would be pleased.

The edge of a sheet of paper between the mount and the backing caught her eye. She widened the gap and tried to see what it was. Not the print itself – that was further inside the mount. She gripped the edge of the paper between thumb and forefinger and gently pulled it out.

It was a letter written in blue ink. The handwriting

was small and upright. Lucasta knew instinctively that it belonged to a woman. There was neither date nor address.

Johnny, The doctor agrees, so there's no doubt any longer . . .

She read to the end. A mistake – it must be a mistake or a forgery.

Pain stabbed at her chest, twisting like a barbed snake. Lucasta screamed. The pain retreated. The snake was biding its time.

She stumbled down the gangway to the hatch. Sobbing for breath, she lowered herself on to the ladder. For once in her life she left the loft with the lights on and the hatch open. The letter slipped from her hand and fluttered to the landing floor.

John, how could you?

Lucasta pushed open the door of Peter's room and went in. She wanted, more than anything she had ever wanted in her life, to pick up her baby and cuddle him: to feel his warmth, to feel his need for her.

'Peter – wake up. It's Mummy.'

But the cot had gone. In its place was a narrow bed, stripped to its horsehair mattress.

'*My baby –*'

As she screamed, Lucasta remembered that she had lost even Peter. As she remembered, the barbed snake slashed across her breast. The pain radiated across her chest and pierced her neck. The snake wrapped its coils around her. She could no longer breathe.

She fell – first to her knees, then forwards on to her hands. The snake squeezed.

The dim light from the landing shone on her hands, the hands of a woman with breasts full of milk for her baby, with a husband working late at school. They were the last thing that Lucasta Redburn saw. The last thing she felt, apart from the pain, was surprise.

She recognized her wedding ring but nothing else.

The finger joints were inflamed with rheumatoid arthritis. The nails needed trimming. Wrinkles and brown spots disfigured the skin. The hands belonged to a stranger.

Two

'Coronary thrombosis.' Hubert Molland sounded surprised that Peter had asked. 'The doctor said it could have happened at any time. I'm afraid it was third time unlucky.'

Third time? Peter thought. *How typical of her not to tell me.* Behind him, the train shuddered and pulled slowly out of the station. The doors of the ticket hall were open. He stared at the darkened forecourt. Molland's rust-streaked Morris 1100, glossy with rain, was the only car in sight. Plumford felt much colder than London.

'How did it happen?'

The old man peered down at him. 'Very suddenly. She can't have felt very much. It looked as if she'd been up in the loft for something, which I suppose was rather rash in her state of health. She managed to get down the ladder. And then she collapsed in one of the bedrooms.'

His voice had the hesitancy of age. It was still flat and harsh. Years before, at Abbotsfield, Kate had told Peter that her father was tone-deaf. As a boy, Peter had been afraid of Hubert Molland.

'Who found her?' he said.

'I did. I went round this morning with the parish magazine. The milk was still on the step and the curtains were drawn. Eventually I called the police and they broke down the door. I found your phone number in her diary.'

'It was kind of you to let me know. You shouldn't have bothered to come and meet me as well.'

'I thought I could give you a lift,' Molland said. 'And there are things we need to talk about, naturally.'

He took a step in the direction of the car. Peter stayed where he was.

'Naturally?'

Molland turned back. He flapped his arms against the long, dark coat he wore. The narrow dog-collar made his neck look even longer than it was. 'Well, for example, the funeral. I've already put the arrangements in hand.'

'*You* have?'

'As her executor.'

'I see.'

'I assumed you knew. She discussed the arrangements with me not long before she died. No doubt she wanted to spare you as many decisions as possible.'

'Will there have to be a post mortem?'

'No. Dr Haines was treating her, so he has issued a death certificate. We shall need to settle a time for the service – the sooner the better. I've already had a word with the vicar and made a provisional booking for Friday afternoon. You'll need to register the death, of course, and lots of other people will have to be notified too.'

'I take it there's a will?'

'Yes – lodged with her solicitor. It's quite straight-forward.'

Peter wanted to ask about the contents of the will but that seemed in slightly bad taste. Suddenly it occurred to him that his mother might still be in her bed at

Number 29, waiting for the undertaker. He had no idea what the procedure was.

'I – er – I assume the house is empty now. There's no reason why I shouldn't stay there tonight, is there?'

'None at all. Alternatively, I booked a room for you at a bed-and-breakfast. But that doesn't matter. In any case, I'll give you a lift.'

'No, really. I can manage by myself.'

'Are you sure? It would be no trouble.'

'Quite sure,' Peter said.

'I made an appointment for us to see Mr Barnes – your mother's solicitor – at ten o'clock tomorrow morning.'

'I'll be there.'

'Number nine Church Row. You know it?'

Peter nodded.

Molland cleared his throat. 'God bless you,' he said gruffly. He limped across the pavement and clambered into his car.

Peter turned up the collar of his coat. He walked down the station approach to the main road, where he turned right. The rain had a fine and penetrating quality about it that reminded him of the oil you squirt from an aerosol can.

The old part of the town lay half a mile away in a shallow bowl, through which meandered the river that gave the town its name. The Christmas lights glittered on the tower of St Clement's Church. From the middle of the nineteenth century, the town had spread east towards the railway and, after the war, crossed over it; now it had flooded over the land between the railway and the new by-pass.

St Clement's clock chimed half-past nine as he reached the beginning of Champney Road. It was a wide street, and cars were parked continuously along both sides. The pavements glistened beneath the yellow lamplight.

He hesitated at the gate of Number 29. The house wore a permanently uncompleted air as if, sixty years before, the builder had intended it to be part of a pair of semi-detached houses but had run out of money or enthusiasm before he started on the second one.

The gate opened silently. Peter walked up the concrete path and let himself into the house. He shut the door behind him as quietly as possible. He was breathing more quickly than usual. He felt automatically for the light switch but did not turn it on.

The first thing he noticed was the tang of disinfectant, mingled with the familiar smells of polish and coal ash. The newel post of the stairs gradually emerged from the gloom, then the mirror on the hatstand and the half-open kitchen door at the end of the hall. A goods train thundered by. The silence returned, and he switched on the light.

Inside the house, nothing had changed. His mother's mackintosh dangled beside her tweed coat on the hatstand. Above them was a trilby that had belonged to Peter's father.

Yellow and brown linoleum stretched down the hall to the kitchen. The hall was a place of shadows. His mother had believed that forty-watt bulbs were perfectly adequate for overhead lights.

Peter pushed open the door to the sitting room. The sewing bag was on one side of Mrs Redburn's chair and a pile of library books, their corners aligned, on the other. His mother had read biographies and history, never fiction. She had listened to the radio occasionally but had never owned a television.

The grate was empty and swept. The coal scuttle was full. Peter suddenly realized how cold the house was. He almost ran down the hall, through the kitchen and into the little utility room that had once been a scullery. The blue pilot light glowed behind the window of the central-heating boiler but the pump was switched off. Peter snapped the knob round to its twenty-four-hour setting. Back in the hall he pushed the thermostat up to seventy-five degrees; he doubted if his mother had ever set it above sixty.

He switched on all the lights downstairs and put the kettle on to boil. He surprised himself by talking aloud: 'A nice cup of tea, that's what I need.' The cold was making him shiver. 'But first I'd better check the bedrooms.'

The ladder was propped against the landing wall. The smell of disinfectant was strongest in the little room that had once been his. The window was open. Otherwise everything was just as he remembered, even the faded yellow curtains decorated with turquoise flowers and green leaves: a relic of the 1960s. The bookshelves were empty and so, he knew, were the drawers and the wardrobe. He had taken what he wanted when he moved to London after leaving university; the rest of his possessions he had thrown away.

In the spare room, the beds were covered with embroidered bedspreads of slippery green satin. As far as he knew, no one had slept in either bed since his mother's parents died. He would sleep in one of them tonight.

Finally, he kicked open the door of his mother's room. Her nightdress was on the pillow of the double bed, her dressing gown behind the door and her hand-bag on top of the chest of drawers.

On the bedside table was a glass of water and a bible. Peter opened the drawer beneath. Inside were three bottles of pills, a card on which was printed a prayer invoking the assistance of the Virgin Mary, and a small black book. The front cover was instantly familiar: gilt lettering set in a white rectangle, with some sort of pattern behind it.

The pattern resolved itself into a jumble of items: an aeroplane, an arrow, a cricket bat, a globe, a boxing glove, a book, a set square, a pair of goggles, a stamp and a football. The title they framed said: LETTS SCHOOL-BOY DIARY. Peter glanced inside. It was a 1964 diary. The title-page was partly covered by a smear of what looked like dried blood.

Downstairs the kettle began to whistle.

Peter opened the diary at random. He was staring at the double-page for the week beginning Sunday 23 August. The thirteenth Sunday after Trinity; a full moon; the 236th day of the year. Only the Sunday had an entry, which read: *Emor. Good lunch. Richard said he saw a raven. Stupid git.*

'Oh Christ,' Peter said aloud.

Towards morning, Peter dreamed the old dream for the first time in months if not years. The diary must have sparked it off, perhaps aided by his mother's death and meeting Hubert Molland.

He was standing on the lawn at Abbotsfield, aware of wet, chilly grass beneath his bare feet, and aware, too, of the sleeping house behind him and the utter silence all around. (Surely the birds must have been singing? No birds sang, either in memory or in the dream.) He followed the path through the old orchard. He saw the pond they called the lake and the grey bulk of the Mithraeum on the farther shore.

The dawn played strange tricks with the pond: it was no longer a muddy puddle, less than ten yards in diameter, but a shining expanse of water, tinted red and silver, and fringed by a belt of trees that seemed more like a forest than the overgrown shrubbery it really was. It was very beautiful. In the dream, but not in memory, a mist rose a few feet above the surface of the water like a veil over a familiar face.

And floating on the water, partly shrouded by the mist, was a great black bird.

At that point Peter woke up, as he always did. The blankets were on the floor and his feet were freezing. Sweat, rapidly cooling, had soaked his pyjamas. A faint yellow light filtered through the thin curtains. For an instant he wasn't sure where, or when, he was. Then the cross-shaped glazing bars of the window told him he was in the spare bedroom of Number 29. Had he screamed this time? Finally he remembered that he was alone in the house, and therefore it didn't matter if he had.

'It's over,' he said aloud. 'It's all over.'

*

17

His mother's death was the first he had been intimately concerned with – his father's hardly counted, because Peter had been only thirteen at the time. He had not realized that there would be so much to do.

Mr Barnes's firm occupied a small Georgian house on the south side of St Clement's. Hubert Molland was in the waiting-room when Peter was shown in. Last night, the old man had seemed much the same as ever, but in daylight the effect of the intervening twenty years was cruelly apparent. Always thin, Molland now looked a caricature of his former self: the flesh beneath the pale, almost yellow skin seemed to have wasted away, accentuating the prominent bones beneath. The coarse, crinkled hair had faded to grey. His black suit, now tinged with green, was shiny at the elbows and knees.

Molland picked up the *Daily Telegraph* lying on the chair beside him and held it out. 'Have you seen this?'

Peter glanced at the newspaper, which was folded in four. A wavering red line enclosed one of the announcements of death:

REDBURN.—On Dec. 12, Lucasta Edith, wife of the late John Henry Redburn, of Plumford.

'Who put it in?' he demanded.

'I did.'

Peter wondered how much it had cost. 'I'm sure she wouldn't have wanted this.'

'As I told you last night, she made all the arrangements herself.' Molland's large blue eyes gazed unblinkingly at Peter. 'This is one of the things she wanted me to do. I can show you the memorandum she gave me.'

'It doesn't matter,' Peter said. 'I was surprised, that's all.'

'She was quite lucid, you know. Lonely, yes, and perhaps a little eccentric. But she knew perfectly well what she was doing.'

A secretary came into the room. 'Mr Barnes will see you now, gentlemen,' she said. She held the door open and waited for them to file through. 'Upstairs and on your left.'

Clive Barnes's room was on the first floor, over-looking the churchyard. He was a wiry man with dark, curly hair, whose cavalry twill trousers and tweed jacket clashed with the pair of trainers on his feet. Molland made the introductions.

'Do sit down.' Barnes darted behind his desk. 'I was sorry to hear about Mrs Redburn.' He rubbed his hands and looked at Peter. 'Are you familiar with the contents of the will?'

'As a matter of fact, no.'

'Mrs Redburn gave me a note about her financial position.' He opened the folder in front of him. 'That was in August, after her first heart attack.'

Peter wondered if he were the only person she hadn't bothered to tell.

'As I expect you know, most of her income dies with her: she had the old-age pension, plus a private occupational pension as the widow of your late father. The will appoints Mr Molland her executor, and you the residuary legatee. Apart from one legacy, the estate will come to you.'

'What legacy?' Peter said.

'Mrs Redburn had a life insurance policy. She's left

the proceeds from that in trust to the parish of St Clement's. Mr Molland and the vicar are the trustees. The legacy is to be used as the trustees think fit.'

'Then what does the rest of the estate consist of?'

Barnes glanced at the sheet of paper in his hand. 'Her personal possessions – jewellery, furniture and so on. Whatever is in her current account at Barclays Bank. Her savings – in August, that was about £1200 in a post-office account, and a little under £4000 in the Leeds Permanent Building Society.'

Peter was surprised his mother had managed to save so much. But £5000 wasn't exactly a fortune.

'And then, of course, there's the house itself.'

'The house? But I thought she rented it.'

Barnes looked puzzled. 'What gave you that idea?'

'I – I just assumed it, I suppose.' Peter shrugged. His mother had always flaunted her poverty as if it were a virtue, so there had been no reason to believe she owned an asset as substantial as a house. 'My mother never talked about money, you see.'

'Your parents bought it in nineteen-sixty from their landlord. Your father had taken out insurance to cover the mortgage, so after his death your mother owned it absolutely.'

Barnes went on to talk about the valuation of the estate, applying for probate and the possibility of Inheritance Tax. The possibility? But that must mean that the estate might run well into six figures.

Peter nodded every now and then, but his mind was elsewhere. He owned a house. A three-bedroom house even in Champney Road must be worth something. It changed everything. With a reasonable lump sum behind him he could afford to throw in his job, sell the London flat and move to the country. It didn't matter where so long as it was cheap. If he were careful, he could survive for years and, for the first time in his life, do exactly what he wanted.

'Right,' Barnes said, glancing at his watch. 'I'll get things moving. It should be quite simple.' He stood up. 'Do let me know if there's anything else I can do.'

Peter tried to detach himself from Molland as they left the solicitor's office. Molland, however, had other ideas, which involved visits to the vicar, the undertaker and the assistant manager at Barclays Bank. These people concentrated most of their attention on Molland, a fellow professional who talked the same language. He fought against the sensation that Molland had strapped him on a sort of conveyor belt in a factory that processed death. It seemed to Peter that everyone else had known his mother better than he had.

Afterwards, Molland drove Peter back to Number 29.

They sat in the sitting room, now unusually warm but still filled with traces of Mrs Redburn, and drank coffee. The old man insisted on taking Peter step by step through everything he had done and everything he proposed to do. Gradually it dawned on Peter that Molland wanted more than confirmation of his decisions and to demonstrate his own honesty: he honestly believed that this numbingly tedious attention to detail was doing Peter a favour by distracting him from his grief.

'I've made a list of payments I have made so far.' Molland took a sheet of paper from his pocket. 'If you'd care to –'

'Please – I've had enough for one day.'

The old man frowned. 'I'm trying to help, Peter.'

'I appreciate that.' Peter hesitated. 'What did you mean by saying that my mother was eccentric?'

A flush spread across Molland's cheeks. 'Nothing to worry about. She didn't get out much, except to church. Her mind was beginning to wander – only in the sense that she tended to get a little confused about time. I think she was rather lonely. This house must have been a lot to cope with. I was trying to persuade her to move to a retirement flat in Waverley Road.'

'I didn't see her very often.'

'No.'

'I thought she didn't want me to come.'

'On the contrary, I think she missed you.' Molland's voice was naturally hard, naturally designed for expressing disapproval.

'No,' Peter said. 'She missed my father.'

When at last he was alone, Peter went back to the sitting room and sat down at his mother's desk. On it was a solitary photograph in a silver-plated frame – of John Redburn as a young man; he was wearing uniform and sported a narrow, black moustache.

He opened the drawers. In one of them he found a collection of cheque stubs and account books that went back to the 1940s. His mother had always been careful with money. She used to dole out weekly pocket money to her husband as well as to her son. Each month, for as long as Peter could remember, she had gone through the bank statement and done the accounts. On one or two occasions the figures had failed to balance; any discrepancy deeply upset her and Peter had learned to avoid her until she had resolved it.

He sorted the contents of the desk into two piles, one for Molland and Barnes to deal with, and the other for himself to look through at his leisure. Neither the current cheque book nor the building society passbook was there. He went upstairs to find her handbag.

On the landing he noticed a piece of paper lying on the floor between the stepladder and the wall. Automatically he stopped to pick it up.

One side was blank. On the other was a letter. The writing, which was in blue ink, was small and upright, as though the writer had used a set-square for each character. The letter began without date or address:

Johnny,

The doctor agrees, so there's no doubt any longer. Darling, it's good news, really. Perhaps it's the best thing that could have happened. I don't think it will be a problem here – quite the contrary in a way. As long as it doesn't look too obviously like you, he'll be thrilled.

This had to end. We knew that from the beginning. We never had a future. Can you imagine what it would be like, for both of us (and both of them), if we did what you suggest?

Now you have given me something permanent to remember you by. I am happy, I really am. Don't write again, please. Too many people could be hurt, including you and me. Goodbye, my love.

M.

P.S. Johnny, please burn this.

Peter read the letter twice before its meaning sank in. As he walked downstairs, he read it a third time to make sure.

The letter had destroyed at one blow a certainty so obvious that he had never even questioned it: his conception of the relationship between his parents. All his life, he had taken it for granted that they loved each other to the exclusion of anyone else. In a sense John Redburn's death had made no difference to Lucasta Redburn. His hat remained in the hall; his photograph in the silver-plated frame, polished twice a week, presided over the sitting room; his memory was invoked, especially during Peter's teens, in sentences that began with the ominous words, 'I know for a fact that your father wouldn't have wanted you to . . .'

Yet the same John Redburn had had an affair – probably after his marriage, and probably with a married woman. He had wanted to continue the relationship but the woman wouldn't let him. He had made the woman pregnant, and the woman had intended to have the baby. And he had been too stupid, or perhaps too sentimental, to destroy her last letter.

Worse than that was the knowledge that his mother had found it, presumably in the loft. It had probably killed her.

What else had she found in the loft? What else had she known? What other surprises were waiting for him?

By a natural progression Peter thought of the Letts School-Boy Diary for 1964. He remembered the diary very well; it had been a Christmas present from his father in 1963. He had resolved to keep it for the whole year, egged on by his father, who had promised him a new bicycle if he succeeded. And Peter had managed nearly two-thirds of the year. But after August 23 he no longer wanted to continue; the present was best forgotten as soon as it slipped into the past. In any case, by Christmas 1964 his father had been too ill to remember his promise and too poor to fulfil it even if he had.

He had no idea what he had done with the diary. In all probability he had thrown it out with the rest when he had moved to London in 1973.

'Are you sure you want to throw all that away?' she'd said. She was standing in the doorway of the sitting room, watching him carry the first of the cardboard boxes downstairs. 'I could store them in the loft for you instead.'

Peter had marched on down the hall. 'I'm not going to want this stuff.' Regiments of Airfix soldiers. *Eagle* Annuals and Dinky Toys, both of which had now become collector's items. Old school exercise books. A Hornby clockwork train and a Number 4 Meccano set, both of which had given far more pleasure to John Redburn than they had to his son. An embarrassing collection of clothes from the 1960s – hipsters, a floral tie and a pair of suede boots that Peter had once loved more than anything in the world.

'Well, it's up to you.' Lucasta Redburn rubbed her hands together as though washing them in invisible soap and water, a sign of displeasure. 'You'll regret it one day.'

At the time Peter had felt a condescending pity: a defect of her personality, no doubt exacerbated by the deprivations of war and the poverty of peace, had made an obsessive hoarder of her.

Now he had to face the possibility that his mother

had combed through the cardboard boxes he had left by the dustbins, searching for things that were too good to throw away and also, perhaps, for clues about himself. God knew what she had found.

Emor. Good lunch. Richard said he saw a raven. Stupid git.

There had been letters, other diaries and all the secret debris of adolescence. He remembered in particular a long and mawkish poem he had written when his father died: an attempt to create emotions that hadn't existed.

Peter picked up the photograph of John Redburn. The eyes were narrowed against the sun. A pipe projected from one corner of the smiling mouth.

On paper, Peter could have described his mother's face in terms of its component parts but he could not visualize it as a whole. When he tried, all he saw in his mind was a blurred grey oval. Oddly enough, his father, whom Peter had known for a much shorter time, was quite distinct in his memory, right down to the smell of Palmolive shaving cream and Gold Leaf cigarettes.

On the last occasion he had seen his mother, which was when he came down to Plumford for lunch at Easter, he had thought that to all outward appearances she was exactly the same as she had always been. Throughout his life, it had seemed to him, she hadn't changed. The same narrow, lined face, the same grey eyes, the same grey hair with the same permanent wave. Circumstances like time and widowhood and loneliness had failed to make a mark on his mother. She was stronger than they were.

It was nonsense, of course – he knew that now. She must have changed over nearly forty years; he'd simply failed to notice.

26

Suddenly he was angry. Deliberately, he lifted the photograph and flung it at the fireplace.

The silver-plated frame winked at him as it turned over and over in the air. It smashed into the pastel tiles above the grate. The glass shattered.

On the afternoon of Friday 15 December, the rain stopped, the sun came out and the temperature rose. To his surprise, Peter almost enjoyed the funeral.

It was not a well-attended affair – perhaps fifteen people, mainly old women, at the church, few of whom came on to the cemetery. During the service, Peter was agreeably conscious that they were all looking at him as he sat in splendid isolation in one of the front pews. His role as chief mourner gave him a certain glamour.

He paid little attention to the service itself. Molland's voice grated away in the chancel. Peter speculated about the rest of the congregation and thought about the future. That morning he had visited several estate agents, and his researches indicated that Number 29 might be worth as much as £80,000. The sale of his flat should raise, once the mortgage was repaid, something in the region of £20,000.

After the service, the other mourners came to offer their condolences. Some of the faces were vaguely familiar. A tall woman of about forty, who had sat at the back, slipped away without speaking to anyone. At the time Peter supposed she was either a connoisseur of funerals or a casual visitor who, finding herself in the middle of the funeral, had stayed because she was too embarrassed to leave. St Clement's was one of the better-known wool-churches of East Anglia, and even in winter it attracted tourists.

The last in the queue to shake his hand was a large, red-faced man of about his own age. He was decorously dressed in a navy-blue overcoat, a black tie and a dark suit.

He seized Peter's hand and pumped it up and down. 'Sorry to hear about your mum. I saw her quite recently. Thought I'd pay my respects.' The accent was local. 'You remember me, don't you?'

'Sorry,' Peter said. 'I left Plumford a long time ago.'

'Wise man. I'm Bill. Bill Coleby.'

The name unlocked Peter's memory: Coleby, a farmer's son, had been in the same year as Peter at Plumford Grammar School. They'd been almost-friends for six years. At sixteen, Coleby left school with two 'O' levels, while Peter went on to the sixth form.

Puzzled, Peter said: 'I didn't realize you knew my mother.'

'Oh yes.' Coleby smiled. 'Look, will you be in Plumford over the weekend?'

Peter nodded.

'Well, why don't we meet for a drink? Or better still for lunch. What about tomorrow?'

Peter said yes because it was easier than saying no.

'Great. Saloon bar of the Angel, 12.45: how does that suit you? We'll take it from there.'

'That'd be fine.'

'Okay.' Coleby smiled, and Peter thought there was a touch of relief on his face. 'Till tomorrow then. Bye.'

Peter watched him as he walked down to the lych gate.

Hubert Molland was at his elbow. 'The cemetery, Peter,' he said sternly. He too was watching Coleby.

'Do you know him?' Peter asked.

'Bill Coleby?' The voice was harsher than before. 'I imagine everyone in Plumford has heard of Bill Coleby.'

Peter had planned a small and solitary celebration for Friday evening. On the way back from the cemetery he visited Sainsbury's and bought half a pound of fillet steak, the materials for a green salad and a bottle of champagne. After dinner he planned to make a proper start on sorting out the contents of the house.

The steak was hissing in the frying pan and he was slicing Chinese leaf on the kitchen table when the doorbell rang. He threw down the knife, turned off the gas ring and stamped down the hall.

But it wasn't Hubert Molland on an errand of Christian mercy. It was the tall woman who had slipped away after the funeral service.

'Mr Redburn? I'm sorry to disturb you. I would have phoned but . . .'

'No, we're not on the phone,' Peter said. 'What can I do for you?'

'Well – I saw the announcement in the *Telegraph*.' The voice was low and hesitant. 'I happened to be in the area and Lucasta Redburn's not a common name, especially in a town the size of Plumford.'

'You knew my mother?' Peter said gently.

The woman smiled. Her hair was short and dark, and she had a long face with a mobile mouth and crooked teeth.

'I met her once, a long time ago. She and your father

stayed with my parents. But in fact I knew you much better. Look, I'm not explaining this very well. You probably won't remember me. I'm Virginia Salperton.'

Peter stared at her. He thought: *Emor. Good lunch. Richard said he saw a raven. Stupid git.*

'Have I come at a bad time?' Ginny said. 'Or perhaps I shouldn't have come at all. Do be honest.'

She took a step backwards, and suddenly he realized that it hadn't been easy for her to come here.

'I can tell you exactly when I saw you last,' Peter said, the urge to surprise her briefly triumphing over the other emotions she aroused. 'It was in nineteen sixty-four. Sunday the twenty-third of August.'

Three

'Lucasta Redburn died on Tuesday,' Ginny Salperton said. 'Did you know?'

Barbara Quest stopped shaking the salad dressing. 'Who?'

'Lucasta Redburn.' Ginny wondered if she had imagined the flash of panic on Barbara's face. 'You remember – Peter's mother.'

'Oh, *her*. No, I didn't know. Why should I? I haven't seen her since I left Plumford, and I saw as little as possible of her before that.'

'There was an announcement in the paper – the *Telegraph*, I think. My mother saw it.'

'Really? Come to think of it, weren't your parents quite friendly with the Redburns at one time?' Barbara had put down the salad dressing and was examining her face in a small mirror. She dabbed at a smudge of lipstick with a tissue. 'It's an extraordinary name, isn't it? Lucasta, I mean. Most inappropriate. Makes you think of – I don't know – buxom Restoration beauties in yards of satin and lace.'

'The literal meaning is "chaste Lucy",' Ginny said.

'Are you sure?' Barbara put down the mirror. 'Would you mind if we eat in here? I've already laid the dining-room table for dinner.'

'Of course not. Who's coming?'

'Just family: James and Kate. I don't suppose you'd

31

like to come too? It's always a little tense when there's just the four of us. You could spend the night if you wanted. The spare bed's made up.'

'David's expecting me. I'd better not.'

Barbara, never the subtlest of people, was trying very hard to change the subject. She was one of nature's ostriches, the sort of person who tries to deal with anything unpleasant by pretending it doesn't exist.

'I went to the funeral yesterday,' Ginny said. 'Hubert took the service.'

'Lucasta was just the sort of woman he used to like. Knew all the responses and had a suitable respect for the cloth. No sense of humour. At least she didn't gossip, I'll give her that. How did she die?'

'Heart attack, I think.'

'She can't have been more than seventy,' Barbara said with a hint of anxiety; she herself was in her middle-sixties. 'Where did I put the peppercorns, darling?'

'Behind the salad bowl.' Another diversion? 'Do you remember the husband? What was he like?'

'John Redburn? Quite human, really, compared with her. Liked a laugh. I think Lucasta bullied him. He was always rather subdued when she was around. And then of course he got ill. Why do you want to know?'

'I just wondered. Seeing the name in the paper triggered a lot of memories.'

'You can ask your parents about John Redburn,' Barbara said, and her voice was unusually sharp. 'They knew him much better than I did. Why ever did you go to the funeral?'

'I was driving back from a conference in Norwich, and I wanted to see the church in any case. It was interesting to meet Peter again. You know he's a writer?'

'Yes, someone did mention it.' Turning her back to Ginny, Barbara tugged open a drawer and took her time over choosing the cutlery. 'Tell me, how did Hubert look?'

So she didn't mind talking about Hubert Molland. That was natural enough. Divorced people almost always nursed a fierce and secret fascination for the subsequent doings of their former partners.

'Old, rather weary. He's retired, according to Peter.'

'And he went back to Plumford? There's no accounting for tastes.'

'Why shouldn't he live in Plumford?'

'Because all the old cats will be sniggering at him behind his back, that's why. Tattling about him over the teacups. And about me.'

'But that was twenty years ago.'

'What's that got to do with it? Hubert's still the clergyman with the flighty wife, the one who used to play cards on Sunday and then did a bunk on him. Oh, they'll remember, all right. They hadn't had such fun for years.'

'I'm sorry. Maybe I shouldn't have mentioned it.'

'Don't be silly, darling. *I'm* not upset. It's just that Hubert was always such a fool when I knew him, and I hoped he might have acquired a little common sense in the meantime. Stupid of me.'

Ginny laid the table while Barbara broke four eggs in a bowl and whisked them vigorously. She seasoned the mixture and poured it into the pan.

'So you actually talked to Peter? Did he recognize you?'

'No – I had to introduce myself.'

A pause. The omelette sizzled in the cast-iron pan. Barbara patted her blonde-rinsed hair. She looked at least fifteen years younger than she was.

'I'm surprised he remembered you. It was all so long ago.'

'We all remember,' Ginny said. 'We had dinner together last night. Peter cooked it – fillet steak and champagne, no less.'

'Lucasta must be turning in her grave. Celebrating, was he? Or consoling himself?'

Ginny shrugged. 'I didn't ask.'

Barbara was bending over the hob, edging a spatula between the side of the pan and the omelette. 'It seems a little odd.'

'The steak and champagne?'

'No. Your going out of your way to see him again.'

'It was an impulse. I suppose I've got to the age when I've started to find the past interesting.'

'Look forward, darling, that's my motto; don't look back. Will you see him again?'

'Maybe. I liked him.'

'When was the last time you met?'

'At Abbotsfield.' *On Sunday 23 August 1964.* Ginny moved towards the window. From there she could see Barbara's profile.

'The omelette's ready,' Barbara said. A tear welled up in her eye and rolled down her cheek, leaving a streak of eye make-up behind it. 'It's the onions. I knew I shouldn't have put any in the salad. They always make me cry.'

*

'So what are you doing with yourself these days?' Bill Coleby asked.

'I work part-time in a library,' Peter said, and as usual a hint of apology crept into his voice. 'Just to pay the mortgage and keep the wolf from the door. Really, I'm a writer.'

As he heard himself speak, he realized he must be a little tipsy. He wasn't used to alcohol at lunchtime. Normally he kept quiet about the writing.

'That's interesting. Stories, is it?'

Peter nodded.

'What kind? I like a good thriller myself but I never have time to read them.'

'Just novels.'

The conversation followed the usual pattern.

'I don't think I've seen your books in the shops. Sell well, do they?'

'I won a prize, actually.'

Coleby looked impressed. 'So you're quite a celebrity.'

'I wouldn't say that.' Peter had won a south-east regional first novel award in 1976 for a book that had sold 2186 copies before being remaindered. Since then he had been trying to write the second book.

Coleby refilled their glasses. They had had two large whiskies in the bar downstairs, and they were now near the end of a bottle of Château Margaux.

'How do you get your ideas? Do you just sit around and wait for inspiration?'

'It's not quite as simple as that. Writing's ninety-nine per cent perspiration.'

Coleby threw back his head and laughed. 'I like it.

Perspiration, not inspiration. That's a good one. What are you working on now?'

'It's a novel called *London*. A metropolitan epic.'

'Sounds fascinating. How long does it take you, a book like that?'

'It depends.' So far *London* had taken Peter over thirteen years, and all he had to show for it was six box files bulging with notes, newspaper cuttings and botched openings. 'This one's going to be big – about a hundred and fifty thousand words. It's not the sort of thing you can dash off in a couple of months. I may have to give up my job in order to finish it.'

'You could afford to do that? Have your publishers given you an advance?'

'Not exactly.'

'Sometimes you have to invest in yourself. Me, I've been doing that all my life.'

Peter seized on the opening. 'Hubert Molland said you're a builder.'

Coleby speared a slice of lamb and grinned across the table. 'Quite a lot of other things, too. Diversify: that's the secret.'

'I thought you were going to be a farmer.'

'Like Dad? Never much fancied it myself. No, we sold off thirty acres to a developer in nineteen seventy-three and that was a lot easier than working. So I developed five acres on my own account and things just went on from there. Can't complain. It makes a decent living.'

Rather more than decent, Peter guessed. He judged by the Bentley in the Angel's courtyard, the Margaux that wasn't even on the wine list and the deference verging on sycophancy that the headwaiter showed towards Bill Coleby. At school, however, Coleby had been one of those brainless nonentities who never belong entirely to any one social group, who seem destined for failure. Plumford Grammar School, like all societies, mysteriously created its second-class citizens and Bill Coleby had been one of them.

'I remember the farm,' Peter said slowly, trying to recall something he and Coleby had done together. 'We used to pelt the pigs with rotten potatoes.'

'So we did. God, the things we got up to.'

'Do you remember Emor?'

Ginny hadn't mentioned Emor last night but her very existence was a reminder of it. And of course the 1964 diary and the Abbotsfield dream had already stirred up Peter's memories, like sticks stirring the bottom of a muddy pond.

'Emor? What was that?'

It was difficult to know how genuine Coleby's ignorance was. True, he had only been on the periphery, a bit-part player who could usefully be dragooned into secondary roles when a little muscle was required.

'A sort of game we used to play. I thought you were involved in it but maybe you weren't.'

A game? Ernor was a lot of things, but to call it a game was doing it an injustice.

'I know some people say their schooldays were the best days of their life.' Coleby finished his wine and signalled to the head waiter. 'Load of rubbish, if you ask me. If someone offered me my life again, I'd ask to be born aged sixteen. Otherwise, no thanks.'

They ordered puddings from the trolley. Coleby

seemed disappointed when Peter turned down the offer of another bottle of wine.

'What are your plans, then? I suppose if you're a writer you can do it anywhere. Must be wonderful.'

'I'm not quite sure. If I leave my job, there's no reason to stay in London.'

'Even for the book?' Coleby looked puzzled. 'I thought you said it was called *London*.'

'It is but it's not that sort of novel.' It was impossible to explain to someone like Coleby that the London of *London* was essentially a metaphor. 'I don't actually have to live there while I'm writing it.'

Coleby wasn't listening: 'But you won't come back to Plumford, will you?'

Returning to Plumford was the last thing that Peter intended to do. Coleby was leaning forward, his small blue eyes gleaming in his bland red face.

'I could do, I suppose,' Peter said. 'You said you'd seen my mother recently?'

'Yes.' Coleby shrugged. 'There's no point in beating round the bush. I wanted to buy her house. I presume it's your house now. I offered her a good price but she wasn't selling. I was hoping maybe we could discuss it.'

'Why do you want to buy it?'

'It's not the house I want, Peter, it's the ground it's standing on. You know the land at the back of your garden? The fields that go down to the railway?'

Peter nodded; and the memories came, unbidden and unwanted: the Field of Mars, the arena and the Dacian swamps where once an army had drowned.

'I own it now. I've got outline planning permission for a shopping complex with secondary access to

Champney Road via that bit of wasteland by your house. The trouble is, it's not wide enough. To be perfectly frank, I need Number 29 if I'm going to go ahead with the scheme.'

'So why wouldn't my mother sell?'

Coleby made a coffee-pouring gesture at the waiter. 'At first I thought she was against the project, full stop. It's aroused a little local opposition. Anything like that always does, even though it's in line with the Structure Plan and the District Council's in favour. So I tried raising the price – that works with a lot of people; you'd be surprised. She wouldn't have got seventy-five thousand for that place, not with the planning permission on the land behind. So I offered her ninety-five. Then a hundred and ten. She wouldn't budge. If you ask me she didn't give a monkey's about the shopping complex or the money. She just wanted to stay in that house. Some people – old folks, especially – get like that: too attached to bricks and mortar for their own good.'

'I see,' Peter said, and waited.

'Well, the offer's still on the table. Tell you what, no point in cutting corners, I'll make it one-fifteen. How does that grab you? And remember, I'm a cash buyer. No messing about with estate agents' percentages and other people's mortgages. I can get you a banker's draft by Monday morning.'

'I'd like to think about it,' Peter said. 'It's a big decision.'

Coleby stared at him across the table. Peter looked away – out of the Angel's big bay window, across Market Street to the Dutch gables of the old town hall.

'But you can't want to *live* there, surely?' Coleby said. 'Not somewhere like Champney Road.'

'I don't know what I want.' Among other things, Peter wanted to enjoy the brief sensation of power that Coleby's offer had given him. 'I just want to think about it, okay?'

'Don't take too long. You never know, I might change my mind.'

'More chocolate mousse, James?' Leo Quest asked, raising his black, bushy eyebrows. 'Sometimes a man must live dangerously.'

'Not for me, thanks.'

'You're probably right.' Leo spooned some into his own bowl. 'It is rather fattening. I imagine you have to watch your figure.'

Barbara Quest exchanged glances with her daughter.

Kate said quickly, 'Have I told you the latest about Carinish Court?'

'No,' Barbara lied. 'Not another disaster?'

'Deathwatch beetle,' Leo said. 'Rising damp. Subsidence in the stables. That worrying crack on the north wall. Repointing, rewiring, replastering, redecorating.' His memory, as always, was uncomfortably accurate. 'That's the trouble with these old houses. They just gobble up money, don't they?'

'No, it's good news, actually.' James smiled at Barbara, and she found herself smiling back; his charm was the kind that, while it is directed at you, makes you feel you are the only person in the world. Its power had nothing to do with sexual attraction, and a great deal to do with wanting to be liked. 'Believe it or not,' he went on, 'the place should be habitable by Christmas.'

'So the builders have nearly finished?'

'I wouldn't go as far as that.' James switched the charm to his wife. 'Did you tell your mother about the drains?'

Kate launched into an account of the problems associated with Victorian drainage, notably lack of maintenance in the past and rats in the present.

Barbara frowned at Leo, who pretended not to notice. Men were so childish. It was not as if James had ever given Leo any justification for disliking him. But Leo, usually the most tolerant of men, had suddenly decided shortly after James and Kate's wedding that he didn't like his stepson-in-law.

He refused to give his reasons. Barbara suspected they boiled down to plain jealousy. Leo was plump, dark and old, and James was lean, fair and young. Leo had dragged himself up from the East End, where his father, a first-generation Jewish immigrant from the Ukraine, had worked as a tailor's cutter; James, on the other hand, had had one of those privileged English upbringings. Leo had climbed laboriously up the promotional ladder of merchant banking to one of the higher rungs, earning every penny of his salary, whereas James seemed to accumulate money without even trying. Leo, bless him, was as ugly as sin; and James had been referred to by more than one gossip columnist as a sex symbol.

All good things come to an end, even drains. When Kate ran out of material, Leo leapt back into the conversation.

'How's the autobiography going?' he enquired. He knew of course, because Barbara had told him, that James had already missed one deadline and was more than likely to miss another.

'Slowly, I'm afraid,' James said. 'Now we've finished the last series of *Pemberley*, I hope I can get down to some serious work on it.'

'I can't tell you how much I'm looking forward to reading it. Who did you say your publisher was?'

'Channel 20 Books.'

'I don't think I've heard of them.' Leo managed to imply that if he, a collector of twentieth-century first editions, hadn't heard of the firm, there must be something seriously wrong with it.

'They're relatively new. They specialize in media-related stuff. Television tie-ins, that sort of thing.'

'You must show me their list some time. Perhaps they're collectable. Have you got a title yet?'

'No, not yet.'

'Well, there's no urgency, is there?' Kate said. 'I'd leave that till last.'

'Anyone like some cheese?' Barbara said. 'Just help yourselves.'

Leo refused to be deflected. 'Perhaps we can think of something. *Salperton on Salperton*? No, too dull. How about *A Person from Pemberley*? Or something straight-forward like *My Life and Times*?'

'I might have a bit of Brie,' Kate said.

Leo passed her the cheeseboard. 'Now, what about –'

'Did I tell you that Ginny came to lunch today?' Barbara said to no one in particular.

'What about *My Struggle*?' Leo suggested.

'She told me Lucasta Redburn's dead. Ginny went to the funeral.'

Leo was interested in other people's deaths. 'And who on earth is Lucasta Redburn?'

'Before your time, darling. Someone we used to know at Plumford.'

'Peter's mother,' Kate said.

Two seconds of silence ticked by. Barbara thought, why did she have to bring Peter into it?

'I remember her,' James said. 'She and her husband stayed at Carinish Court.' He looked from Barbara to Kate. 'It was years ago, wasn't it? When Peter was at Abbotsfield with you.'

Usually none of them talked about Abbotsfield, including Leo, who knew the outline of what had happened.

'Your mother saw the announcement in the paper,' Barbara said to James. 'And Ginny was in the area so she decided to go.'

'Was Peter there?' Kate said.

Barbara nodded. 'They had dinner together.'

'How *is* old Peter?' James asked, contributing to the elaborate pretence that everyone was thinking about the Redburns, not Abbotsfield.

'Apparently he's a writer,' she said.

'Always had a lot of imagination.' James dropped a crumb of Stilton on the tablecloth. Frowning, for he was fastidious in all his personal habits, he picked it up between thumb and index finger, deposited it on his plate and wiped the soiled fingers on his napkin. 'Where's he living these days?'

'London, I think.'

'Perhaps he could give you a few tips,' Leo said. 'I'm sure he'd be only too glad to help a fellow author.'

'Well, I hope you're satisfied,' Barbara said when Kate and James had left.

'Yes, indeed.' Leo was stacking plates and bowls in ascending order of size on the dining-room table. 'A wonderful meal.'

'You know what I mean.'

'I would be if Kate were happy.'

He looked at her and for once he wasn't smiling; the mischief had drained out of him. From the first Leo had treated Kate as his own daughter and her marriage to James hadn't changed that. Kate was family: she mattered to him.

'But it's ridiculous. I've never seen such a perfect couple.'

'A marriage made in heaven?'

'I should know if there were something wrong. You know what I think it is? You've got a chip on your shoulder about James.'

'Perhaps.' Leo carried the pile of crockery into the kitchen and began to load it into the dishwasher.

Barbara followed. His quietness frightened her. 'What's wrong with him?'

At last Leo exploded. 'On the contrary, everything is almost offensively right. The way he looks. His haircut, with that floppy bit of hair at the front he always has. Know why? So he can look boyish and appealing when he sweeps it back off his forehead. And those oh-so-perfect suits he wears. The charm he switches on and off like an electric fire. The flat in Montpelier Square. And now Carinish Court. As far as he's concerned, Kate's part of it. Don't you see? To him she's not a person. She's just a prop. Part of his setting, if you like. Another slice of perfection that is now the exclusive property of James Salperton.'

'You don't mind Ginny.'

'What's Ginny got to do with it? It's her brother who's the problem.'

Ginny was now living on a part-time basis with David, Leo's son by his first marriage; Leo hoped that Ginny and David would marry and produce a host of little Quests for him to dote on in his old age.

'This autobiography,' Leo went on, cramming forks into the dishwasher. 'It's typical. He agreed to do it because it flattered his ego. Never mind he can't string two sentences together – he'd never admit *that*. What makes him think he's so wonderful?'

'It's what Kate thinks that counts.'

'That's the whole point.' Then, with the massive illogic he was sometimes capable of, Leo said in a quieter voice: 'That's what I've been trying to say. Kate's scared of him.'

Kate scared of James?

The idea circled round Barbara's mind. Beside her, Leo was snoring gently. Every minute or so, the snores would stop, he would snuffle like a satisfied baby coming off its mother's breast, and then the snores would start again. His ability to sleep annoyed her. When they had a quarrel, it was always she who lay awake afterwards.

45

The whole world seemed to be sleeping, apart from Barbara. It was nearly 3 a.m. She got out of bed, slipped on her dressing gown and tiptoed to the window. She looked down on a motionless gathering of Mercedes, BMWs, a Range Rover and the occasional Rolls. Lavender Lane was reputed to be the wealthiest road in Edgware. Nevertheless, the people who lived here were only comfortably rich, not seriously rich like those who lived, say, in the Bishops Avenue.

James was said to have made a fortune after the divorce from Ursula, his first wife. An unpleasant business all round. Barbara preferred not to think about it. What did it matter, anyway? Was Kate afraid of him?

Leo had refused to give reasons for his belief. Like so many men he sneered at women's intuition but conferred a quasi-biblical authority on his own.

'Little things,' he'd said when, just before he fell asleep, she'd asked him the question once more. 'Don't ask me for chapter and verse. You have to trust your gut-feelings.'

Barbara remembered last Wednesday and the odd little incident in Harrods. The cashmere shawl hadn't been expensive. Only just into three figures, which was nothing these days, and in any case the money couldn't have been important. Kate had liked it: you could tell by the way she fingered the material, by the way she looked at herself in the mirror with her chin lifted just a little higher than usual.

'It's perfect,' the woman had said; and for once a shop assistant had said no more than the truth. 'It brings out the colour of your eyes.'

'It's lovely, darling,' Barbara said. 'Go on. Treat yourself.'

'I'm not sure.' Kate draped the shawl on the counter. 'I'll think about it.'

As they left, Kate glanced back, her eyes searching for the shawl. But the woman had already put it away.

Later that same afternoon, they had walked to Montpelier Square for tea.

'Where's James?' Barbara had asked as they went in.

'He was having lunch with his agent and some Americans.' Kate pulled off her coat and turned away to hang it in the hall cupboard. 'So he said.'

The tone of the last three words was neither bitter nor jocular, merely neutral, as befits a statement of fact. Barbara caught the possible implication at once, that what James said was not necessarily the same as what James did.

'Is there anything I can do?' she asked with deliberate ambiguity.

'No. Why don't you go and sit down? The tea won't be a minute.'

Barbara didn't want to think about it. Anyone could tell that Kate and James had everything they wanted – except, perhaps, children, and there was still time for those.

She shivered; the central heating was off. Hadn't she earned a little peace and quiet? A girl needed her beauty sleep. The grandmother clock in the hall whirred, then struck three times.

Barbara padded across the carpet to the en-suite bathroom and opened the medicine cabinet above the basin.

*

At 3 a.m. in the morning of Sunday 16 December, Peter Redburn was also awake. He was in the loft of 29 Champney Road.

He was too excited to sleep. £115,000 needed a lot of thinking about. Coleby was a shark, not the sort of man to pay more when he could pay less. If the offer were a serious one, why should Peter be content with £115,000? If Coleby needed the land the house stood on, he would be prepared to negotiate.

The loft was very cold, very crowded and very tidy. Apart from the central gangway it wasn't boarded. Peter had never been up here before. When he was a child, the loft had been out of bounds. As an adult he had had no interest in it. He would never understand how his mother had managed to manoeuvre so many bulky items up the stepladder and through the hatch.

From their discarded belongings she had made a museum that recorded forty years of family history. He found his father's suits, carefully folded and smelling even now of camphor, and his mother's wedding dress, the silk rotting and the lace yellow with age.

The *Eagle* Annuals were here, the Dinky Toys, the Hornby train and the Meccano set. Even the hipsters – a purple and blue check, with a wide black plastic belt – had been preserved.

In the same tea chest he came across a cube-shaped case made of orange plastic. It contained his collection of singles and EPs from the early 1960s: the Beatles, the Rolling Stones, Cliff Richard.

One of the singles was 'A Hard Day's Night'. They'd seen the film that summer at Abbotsfield. Mr Salperton had paid for them to go. He still remembered the excitement generated by the opening chord of the title song and remembered, too, Kate saying afterwards, 'I'm going to buy the record.'

'The single?' he'd said, knowing that she hadn't any money.

'No. The LP, of course.'

She'd run on ahead to join James, her bare legs flashing in the sunshine.

He brushed a cobweb out of his hair. Damn James, damn Kate. He thought too much about them. Every time he'd had a few drinks, they took starring roles in the fantasies that played themselves out in his head. It was time to go to bed.

As he turned, his foot slipped off the joist. His ankle twisted. He fell on to the tea chest. A metal-rimmed corner dug into his side, and he shouted with pain. He rested his hand on a cardboard box behind the tea chest and pushed himself up.

The box looked familiar – but then almost everything in the loft looked familiar. It was a sturdy affair that had once contained twelve bottles of South African sherry. Tugging out the tea chest, he brushed the dust from the top of the box and pulled open the leaves of the lid.

The first thing he saw was a buff-coloured exercise book. The royal monogram ER was on the front cover and immediately beneath the monogram were the words SUPPLIED FOR THE PUBLIC SERVICE. EXERCISE BOOK NARROW RULED. Peter opened the book. The metal clips that held the pages together had left smears of rust on the paper. Each of the narrow lines was filled with small round handwriting in blue Biro.

The light was bad but Peter deciphered the first few lines of the left-hand page.

. . . was made Chancellor of the Exchequer, Guillielmus Colbiensus was Chief of the Secret Police, and Josephus Sartor was secretary to the Emperor and Director of Foreign Trade and Commerce. The reign began badly when the IX Legion, commanded by an incompetent Legate, was lured by treacherous barbarian allies into the swamps of Dacia, and completely wiped out. Meanwhile the Chancellor was shocked to discover that the Civil War of the previous reign had swollen the National Debt to a record level . . .

Peter turned back to the front of the book. There was a title page decorated with red, green and blue Biro.

The Secret History of Emor
Volume I
As from the death of the Emperor
Josephus Sartor Imbecillus
In the Year of Rome 862
Compiled by the official Historian of Emor
Gaius Marcus Mollandius
and by his posterity

The past exerts a sly but terrible fascination. It is sly, Peter thought, because the fascination masquerades as harmless nostalgia. You don't realize that nostalgia is addictive. The pleasure it gives is rapidly subsumed by emotions that squeeze the heart. Worst of all is the sense of utter futility because it is far too late to change anything.

Peter rummaged through the top layer of the box's

contents. He found bundles of Emorian bank notes, a membership card for the casino, despatches from Dacia and Tunisia, an immensely detailed drawing of the Imperial Trireme ('With the compliments of Gaius Marcus Mollandius, Lord High Admiral'), and a map of the empire which Peter remembered tracing with uncharacteristic patience from the original in Hubert Molland's classical atlas.

Even now Peter didn't want to think about Emor, because Emor led to Gaius Marcus Mollandius, who led in turn to Richard Molland and the raven on the water. He remembered when Barbara Molland had given him the box. That had been in May 1970, almost six years after the end of Emor.

'Richard wanted you to have it,' she'd said. 'When I was clearing out after Kate left, I found a sort of letter.'

Barbara had been standing very close to him, and he had been conscious of the nearness of her left breast and the faint smell of perfume mixed not unpleasantly with sweat.

'Kate's left?'

'Didn't she tell you?'

'Kate's *left*?'

And Kate's mother had put her arm around him and pulled him towards her. What he remembered most about that was the sense of unreality. Panic, too, and also an unbearable excitement like an itch you were forbidden to scratch.

'You poor darling,' she said.

Four

In 1970 – if you were eighteen and could lay your hands on a little ready money – it was almost *de rigueur* to travel overland to Greece where, in an idyllic island setting, you could hang out in the coolest way imaginable with amiable drug-dealers and liberated chicks.

Peter planned to beat the rush by leaving at the end of May. He had left school the previous December, having failed to get into Cambridge, and was due to go to Essex University in September. To raise the money for Greece he went to Ipswich, the nearest city to Plumford, and worked as a labourer at a warehouse belonging to a mail-order company. He earned nearly £22 a week and lived in a bedsitter. On two occasions he failed ignominiously to lose his virginity to a girl called Rosie in the packing department.

'Stop messing about,' Rosie had said at his first attempt. 'Who do you think I am?'

The second time she was blunter: 'Why don't you piss off?'

In the third week of May he went back to Plumford to prepare for the journey. However, Peter didn't go to Greece that summer. Instead he renewed his acquaintance with Kate Molland.

If he'd arranged the circumstances himself he couldn't have done much better. At nine o'clock on his second evening at Plumford, he was sitting on the terrace of the Ferry Inn. Joe, a friend from school, had been due to meet him there, half an hour earlier.

Joe's absence almost certainly meant that he had succeeded in persuading a girl called Jill into going out with him. Peter was feeling irritable, partly because Joe's putative success contrasted with his own failure to acquire a girlfriend, and partly because Jill was reputed to be hot stuff, a chick who positively demanded to go all the way.

Peter, now on his second pint of beer and his fourth cigarette, was picking his way with some difficulty through *Les Fleurs du Mal*. He looked up, and there was Kate, hesitating in the doorway that led to the bar.

In the last six years he had seen her occasionally – in the street, at the Ritz (Plumford's only cinema, which was known locally as the Fleapit) and once at a party. Before Abbotsfield, he had been to all intents and purposes an honorary member of the Molland family. At Abbotsfield itself he had lived in the same house as Kate for nearly a month. But since then there had no longer been a reason for them to meet. Quite the contrary. He knew, because in a town the size of Plumford everybody knew these things, that Hubert Molland had been given a combined parish a few miles outside Plumford, and that the Mollands were now living in Champney Crucis; he knew that Kate had left school and was now doing something at the technical college; and, more importantly, he had heard from Joe that she was going out with the local MP's youngest son, whose name was Julian and who drove a Triumph Spitfire.

Peter often tried to describe what Kate looked like as she stood in the doorway, half in, half out, glancing at her watch and swinging an embroidered bag barely large enough to take a packet of cigarettes. She was dressed very simply in a short blue dress belted across the hips. She wore leather sandals with straps that came halfway up her calves. The belt and sandals were fashionably ethnic – the sort of accessories that were made of buffalo hide by a little man in Kabul. Usually her blonde hair stretched down to her elbows but on that evening she wore it up, tied with a black ribbon. Her head swayed like a heavy and exotic flower on a delicate stalk. Huge blue eyes floated in pools of mascara.

She stood there for perhaps three seconds. Her eyes glided over Peter, apparently without recognizing him. He couldn't stop looking at her. Kate was like a natural force – an earthquake, perhaps, or the movement of the tides: inevitable, invulnerable and irresistible.

'Looking for me, darling?'

A man in a tie-dyed tee-shirt and cut-off jeans loomed beside her in the doorway. Tattooed women snaked up his forearms and his belly gaped like a mouth between the bottom of the tee-shirt and the waistband of the jeans.

Kate glanced round, saw him, and stumbled on to the terrace.

The man followed. 'What's a nice girl like you doing in a place like this?'

Peter stood up. His chair fell over. Around him conversations faltered and people stared.

'Kate – over here,' he called.

This time she recognized him and waved. Without a backward glance she walked slowly towards his table.

The man blundered after her, colliding with one of the cast-iron tables. Peter wished that he had some kind of weapon. Kate nodded to him and sat down. She didn't look at her pursuer, who stopped inches away from Peter.

'She's with you?'

Peter tried to speak, failed and cleared his throat. 'She certainly is,' he said in a voice that hardly quavered at all.

'Okay. Just wondered. Always worth a try. You never know, do you?'

'No,' said Peter. 'You don't.'

The man swayed. He was not much older than Peter and he looked puzzled, as if wondering not only how to end this conversation but how he had begun it in the first place.

'Keith!' someone shouted in the bar. 'It's your round, you bugger.'

'Got to go,' the man said. 'Nice meeting you.' His eyes lingered on Kate but he spoke only to Peter. 'See you, mate.'

Kate opened her bag and took out a packet of Consulate.

'Are you going to buy me a drink as well?' she asked. 'Or do I just get rescued from a fate worse than death?'

'Of course.' Peter was still standing. 'What can I get you?'

'Gin and angostura, please. With ice.'

'Gin and . . . ?'

'Just ask for a pink gin. And don't forget the ice.'

Inside, Keith was propping up the bar and waving a £5 note at the landlady. He made room for Peter.

'Jesus,' he said. 'What's the secret? How d'you get a girl like that?'

Peter said with perfect truth that he wished he knew.

'What are you having then?'

When Peter told him, Keith insisted on including Kate's pink gin and Peter's pint in his order. 'It's my round,' he kept saying. 'Jesus, what a girl.'

Peter carried the drinks outside. Pink gin seemed a wonderfully sophisticated choice; he had only read about it before. He was prepared to find that Kate had gone, or that in the meantime her boyfriend had turned up. But she was still at the table, alone and looking across the river. Peter's eyes lingered on the line that swept from her head down her neck to her shoulder and along her extended arm. She smiled at him as he put down the drinks.

'Julian was meant to be meeting me.' She took it for granted that he would know who Julian was. 'He's stood me up.'

'That makes two of us. I was meant to be meeting someone too.'

'It's turned out rather well.' She sipped the pink gin, and for a few delirious seconds Peter wondered if it had turned out well because she had met him instead. 'I've been trying to find a tactful way to drop him for ages.'

'What's wrong with him?'

'Julian? He's *dull*. Who were you meeting?'

'Just someone I know.'

'A girl?'

He nodded, adding. 'No one important.'

'Someone said you'd gone to university.'

The fact that she'd remembered him gave him pleasure, even though she had evidently misheard what had been said. He explained about the year off and told her about hitchhiking to Greece to sleep on beaches beneath the Mediterranean sky. He hoped that at the very least she would approve of the idea, and at the back of his mind there was a fantasy in which she offered to come with him.

'I'd prefer to fly there, and rent a villa,' she said. 'Why Greece, anyway? Everyone goes there. I'd rather go to Kashmir or Goa.'

Peter said feebly that he was thinking of going to India next year. Then he asked what she was doing.

She told him about the secretarial course at the technical college and her plans eventually to go to London, perhaps to model.

'What does your dad say to that?' Peter asked.

'I haven't told him.' Kate smiled, making them conspirators, and offered him one of her menthol cigarettes. 'Would you?'

They had a second round of drinks and talked for another twenty minutes. Kate borrowed his denim jacket, which she draped across her shoulders. It was the first time they had been alone together since Abbotsfield.

Afterwards, Peter remembered far more about his feelings than the content of their conversation. The feelings retained their freshness in his memory: the delicious agony of watching her; the frustration of not being able to touch her; the pleasure he had when someone he had known at school passed along the towpath, looked up and saw him, Peter Redburn, having a drink with Kate Molland. He also remembered the goose pimples that appeared on his arms as the evening grew cooler, and how he didn't suggest they went inside because he was afraid she would say that it was time to go.

Suddenly she looked at her watch. 'Oh Christ.'

'What is it?'

'I've just missed the last bus. Julian usually drives me home. I'm just not used to thinking about buses.'

'I'll take you back,' Peter said.

'It's six miles to Champney Crucis. Have you got a car?'

'I'll phone for a taxi.'

When the cab came, Peter ushered Kate to the road and opened the door for her. He wasn't sure what she expected him to do. To his relief she wriggled across the seat, leaving room for him to get in beside her.

The journey was the best part of the evening. The driver didn't talk and nor did they. He was very aware of her body beside his, of the long legs that shimmered in the semi-darkness, and of the smell of her perfume. Once when they went round a corner she swayed against him and caught his arm to steady herself.

At Champney Crucis Kate directed the driver up a lane beside the dumpy little church. She told him to stop just after they had passed a small, modern house with a Mini Clubman parked in the drive. Peter managed to get out first. He ran round to open Kate's door for her. She handed him his denim jacket and swung her legs out of the car.

'Is that the Rectory?' he asked, nodding towards the little house. He'd been expecting something like

Abbotsfield or the decaying Georgian splendours of St Clement's Vicarage in Church Row.

'Yes,' she said in a colourless voice and began to walk away from him.

'Kate?' He moved after her.

She turned. 'No, don't come up to the door. It'll only cause problems.'

'Okay.' The fear of never seeing her again swamped his other feelings, even lust and shyness. 'I was wondering if you were doing anything tomorrow night.'

'Maybe. Why?'

'They've got *Midnight Cowboy* at the Fleapit.'

'I saw it in London.'

'Just an idea.' The shyness flooded back, and he desperately wished he had left the invitation unsaid. 'Maybe something else, another time.'

'I didn't say I didn't want to see it again.' She moved a little closer to him. 'It's a good film. Why don't you pick me up at the Tech? I've got a meeting so I'll be staying late. Six-thirty in the car park?'

'Yes. Yes, of course.'

The technical college was on the outskirts of town, miles away from the cinema. He could hardly expect her to queue at a bus stop. It would mean another taxi. Well, why not?

'Great,' Kate said. 'Well, goodnight, and thanks for the lift.'

She came a step closer, rested her hands lightly on his shoulders and kissed him full on the mouth. The kiss was so brief, and he was so surprised, that he had no chance to respond.

Kate walked away, swinging her bag. She might have

been alone in the world. Peter stared after her. His lips tingled. The taxi-driver revved his engine.

'Goodnight,' Peter whispered.

Kate didn't answer.

Peter saw Kate the next evening, which was a Thursday, again on Saturday, three times the following week, and twice the week after that.

He couldn't believe this was happening to him – that he was going out with Kate and that the whole world could see it. On the days he was going to see her, he woke up feeling that anything was possible, that the world was his for the asking.

On the second Saturday they took the train to London. Kate wanted to go to to Biba in Kensington High Street and Peter wanted to be with Kate. In Biba she tried on a black, floppy hat and a midi-dress, and they browsed among tasselled lampshades and satin sheets; but neither of them bought anything. Later, however, in Kensington Market, at a booth that was so saturated with the stench of joss-sticks that Peter couldn't stop coughing, he bought her a pair of boots in maroon suede. The boots had platform soles and they cost him more than his weekly wages at the warehouse.

When they were in the market she insisted on his buying a pair of white loons, which were just coming into fashion. The bell-bottomed trousers were so tight round his hips that he could hardly walk in them. If you wanted to take them off or even go to the lavatory, you had to undo a complicated buttoned flap at the front. Considered objectively, they were an instrument of torture; but the discomfort they caused was a small price to pay for the knowledge that Kate had persuaded him to buy them. *She* wanted to see him in loons; *she* let him buy her those boots. These things were symptoms of intimacy, like the way she talked of Julian or the things she said about her father.

She kissed him goodnight on two other occasions, briefly but hard on the lips. Sometimes they held hands. Once, in Ipswich, she clung to his arm during a sudden rainstorm that plastered her Indian shirt to her body. She wasn't wearing a bra and, when he glanced down, he saw her left nipple quite distinctly beneath the thin and now almost transparent cotton that covered it.

She came with him to Joe's birthday party and danced mainly with Peter, though in the slow numbers she gave him no encouragement to smooch with her; and when she danced with other people he thought that, quite literally, he was going to die of pain.

Early in their relationship Peter learned that he must not try to take more than Kate was prepared to give. When he reached for her hand, it slid away from his. Often she would leave him unkissed at the Rectory gate and forget to wave when she went inside the house. He decided that this must be because Julian had hurt her more than she cared to admit. Julian had made her shy away from physical contact. The solution was to let her initiate everything, to allow her to come towards him in her own time. He constructed an agreeable fantasy in which Julian pestered Kate and he, Peter, rescued her, showing in the process his immense spiritual, intellectual and physical superiority over Julian; immediately after the confrontation, Kate fell into his, Peter's arms.

He made his preparations. The packet of Durex,

bought in a chemist's at Ipswich to meet an eventuality that Rosie had never allowed to materialize, lived permanently in his wallet; he put them in a brown envelope in case a chance sighting made his intentions too crudely obvious. To guard against accidents – such as the loss of the first packet, for example, or a furious spate of activity when the chemists' were closed – he bought another packet of condoms and secreted them under the lining paper of his sock drawer.

In the space of seventeen days, Peter saw Kate eight times. The period stood out as something qualitatively different from what came before and what came afterwards. It was as if he had been running a high temperature or tripped out of his head on acid. Everything was more intense, not just his emotions. Colours were brighter. The books he read and the music he listened to took on profounder significance than ever before.

She even affected his attitude to his mother. For the first time in his life, Peter found her pitiful, a tiny figure who had made a cage of her routines and spent her life staring through the bars at the glorious unpredictability of the world outside. He never took Kate home or mentioned her to his mother. He had a superstitious fear that talking about Kate would mean losing a part of her, would be a sort of sacrilege. Besides, what could his mother know of love? It was only with the greatest difficulty that Peter could imagine the mechanics that must have led to his own conception.

'When are you going to Greece?' his mother asked on the Wednesday of the second week, while they were doing the washing-up.

'I don't know,' Peter said, dragging his mind away

from Kate and not bothering to conceal his irritation. 'I might stay here and get another job.'

'Why?'

He shrugged, and that was the end of the conversation.

The future shrank. All that mattered was the next time he would see Kate; beyond that he looked forward with an urgency that hurt to the first time they would make love. And in the far distance beckoned the possibility of marriage, a state so close to paradise that he hardly dared imagine it.

His savings were evaporating. At the beginning of May he had had nearly £300 in his bank account; the balance was now down to double figures and falling fast. Usually Peter paid for whatever they did. It was a privilege to spend money on her; she could measure his love by his diminishing bank balance. Even if he had wanted to, he could no longer afford to go to Greece. But he didn't want to go if it meant leaving Kate behind.

On one of their trips to Ipswich, Kate insisted on buying him a present, a Ronson Varaflame gas lighter. That night and for many nights afterwards he took the lighter to bed with him, and lay there, thinking of Kate and feeling the metal growing warm in his hand, until he fell asleep.

Another episode that gave him much reassurance was the time when Kate invited him in for tea at the Rectory. Hubert Molland wasn't there. Peter stayed for an hour, feeling that the visit confirmed him as Kate's official boyfriend. Barbara was wonderful: unlike some people who had known him as a child, she treated him as an adult. It was difficult to believe that she was only a few years younger than his mother; both mentally and physically she belonged to a different generation. They talked about travel.

'I wish I was your age again,' Barbara said. 'I wouldn't just go to India. What about Burma? Thailand? There's a whole world out there.'

'You'd hate it,' Kate said. 'Think of all the bedbugs and snakes and surly natives.'

'I'd find myself a rich protector. Travel on his yacht. *Much* more civilized.'

None of them mentioned Richard or Hubert Molland; nor did they refer to the last time they had all had tea together. Peter endowed the occasion with an atmosphere of reconciliation: the fact that he and Kate were together somehow made up for Abbotsfield; there was no longer any need to feel guilty.

On the last day they met, a Friday, Peter realized at once that something was wrong with Kate. Lovers are the most sensitive animals on earth, though often the strength of their feelings warps their interpretation of the signals they receive.

It was lunchtime and they were on the river. Kate had decided to skip the afternoon's classes and arranged to meet him at the boatyard near the Tech. They hired a punt, which for Peter was a craft bristling with erotic potential. He had come equipped with a bottle of white wine, paté, French bread and fruit.

Peter poled upstream, away from other people. He didn't talk because he was afraid of losing the pole or, worse still, falling in. Every now and then he glanced down at her. She was lying on the cushions, smoking a cigarette and paying no attention to him. She wore flared jeans and a tight shirt, a sort of cotton grandpa vest that outlined her breasts, and her feet were bare. Peter waited until they had left the spectators behind before he risked speaking.

'Do you want to open the wine?'

Kate nodded, and rummaged in the carrier bag for the bottle and the corkscrew.

'Can you manage? I'll do it if you want.'

'Don't fuss. Peter, this wine is practically hot.'

'Sorry.'

'It should be chilled.'

'I know but I didn't have time.'

'Then why didn't you hang it over the side of the punt?'

'Sorry.'

'Where are the glasses?'

'Oh hell, I forgot.' He fought back the word 'sorry', which was threatening to erupt for the third time. 'Can't we drink from the bottle?'

Kate shrugged. 'It looks like we'll have to.'

'Shall I find a place to stop? There's a willow tree coming up.'

'All right.'

He rammed the punt into the trailing branches. It bumped into the bank just as Kate pulled the cork from the bottle. Peter nearly lost his balance. Kate spilled wine on her jeans and swore. Peter apologized.

He joined her on the cushioned seat. Their hands touched as she passed him the bottle. I burn with unrequited lust, he thought, surprised that a cliché should so accurately express what he was feeling.

'Do you want to go to a party tomorrow night?' he asked.

'Whose is it?'

'Bill Coleby's. Joe told me about it. Bring a bottle. Everyone's welcome.'

'I can't.'

'Look – what's wrong? Have I done something?'

She turned her head. 'It's nothing to do with you. Why do you have to take everything so personally?'

'Then what is it?'

'What do you think? My bloody father. We had another row on Wednesday. He thinks most of my clothes are – and I quote – "indecent". He doesn't approve of the way I spend my free time. He says I don't give my mother enough help around the house. Oh, you know – it's the same old story. Story of my life, really. But this time he's put me under a curfew. Jesus, I might as well go into a nunnery and be done with it.'

'What did your mother say?'

'Not much. She's even more stuck with him than I am.'

Greatly daring, Peter put his hand on her thigh. She stared at it.

'I'm sorry,' he said. 'I really am.'

'So am I.' She was still looking at his hand. 'But being sorry doesn't help, does it? And nor does having your hand on my leg.'

He snatched it away.

She grabbed the French loaf and wrenched it into two unequal halves. 'Let's eat, shall we?'

They ate in silence. Neither of them had much appetite but they finished the wine.

'I'm sorry too,' Kate said. 'I'm not very good company today.'

'It doesn't matter.'

'You can come over tomorrow afternoon, if you want. Around teatime.'

'To the house? But won't your dad –'

'He won't be there.'

A little later, Kate said she wanted to go home. Peter punted back to the boatyard. He hadn't enough money for a taxi so they took the bus back to Champney Crucis. Neither of them said much on the way. Peter felt he had missed an opportunity. He had failed her and he didn't even know how.

The following afternoon he struggled into the white loons, which he had washed and ironed himself. He caught the bus to Champney Crucis. Barbara Molland opened the front door of the Rectory. She was wearing a short, summery dress and no stockings. Peter thought she was more like Kate's elder sister than her mother.

'I'm glad you've come,' she said. 'I've got a box for you.' Her lips were trembling. 'Richard wanted you to have it. When I was clearing out after Kate left, I found a sort of letter.'

The world became a place that Peter no longer recognized, an unmapped wilderness.

Kate had gone to London, Barbara said. They'd left early this morning.

'They?' Peter said. He felt the warmth of Barbara's arm against his cheek, and her breast pressing into his body.

'She went with Julian.'

'I thought she'd finished with Julian. When's she coming back?'

'She said she isn't.'

'But her clothes, all her things . . .'

'She took everything she wanted. Told me I could burn the rest for all she cared. Peter, I am sorry – I thought you'd know.'

'But where will she go? Where will she stay?'

'Julian's sister's flat. She's going to get a job and look for a place of her own.'

'Why?' he said. 'Why?'

'It had to happen sometime,' Barbara said. 'She couldn't stay here all her life. Anyway, you know that Kate doesn't get on with her father.'

Peter pictured Kate and Julian in the little red sports car, hurtling through the sunshine to London on a straight, empty road. She was laughing at something that Julian had said and her hand was resting on his leg.

'Kate's *gone*?' he said, yet again.

'Poor darling,' Barbara said.

Suddenly she was kissing him and he was kissing her back.

Peter didn't open the box containing the Archives of Emor. In 1970, the last thing he wanted was to be reminded of Richard and the silly game they used to play.

Barbara Molland had found the box in a trunk that stood under the window in Kate's room. A few of Richard's toys were there as well, and some that had belonged to Kate. And underneath the toys she found the letter. It was dated 19 July 1964, just before they went to Abbotsfield.

To Whom It May Concern:

If I should die, I leave my possessions to Charity, except any documents whatsoever that relate to Emor, which I leave to my friend Peter Redburn.

Signed (in my blood),

Richard F. Molland.

Kate went away on Saturday. The following Monday Peter packed his rucksack and caught the train to Ipswich. He left the cardboard box on top of his wardrobe, where it remained until 1973, when he cleared away every trace of himself from 29 Champney Road. He failed to allow for the fact that Lucasta Redburn could not bear to throw away anything that might one day come in useful.

Peter went back to the bedsitter, back to the same job at the mail-order warehouse. He got drunk three times a week and made copious notes about Kate Molland and the human condition in his journal. Now that he was no longer a virgin and now that it no longer mattered very much, he succeeded in seducing Rosie.

Five

'Don't get me wrong,' Ginny Salperton said. 'There was never anything like that. We were much too young.'

'Balls.' David Quest took a forkful of Ginny's scrambled eggs. 'You were what? Nearly fifteen? And he was maybe a year younger.'

'Exactly. Much too young. Not to mention innocent.'

'At that age, the kids round here are copulating like rabbits.'

'This is here and now, that was then and there. Anyway, in those days Peter was all teeth and nose.'

'But he's improved a bit since then?'

'Yes. Nowadays he's gaunt and interesting.'

'Instead of fat and boring like me?'

'Would I be here if you were boring? I can live with fat. Peter's got one of those lined foreheads a woman longs to soothe. He made me slightly tiddly on champagne so perhaps he *was* trying to seduce me. Do you think so?'

David said nothing because his mouth was fully occupied by the last of Ginny's breakfast. Still chewing, he balanced the plate on the top of the pile of books on the bedside table, put his arm around Ginny and squeezed.

'Have I made you jealous?' she asked.

With his free hand he flung back the duvet, demonstrating that she had aroused quite different emotions.

Ginny twisted towards him and they slid down the bed. The phone began to ring.

Ginny tried to pull away from him.

'Leave it,' he said.

'But it might be urgent.'

'I doubt it. If it is, they'll call back.'

In a while the ringing stopped. Only then was Ginny able to enjoy what was happening. As always, the pleasure was heightened by the sense of guilt that accompanied it.

When she was a child, Ginny Salperton followed the forms of religion that her school and to a lesser extent her parents laid down for her. Towards the end of August 1964, she officially embraced atheism. What happened at Abbotsfield that summer left her with a distaste for all religions, not just Christianity. You could say that Mithras was as much to blame as Jesus Christ.

If there were a loving God, she argued, he would never have allowed it to happen. Therefore, either God did not exist or, if he did, he was not noticeably loving. Atheism was a satisfactory response to both alternatives: if God did not exist, atheism was merely a recognition of the truth; and if he did, atheism was the spiritual equivalent of Ginny's giving God's face a well-deserved slap. This phase lasted until after university, though Ginny flirted with agnosticism in times of stress.

Neither position proved to be tenable in the long run. The trouble with atheism was that it was no more susceptible to proof than the notion that God was a bearded gentleman of advanced years. Agnosticism wasn't much help either, not when God kept talking to

71

her. It was most inconvenient and she often wished he would leave her alone. Why me, for God's sake? He sidled into her mind, usually when she was by herself but not always; he wasn't shy. The salient impression he left behind him was one of calmness and loving kindness. Put baldly like that, her experience of God sounded like a symptom of madness. But she didn't feel mad, just harassed.

'Sometimes he doesn't actually talk,' she had explained to David Quest soon after they met, which was at the wedding of Kate Molland and James Salperton. 'But it's as if he's in the same room. Do you think I'm mad?'

'I think we're all mad,' David said. 'My father says I'm mad practically every time I see him. Your sort of madness sounds quite pleasant.'

'It isn't always,' Ginny said, wondering what on earth (or in heaven) was making her talk like this to a little man whom she'd met only once before; she hoped it wouldn't put him off her. 'Sometimes I know he wants me to do something and usually it's something I don't particularly want to do. And when I do it, whatever it is, I feel glad and I think he does too, but that's not much consolation before I do it. Besides, I don't like being manipulated.'

'You've considered the standard explanations? Other than madness, that is.'

'Of course. For all I know one or more of them is right. But that doesn't alter how I feel. It's like being a very little fish on the end of a very long line.'

'And the divine angler is slowly hauling you up to heaven?'

'You're laughing at me.'

'Of course I am. Do you go to church regularly?'

'I try. I don't like it much, I'm afraid, or most of the people you meet there. Aesthetically it's a dead loss now that they've tried to modernize everything. But it seems logical to go. Or rather it would be a bit dishonest if I didn't. Do you understand?'

'I think so – as far as I can, bearing in mind that I'm Jewish and that I've never been remotely religious. Does this mean you won't come to bed with me?'

'No,' said Ginny, trying to conceal the relief she felt. 'It just means that I'll feel guilty about it.'

'So what does God think about me?'

'I think he rather likes you,' Ginny said. 'But that may just be wishful thinking.'

The phone rang again when Ginny was in the bath.

David appeared in the doorway with a towel round his middle and the cordless phone in his hand. 'It's your brother,' he said, holding up the phone so she could see that he was pressing the mute button. 'Do you want to talk to him, or shall I say you're otherwise engaged?'

'No, I'll take it.'

Ginny wiped her hand on David's towel and took the phone from him. Her immediate reaction was to fear that something had happened to one of their parents. She and James were not in the habit of phoning each other regularly.

'Hello, James. How are you?'

'Fine. Sorry to bother you on a Sunday morning.'

'What's up?'

'Nothing's up. Barbara said you'd seen Peter Redburn.'

Ginny frowned. 'His mother's just died. Mum saw it in the paper.'

'Do you have a phone number for him?'

'*You* want to see him?'

'Why not? Nice to make contact with an old friend. Besides, if his mother's just died, he's probably feeling a bit low.'

Ginny switched the phone from one hand to the other. She didn't believe James for a moment. He was not the sort of man who gets sentimental about old friendships. Maybe Kate was behind the approach: she must have known Peter far better than either of them. The phone was now covered with bath foam. Ginny tried to blow it off.

'Are you still there?' James said.

'Yes. I've only got his London number.'

'I've got that. It's in the phone book. But no one's answering.'

'He's probably staying in Plumford for a while. The house isn't on the phone. I can remember the Plumford address. Would that be any use?'

'I might as well have it. Just in case.'

'Twenty-nine Champney Road.'

A pause. 'Are you staying in Bristol?'

'No, I've got to get back. Ralph's coming to stay. I'm picking him up after lunch.'

'Rather you than me.'

'I'd feel just the same,' Ginny said. 'Or rather I would if you'd give me the chance.'

'He doesn't get on with me. Anyway, he drives Kate round the bend. How was Mother when you saw her?'

'She's fine.'

'How long is she going to be in the Lake District?'

'Well into the new year, I think. She feels she deserves a bit of pampering.'

'What's new?'

Ginny agreed with him. Their mother had made a career out of being cosseted since she had left their father. She was fortunate in that her income came from a family trust fund, so Ralph had never been able to get his hands on the capital. They had separated in 1976 and Mrs Salperton had immediately embraced the privileges of old age. She lived in Putney, in a flat at the top of a mansion block overlooking the river. Two or three times a year she exchanged the cushioned existence she had constructed for herself for something different but equally restful, like a prolonged stay at a good hotel in the country or a cruise on the QE2. 'The change does me good, dear,' she would explain gently but firmly to anyone who would listen. 'At my age, one deserves it, don't you agree?' She was sixty-seven.

'How long have you got to put up with Ralph?' James asked.

'Three nights. I don't suppose you'd like to ask him to dinner?'

'Sorry. We're fully booked up.'

'Of course you are,' Ginny said. 'It was just an idea.'

The bath water was getting cold and her spirits were dropping with the temperature. Talking with James often had that effect on her. She sent her love insincerely to Kate and hung up.

David came back as she was getting out of the bath. He was wearing paint-stained jeans and a baggy jersey with holes at the elbows. His black hair sprouted at all angles from his scalp and he still hadn't found time to shave.

'What did wonder boy want?'

She told him. 'You'd think Peter would be the last person James would want to see.'

'After Abbotsfield?' David took the towel from her and began to dry her back. 'Did he ask you why you went to see him?'

'No. But he wouldn't though. James isn't curious about other people except when it affects him.'

'I except he has his reasons. He usually has.' David ran a finger down her spine. 'Like you had your reasons.'

Ginny pulled up beside Wistaria Cottage and said, 'Shit'.

Ralph Salperton was standing at the living-room window. He must have seen her but he didn't wave. The tip of his cigarette glowed on the other side of the glass and then vanished into the darkness of the room behind. As she was getting out of the Metro he opened the front door.

'You're late.' He was wearing his raincoat and behind him in the hall stood his suitcase and a scuffed, imitation-leather flight bag. 'It's two thirty-five, you know.'

Ginny braced herself and kissed him. His cheek smelled of aftershave and stale tobacco. His hair, which was smothered with grease, badly needed cutting. She wondered when he had last had a bath. He accepted the kiss but did not return it.

'I said I'd get here *about* half-past two. How are you?'

'Me? Oh, I'm all right. Anyway, I'm all ready. Shall we go?'

Without waiting for an answer, he picked up the case

and the bag, deposited them on the path and fumbled for his keys.

'Damn,' he said. 'I forgot to plug in the timer.'

She followed him into the house. 'The timer?'

'It was an offer in one of those magazines,' he said, suddenly animated. 'You plug it in when you go away and it switches on the light for you at the same time every evening, and switches it off too. Marvellous things. You should get one.'

Ginny had owned a timer since 1977. Ralph was the only person she knew who believed that the special offers in magazines actually were special. Had he seen the timer in a shop window at half the price, he would have ignored it.

'Bloody thing won't work,' he said a moment later. 'Can't make head or tail of the instructions.'

'Shall I try?' Ginny said. 'What times do you want it set for?'

He told her; and he watched suspiciously as she glanced at the sheet of instructions, set the timer and plugged it into the power point that controlled the standard lamp.

'There,' he said, claiming her achievement as his own and inflating it in the process. 'Marvellous things. If everyone had one of these, the crime rate would drop by about fifty per cent.'

Ralph hustled her out of the house, locked the door and preceded her down the path to the car. He was in a hurry. He was always in a hurry to get where he was going and always in a hurry to leave it when he got there.

They drove up to the crossroads at the centre of the

town. Paulstock wasn't architecturally distinguished but the church and the stone-faced cottages looked their best in the thin winter sunshine, like a faded watercolour by a gifted maiden aunt. The signpost outside the post office told her that it was ten miles to Abbotsfield and twenty-five to Bristol.

They did the journey to London within two and a half hours. Ginny had driven this route dozens of times, in the last year to Paulstock and before that eight miles further south to Carinish Court, which lay in a fold of the hills on the Paulstock side of Abbotsfield. Ralph spent most of the time studying his newspaper. He was not a man who bothered with small talk.

As they drew closer to London, Ralph abandoned the paper and stared out of the window. Occasionally he grunted or coughed. Ginny stopped at a zebra crossing in Fulham Palace Road. A West Indian woman wheeled a pushchair slowly across.

'Where do they all come from?' Ralph asked. 'It beats me. In a couple of years we'll be outnumbered.'

Ginny's flat was in Wandsworth. Every time she crossed Putney Bridge she could see her mother's windows high above the north bank of the Thames. A few minutes later she turned into Varney Street, a cul de sac west of the common, and parked outside a late-Victorian terraced house near the end.

Ralph looked at his watch. 'I'll unload, shall I?'

Ginny left him to it and went inside. Her flat was on the ground floor. The few rooms were large and high and she had painted the walls in pale yellows and greens. Keeping furniture to a minimum, she had filled the place with books and plants.

She walked through the living room to the long window at the end. The back garden belonged to her as well. When she'd moved in, it had been no more than a yard full of builders' rubbish. Now she grew herbs along the south-facing wall at the end; and in summer she sat on the tiny lawn, smelling the yellow roses and watching the clematis creeping over the fence from next door.

The flat and garden were private property like her relationship with God. She could count on the fingers of one hand the people she actually enjoyed having on the premises; most of her other vistors she merely tolerated and a few of them had the power to make her feel violated.

Ralph poked his head into the living room. 'I'll just put my bags in my room, all right?'

Ginny put the kettle on and went back to the car for her bag, which Ralph had left on the back seat – not so much from laziness but because he was not in the habit of thinking of others. He was waiting in the hall when she came out of her bedroom. He padded after her. She gave him his tea and put the plate of chocolate biscuits on the table beside his chair; he had a sweet tooth.

Ralph ate five biscuits, drank his tea, accepted another cup and lit a cigarette. At this point he departed from the script that Ginny, on the basis of previous visits, had laid down for him. According to the script he should have suggested that she turn on the television.

Instead he grunted and said, 'Something I want to talk to you about. I'm seeing my solicitor tomorrow.'

'So you told me on the phone.' Ginny had never

been able to understand why Ralph continued to put up with the expense and inconvenience of a London solicitor; the legal advice he received at Lincoln's Inn was available far more cheaply in Paulstock.

'I'm changing my will.'

'Really?' She was surprised he still had anything left to leave. Debts had swallowed up most of the money he had got for Carinish Court. Wistaria Cottage wasn't worth much and in any case he had talked at one point of trading it in for an annuity.

'You know why?'

Ginny shook her head. She didn't want to know why, either.

'There's a fellow I sometimes see in the Dragon.' The Dragon was the main hotel in Paulstock. 'Robert something – can't remember the name.' Ralph chewed his lower lip. 'Doesn't matter anyway. Point is, he's an estate agent. We got talking one evening last week, and he was asking about Carinish Court. He knew the place, you see – he'd been over quite recently to do a valuation for insurance. "Marvellous house," he said. "Marvellous." Well, he'd had a few – I mean, he probably shouldn't have said what he did. I happened to let slip how much James gave me for it. He was shocked. He said I'd been cheated.'

'Not necessarily,' Ginny said. 'The sale was nearly two years ago. And you said yourself that the house was in a terrible condition.'

'I told him all that. Didn't make a blind bit of difference. "You've been cheated, old man." Those were his very words, I promise you.'

'But didn't you have it valued before the sale?'

'James did all that. Said he'd save me the trouble. Some man came round, and James phoned me afterwards, told me what he'd said. I never saw anything in black and white.'

'Maybe James was making allowance for the fact it was a private sale. No estate agent's commission.'

Ralph grunted. 'Some commission. Robert reckoned I'd dropped thirty or forty thousand pounds.'

'You can't be sure. This man didn't know the house before James started to have it renovated. He's probably making a mistake. You said he was drunk.'

'I said he'd had a few. That's not the same thing. No, there's no doubt in my mind. And that's why I'm going to change my will. When I pop off, everything will come to you. That little bastard won't get his hands on another shilling.'

Peter Redburn wasn't altogether surprised when, at five o'clock in the afternoon of Sunday 17 December, he opened the front door of 29 Champney Road and found James Salperton on the doorstep.

For the last few hours he had been thinking about James and Kate and the rest of the Mollands, the Salpertons and the Redburns; and it would not have shocked him if any or all of them who were still alive had turned up unannounced at Number 29. The Jungian concept of synchronicity was much on his mind because he was toying with the idea of using it to underpin the narrative structure of *London*. The novel would deal with a single moment in the life of the city; and one of its themes was that there was an acausal link uniting all its apparent diversities into a single interdependent whole.

81

Outside it was already dark and a squall of rain burst into the house when Peter opened the door. He recognized his visitor at once. He had seen him often enough on TV, and when you hate or love a person you know his face as well as you do your own.

James was wearing a full-length waxed coat. His head was bare and his smile was just a little rueful, as if he were uncertain of his welcome. A silver Mercedes was parked beneath the streetlamp outside the house.

'Peter?' he said. 'Peter Redburn?'

'Yes. Come in, James.'

James stepped into the hall. 'You recognized me.'

They shook hands.

'I imagine most people do.'

'Even so, I'm impressed.' James shrugged off his coat. Underneath it he was wearing a thick cream jersey, dark green corduroy trousers and brown shoes that looked hand-made and probably were. 'After all these years, who'd have thought it?'

'Come and get warm by the fire. Would you like a drink? Some tea?'

'Whatever you're having. Tea, perhaps; I'm driving.' James glanced round the living room, moved towards the fire and held out his hands to the heat. 'I happened to be passing – hope you don't mind me barging in like this. Kate and I have been meaning to get in touch for ages.'

'It's been a long time.'

'Far too long. Ginny told me about your mother. I'm so sorry.'

'One of those things,' Peter said. 'Sorry about the mess in here – I'm trying to do some clearing out.'

The Secret History of Emor lay open on the arm of his chair. Peter picked up the exercise book and slipped it into the box he had brought down from the loft. He pushed the box with his foot behind the chair.

'I remember her staying with us at Carinish Court,' James was saying. 'A nice woman; I know my mother was fond of her too. I say, I hope I'm not interrupting you? I'm sure you must be awfully busy.'

'Glad to have an excuse to stop.' Peter felt the impersonal force of James's charm as James was feeling the warmth of the fire. 'I won't be a moment. I'll just put a kettle on.'

'I can't tell you how nice this is,' James said. 'It's as if the last time you saw me was yesterday.'

Not yesterday, Peter thought grimly, as he stood at the kitchen table laying the tea tray with his mother's china; but certainly last week or the week before. It wasn't easy to avoid James Salperton.

For a start there were the Trumper's advertisements on TV – a whole series of them, which had been running for years. Each was a romantic saga in miniature and each had the same basic plot: in a variety of vaguely 1930s settings, James played a wealthy philanderer who appeared to have a fetish about tea since the common feature of the married women he pursued was their taste for Trumper's Tea Bags. A traditionally minded bishop had given the advertisements a welcome boost by complaining in the pulpit and in *The Times* that the campaign glorified adultery as well as Trumper's Tea Bags. When the gossip columns got hold of the business with Ursula Salperton, almost everyone was delighted

– including the bishop, who felt that events had proved him right.

Pemberley, however, was the main reason why James Salperton was famous. Peter Redburn hated *Pemberley* and he had fed his hatred by watching every episode. Everyone else appeared to love it, not just in Britain but throughout the English-speaking world. During the first series, people stayed in to watch it. Dinner parties were built around the episodes. The second series established *Pemberley* near the top of the TV ratings. The third series kept it there. A supermarket chain gave the name *Pemberley* to its own brand of champagne. Enterprising entrepreneurs set up *Pemberley* Trails and *Pemberley* Weekends. You could buy *Pemberley* calendars and *Pemberley* diaries. Sales of *Pride and Prejudice* rose. The fourth series was due to be shown in the spring. They said that James Salperton had turned down the offer of a fifth series and the producers were unwilling to continue without him.

Success breeds success. To add to the unfairness, James was independently wealthy. And to add to the unfairness still further, he had Kate.

'Kate sends her love,' James said. 'I told her I'd try and see you while I was down in this part of the world.'

'How is she?' As he poured the tea, Peter wondered if she'd told James about how she'd made a fool of him; perhaps they had laughed at him together.

'Blooming. She said if I found you I had to ask you to dinner. Do you think you could manage it? Once you're back in town, I mean.'

'I'd love to,' Peter said.

'Great. I'll give you a ring when you're back. We're quite central – Montpelier Square.'

'I know.'

'You know?'

'There was an interview in one of the colour supplements.'

'I keep forgetting our lives are public property. We get people hanging around outside the flat. Very tiresome. You know I bought Carinish Court from my father? We hope to spend a lot of our time there. Much easier to be private in the country.'

'It's a lovely house,' Peter said. 'I envy you.'

'You remember it?'

'Very well.'

'I don't mind telling you we nearly lost it. Ralph – my father – let it get very run down. And then he just couldn't afford to live there, and he had to sell it. It all happened very quickly. It was only by the grace of God I could afford to buy it.'

The grace of God and the acumen of Ursula Salperton. Peter said, 'I thought your parents were very comfortably off. Or rather they seemed to be.'

James shrugged. 'They were. But that was before inflation, and Ralph's not much of a businessman. Between ourselves, he's gone downhill recently in more ways than one. Did you know that he and my mother have separated?'

Peter shook his head, surprised by the suddenly intimate turn the conversation had taken.

'Not divorced,' James went on, as if the precise terms of his parents' separation were important. 'They just decided they'd be happier living apart.'

'Talking of parents, I suppose you must see something of Kate's mother. She lives in London, doesn't she?'

'Barbara? Good lord, yes. We had dinner with them last night. You know she's married again? Chap called Leo Quest – works for a merchant bank. It was she who told me you're a writer.'

'Only a part-time one.'

'You'll have to forgive me but I've never read any of your books. It's something I shall remedy. Barbara said that one of them won a prize.'

'*The Babylon Baby*,' Peter said. 'As a matter of fact, it's the only one that's actually been published.'

'It's in print?'

'I'm afraid not. You might be able to get it from a library. Alternatively, I could let you have a copy if you'd really like one. I've still got a few spares.'

'I'd love it,' James said. 'I do envy you, you know. There's something so permanent about a book. Whereas with acting you're here today and gone tomorrow. The sort of stuff I do isn't exactly high art.' He hesitated, perhaps waiting for Peter politely to disagree. Then: 'I know from personal experience how difficult it is to write a book. I just wish I had your talent.'

'I didn't realize you wrote.' Peter's curiosity momentarily swamped his irritation. If James wrote a book, it would no doubt be a bestseller, which would make another point of contrast between the two of them.

'That's the problem. I don't.' James flicked his hair off his forehead, and his signet ring glowed orange in the firelight. 'Do you know an outfit called Channel 20 Books?'

'I don't think I do.'

'They commissioned me to write my autobiography – oh, it must be eighteen months ago. I'm still on page two. It's not for want of trying.'

'What's the difficulty?'

'I don't know. I just can't cope with the written word, I suppose.'

'Can't you just explain that to your editor? If you repaid the advance, I'm sure they'd let you off the hook.'

'Too late for that. It's my own stupid fault. My first deadline was the end of last March, and I hadn't even started thinking about it by then. So I got the woman – Clare, she's my editor – to extend the deadline until the end of next month. I didn't want to tell her I'd done nothing at all so I told a sort of white lie – said I was halfway through the first draft. And of course she leaked that to the press. You know what these publishers are like: they'll do anything to whip up a bit of interest in a book. The result is, I'm stuck with it. I can't just turn round and say, "Sorry, chaps, it was all a mistake."'

'Why not?'

'Think of the publicity. People have got nasty minds: believe me, I know. They'll either hint I was downright dishonest to sign the contract in the first place or they'll make out I can't even spell my own name. I can't win.'

'You could explain to your editor and ask her to find you a collaborator, a ghostwriter.'

'If I'd had the sense to be frank with her last March, maybe I could have done that. But it wouldn't work now: I've got to have something to show her, otherwise she'll know I lied to her. Anyway, publishing's like acting. It's a small world. Even if she guaranteed the discretion of the ghostwriter, everyone would know.' He hesitated and added softly: 'I don't think I could bear that.'

Peter lifted the teapot. James passed his empty cup.

'I was wondering whether you'd be willing to help.'

'Me?' Peter's hand wavered. Tea spurted into the saucer. 'How?'

'Would you write the bloody thing for me?' As in the past, James's smile promised everything but gave nothing away. 'Would you be my ghost?'

Six

'But why Peter?' Barbara Quest said.

The phone hummed and crackled. Kate said, 'How should I know? James got the address out of Ginny and drove up to Plumford yesterday afternoon. He didn't discuss it with me beforehand, just told me when he got back.'

'He must have a reason for choosing Peter.'

'I think it's because he used to be a sort of friend.'

'What do you mean?'

'James likes everything to be on a personal basis. Like he always has his hair cut by the same man. He was at school with his solicitor. I don't think he likes strangers very much.'

Barbara wondered if that were part of the reason for his marrying Kate. 'How do you feel about seeing Peter again?'

'Me? Why not?'

'I think he felt very bitter.'

'That was years ago. Anyway, we were just friends.'

'I'm not sure Peter saw it like that.' Barbara groped for another objection. 'I thought James was going to write the book himself.'

'He says he hasn't the time to do a good job. Actually, I think he's found it harder than he expected and he needs help.'

'If you ask me, the whole thing's a mistake.'

'Look, there's nothing to worry about. It's still James's book. All Peter will be is a sort of glorified secretary.'

'All it needs is for a journalist to go down to Abbotsfield.'

'Mum, you're overreacting.'

'If people read the autobiography, they'll start thinking about the past, James's past. Once someone makes the connection, there's nothing we can do.'

'But it doesn't matter if they –'

'It matters to me, darling. And it would matter to James, too. With all the publicity he's had, I'm surprised no one's mentioned it already. That you knew each other when you were children, I mean, and what happened that summer.'

'We were only there for a few weeks. Why should anyone remember?'

'The Timballs might.'

'Who?'

'Timball was the vicar at Abbotsfield. Didn't you meet his son?'

'Frank? Yes, I think we did.' Kate sighed. 'Anyway, I couldn't stop James, even if I wanted to. I really don't see what's worrying you. When James and I got married there was a lot of publicity. All that business with Ursula, remember? If anyone was going to make the connection, that was when they'd have done it – when all the muckrakers were going full blast. This book is nothing in comparison. Just a bit of PR.'

'I hope you're right.'

'Do you and Leo want to come to dinner on Tuesday? Peter's coming.'

Barbara wished they were talking face to face. Nothing in Kate's voice revealed her feelings. She made Peter sound like just another duty guest.

'No. I'm afraid we can't.' Barbara swiftly invented a reason: 'Leo's got something arranged. He told me this morning.'

'Shame. Oh, and talking of Leo: James is a bit sensitive about Peter helping him with the book.'

'You mean you don't want me to tell him?'

'Only under oath of secrecy. Personally, I don't care one way or the other but James wouldn't be very happy if he knew that Leo knew.'

'Is everything all right with you and James?'

'Of course it is. Why do you ask?'

'Oh, I just wondered. Sometimes these little problems can —'

'What problems?' Kate interrupted with an urgency that made Barbara instantly suspicious. 'Everything's fine. We have the occasional argument. Who doesn't? But we don't have problems in the sense that you and Dad used to have.'

The problems with Hubert had begun if not on their wedding day then certainly during the honeymoon. Barbara married him in 1950, early in September. She wanted a church wedding with as many of the trimmings as they could possibly afford.

'I'll only get married once in my life,' she'd said, inaccurately as it turned out. 'I'd like it to be something to remember.'

'You don't mind that I'm an atheist?' he'd said with a frankness that at the time she'd admired.

'Of course not, darling. I think I am, too.'

'The point is, in my job it's not something you can afford to shout from the roof tops. The Thirty-nine Articles are practically part of the curriculum. I don't like to be hypocritical about it but in fact I haven't any choice.'

Barbara, who was uncertain what the Thirty-nine Articles were, patted his hand. 'I do understand. As far as I'm concerned, it doesn't matter.'

Looking back, she could see that she had married for all the wrong reasons. She was afraid of staying single all her life and everything she had ever been told supported the belief that a woman's highest ambition was to become a wife and mother.

When she met Hubert Molland she was working as a secretary in London. Her boss was the managing director of a firm that sold fertilizers and animal feeds. In July 1950 he asked her to drive down to Cambridgeshire and collect his son from boarding school.

Barbara liked Rosington immediately. It conformed to her image of what a public school should look like. It had ivy-clad buildings that looked old even if they were not, rolling lawns, elm trees, a small lake and a chapel with a portico. It had the glamour that attaches to other people's privileges; Barbara did not resent the lack of advantages her own parents had given her, but she wanted those advantages for her own children. Perhaps, she thought later, it was Rosington she fell in love with, not Hubert.

Once at Rosington the car refused to leave. Hubert, who was the boy's housemaster, summoned a mechanic and invited Barbara to lunch. During lunch he treated

Barbara with a grave courtesy that she later realized was a mask for his shyness. Nevertheless, she was both surprised and touched when, with an obvious effort, he said that he would be in London at the weekend and wondered if he might have the pleasure of taking her out to lunch.

Lunch on Saturday led to dinner on Monday. On Tuesday they spent the day together, and he proposed. On Wednesday she handed in her notice to the managing director, who was touchingly reluctant to accept it.

The honeymoon lasted only a week because Hubert had to be back at school for the start of the Michaelmas Term. They went to the Highlands, which was where the problems began. Hubert wanted to tramp across as many mountains as possible, and he assumed that Barbara wanted to do the same. In her memory it was always raining and always cold. On the third morning, she slipped in the omnipresent mud and sprained an ankle. This at least meant that she was no longer expected to walk.

'What awful luck,' Hubert said. 'Will you be all right here if I go and stretch my legs for a while?'

'Yes darling of course,' Barbara said, hastily revising her ideas about the purpose of honeymoons.

It wouldn't have mattered so much if the nights had brought the compensations she had been led to expect. However, on their first night she felt like a patient strapped to an operating table without the benefit of an anaesthetic; and the surgeon was not only blind but expected the patient to give him directions.

'Left a bit.' She wriggled beneath the weight of Hubert's big, bony body. 'No, not there. Actually, it *is* hurting rather a lot. Try it from the side. Yes, that's it. Oh dear, I think it's come out again. Never mind, try again.'

On subsequent nights their fumblings in the darkness were equally painful and messy. Barbara, whose previous experiences in that line had been few but enjoyable, remembered with guilty nostalgia the handful of nights she had spent with the managing director at the Royal Albion in Brighton. After the honeymoon she and Hubert slept in the same room but in single beds.

'I don't want to disturb you if I work late,' Hubert explained.

She felt starved of physical contact. Hubert would kiss her on the cheek in the morning and when she went up to bed. If they were walking he would sometimes take her elbow – less to support her, she thought, than to steer her. Apart from that, Barbara had to be content with what happened on almost every Saturday night of their life together.

Hubert would stand in his dressing gown beside her bed. 'May I?' he would say, as if asking her to dance.

They never made love with the light on and the act itself was too brief and impersonal to give her any pleasure. But she thought these occasions were important to him and perhaps constituted another reason why he wanted to marry her. If nothing else, she enjoyed feeling needed; but sometimes she dreamed with disturbing vividness about the managing director, who had believed in full-length mirrors, bottles of champagne and the importance of taking one's time.

In return Hubert gave her security, pleasant surroundings, a degree of social standing and, of course, the twins. Richard and Kate, the fruit of her weekly meetings with Hubert, were born in July 1951. They chose to arrive prematurely – on Speech Day, as it happened, which was most inconvenient for their father. The twins were demanding – in the first few years she thought she would go mad from lack of sleep and overwork – but at least they touched her and hugged her and kissed her and loved her.

Hubert was intensely ambitious. He worked very hard, even in the holidays: he threw himself into all the activities of the school and contributed a number of well-received papers to conferences on education. Barbara thought that he was driving himself too hard. She knew that he often slept for less than four hours a night. Occasionally he talked in his sleep but she could never make out what he was saying.

His efforts to move to a better school were unsuccessful. On the other hand he became Deputy Headmaster of Rosington in 1957. In 1959 he applied for the headship of another minor public school, which had the disadvantage of being in Northumberland.

'I'm getting older,' he said to Barbara. 'The money's good, and I think there's a lot of potential for expansion there. It'll be a useful stepping stone.'

Hubert went for one interview, along with six other candidates. He liked what he saw of the school and got on well with the Chairman of the Governors, a fellow classicist. His optimism grew as he made his own assessment of the other candidates. A few weeks later the appointments committee asked him back for another interview; only one other candidate remained on the shortlist.

'I don't think there'll be any problem,' he assured Barbara as she drove him to Rosington station; he hadn't slept the night before. 'The other man's a make-weight – an insurance for them in case I withdraw. This is really just a formality.'

Hubert was nearly right in his assessment of the situation. But he was the makeweight. The following afternoon, the appointments committee told him that they had offered the job to the other man and that he had accepted.

As he told Barbara afterwards, he had never felt more depressed. The long railway journey added to his distress. One train broke down, causing a two-hour delay. At Newcastle station, the buffet was closed and someone stole his wallet. Reporting the theft delayed him even longer. It was after midnight by the time he was able to continue his journey.

Somewhere south of York, Hubert was alone in a second-class non-smoking compartment. He was tired, hungry and humiliated. 'I was actually thinking about suicide,' he confessed to Barbara.

The door to the corridor slid open. He looked up, angered by the intrusion. A man came in and sat down in the seat opposite him. Later, Hubert had no memory of the newcomer's face or clothes. He remembered only the hands.

The man leaned forwards and spread out his hands. According to Hubert, blood oozed from the centre of the palms. Several drops fell to the floor.

'My son,' the man said to Hubert Molland. 'It is time for you to serve me.'

*

Leo had chuckled when Barbara told him the story of Hubert's conversion. They were in the middle of a leisurely Saturday lunch, the sort of meal that stretches imperceptibly into afternoon tea. In the interests of discretion – Leo was always discreet – they had driven out of London to Faringdon.

The hotel was just outside the town. It was a warm day, one of the best that summer, and they ate on the terrace. The lawn glowed green below them, drawing the eyes down to the sparkle of the stream at the bottom of the garden. It was August 1980 – after her divorce from Hubert had been made absolute.

The miracle, if that is what it had been, was something that she'd never discussed with anyone. The whole business sounded so ridiculous, and in any case the past was the past and she preferred to live in the present. She talked about it today partly because she was warm, relaxed and happy, but more because she felt she owed it to Leo. He had just told her about Miriam, his first wife and David's mother, who had eloped to Dayton, Ohio, with a dentist whom she later married. By that time Barbara knew Leo very well, and she guessed how much it had cost him to tell her the whole unsavoury story. One confidence deserved another. In August, she was still working at Chessington-Harris as Leo's secretary; but for over a year their relationship had been considerably warmer than any of their colleagues realized.

'Like Saul on the road to Damascus,' Leo said. 'A traditional volte-face, from one extreme to the other. But why did he have to leave his job? After all, he was teaching at a Christian school.'

'Because that's what God wanted him to do.'

'He was quite a good teacher, right?'

'Yes. At least I think so. Everyone used to say he was. He got results, and he knew how to keep the boys quiet. I'm not sure how much he enjoyed it. What he really liked was the administration.'

'And what was he like as a priest?'

'He tried hard. But people tended to be afraid of him or he was afraid of them. Everything was too messy for him to cope with.'

'Then I think God made a mistake,' Leo said. 'Or Hubert did.'

'The funny thing was, no one would believe him. He went to see the bishop, the Bishop of Rosington, to ask about training for the ministry. I think the old man thought he was mad. Tried to argue him out of it, even suggested – very tactfully – that he saw a doctor. I got the impression that the Church of England doesn't like you to have visions. But Hubert just wouldn't accept that. He said to me that God had given him a chance to expiate his past life, and that was what he was going to do. He didn't care about the effect it had on the rest of us. It was his soul that counted, that's all.'

'Then why didn't you leave him to it and get on with your own life?'

'I don't know. The children – that's what I told myself when I thought about it. But I think force of habit came into it, too, and fear of what people would say. And also I was a little sorry for him. Everyone in Rosington seemed to be laughing at him behind his back. He knew that. He isn't a fool. He said it was part of price he had to pay.'

'Perhaps the bishop was right.'

Barbara shrugged. 'Anyway, Hubert got what he wanted in the end. He ws ordained. The first place they sent us to was a parish in the East End. He nearly had a nervous breakdown so they made him go to Plumford. A senior assistant curate, no less – do you know what that is? Just about the lowest of the low.'

She was silent for a moment, thinking of the drudgery to which Hubert's vision had condemned her and of the advantages it had denied the children.

'Seven years later they gave him a parish of his own. Do you know, he was in two minds about accepting? Honestly, he wanted life to be as hard as possible. I think he even thought that what happened to Richard was all part of God's plan for him, Hubert.' Her voice rose, and she knew she was close to tears. 'Something to be grateful for.'

'Tell me something. After you'd stuck it out for so long, why did you leave?'

'Once Kate had left home, there was no need for me to stay. I couldn't leave her there with Hubert and I couldn't afford to take her with me.'

'There was no other reason?'

'What do you mean?'

'I thought perhaps you might have had an affair. A trigger of some sort. Something that finally made up your mind for you.'

'Nothing worth mentioning,' Barbara said.

Leo looked at her for a moment. Then, changing the subject, he told her that he was going to be the new head of economic analysis at Chessington-Harris. The promotion would bring a seat on the board.

'But, darling, that's wonderful.'

'They'll make it official on Monday.'

'What do you want me to do? Move with you?'

'No. I'd like you to resign.'

'Are you giving me the sack?'

Leo picked up her hand and planted a kiss on it. For an actuary, he was a very romantic person and he had no inhibitions about showing it. 'I want you to marry me,' he said. 'Please say yes.'

On Monday morning, Peter Redburn walked down to Market Street. At Barclays Bank he paid in the cheque from James Salperton and cashed a cheque of his own. Then he found a telephone box and made three calls.

The first was to the area librarian whose responsibilities included the branch library where Peter worked.

'When do you think you'll be able to come back?' she said. 'Don't think I'm hurrying you but we're rather short-staffed what with Christmas and everything.'

'That's what I was phoning about,' Peter said. 'I'm not coming back. I'm resigning.'

'But, Peter —'

'Don't worry. I've written to the Borough Librarian so it's all official. I know I should give a month's notice but I've got some leave due; you can take that instead.'

Afterwards he dialled Bill Coleby's number. A secretary answered. She said that Mr Coleby was in a meeting and offered to take his name and a message.

'Would you just say Peter Redburn called?'

'Oh, Mr Redburn.' Suddenly the secretary's voice was warmer, almost flirtatious. 'I'm sure Mr Coleby wouldn't mind if I disturbed him. Could you just hold a moment?'

'Actually, I'm in rather a hurry. It doesn't matter. Goodbye.'

Finally he phoned the solicitor. Mr Barnes was delighted to hear from him, which made Peter suspect that he knew of Coleby's interest in 29 Champney Road. Peter explained about Coleby's offer of £115,000.

'Will you accept?'

'No,' Peter said. 'He'll go higher.'

'Can you be sure of that, Mr Redburn? If Coleby's overheads at the development stage go a certain figure, he may decide that the game's not worth the candle. He's not fully committed yet. Or he may have an alternative up his sleeve.'

'I think he'll raise the bid. On the assumption that he does, and that we reach agreement, would you be ready to handle the sale?'

'Of course, with pleasure.'

'And I wonder if you could recommend an accountant.'

Again, Barnes was only too pleased. Then: 'Don't think I'm prying, but why are you so certain that Coleby's prepared to raise his offer?'

'Call it intuition,' Peter said. 'Did you know that he and I were at school together?'

Peter's near-certainty had a little to do with intuition and a lot to do with the Letts School-Boy Diary for 1964. If used properly, the diary was a mine of information.

Peter had begun to study it on Sunday, chiefly to discover what he had had to say about Abbotsfield. The entries were not much immediate use to him. You could read very little into *Went to see A Hard Day's Night – Fab* or *Went swimming at CC. Ginny lent me The King Must Die*. The Mithraeum wasn't even mentioned, though on August 9 he had written: *I AM NOW A RAVEN!!!*

At first he was disappointed that he had recorded so little. Gradually, however, he realized that he could become a detective investigating his own past and that what he gleaned might have a bearing on the present. After all, there was plenty of material. He had three main sources of information: the diary, the Archives of Emor and his memory. It was not easy to combine them. His memory was often inaccurate. Many of the documents in the Archives were dated either not at all or according to an incomprehensible Emorian system invented by Richard; and it sometimes proved impossible to link the events they recorded with events in the world beyond Emor. The diary entries were tantalizingly brief. But the three sources complemented one another and their sum was greater than their parts.

Peter thought it best to start with the diary because it provided a chronological framework. Charles Letts and Co Ltd had clearly believed that the average schoolboy had a voracious and undiscriminating appetite for facts. The first sixty-four pages of the little book included information on everything from jet engines to German strong verbs.

He turned to the entries he had made himself. Many of them recorded complicated transactions in cash and kind, often accompanied by the laconic comment 'massive profit!' Several of the deals had been with Bill Coleby: 'Got 2/6 off Coleby for Yugoslav note worth 1s' was one which Peter did not remember. Another, however, jogged his memory: 'Coleby gave me 10s for my old penknife – very massive profit!'

In those days Peter had haggled as a matter of course. Scenting the strength of Coleby's desire for the knife, he had beaten him up from two shillings to ten over a period of three days.

Peter wondered how much people really changed. In 1964 he had been prepared to back his hunches. In the past Coleby had paid over the odds for things he wanted. His offer for Number 29 had already increased. It was time to gamble again. Peter remembered the motto he had chosen for the Emperor's Luck Casino in Emor. The motto formed part of the coat of arms he had designed for the establishment – five poker dice surmounted by an imperial crown.

'The gods help those who help themselves.'

The Bentley arrived before lunchtime on Monday.

Peter, who was in the front room, saw the brown car pull up outside. Even though he had been expecting it – hoping for it, really – he resented the interruption because it broke his chain of concentration. Also, of course, he was nervous; these days he was unused to gambling. He shovelled a handful of Emorian documents back into the box and reached the front door before Coleby had time to ring the bell.

'Peter. Good to see you.' Coleby stepped into the hall and stamped his feet on the mat. 'My secretary told me you'd rung. Stupid woman – I'd told her to put you through if you called.'

'It wasn't her fault,' Peter said. 'I didn't want to disturb you in the middle of a meeting.'

Coleby kept on his overcoat. Without waiting for an invitation, as if the house were already his, he led the way into the sitting room. Peter followed, thinking how such behaviour would have infuriated his mother, and how it strengthened his own position.

'Thank you for lunch on Saturday,' he said. 'I really enjoyed myself.'

'Well, what's the verdict?'

'I don't know. It's a difficult decision.'

Coleby turned slowly to face him, like a liner man-oeuvring to ram a tugboat.

Peter held his ground. 'Would you like a cup of coffee?'

'Coffee?' Coleby frowned at the idea. 'No, I can't stay long. What's the problem?'

'It's a very generous offer and all that.'

'You won't get a better one. And maybe I should remind you that it won't stay open for ever.'

'The point is, I'm wondering about living here myself.'

'Why, for God's sake?'

'Difficult to explain,' Peter said. 'Another writer would understand. I seem to be able to work here.'

'Surely you can work anywhere?'

'In theory, yes; but some places are more conducive than others. It's a matter of atmosphere.'

'Have you thought what the atmosphere will be like once the building starts?'

'*If* the building starts.'

'Not if: when. Something'll go up on that land behind the house. I can promise you that. Simple economics – I can't afford to leave it lying idle. Take light industry, for example, which wouldn't have the same access requirements. Have you thought what that would mean? I'll tell you: a lot of dirt, a lot of noise, a lot of traffic. Wouldn't do much for the value of the house, either.'

'I could live with that. Money's not the only consideration, is it? As for the noise, my flat in London is on a main road, and the noise never really stops. It doesn't worry me. Besides, it's the house itself I like, not the setting.'

Coleby glanced around the little sitting room. His face darkened.

'I'm not saying that I shall live here,' Peter said. 'Only that it's a possibility. I thought it only fair to let you know.'

Coleby plunged his hands into the side pockets of his coat. 'When are you going to decide?' he said. 'I can't wait for ever.'

'Of course you can't. A few days, perhaps.'

'You'll be staying in Plumford while you make up your mind?'

'Some of the time at least. I've got to go up to London.'

'If I go up to one-twenty, will that help you make up your mind?'

'It could be a factor,' Peter admitted. 'Oh, while I remember: there was something else I wanted to mention. At the Angel, you were asking about my book. *London.*'

Coleby grunted and began to move towards the door.

'And I asked you if you remembered Emor.'

'Yeah, the game you said we played. What about it?'

'I think I might be able to work it into *London*. The fantasy city that interacts with the real one.'

'I see,' Coleby said. 'Well, good luck to you. As I told you, I hardly remember it.'

'I wondered if you might have any papers relating to it.'

'Papers?'

'Emor generated a lot of paper,' Peter said. 'Don't you remember? A typical bureaucracy, when you come to think about it.'

'If you say so.'

'Do your parents still live at the farm? In the same house, I mean.'

'As a matter of fact, they do.' Coleby was frowning now. 'What's this all about?'

'Well, it's just possible that anything you had from Emor might still be there. In your old bedroom. Stuffed at the back of a drawer. Or in the attic, maybe. And if there is something, I'd like to see it.'

'If you think –' Coleby thought better of what he had been going to say. He jingled his car keys and said in a quieter voice: 'Has this anything to do with whether you keep this house or not?'

'It might do,' Peter said. 'To be honest, I'm not sure. Put it this way, Bill: if you can come up with something from Emor – despatches, that sort of thing – I'd really appreciate it. You'd be doing me a favour. One good turn deserves another.'

Coleby looked as if he thought Peter were mad. He marched into the hall and opened the front door. On the step he turned back.

'You want this stuff for the book?' he said in a voice

that was nine parts disbelief to one part disgust. 'Are you having me on?'

'Why on earth should I?' Peter said. 'I'll be in touch. Goodbye.'

When Coleby had gone, Peter leaned against the wall and stared down at the worn linoleum. He was trembling – partly from exhilaration and partly from anxiety. Coleby hadn't really changed for all his success. Underneath the mohair coat and the surplus flesh lurked the second-class citizen they had grudgingly tolerated at Plumford Grammar School. More to the point, Peter hadn't changed either.

He had lied to Coleby, and done it convincingly, as part of the negotiations to drive up the price of Number 29; he was still capable of taking risks. And Coleby was as hampered now as he had been in Emor by his lack of imagination: get him away from a straightforward discussion of bricks, mortar and money, and the man was lost; give him a load of crap about the artistic temperament, and his sense of smell deserted him.

Peter began to laugh. If he kept his nerve he would squeeze more money out of Bill Coleby. If he were very lucky, he would also get a bonus: Coleby might provide him with evidence of murder.

Seven

On Monday evening Ginny left the office without her usual sense of mild relief. She worked for the British Council in the monolithic Spring Gardens building between the Mall and Trafalgar Square. Normally she tolerated her job and relished her home. At the present the position was reversed.

The streets were more crowded than usual. Ginny waited for a bus and watched people darting along the pavements and in and out of shops. All they had in common was their sense of urgency: the mass hysteria that characterizes the week before Christmas.

A bus came and she squeezed aboard. As it trundled towards Wandsworth, Ginny thought about Christmas. There was only a week to go. She hadn't even started to buy presents and make preparations. She and David planned to spend the long weekend alone in Bristol. Last night, however, Ralph had begun to angle for an invitation by reminiscing about the joys of the traditional family Christmas at Carinish Court. It astonished her how the passage of time had censored from his memory everything except the trimmings like crackers, turkeys and mince pies; and he'd imagined, in the place of the emotional strain and physical surfeit he'd forgotten, a wholly fictitious jollity.

At Wandsworth, it was a seven-minute walk from the bus stop to the end of Varney Street. Ginny bought some milk from Mr Ahmet's Corner Emporium & Newsagent's on the corner. When she let herself into the flat, Ralph was waiting in the hall. She guessed that he had been standing at the window or listening for the sound of her key in the lock. The television was on in the living room. The flat smelled like the lair of a strange animal.

'Hullo,' he said. 'Still raining? There's something I want to show you.'

Ginny wished that he had allowed her to take off her coat before he started. She followed him into the bathroom. The basin was ringed by a tidemark composed of specks of hair and shaving cream.

'See this?' Ralph wrapped his hand round the cold tap of the bath. 'It drips. If you ask me you need a new washer. Quite apart from the waste, it'll stain the side of the bath if you're not careful.'

'Yes,' Ginny said. 'You're right.'

'Just thought I'd mention it. Hope you don't mind. Oh, and another thing. You're getting very low on milk. I think there's about half a pint left. Not much, when you think of breakfast.'

'It's all right. I got a couple of pints on my way home.'

Ralph looked disappointed. 'There was something else. I should have made a list. What the hell was it?'

Ginny tried to back out of the bathroom.

'I know,' he said. 'You had a phone call. I made a note of it on the pad.'

It couldn't have been David because David knew she would be out at work, and knew that Ralph was staying with her. The pad wasn't beside the phone in the hall.

Ralph searched the flat, clucking anxiously. Ginny managed to take off her coat, put the milk away and turn on the oven before he ran the pad to earth on the table beside his armchair.

'It was about four o'clock,' he announced. 'Chap called Peter something.' He peered at the piece of paper. 'I said you were at work but I didn't let him have your number. Just in case, you know.'

In case of what? Ginny could only suppose that Ralph thought he was protecting her from a possible nuisance. Perhaps he thought British Council employees who received personal calls at work were instantly dismissed. Perhaps he suspected that Peter Redburn intended to whisper obscenities in her ear.

'Did he leave a message?'

'Said he'd ring back later. Hope I did the right thing?'

'Yes, fine,' Ginny said, and her irritation with Ralph was suddenly replaced by pity. 'I think I'll have a drink. Would you like one?'

'I wouldn't say no to a small G and T.'

She carried their drinks into the living room and asked Ralph if he had managed to see his solicitor; the appointment had been at 2 p.m.

'Oh yes,' he said. 'Do you know they've got a Jew in the partnership now? Incredible, isn't it? They get everywhere. Even James married a Jew's stepdaughter. I honestly don't see what Barbara Molland sees in that fellow Quest. An attractive woman like that could have had anyone.'

And I sleep with the same Jew's son, Ginny thought, whenever I can.

'What we need is a sensible immigration law,' Ralph

said. 'There was something in the paper.' He pawed at the *Daily Telegraph* but failed to find whatever he was looking for and lit a cigarette instead. But he had not exhausted the subject. 'In my humble opinion –'

'How are you getting on with the family history?' Ginny interrupted.

'Eh?' Ralph switched from one hobbyhorse to another. 'Oh, there's a lot still to do. There would be with a family like the Salpertons. God knows how many generations – right back to the Conquest. Backbone of England.'

When Ralph Salperton sold the business his father and his grandfather had built up, he had announced his attention of devoting much of his newly won leisure to compiling the family history. In her late teens Ginny had surreptitiously investigated the notes he had made. It had not taken her long. Ralph had succeeded in proving his descent from his great-grandfather, a grocer in Whitstable, who had married in 1838. Thereafter his researches had moved into the realms of fantasy. There had indeed been a family of minor gentry called Salperton in the later Middle Ages though they had no demonstrable connection with the Conquest. Their last known descendant, Nathaniel Salperton, was among those executed after the Monmouth rebellion in 1685. By an act of faith that spanned one and a half centuries, Ralph had assumed that Whitstable grocer must be the lineal descendant of the Protestant rebel.

'Trouble is,' Ralph was saying, 'it involves a lot of work, a lot of travelling. In fact I was wondering if you could give me a hand.'

'I wish I had the time. Perhaps James would help.'

'I wouldn't ask him for a drink of water if I were dying of thirst. I meant what I said last night. I'm changing my will. Mark my words, he'll regret it.'

Regret a half share of nothing in particular?

'And to think I was pleased,' Ralph said. 'Keep the old place in the family, I thought – best thing that could happen if I couldn't stay there myself. Goes to show: you can't trust anyone. When I think what I've done for that boy. He wouldn't be where he is today without me.' He stared into his gin and tonic. 'Beautiful house. We used to have super parties there.'

'When was that?' Ginny asked. Carinish Court was a safer subject than James, less objectionable than Ralph's views on racial purity and closer to reality than the history of the Salpertons.

'Eh? In the first few years. We moved in, let me see, it was a wedding present from my father: that would make it nineteen forty-seven.' He rubbed his chin. 'I'd just come out of the army. We did a lot of entertaining. Though I say it myself, your mother and I knew how to throw a party. I remember old Johnny Redburn saying, "I've got to hand it to you, Ralph, you know how to make things go with a swing." Poor old Johnny.'

'I remember him coming to stay.'

'When was that?'

'Nineteen sixty-four, I think,' Ginny said carefully.

'Must have been the last time I saw him. Came with his wife, didn't he? Can't recall her name. Of course, he was dying then. But he used to be very different. We had some great times in the army. You know he was my best man?' Ralph's eyes were watering. 'All gone now,' he said. 'All gone.'

Ginny stood up. 'I'd better do something about supper.'

Ralph appeared not to hear her. 'Johnny liked Carinish Court. He stayed there once – by himself, without that dreary wife of his. Must have been the same time I did my leg in. I remember him outside the front door, getting out of the taxi. He looked up at the house, at your mother and me in the doorway. You know what he said? "I envy you, old man. Christ, I envy you."'

Carinish Court had aroused some people's envy: that at least was true, even if Ralph had perhaps been mistaken about Johnny Redburn's reaction to the place.

Ginny left him brooding on the past in front of a game show on television. ('Load of nonsense,' he always said about television; nonetheless, he liked to have it on.) In the kitchen, she opened the freezer and found a Chicken Kiev for two, which she put in the microwave to defrost. She stared at their supper as it revolved on the turntable.

Ginny used to think that Carinish Court tried too hard to be something that it wasn't. The entrance to the drive, for instance, was marked by stone piers surmounted by pineapples, but the piers were stunted and the pineapples crudely carved: had anyone really been fooled?

James had always loved the place. In summer, he used to take friends through the drawing room, out of the French windows and on to the terrace. And there in front of them was the blue rectangle of the swimming pool, framed by the green of the grass and the darker green of the box hedges that acted as windbreaks. If the friends weren't expecting to see the pool, their eyes would widen and James's lips would twitch.

'If you'd like a dip, we can lend you a costume,' James would say casually. 'Unless you'd rather play tennis, that is.'

To reach the hard court, you walked out of the garden door of the house, over the lawn, past the cedar of Lebanon, and there it was, between the rhododendrons of the drive and the wall of the kitchen garden. Ralph had laid it down in the 1950s. In those days he still played a good deal of tennis. One of Ginny's earliest memories was of the contrast between the white of his shirt and shorts and the brown of his skin; his legs and arms had been heavily muscled and covered with a sprinkling of dark hairs, and beads of sweat on his upper lip drained into his thin moustache.

It was true that both the house and the grounds had the curious quality of seeming larger than they were. Carinish Court had once been a farmhouse. Its origins were Queen Anne but it had been remodelled several times, most radically at the turn of the century when it had become the holiday home of a London architect. The drive wound through tall trees and bushes, creating the impression that the house was much further away from the road to Abbotsfield than in fact it was. Suddenly the drive ended in a gravel sweep and the house reared up on the left.

The frontage was stately and symmetrical, promising similar qualities within. Apart from the drawing room, however, the rooms were small and low. There were winding passages, interconnecting rooms and two staircases. Some of the bedrooms were at mezzanine level between the main floors. The kitchen wing was at the back and to the side so the house was L-shaped; and beyond the kitchen was a cobbled yard bounded by the stables, where they kept the cars.

The house was an ordeal for visiting children, who were always getting lost. It made a perfect setting for Murder in the Dark. The memory of that game brought Ginny back to Johnny Redburn: the last time Ginny remembered playing it was when he and his wife came to stay in August 1964. The whole weekend had been unsettling, which was perhaps why the game had stuck in her mind. The adults had gone out. The five of them were alone in the house: herself and James, Kate and Richard Molland, and Peter Redburn.

The game had been James's idea. Richard had been the detective. Ginny had hidden in the big cupboard in the dining room. Richard, whom they had left counting to a hundred by the mains switch in the hall, turned out the lights.

At her age – almost fifteen – Ginny was far too old to take the game seriously. That was what she'd told herself. She was only joining in for the sake of the others because Murder in the Dark is more fun with five than with four. In fact the darkness, the whispers, the creaking floorboards, the footsteps and the thought of a stalking murderer had had their usual effect on her: a state of fear that had little to do with pleasure. The cupboard smelled slightly of damp and even on a warm summer evening Ginny felt the prickle of goose pimples rising on her bare arms.

The house grew still but it was a menacing stillness, like that of a cat about to spring. Ginny's breathing became fast and shallow, and she had difficulty swallowing. She had left the dining-room door open and the cupboard door slightly ajar. She wondered if the others were playing a joke on her: perhaps they'd gone out for a walk; perhaps, at this very moment, they were laughing at the thought of her waiting for a killer who would never come.

Then someone screamed.

Ginny had no idea who it was or where the scream came from. Why hadn't Richard turned the lights on? She burst out of the cupboard, stumbled across the dining room and felt her way down the hall to the cupboard where the mains switch was. She grazed her knuckles on the corner of the fusebox. At last she found the switch.

The lights came on. Richard Molland was clinging to the newel post at the foot of the stairs. His pupils were so enlarged that his eyes looked black.

Ginny smoothed her hands on her dress and got her breathing under some sort of control.

'Who's dead?' she said, trying to sound amused, an adult among children.

He looked at her.

'Who's dead?' she repeated, irritably because she was ashamed of having been scared. 'Do you know? Who screamed?'

'I screamed,' Richard said.

'But you can't be dead. You're the detective.'

Ginny heard the rising note of a car engine and the crunch of tyres on gravel. Peter clattered downstairs. James and Kate came along the passage from the kitchen; they were whispering and giggling. The game was over. Ginny never learned the identity of the murderer.

In the real world, the safe world of the present, with nothing harder to handle than Ralph in the next room, the phone began to ring.

Ginny ran into the hall and picked up the handset. Ralph appeared in the doorway of the living room. Other people's phone calls excited him strangely. It was as if he were always expecting bad news to be relayed to him.

'Hello,' Peter said. 'I'm back in London for a couple of nights. I wondered if there was any chance of our meeting. How about lunch tomorrow?'

Ginny gave him the address and phone number of her office, and arranged to meet him there at 12.45.

'I don't know if you've heard,' he went on, 'but James came to see me yesterday.'

'That was my fault. I hope you don't mind. I gave him your address.'

'You know this book of his? He wants me to help him with it.'

'Do you think that's a good idea?'

'Why not? He's paying quite well.'

'Knowing James, you may end up with more than you bargained for.'

'Don't worry. I remember what he's like. He hasn't really changed.'

'Have any of us?' Ginny said.

'I'm beginning to think we haven't. I've got very vivid memories of that summer, about Abbotsfield and Carinish Court. I'd like to talk about it some time.'

'Okay. If you want.'

They said goodbye and she put down the phone. Ralph was still waiting in the doorway.

'Everything all right?' he said. 'Who was that?'

Ginny wondered how he would react if she told him the simple truth. 'Just a friend,' she said. 'Supper will be ready in about ten minutes.'

Abbotsfield and Carinish Court: Peter had heard the two names for the first time on the same evening in July 1964.

After he had said goodbye to Ginny, he sat down in front of his work table and opened the Letts School-Boy Diary. He had brought it to London with him from Plumford, together with a selection of Emorian documents and one of his mother's account books.

According to the diary, it must have been Friday 17 July. *Good day. Went swimming – temp 73 degrees! Holiday with GMM?* The last sentence could be expanded to 'I may be going on holiday with Richard Molland but I'm not sure.'

July 17 was towards the end of the summer term when the evenings seemed to last for ever. Peter had been outside in the wasteland. By the time he got back to the house, it was after nine o'clock. He opened the door and slipped into the kitchen. Technically he was meant to be in bed.

His parents were in the sitting room. The door was slightly open. Peter hesitated in the hall, not so much to eavesdrop as to prepare himself for a noiseless ascent of the stairs.

'I talked to Barbara Molland today,' his mother was

saying. 'She said they'd have plenty of room, and one more wasn't any bother as far as she was concerned.'

His father cleared his throat and said in a voice that was now almost a whisper: 'So it's all settled then?'

'Not quite. She wants to ask Hubert.'

'He won't object, will he?'

'It's nothing to do with him. *He* won't have the extra work.'

'When are they going?'

'Probably the thirty-first of July. I haven't mentioned it to Peter yet.'

'I think you should.'

'Better not. Wait until it's absolutely certain.'

'Where are they going?' his father asked.

'It's in Somerset. A place called Abbotsfield.'

'Good God, that's not far from Carinish Court. You know, Ralph Salperton's place.'

'Oh yes,' his mother said. 'I suppose it must be.'

'Perhaps I should drop Ralph a line. His kids must be about the same age.'

'Are you sure that's sensible?'

'Oh, Ralph's a good sort. Very hospitable. It'd be nice to see them again, wouldn't it? For us to see them, I mean. We've got a standing invitation. Maybe we should take them up on it.'

His mother didn't reply.

'You never liked him much, did you?'

'What I think about him is neither here nor there. He's your friend.'

Peter backed down the hall and into the kitchen. He opened and closed the back door, taking care to slam it, and returned to the hall, whistling a Beatles' song, 'Can't Buy Me Love'.

'Is that you, Peter?' his father called.

Who else could it be? He went into the sitting room.

'Come to say goodnight, old chap?'

Peter nodded.

'You're late,' his mother said. 'Those jeans will have to be washed. And mind you get your nails clean before you get into bed.'

He kissed his mother on the cheek. His father twisted in his chair and gripped Peter's wrist.

'Are you all right, old son?' he said with an anxiety that infuriated Peter – and also upset him because John Redburn's anxiety was a sign of his vulnerability. Until very recently, Peter had assumed that all adults – and in particular his father – were invulnerable, almost by definition.

'I'm fine,' he said, pulling away. 'See you in the morning.'

Upstairs Peter looked up Abbotsfield in his Philips school atlas. The town or perhaps village was south of Bristol. It looked even smaller than Plumford. All he knew about Somerset was that they had a cricket team and that the yokels drank cider and pronounced it 'zyder'. He wondered what he had done to make his parents want to get rid of him for most of the summer holidays.

At school the next day, he talked to Richard in break.

'Have you heard the news?'

'No. What?'

'It looks like I may be coming with you to Abbotsfield. But keep it quiet. It's not official yet.'

'Great,' Richard said. He squared up to Peter and punched him lightly on the shoulder. 'How do you know?'

Peter winked at him. 'Ve haf vays of making zem talk.' And as he was emperor that week he added, 'My secret police are very efficient.'

If anyone had asked him, Peter would have said that the Mollands had invited him to spend the summer with them at Abbotsfield simply for the pleasure of his company. His mother's account book revealed a different story.

30th July – To H. Molland (for P.) – £5–5–0.

It seemed cheap at the price – five guineas for travel and a month's board and lodging. At the back of the same red Lion Brand Cash Book was a note in his mother's handwriting to the effect that she had given Peter £1 for pocket money.

Before the end of the summer term, he had tried to get more information about Abbotsfield from Richard.

'You never know with a locum,' Richard had explained. 'Sometimes it's awful, sometimes it's great.'

'What does your father have to do?'

'Just take the services on Sunday, I think.'

'What about the other ones? Marriages and funerals and so on?'

'It depends, doesn't it?' Richard said. 'Sometimes we get a funeral. Do you want to see the advert?'

They were in the Mollands' house – not the modern Rectory at Champney Crucis but the Vicarage at Plumford; old Hubert was still Senior Assistant Curate at St Clement's. It was a rambling house and the Mollands lived in what had once been the servants' quarters; the vicar had the rest of the place to himself. Richard went into his father's study and Peter trailed after him. On the desk by the window was an April issue of the *Church Times*. One of the advertisements had been ringed in green ink.

House for duty, 4 Sundays from August 2. PB Catholic. Somerset village. Write: Timball, The Vicarage, Abbotsfield.

'"House for duty"?' Peter said.

'Clerical duties. Taking services. And in return the locum can use the Vicarage rent-free. "PB Catholic" means Prayer Book Catholic, which is sort of high church like St Clem's. You know, incense and crossing yourself.'

Peter, who resented the air of omniscience that Richard assumed on matters ecclesiastical, stared out of the window. The study overlooked the churchyard. Kate was walking towards the Vicarage, arm in arm with a schoolfriend. They wore light-blue blazers and short gingham dresses, and their heads were very close together. Until recently, Peter had thought of Kate as someone to be avoided: a member of an alien species who happened to be Richard's sister. Lately, however, he had begun to be curious about her – almost against his will. He wondered if her hair were as soft as it looked.

Richard had seen them too. 'I bet they're talking "secrets" again. Typical girls.'

Peter, hoping his interest in Kate had not been obvious, turned his back to the window. 'Look here, we've got to have a conference about the Sinking Fund.'

The front door banged.

Richard put a finger to his lips. 'We'd better go up to my room, Your Majesty. This is no place for state secrets.'

The secrets of Emor.

Peter pushed back his chair and stood up. There had been so many secrets. He stood at the window, watching the traffic on Willesden High Road. On the opposite pavement, three West Indian boys waggled their bodies in time to music coming from a nearby shop.

How old were they? It was hard to tell: perhaps no more than twelve or thirteen. Peter wondered whether they had secrets, whether they lived much of their lives in private worlds. The public fantasies of television might have destroyed the need for private ones. They must still have secrets, though; everyone needed secrets.

The secrecy that surrounded Emor had been a large part of its charm. At school they concealed it automatically from masters and other boys: the secrecy was enjoyable for its own sake, and in any case Emor would have been labelled 'childish' – the sort of behaviour that was only one step removed from taking a teddy bear to bed with you at night.

Emor had similarities with Freemasonry or Rosicrucianism. On impulse Peter crossed the room to the bookcase and took down Jung's *Memories, Dreams, Reflections*. It was years since he had read it but he thought Jung had said something about the universal need for secret societies. He checked the index and found the reference.

There is no better way of intensifying the treasured feeling of individuality than the possession of a secret which the individual is pledged to guard. The very beginnings of societal structures reveal the craving for secret organizations. When no valid secrets really exist, mysteries are invented or contrived to which privileged initiates are admitted . . . The need for ostentatious secrecy is of vital importance on the primitive level, for the shared secret serves as a cement binding the tribe together . . . The secret society is an intermediary stage on the way to individuation . . .

The chronology of *The Secret History* recorded the events of more than 200 years. In real time, Peter worked out, Emor began towards the end of 1963 and flourished for nearly two years. In the outside world the Profumo scandal and Philby's defection rocked Macmillan's last government; President Kennedy was assassinated; the United States made its first air raids on North Vietnam. He and Richard must have heard about these things but in general they had failed to register. News headlines were part of a game that adults played.

Peter returned the book to its place on the shelf and went back to the table. He leafed through a pile of documents until he found a sheet of paper torn from an exercise book. It was a formal agreement between himself and Richard, signed in their mingled blood on 29 November 1963. They had pledged eternal friendship between the Gens Redburna and the Gens Mollandia.

In Article 3 of the agreement, each had promised to avenge the violent death of the other with the blood of the murderer.

*

'Emor?' Ginny said. 'Oh, I remember.'

'But you weren't really involved, were you?' Peter said. 'You were too old. The only girl we allowed in was Kate and that was only right at the end.'

It was Tuesday lunchtime, and they were sitting in the restaurant at the Institute of Contemporary Arts in the Mall; Ginny often ate there when she had had enough of the food and the company in the canteen of the British Council.

'I probably knew more than you realized,' she said. 'James told me a lot. He wanted me to give him ideas. One of my ideas was Mithras.'

'Don't blame yourself for that.'

'Easier said than done.'

'In a sense we were all to blame. And me more than most.'

She smiled across the table, grateful that he'd understood.

Peter fiddled with the handle of his coffee cup. He looked very tired. 'Emor was extraordinarily detailed by the time we got to Abbotsfield. Have you ever come across anything like it?'

'Not directly,' Ginny said. 'But it's not uncommon, is it? The Brontë children had a fantasy world, and C. S. Lewis and his brother. You've got respectable literary antecedents.'

'I found the Archives in my mother's loft. That's what started me thinking about it.'

'I never really gathered how Emor began.'

'By accident. I'd swapped some toy cars for a set of poker dice in a red leather case. Richard and I used to play with the dice at school. We started gambling with scraps of papers because we hadn't any real money and matchsticks were forbidden. We marked the papers into denominations – ones and fives and tens. And then one of us said, "Let's make them sesterces." It just went on from there.'

Rome, which was reversed to Emor for reasons of secrecy, grew out of a set of poker dice. Richard and Peter acquired roles to match the sesterces, and names to go with the roles: Gaius Marcus Mollandius and Petronius Redburnus. Since he owned the poker dice, Peter claimed to be the proprietor of the Emperor's Luck Casino, which proved to be a far-sighted move. As time went by, the casino diversified to embrace other gambling games – pontoon, for example, knock-out whist and finally bezique.

Long before that, however, Emor had developed its own momentum. The casino demanded a context – and soon the context was far more important than the casino itself. The great merit of Emor was that it could be adapted to suit the requirements of almost any activity you cared to name. It hovered like an invisible metaphor over their lives, transforming a school lunch into a banquet, a classroom scuffle into a gladiatorial duel, haggling into cabinet-level negotiations.

As the scope of Emor expanded, so the available roles increased. One by one, other boys were absorbed into the empire. Peter could not remember asking them to join; he thought they had volunteered, driven by the craving for fantasy that is common to all children. At the empire's peak in July 1964, there were seven boys at Plumford Grammar School who played parts of varying importance.

Nevertheless, Richard and Peter remained at the centre. They had invented Emor; they did ninety per cent of the paperwork, agreed the salaries of the officials and devised most of the activities. There was plenty of material to work from: Latin was compulsory at Plumford Grammar School; the English master had drummed into their memories large sections of Macaulay's *Lays of Ancient Rome*; they had read novels with a Roman background, like Rosemary Sutcliff's *Eagle of the Ninth* and Robert Graves' *I, Claudius*; and they could plunder Hubert Molland's classical library for further information as the need arose.

As time went by, Emor grew increasingly cerebral. Planning its history became more important than acting it out. They laboured to make the empire internally consistent. He and Richard had sensed that Emor had its own self-generated laws of existence, and that these laws must never be broken.

The imperial succession was a case in point. Fairness demanded that the throne be rotated among the players, usually on a weekly basis. They developed a rationale to explain this in Emorian terms. From the earliest days, no one in Emor was a mere individual: he was also the current representative of a *gens*, one of the great Emorian dynasties that dominated the political life of the empire. In practice the crown passed from one *gens* to another. Richard and Peter devoted a great deal of thought to the theory underlying the succession, and made sure that there was a plausible Emorian reason for each change of emperor.

If he had no children, an emperor might adopt a son from another *gens*, or he might leave the throne to his sister's son, who would of course bear the name of another family. Sometimes the Senate would decree that the son of a deceased emperor was unfit to succeed his father. Perhaps the son was a traitor or a criminal, which led to the exciting possibility of civil wars in later reigns. Perhaps he had been kidnapped or for some reason forced to adopt another identity, in which case he could be trusted to reappear, several reigns later, cover himself in glory and inherit the throne. Perhaps he was too young to assume the purple, in which case the Senate would either appoint a Regent (who usually proclaimed himself emperor and murdered his young rival) or declare that, owing to an emergency (the impending bankruptcy of the empire, for example, or yet another insurrection in Dacia), the throne would pass to a full-grown man. Once – after the reign of the philosopher emperor Gaius Marcus Mollandius Sapiens – Peter and Richard briefly experimented with a republic but this was not a success.

The *gens* system gave Emor an element of continuity. As *The Secret History* and other records showed, most of the great statesmen and admirals of Emor came from the Gens Mollandia, and the Gens Redburna produced an astonishing number of first-class generals. Another advantage of the *gens* system was that you could keep the fortune you had amassed in one incarnation and use it in the next. That was how the Gens Redburna came to dominate the imperial economy.

Petronius Redburnus was a daring and fortunate gambler. As proprietor of the casino he demanded and often received ten per cent of the others' winnings. The Chancellor of the Exchequer had the tedious task of creating more money – of writing out Emorian bank notes to pay the weekly salaries. Successive chancellors found it easier to borrow the ready-made currency in the possession of the Gens Redburna in return for Imperial Notes of Hand; interest was paid on the loans. The sums involved grew larger and larger for the sesterce was bedevilled by inflation. The denominations of bank notes rose; banker's drafts were often used to replace cash; and by the end of Emor several million-sesterce notes were in circulation. Peter Redburn had owned them all. Technically, in fact, he owned a majority share of the treasury as well since most of the money it contained was his. In Emor he had been rich beyond the dreams of avarice.

Suddenly Peter flushed, which made him seem much younger than he was. 'I'm sorry. I think I'm getting obsessed with Emor all over again. It must be incredibly boring.'

'Don't be silly,' Ginny said. 'It's fascinating. Emor's part of my past as well as yours.'

'I'll get us some coffee, shall I?'

She watched him as he queued at the counter. He'd had a haircut. His jacket looked new and he was wearing a tie. In a curious way he seemed more formidable than before. When he came back, they sipped their coffee and avoided each other's eyes. Ginny waited for him to break the silence.

'It's odd we should be talking like this,' he said at last. 'I mean, you hardly know me.'

She hesitated, even opened her mouth; but, before she had time to grasp it, the moment had gone.

'It was a bit like this with James,' he went on, playing with the spoon on his saucer. 'Not to the same degree, of course, but on Sunday there was the same feeling – as if we were continuing a conversation we were having yesterday, as if nothing had really changed. Does that make any sense to you?'

'You'll be careful, won't you?'

'What do you mean?'

'With James. He uses people.'

Peter laid the spoon on the table. Then he looked at her, raising his eyebrows. The restaurant felt very hot.

'Between ourselves,' she said, 'Ralph claims that James cheated him over the sale of Carinish Court. It might well be true.'

'But how could he harm me?'

'I don't know. It's just a feeling.' Embarrassed, Ginny glanced at her watch. 'I should be getting back.'

In the foyer, however, she paused by the bookshop.

'What are you doing for Christmas?'

'I haven't decided yet. I'll probably be by myself – maybe at Plumford; there's a lot of sorting to be done. What about you?'

'I was going to spend it with David in Bristol. I told you – Barbara's stepson. But there's Ralph to consider. So I'm not quite sure what we'll be doing.'

'Have you always called him Ralph?'

'Since I was about eighteen. James does, too. Somehow it's easier.'

He glanced at her. 'You sound as if you don't like him much.'

'I wish I did. He was never very kind to my mother.'

Peter moved towards the door and held it open for

her. 'Don't think I'm prying,' he said as she passed him, 'but is it true that Ralph had an affair with Barbara Molland?'

Eight

'It's a monster,' said James Salperton. 'There's something devilish and uncouth about it, so I call it Caliban. When you switch it on, a little green eye winks at you. I wish I'd never got the beastly thing.'

The shiny personal computer stood on a leather-topped pedestal desk between two glass-fronted bookcases with cupboards below and scrolled pediments above. The room was uncomfortably chilly. The few pictures – mainly landscape watercolours in gilt frames – were conservative, unobtrusive and probably valuable. Pride of place went to an architect's drawing of Carinish Court over the fireplace.

'I'm thinking of buying a PC,' Peter Redburn said, strolling away from the desk. 'A friend lent me hers for a few weeks. They're addictive.'

'You can borrow Caliban if you want.'

'I might take you up on that.'

Peter examined the drawing of Carinish Court. It showed the east façade of the house. The ground level appeared to be slightly higher than he remembered and there was no sign of the seven semi-circular steps leading up to the front door. The drawing was signed and dated in the bottom right-hand corner. Carinish Court as seen in June 1904 by someone with an illegible signature.

'Charles Curran,' James said. 'He was the chap who

owned the place around the turn of the century. Quite well-known in his way. He was an architect who worked with Lutyens.'

'Was it he who added the steps? And isn't the pitch of the roof rather higher nowadays?'

James nodded. 'Yes, and the roof's hipped and sprocketed now, which it wasn't then. That was Curran's doing. Otherwise it's remarkably unchanged, don't you think? Or perhaps you don't remember?'

'Oh, I remember quite well. By the way, I brought you a book.'

Peter took a copy of *The Babylon Baby* from his brief-case. He had signed the title page and added a dedication: 'For James and Kate, with all best wishes.'

'You didn't forget. Wait till Kate sees it.' James studied the title page and for twenty seconds pretended to be fascinated by the contents of page one. 'Wonderful. We'll fight over who reads it first.'

'I hope it won't disappoint you. Now, what about your book?'

James laid *The Babylon Baby* beside the PC. 'I suppose we'd better make a start. We won't be disturbed for an hour and a half at least – Kate's out, and then she'll be seeing to the meal. How do you think we should play this?'

Peter relaxed. Since he'd arrived at Montpelier Square he had been listening for the slightest movement else-where in the flat. By now it was nearly six o'clock. James had asked him to come early so they could do some work on the autobiography before dinner.

'It would be useful to talk in general terms about how you see the shape of the book,' Peter said. 'And

I'd like to get an idea of the raw materials I can use – press cuttings and so on.'

Hitching his trousers to prevent them kneeing, James knelt in front of one of the bookcases and unlocked the cupboard doors. 'Videotapes,' he said. 'Just about everything I've done for film and TV. Underneath I've got the scrapbooks. Have a look. Everything's labelled.'

The scrapbooks were sturdy foolscap-size volumes, bound in black cloth and with the dates they covered marked on the spines. Peter opened one at random and found himself looking at a photograph of Kate. She was climbing into a car and the camera had obviously taken her unawares. Her collar was turned up, masking the lower half of her face. Peter had the impression she was trying to run away. The caption read: 'Is this the new love in Darcy's life?'

James sighed. 'You just wouldn't believe the things they say.' He took the scrapbook and restored it to its place on the shelf. 'In the other cupboard, I've got a collection of memorabilia. School reports, theatre programmes, that sort of thing.'

'The Salperton Archive?'

'Exactly.' James either ignored or failed to notice the undercurrent of mockery in Peter's voice. 'Here, I'll show you.'

He unlocked the other cupboard, opened both doors and ran his finger along the top shelf. 'This section is birth to RADA. Next we've got from RADA to the start of *Pemberley*; that goes up to there.' He pointed to the second shelf, a third of the way along from the left. 'And the rest of that shelf and all of the bottom one covers *Pemberley* to the present.'

'You're very well organized. We could use those as the main divisions of the book.'

'Yes, that's what I thought.'

'With the third as the longest, presumably. That's what people will be interested in.'

'In Mr Darcy.' James swept the hair off his forehead and glanced at Peter. 'I'm sick of him. You know, when they stop me in the street, at least half of them call me Mr Darcy. It's infuriating. I know one shouldn't bite the hand that feeds but sometimes I feel that the roles are reversed: that I'm really William Darcy, and I'm playing the part of James Salperton.'

'Is that why you turned down the fifth series?'

'Partly. Also, I've had offers elsewhere. Even if I'd agreed to a fifth series, *Pemberley* wouldn't have lasted for ever.'

Peter waved towards the cupboard. 'Just going through all that will take quite a while.'

'We haven't got much time,' James said. 'That woman from Channel 20 Books phoned me yesterday.'

'To see how you were doing?'

'Yes. And also to say that one of the Sundays has expressed interest in doing an extract. Clare wants to tie in the publication with the fourth series. It's scheduled to start in April.'

'That's incredibly fast. Publishers usually need about nine months to process a book.'

'So she said. Which is why we've got to get the typescript to her by the end of January. We can do it, can't we?'

'I'm sure we can,' Peter said.

'We'll go through the material together. It looks more

formidable than it is, and of course we'll only use a fraction of it. I've tried to make a start already. Listen to this.' He pulled out a folder from the top shelf. 'My first review – in the school magazine.' It took him only a few seconds to find the page he wanted. '"Salperton made a creditable stab at Ophelia, though"' – Peter grinned – '"though his voice was a little husky for the part." *Hamlet*, nineteen sixty-five.' James looked up and added sharply, 'What's funny?'

'The reviewer's phrasing,' Peter said. 'It's unintentionally ambiguous.'

'Oh lord, so it is.' James frowned. 'I'd never noticed.'

'Could be useful. Add a touch of humour to the first chapter.'

'Perhaps. I suppose you're the best judge of that.' James moved towards the desk. 'I've chosen the photographs, by the way. That's one thing you needn't worry about. Would you like to see them?' Taking Peter's agreement for granted, he opened one of the bottom drawers of the desk and removed an envelope file. 'Clare wants sixteen pages of black-and-white. I thought she could make a selection from these.'

Peter sat down on the leather sofa, which was as uncomfortable as it looked, and went through the folder. The photographs were like a comic-strip biography: Salperton in pictures. James in a pram, with his parents poised above him. James on a stout little pony beside the cedar tree at Carinish Court, and Ginny, squinting at the camera, standing on the grass with the reins dangling from her hand. James in short trousers and a blazer; James in cricket kit; James in the boxing team of his public school. James carrying a spear for the

Royal Shakespeare Company. James mingling with the famous, on and off the screen. James in a toga; James in a top hat; James as Darcy. James chatting with the Earl of Farrow outside Farrow Hall, which had been used for many of the exterior shots in *Pemberley*. James shaking hands with Lord Olivier, whose mind was obviously elsewhere, and with the Princess of Wales, who looked puzzled. James and Kate at their wedding, at which Lord Farrow had been James's best man. James and Kate divided by a tea table on the terrace at Carinish Court.

'That was taken in late September,' James said, perching in the arm of the sofa. 'I wanted to have one of us at the house.'

Peter leafed back through the photographs. He paused at James in his pram. 'Your parents made a good-looking couple, didn't they?'

'Not bad. I'm told I take after my mother's side of the family.'

'No pictures of Ursula.' Peter returned the photographs to the folder and handed it to James. 'Is that intentional?'

'I didn't want to upset Kate.'

'We'll have to mention Ursula in the text.'

'I suppose so. I hoped we could gloss over my first marriage as much as possible.'

'As you like, of course. But people will notice. They'll want to hear your side of it.'

'I can't say what I really think about her. She'd sue me.'

'Silence might be construed as an admission of guilt.'

'Guilt? For what? Ursula made my life intolerable. If you ask me, jealousy was at the root of it. When we got married she was a lot more successful than I was. She was two years older so it wasn't surprising. But she just couldn't take it when I started pulling ahead. That was the real reason why she left acting, that and the fact that she was losing her looks.'

'There was a lot of talk about the time when she and Kate —'

'Kate was just trying to defend herself. Ursula leapt at her, completely out of the blue. We were damned unlucky, actually. If only the photographers hadn't been there, we might have been able to hush it up.'

'And the money?'

'Must we go into that?'

'Other people will.'

'I just don't see what upsets them.' James slid off the arm of the sofa and stuffed his hands in his trouser pockets. 'Damn it, it's so unreasonable. Why not blame my broker? It was he who advised the sale. I happened to make a shrewd investment in 'seventy-eight, and a couple of years ago I sold out. That's all there was to it.'

'The timing was unfortunate.'

'That wasn't my fault. Yes, I knew about the takeover — I could hardly avoid it — but that was Ursula's headache, not mine. The negotiations had driven up the share prices, which was wonderful. As far as I was concerned, it made it the logical time to sell. The fact I used to be married to Ursula is completely irrelevant.'

'Yes, I can see that,' Peter said. 'I'm sure that in your place I'd have done the same. Still, it cost Ursula control of the Hair House, didn't it? And everyone knew you'd quarrelled. The point is, to an outsider who didn't know better, your actions could appear vindictive.'

'Rubbish.'

'Of course it is. But people listen to rubbish.' And watch it on their televisions, Peter thought. 'Leave it me,' he went on. 'A paragraph or two would do it, make it clear that you've been unfairly treated. I think it would be best if you came across as nobly resigned: "How could she stoop to do this to me" – something along those lines – without going into too much detail. We can hint that a less honourable man could have ground her up to mincemeat.'

He wondered if he had gone too far; but James was nodding approvingly.

'I can see I made the right choice,' James said. 'You've got a talent for this. Ever thought of trying public relations as a career?'

'No.'

'Just a thought. Shall we make a start on the taping?'

Peter took a pad from his briefcase. 'I've roughed out a few questions but they're only a guide.'

James opened another drawer in the desk and produced a cassette recorder with a built-in microphone. He put the machine on the round table in front of the sofa, plugged it into a socket and sat down in the nearest armchair.

'I assume you'd like to work chronologically.' He inserted a tape in the recorder. 'Where do we begin?'

'Family background?'

James leant forward and switched on the recorder. 'Testing, testing, one, two, three.' The needle in the level indicator jumped towards the red. 'That's all right.' He gestured towards Peter. 'Over to you.'

'Tell me a little about your parents.'

'Well, Ralph used to be a tea importer, third generation in a family business. Salperton's Quality Teas. He's
a bit of a genealogist – claims the family goes back to
the Normans. Minor country gentry, I suppose. Is this
the sort of stuff you need? Seems rather boring to me.'

'It's fine,' Peter said. 'Every picture needs a frame.
Do go on.'

Now the recording had started, James's voice had
changed: it was richer, more assured; Darcy had pushed
aside Salperton.

'My mother was the daughter of a regular army officer
– a lieutenant-colonel in the North Staffordshires. They
met while Ralph was in the army. It was in the war,
I think, and –'

A door banged. Peter shifted on the sofa, and a
spring twanged dully beneath him. James cocked his
head.

'Ah,' he said. 'Kate's back.'

An hour later, James pushed open the drawing-room
door. 'Darling,' he said. 'Here's Peter.'

Kate was sitting on one of the two deep sofas that
stood at right angles to the fireplace. As Peter and James
came in, she threw down the magazine she was reading,
stood up and came towards them. She was dressed in
a cream shirt and navy-blue slacks that fitted snugly over
the hips; the only jewellery she wore was a platinum
wedding ring. Her movements were fluid, economical
and beautiful to watch, like those of a good swimmer.
She laid her hands on Peter's shoulders and kissed him
on the cheek.

'Peter,' she said.

That was all. Unlike the others, she didn't rush to say how pleased she was to see him after all this time; she didn't make polite small talk about Lucasta Redburn's death. Just 'Peter', and a kiss.

'You're cold. Come and sit by the fire. James always keeps the study at sub-zero temperatures.'

'Are you cold?' James said, surprised. 'I can't think straight if a room's too warm. It tends to affect my sinuses, too.'

'Dinner will be ready in about fifteen minutes. Why don't you get us all a drink, darling?'

'What will you have?' James said to Peter.

'Have you any angostura? I'd like a pink gin.'

'What a lovely idea,' Kate said. 'I'll have one too.'

James fussed over the drinks tray, which was on a table behind one of the sofas. Kate sat down on the sofa beside Peter.

'Mum sends her love,' she said. 'I'd hoped she and Leo could be here tonight, but they had another engagement.'

'How is she?' Peter said.

He listened less to the answer than to Kate's voice, and, as he listened, he watched her face. She sounded huskier than he remembered; she spoke slowly, the full lips lingering on words as though reluctant to part with them. She'd cut off her hair, which he already knew from seeing her photograph in the papers; it had the effect of making her head seem less of a burden on the slender neck. There were tiny laughter lines at the corners of the eyes. The eyes themselves were the same arresting blue that you see so infrequently. It astonished him that her outward appearance had changed so little.

James handed round the drinks; he had poured himself a tonic water with a slice of lemon.

'We've made a good beginning,' he said, interrupting Kate's account of how Ginny Salperton had met David Quest. 'Almost an hour on tape.'

'Oh good.' Kate was still looking at Peter but she accepted the change of subject smoothly, like a skilful footballer changing tack to cope with a pass from an unexpected direction. 'How will you actually do it? Isn't it terribly hard, pretending to write as someone else?'

'It's what a novelist does all the time. No, the idea is, I'll transcribe the tape more or less verbatim and then work in the other material.' Smiling, Peter glanced up at James. 'Like how you made a stab at Ophelia in nineteen sixty-five.'

Kate giggled. 'Do you think you'll get it finished by the end of January?'

'I don't see why not, if we work flat out.'

'Isn't this interfering with your own writing?'

'I can manage.'

'Talking of which,' James said, 'Peter's brought us a signed copy of *The Babylon Baby*. Isn't that kind? It's in the study – I'll fetch it.'

When they were alone, Peter said, 'You don't have to read it, you know. It's rather precious and juvenile.'

'Of course I shall read it,' Kate said. 'And I'll tell you exactly what I think about it.'

James came back with the book. She glanced at the dedication and at the cover.

'Terrible jacket, isn't it?' Peter said.

She wrinkled her nose. 'At least you needn't blame yourself for that.' She put down the book and said abruptly: 'I gather you've seen something of my father?'

'He's my mother's executor,' he said. 'He took the funeral service.'

'Is he all right?'

'As far as I know. He's retired, of course, but he helps out at St Clem's and he's still very vigorous. Do you mean you don't see him at all?'

'That's not our fault,' James said. He picked up his glass and sank into the armchair near Kate's end of the sofa.

'He never really forgave me for leaving home,' she said to Peter. 'You remember? When I was eighteen?'

'I remember.' Peter thought about Julian and the red Triumph Spitfire, and about Barbara Molland in the hall of the Rectory at Champney Crucis.

'He saw it as – I don't know – a sort of betrayal? Later, I tried to smooth things over, but he wasn't interested. He knew I was living with someone, living in sin.' She patted James's hand. 'Before your time, darling. Anyway, that made me a scarlet woman.'

'We asked him to our wedding,' James said.

'Yes, but he wouldn't come because it was in a registry office. Not valid in the eyes of God. As far as Dad's concerned, marriages are eternal. James was divorced, so that makes us both adulterers.'

'It's primitive.' James shrugged. 'But what can one do? He's too set in his ways to change.'

'Sometimes I feel I should have made more of an effort with him,' Kate said. 'Maybe it's not too late.'

'You've done all you can,' James said. 'No point in making yourself ridiculous. Let's face it – we're all friends here; Peter won't mind my talking about it

– your father's a little eccentric, and that's putting it kindly.'

Kate stared at the fire. A lump of coal cracked and a tongue of flame spurted out of it. While the others were talking of Hubert Molland, Peter had felt like a spectator at a play – as if he were watching a scene that had been rehearsed so many times that the actors spoke their lines mechanically, hardly caring about the meaning. Were the 'darlings' and the hand-pattings equally mechanical? And if they were, what did that say about the relationship between James and Kate?

'Darling.' James smiled at Kate. 'I just don't want you to get hurt again, you know that.'

'I know.' She smiled back and turned to Peter. 'Was it very strange, going back to Plumford?'

'A little. Like dreaming about a familiar place, and in the dream it fails to correspond to your memory of it. Unsettling.'

Kate nodded. 'It's the same when you dream about people doing things that you know they'd never do in real life.'

For the next five minutes all three of them talked about dreams. The conversation was natural and easy. And why not? James and Kate were a happily married couple, and Peter was an old friend. Peter thought that he'd been a fool to imagine that there might be something wrong between his hosts; he put it down to an overactive imagination coloured by wishful thinking.

Kate brought them back to Plumford. 'It's the last place on earth I'd want to live.'

Peter nodded. 'As soon as I'm shot of the house, I'll be off.'

'Can't you let an estate agent handle that?' James asked.

'Not really. The circumstances are unusual.' Peter explained about Coleby's offer and the planned shopping development. 'I'd rather handle the negotiations myself.'

'Do you think he'll give you the price you want?'

'Eventually.' Peter saw no reason to conceal the figure; Petronius Redburnus had never been modest. 'I'm ready to wait if I have to. A quarter of a million pounds is worth waiting for.'

'What will you do with the money?' Kate said. 'Or shouldn't we ask?'

'Buy a house, probably, and write.'

'What about your job?'

'I've chucked that in.'

'You're lucky to have so much freedom.' Kate stirred beside him on the sofa, and Peter smelled her perfume. 'It must be intoxicating.'

'Oh, it is,' Peter felt light-headed, tipsy on a small pink gin, but still completely in control. 'Like wine.' Or, he thought, to be more precise, like the smell of a desirable woman.

'Talking of freedom,' James said, 'Kate and I were wondering what you were doing for Christmas.'

The euphoria dissolved. Peter said, 'I've nothing planned.'

'Would you like to come down to Carinish Court for a few days?'

'You wouldn't want me there.' Peter was aware of his heart thudding in his chest. 'Not at Christmas, surely?'

'It would be lovely,' Kate murmured.

The words were all right but the lack of emphasis made Peter suspicious. He glanced at her, wondering if this were the first she had heard of the proposal. She met his eyes and smiled.

'You'd be our first house guest,' James said. 'We'd love it. And also, of course, I'm being selfish. I was hoping we could get through a certain amount of work.'

'At Christmas, darling?'

'Now, don't worry. I'm not suggesting that we chain Peter to Caliban for eighteen hours a day. But we'd be able to cover a lot of ground. For one thing, there won't be the interruptions we get here.' He turned back to Peter. 'Look, we're going down on Saturday. We're thinking of staying about ten days – into the new year, anyway. You'd be welcome to stay as long as you wanted. You can have a room to work in, anything you need.'

'What about all the documents?' Peter asked. 'The scrapbooks and so on.'

'Easy. We'll take the Range Rover. Plenty of room for everything. Do say you'll come.'

'It's very kind of you.'

'Not kind,' Kate said. 'You'd be doing James a favour. Me, too, come to that – if you don't come, he'll spend the whole time fretting about the book.'

'You'll come, Peter, won't you?' James raised one of his eyebrows, puckering the skin of his forehead, and his lips twitched in the sort of smile that invites complicity. He was very sure of himself. 'Look at me,' his expression said. 'I'm pleading with you and mocking myself at the same time: how can you bear to resist?'

'Of course I'll come,' Peter said. 'If you're both certain. Remember, you hardly know me.'

Beside him on the sofa, Kate let out her breath in an almost silent rush of air – too quietly for James to have heard. To Peter, it sounded like a sigh of relief.

'That's wonderful, isn't it, darling?' James said. 'If you want, you can drive down with us.'

'If you don't mind, I think I'll hire a car. In fact, I've been considering buying one.'

'Whatever you prefer. Let's hope it doesn't run out of petrol, eh?' James glanced from Peter to Kate. 'Surely you haven't forgotten? That's how we all met.'

The car that ran out of petrol on 31 July 1964 was a six-cylinder Rover belonging to Commander Molland, Richard and Kate's grandfather. Like the commander, whom Peter met at Plumford Vicarage just before they left for Abbotsfield, the car had seen better days.

Commander Molland, a widower, was intending to spend August abroad. He had offered the car to Hubert for the summer on condition that everyone promised never to stand on the running boards, because they were threatening to fall off. Like its owner, the Rover was large and upright. It was a maroon colour, now much mottled, which was another point of resemblance between them. The seats, upholstered in dark red leather, held you high above the surface of the road and shed a certain dignity on your journey; you did not so much travel as process.

A car was a novelty to both Peter and Richard, since neither of their fathers owned one. At Plumford, they bombarded the commander with questions about it. He said the Rover was about thirty years old ('and that's a damn sight younger than I am') and that it did only sixteen miles to the gallon.

'But look at the coachwork. Beautiful. That's quality. Open the door and shut it, young man. Hear that? No, not the squeak. Just needs a drop of oil. I mean the way it went "clunk". Perfect craftsmanship. These days, if you want to hear a car door close like that, you have to buy a Rolls-Royce.'

The windows were tinted yellow and in places were now almost opaque. The interior smelled of the commander's pipe, and the worn carpet was grey with ash. The dashboard and the other wooden fittings were made of walnut.

'How fast will it go?' Richard asked.

'Oh, she'll reach fifty quite easily. But I wouldn't advise it. You get a smell of rubber if you go that fast.' The commander puffed his pipe and looked puzzled. 'Bit of a mystery, actually. Never been able to find out where the smell comes from.'

'Where's the boot?'

'She doesn't have a boot,' the commander said. 'In those days your servants looked after the heavy luggage. But there's plenty of room on the roof rack.'

The drive to Abbotsfield was a slow and unpleasant experience for all of them. Hubert Molland was an unpractised driver and his nervousness seemed to communicate itself to the big car, which juddered and groaned alarmingly. Even at forty-five m.p.h. the smell of burning rubber would have been overpowering if they had not had the windows open. He drove with fierce concentration, and sometimes his fierceness spilled over on to the passengers – especially on to Barbara, who sat beside him and navigated.

'Can't you keep those children quiet? Which way do we go here?'

'Left, I think.' Barbara swivelled in the seat and mouthed threats at Richard and Kate.

'What on earth's that lorry doing? That fool shouldn't be allowed on the roads.'

'Oh, Hubert – that signpost said Bristol. I've an awful feeling we should have gone right at the last junction. I am sorry.'

Peter, who was sitting on the nearside at the back of the car, could see a muscle jumping in Hubert Molland's cheek. On one occasion he thought he heard Hubert's teeth grinding; but it was difficult to be sure because of the roar of the engine.

Richard was sitting in the middle of the back seat, separating Peter from Kate in the other corner. Stacked on the floor around their legs was all the luggage that wouldn't fit on the roof rack. The children were wedged so tightly that it was difficult to move.

Peter would have liked to sit next to Kate but he had lacked the necessary social agility to secure the centre position. He was nervous, too, because he was stuck with the Mollands for the next four weeks, and he was terribly afraid of feeling homesick. He didn't mind being with Richard – being with Richard was almost like being with himself – and he liked what he knew of Mrs Molland. Kate was curiously fascinating, but mixed in with the fascination was a sort of fear; and over the last few months she had made it quite clear that the less she had to do with him, the better she would like it.

Most worrying of all was the prospect of spending a month in the same house as the Reverend Hubert Molland. Even Richard was afraid of his father. Mr Molland was like all the unpleasant masters at school rolled into one, with the additional drawback of a dog collar round his neck.

The Rover ambled across England from east to west. The children read, played games and looked out of the window; they complained about the hardness of the seats and squabbled.

They had started early, when the day was still cool, but soon it grew very hot. The squabbling became more bitter, and the adults began to snap at the children. Twice they had to stop because Richard thought he was going to be sick. At lunchtime they pulled into a lay-by for a picnic; and later in the afternoon they had tea in a transport café where three lorry drivers stared at them, whispered to one another and laughed.

'How far is it now?' Richard and Kate kept asking until Hubert Molland shut them up. 'Are we nearly there?'

The atmosphere improved when they were past Bristol. By now it was after five o'clock. Barbara Molland's navigation became faultless. When they reached the town of Paulstock, Hubert Molland even made a joke.

'Paulstock, eh? We must see if there's a Peterstock.'

Peter tried to smile.

'Keeps your eyes skinned for a garage, everyone,' Hubert said. 'I'd like to get some petrol.'

'We're still half-full, aren't we?' Barbara said.

'I think the fuel gauge has jammed.'

'Look at that signpost,' Kate shouted. 'Only ten miles to Abbotsfield.'

Mr Molland grunted. 'Thank heavens for that. I was beginning to wonder if the place actually existed.'

Eight miles later, when they were coasting down a long hill, the engine spluttered. After a few seconds it cut out completely. The heavy car rushed on. Only the wind made a sound as it streamed along the sides of the Rover and poured through the open windows.

'Perhaps we'll roll all the way to Abbotsfield,' Richard whispered.

All of them were sitting forward in their seats, as if bracing themselves for a collision. The ground levelled out. Peter saw a church tower in the distance. The Rover slowed. Soon it was moving at the speed of a trotting horse between a high hedge on the right-hand side and a stone wall on the left. As the wind dropped, Peter heard the squeaking of the car and Richard's fast, excited breathing. No one spoke.

Hubert Molland pulled over towards the wall and stopped across the entrance of a drive.

'What's that?' Kate said, pointing.

'It's a pineapple,' Richard said. 'Look, there's another.'

'There's someone coming,' Barbara said.

A tall boy was walking unhurriedly down the drive towards them. Fair and slim, he wore a white shirt, tight blue jeans and black, Cuban-heeled boots.

Peter heard Kate sigh with pleasure. He felt hot and inexplicably angry.

'He looks like a pop star,' she said.

Nine

Ginny had arranged to take the Wednesday off work. She wanted to celebrate Ralph's departure by cleaning the flat and doing some Christmas shopping. That was before Ursula phoned late on Tuesday evening, after which she modified her plans.

First, however, Ginny took Ralph to Paddington. Though he had never said as much directly, she guessed that he was afraid of London, and particularly afraid of being mugged on the Underground. On tube trains his head turned ceaselessly to and fro, his eyes were large and anxious, and he clung to his bag.

When they reached the station, she stood with him while he bought a ticket to Bristol, helped him find the right platform and installed him in the smoking carriage near the front of the train. He lined up lighter, cigarettes and *Daily Telegraph* on the table in front of his seat.

'I'll be off then,' Ginny said.

'So I'll see you next on Christmas Day?' Ralph asked for the third time that morning.

'I'll collect you about eleven o'clock. I'll phone before I leave David's.'

'David Quest,' Ralph said, like a boy repeating a lesson he has by heart but does not fully understand. 'Leo's son. He lives in Bristol. And you'll take me back to Paulstock after lunch?'

'Of course.'

'Sorry to be such a bother,' he said. 'I like to get things straight. Just a minute – I'd better check I've got enough money for the taxi at the other end.'

Ginny wondered whether Ralph was subtly implying that she ought to have driven him back to Paulstock. Probably not, if only because subtlety was not Ralph's forte. The delay was completely unnecessary because he'd counted the cash in his wallet last night, and they both knew he had enough.

'Right,' Ralph shut his wallet with a snap. 'No problem there. Thank you for all your hospitality.'

Again, had Ralph been a subtler man, Ginny would have suspected him of sarcasm. As it was, she suspected him merely of insincerity. He offered his cheek to be kissed and they said goodbye.

She walked quickly along the platform. As she passed his window she waved. He didn't look up. He was already engrossed in the *Daily Telegraph*.

From Paddington Ginny caught the tube to Oxford Circus. Ursula's flat was only a few minutes' walk away.

Unlike Ginny, who liked to relish pleasures in advance, Ursula Salperton believed in spontaneity, at least in her personal relationships; she had a different set of rules for business. Last night, just before midnight, she'd phoned out of the blue. Both the time and the unexpectedness were typical.

'Hello, Tonic,' she'd said cheerfully. 'How's tricks?'

'Fine.' Ginny noticed that Ralph was waiting expectantly in the doorway of the spare room. Once Ursula started she might go on for hours. 'It's rather difficult just now. Could I call you back tomorrow?'

'All right. Or come and see me if you'd rather.'

'In the morning? Between ten and eleven, say?'

'Yes, okay. I'll be at the flat, not the office.'

When Ginny put down the phone, Ralph advanced into the hall: 'Who was that?'

'Just a friend,' Ginny said. Ralph and Ursula had never liked each other.

'Bit late to phone, isn't it?'

'No harm done. Goodnight.'

'Night, night. Sleep tight.'

Ursula owned three homes – an apartment in Manhattan, a house in Paris and a small flat above an Italian restaurant in Beak Street, Soho. She had bought the flat in the early 1970s, long before she met James. In the first years of their marriage, when they were living in Notting Hill, James had tried to persuade her to let it or, failing that, at least to refurbish it.

'But I like it how it is,' Ursula had wailed. 'I like squalor. Ginny, can't you make him understand?'

The flat was on the north side of Beak Street in a house with a typical Soho exterior: on the ground floor, everything was brash plate-glass and twentieth-century tiles; but the floors above were still faced with grey bricks and lit by neat eighteenth-century windows; and from the slate roof poked Victorian dormers with rotting frames.

The black door was tucked between the restaurant and the ironmonger's next door. Apart from the spy-hole, the door looked as though no one had touched it for at least a century; but Ursula had installed new locks, a steel frame and a burglar alarm. She might be eccentric but she wasn't stupid.

There were two bells, one labelled Frisby, which was Ursula's maiden name, and the other blank, as it had been for the past six years. Ginny suspected that Ursula had bought the lease on the flat above hers, and possibly the freehold of the entire building. Everything changes, Ginny thought; nothing stays the same unless you can afford to keep it that way. Over a period of time even squalor becomes a luxury.

Ursula opened the door and drew Ginny into the narrow passage that served as a hall. Her long grey hair was drawn into a ragged ponytail and secured by an elastic band. She wore a blue silk dressing gown, which had once belonged to James and before that to Ralph, over jeans and a khaki army-surplus jersey. The silk had torn below the left armpit. The dressing gown was far too large for her and the hem trailed along the floor, gathering dust and cat hairs.

Ursula smiled. 'Hello, Tonic.'

'Hello.'

'Playing hooky from the office?'

'I've got the day off work.'

They kissed each other. Ursula led the way up the narrow stairs, the soles of her slippers slapping against the uncarpeted treads. The nickname dated from the time when her marriage to James had at last reached the point of no return. Ginny, who had just separated from David's predecessor, had spent an evening with her in Beak Street. Each of them drank a bottle of Bollinger and promised to help the other rebuild her life. In honour of the promised they had bestowed new names on each other; Ursula's had been 'Little Bear'. The new lives were not very different from the old, but

Ursula often called Ginny 'Tonic' when they were alone. 'Little Bear', however, had fallen into disuse because Ginny, whose blurred memory of that evening embarrassed her, had rarely been able to bring herself to use it.

One of the cats was waiting at the top of the stairs – a slender tortoiseshell creature named Teresa. Ursula scratched the cat's head as she passed. The living room was small, with a glowing gas fire and a single window shrouded with net curtains.

'Make yourself at home,' Ursula said.

This was easier said than done because the other cats were asleep on the two easy chairs – Mona, a small tabby, and Daisy, who was large, half-Persian and inclined to give herself airs. Ginny sat down at the table by the window.

'Tea?' Ursula said, dragging another hard chair up to the table.

'Thank you.'

Ursula fetched a cup without a saucer from the kitchen. When she sat down, Teresa leapt on to her lap. As usual the tea was very black Earl Grey, poured from a large brown teapot.

'What do you do with the cats when you're abroad?' Ginny said. 'I've often wondered but I never remember to ask you.'

'They stay here. Dorabella feeds them.' Ursula jerked her thumb downwards, towards the restaurant. 'The longer I'm away, the fatter they get.' She added without rancour: 'They love Dorabella much more than me.'

She had a fat red face and beautiful green eyes. When Ginny first knew her, Ursula had been plump and pretty with dyed ash-blonde hair; she had earned a comfortable living from playing barmaids, prostitutes and mistresses.

'I'm a character actress,' she used to say. 'I'll do anything as long as it's dead common and has big tits.' Even then she had been casting around for another career: 'Beddable blondes have a limited shelf life.'

'I hope I haven't dragged you up to town.'

Ginny shook her head. 'I've just taken Ralph to Paddington.'

'Ah, that's why you couldn't talk last night. The ever-listening ear.'

'He stayed for three whole nights.'

'Your own fault. You shouldn't let him get away with it.'

'And he dragged me away from a weekend with David.'

'When are you two going to make up your minds about each other?'

'Don't bully me,' Ginny said. 'David's made up his mind. I'm the one who isn't sure.'

Ursula tapped her cigarette against the ashtray. 'I wouldn't leave it too long. He struck me as the sort of man who's in search of permanence.'

'David?'

'And if he doesn't find it with you, he'll eventually look elsewhere. But maybe that's what you want.'

'No,' Ginny said. 'I don't think it is. I told Ralph about him yesterday.'

'He didn't know before?'

'Well, no. There never seemed any point in upsetting him.' Ginny stopped, hoping she had said enough. But

Ursula's lips were pursed and her eyes were full of accusation. 'It wasn't as if I'd committed myself. And then of course David's Jewish, and he makes his living painting houses, and not a very good living at that. I know he's an artist too, but he's only sold about three pictures in his entire life. Anyway Ralph thinks all artists are immoral, and even worse if they haven't any money.'

'You chickened out, Tonic. Be honest. You hate things to be unpleasant.'

'I didn't chicken out. Oh, all right, I suppose I did. Anyway, I had to tell him last night because of Christmas. Ralph wanted me to cook his Christmas dinner and pull crackers with him. But I'd already arranged to be with David. And when I talked to David about it, he suggested asking Ralph for Christmas lunch. Just for lunch, which, incidentally, David's going to cook. A sort of compromise, you see. Everyone gains something. The only problem was, I had to tell Ralph about David.'

'You should have done it ages ago. What did he say?'

'That was the weird bit. He said he was glad to hear about David because he'd been worried about my being on my own. Then he started talking about how happy he and my mother had been. The whole thing was so out of character I just sat there with my mouth open.'

Ursula blew out smoke. 'I expect Ralph has his reasons. Has James been upsetting him?'

'Ralph's just cut him out of his will,' Ginny said, wishing that Ursula were less shrewd and less inclined to attack her exhusband at every possible opportunity. 'He's convinced that James cheated him over Carinish Court.'

'Wouldn't surprise me in the least. It would explain why Ralph's being nice to you. You know, the last remaining prop of his old age.'

Ginny shrugged.

'I like David,' Ursula went on. 'Why don't you take him for a dirty weekend in Paris? You could use the house.'

'I'm not sure he'd belong in the Sixteenth Arondissement.'

'That man would belong anywhere. Ask him. See what he thinks. And now I want to ask you something. When I got back from the States yesterday, there was a sheaf of messages at the office. Someone called Peter Redburn wants to get in touch with me.'

'Peter?'

'You do know him, then? My secretary – you remember Simon? – told me he claimed to be having lunch with you yesterday. In other words, I thought, this Redburn knows you and I are friendly and he was trying to use you as his passport. According to Simon he was very persistent, very polite. Not a journalist, though, or so he said. So who is he?'

Ginny hesitated. 'You could call him an old friend, I suppose. James and I knew him when we were kids, and so did Kate. We met again last week. I remember mentioning that I saw more of you than I did James. What does he want with you?'

'"Personal business." Whatever that means.'

'He's a writer. He's going to ghost James's autobiography.'

'I can't help him with that. Or not in a way that James would approve of.'

'Then maybe it's something else. Background information?'

'I know what he wants,' Ursula said, coughing and laughing at the same time. 'He's planning blackmail. James has given him the dirt on me. I wee in the bath. I bite the heads off live chickens.' She stopped laughing and squinted through the smoke at Ginny. 'What's wrong?'

'It worries me.'

'Why should it? I can handle James.'

'But I doubt if James knows that Peter's trying to see you. I'm not sure that Peter even likes him.'

'A point in Peter's favour. So why are you worried?'

Ginny drank her tea to postpone having to answer.

Ursula put her head on one side. 'You fancy him? Is that it?'

'No, it's not that.'

'Then what is it?'

'Peter keeps asking questions. Like, did Ralph have an affair with Kate's mother in nineteen sixty-four?'

'Did he?'

'I'm not sure. Possibly. But why does Peter want to know?'

'Ask him.'

'I did. He said it's for a book he's writing – not James's autobiography: a novel called *London*. He's interested in the relationship between reality and memory, and he's making a sort of case study of his own past to explore the overlap between them.'

'Sounds like a poncy way of trying to justify being nosy. Why don't you tell him to piss off?'

'I don't want to do that.'

'Are you going to explain? Or shall we talk about something else?'

Ursula waited. Ginny listened to the traffic in Beak Street, to the hum of a Hoover downstairs, to Teresa's purring. And then, because she wanted Ursula to know and it might as well be sooner rather than later, Ginny explained about Peter Redburn.

The doorbell rang for the third time.

Barbara Quest tiptoed away from the spyhole. She felt harassed, cowardly and ridiculous: an unpleasant combination. As she climbed the stairs, she clung to the banisters.

She'd recognized Peter Redburn at once – despite the passage of twenty years, despite the fish-eye distortions of the spyhole's lens. Why hadn't he phoned? There was an easy answer to that: a caller on the doorstep is harder to rebuff.

The house felt like a spacious padded cell. Barbara slipped into the bedroom she shared with Leo. Fortunately she was alone. Ignoring the doorbell requires explanations. She padded over to the window and peered out.

Lavender Lane was empty. The half-timbered houses across the road might have been deserted. The monkey-puzzle in the front garden looked like a child's construction made of giant green pipe-cleaners. A bedraggled swan swam sluggishly across the grey surface of the round pond on the corner of the lane; nothing else moved. Barbara's breath misted the glass. She changed her position so that she could see the roof of the porch below.

At last Peter gave up. She saw a dark head and a tan raincoat emerge from the porch. She backed away from the window and crouched down. He might look back at the house and see her watching. Rationally she knew that he wouldn't have been able to see her unless she were right up against the leaded panes.

She sat on the floor, leaning back against the bed. Everything was so muddled. Leo had once counted the reasons why he loved her: 'And fourthly, my pet, I love you because you are not logical.'

Peter might be waiting, suspecting that she was inside. He might be snooping round the back of the house or hiding in the garden. He might have gone to fetch something from a car parked just up the road; probably he was walking back to the house.

She stood up – slowly and a little painfully because her joints had already begun to stiffen. She hobbled on to the landing and listened. He must have gone. Why should he bother to stay? Barbara tried to persuade herself that anyone would have acted as she had done. The past was the past: dead and buried. She and Peter had nothing left to say to each other. There was no point in seeing him again. Also, he might upset things.

Peter had been an observant boy. It wasn't that she couldn't cope with an adult Peter or with what he might tell Leo. It was merely that, given the choice, it was wiser to avoid trouble than to meet it head-on.

The idea crossed her mind that none of this would have happened if she had been entirely frank with Leo from the outset. She pushed the thought away. Leo was a romantic. It would have been unkind to destroy his illusions. Besides, none of it had really been her fault.

Everything was so unfair. She wasn't to blame for the car running out of petrol.

'The gauge has jammed,' Hubert had explained to the beautiful boy. 'I wonder if your parents would sell us a drop of petrol or let me telephone a garage. We're not going far. Just to Abbotsfield.'

The boy had seen the dog collar. 'Are you the locum, sir?'

'That's right. I'm standing in for Mr Timball.'

'I'm sure we've got some spare petrol. I'll go and get it.'

'I think I should first have a word with your father or mother.' Hubert was always a stickler for such formalities. 'If it's convenient, that is.'

'Of course. My father's up at the house.'

Hubert got out of the car. 'My name's Molland, by the way. And this is Mrs Molland; our children, Kate and Richard; and their friend Peter Redburn.'

'Not my friend,' Kate muttered.

'How do you do. I'm James Salperton.'

The beautiful boy had manners to match. Curious to see his parents and the house where they lived, Barbara opened her door.

'I think I'll come too.'

'There's no need, dear.'

'I'd like to stretch my legs.' Barbara grimaced at Hubert. 'The children can stay here.'

He avoided her eyes. 'As you wish.'

James rushed round the car to hold the door for her.

In some respects Hubert was easy to manage. She knew the grimace had worried him and that he wouldn't dare to ask her what it meant, not in front of James.

He would interpret it either as a pressing need to use the lavatory or as evidence that Barbara thought it would be uncivil not to meet the Salperton parents. He was surprisingly sensitive about how other people saw him and his family; and his sensitivity was increased when they were away from home. He would hate to make a bad impression at Abbotsfield.

The children murmured rebelliously but Hubert refused to allow them to come. He took Barbara's arm. The winding drive was was a cool, green tunnel with a floor of recently raked gravel. Rhododendrons were massed along one side, and on the other was a belt of deciduous trees, mainly beeches and elms.

'It isn't far,' James said. 'Round the next corner.'

Suddenly they were back in the sunlight. In front and to their left was a tall house, its face in shadow.

'Hello.'

A man in tennis clothes was sitting on the stone balustrade that bridged the gap between the corner of the house and a box hedge in the garden. The sun was behind him, which made it difficult to see his features; he cast a long, hunched shadow across the gravel. He flicked his cigarette into the hedge, slid off the balustrade and came towards them.

'This is my father,' James said. 'Dad, this is Mr and Mrs Molland.'

'Molland? You must be the new padre. George Timball said you were coming today. I'm Ralph Salperton.'

'I'm afraid we've run out of petrol,' Hubert said. 'Sorry to impose on you like this.'

'Not at all.'

Everyone shook hands. Mr Salperton was dark and quite good-looking. He had a thin black moustache and he smelled faintly of sweat. Barbara enjoyed the way his eyes lingered on her. It was nice to feel that men still found her attractive. Between them, Hubert, motherhood and Plumford had eroded much of her self-confidence.

'My wife's out, I'm afraid,' Mr Salperton said. 'But my daughter's around somewhere. You'll stay for a cup of tea, won't you?' He glanced at his watch. 'Or even a drink.'

'Another time, perhaps,' Hubert said stiffly. 'We shall have a lot to do at the Vicarage. And then there's the children to think of.'

Barbara was infuriated. She could think of nothing more pleasant than sitting in a deckchair with a long, cold drink in her hand.

'James would fetch the children for you,' Mr Salperton said.

'It's very kind of you.' Hubert was becoming agitated. 'But we really should be on our way.'

'Well, you know best. As you say, another time. James, nip round to the stables, will you? There's a tin of petrol in the boot of the Jaguar.'

'What a lovely house,' Barbara said.

Mr Salperton smiled at her. 'We like it. You must let me show you round when you're next here.'

A few minutes later the four of them walked down the drive.

'Just a minute,' Mr Salperton said to Barbara. She waited while he bent down to tie the lace of one of his plimsolls. The others walked on. Hubert was making laboured conversation with James. She heard him say, 'Where do you go to school?'

'I shall be going to Harrow in September, sir.'

'Ah, Harrow,' Hubert said, and perhaps there was a ghost of regret in his voice. 'Once upon a time I used to be a schoolmaster myself. Classics was my subject.'

Mr Salperton stood up and laid a hand lightly on Barbara's arm. 'See that?' he whispered. 'A red squirrel.'

She gazed into the beech tree above their heads. Hubert and James disappeared round a bend in the drive.

'I can't see it.'

'Those little blighters move like greased lightning.' Mr Salperton was still holding her arm, just below the elbow. 'Shame you didn't fancy a drink.'

She moved her arm away. His hand dropped, as if by accident, on to her waist, just below her left breast. He ran his fingers quickly down her thigh. Barbara gasped, and jumped away from him.

'Oh – the others are out of sight,' she said, refusing to believe what had happened. She set off after them.

'Mrs Molland?'

By now she was well beyond the reach of his arm so she stopped and looked back. It would look very odd indeed if she dashed back to the car with Mr Salperton in hot pursuit.

'What?'

'There it is again. The squirrel.'

Once again he pointed. She was willing to take part in the charade for the sake of appearances. For both of them it served as a way of bolstering the necessary pretence that nothing had happened. Also, her breathing was fast and shallow, and she was glad to have a chance to bring it back to normal before they rejoined the others. Perhaps, she thought, Mr Salperton's hand had slipped by accident. Perhaps there really was a red squirrel.

However, she didn't see a squirrel. She saw Peter Redburn, his face pink with embarrassment, peeping round the trunk of a tree.

'Is this it?' Kate said, astonished.

'No, dear,' Barbara said. 'This is the churchwarden's house. We have to collect the keys.'

Hubert got out of the car. The others watched as he knocked at the door of the cottage. The woodwork and the rendering were pink, and so were the flowers in the tiny front garden. A plump man with a neat grey beard appeared in the doorway. A napkin was tucked into his collar. He was almost entirely bald. The dome of his head was as pink as his roses.

'His name's Mr Nimp,' Barbara whispered. 'Honestly. Albert Nimp.'

'Nimp the pink,' Kate said.

Richard giggled. 'Pimp the nink.'

'Richard, you mustn't say that.' As she spoke, Barbara realized that Richard was too young to have heard of the word 'pimp'. Kate was laughing now; and Barbara herself started to giggle. The scene at Carinish Court must have made her slightly hysterical.

Peter did not join in the laughter, which made her a little uneasy. She hissed at the children to shut up; the windows were open. A moment later Hubert returned to the car with a bunch of keys in his hand.

'Mr Nimp was in the middle of his evening meal,' he murmured to Barbara. 'It was rather awkward.'

'Did you ask the way to the Vicarage?'

'Up the street, take the turning by the church and the drive's a few yards up on the right. Mr Nimp said our trunk has arrived. It's in the hall.'

'Thank heavens for that.'

The trunk, sent ahead by carrier, was vital to the smooth running of the holiday. At their first locum it had arrived two days after the Mollands, which had involved them in the expense of buying new sheets and towels.

They drove slowly down the street, past a hotel and a row of small shops. The church was set back from the road on a mound dotted with gravestones.

'Where's that turning?' Hubert said.

'It must be there.' Barbara pointed. 'By the pillar box.'

The road was little more than a lane running between the churchyard on the left and a redbrick wall on the right.

'Quite a contrast to the Salpertons',' Barbara said.

The surface of the drive was composed of rutted, sun-baked mud, with a strip of ragged grass growing along the centre. Bushes pressed in from either side; and an elder tree, surrounded by a huge clump of nettles, had actually encroached on the drive. They could see the Vicarage from the road – a long, redbrick house with a battlemented porch.

'It looks like a church,' Richard said.

Hubert engaged first gear with a loud grating noise. The Rover nosed up the drive. Branches brushed against the sides of the car, and Hubert muttered under his breath about the possibility of damage to the paint-work. At the front of the house the drive divided: the left fork led up to the porch and the other snaked round the end of the house to a row of outbuildings.

'Can you see a television aerial?' Kate asked.

'The garden looks huge,' Richard said. 'Do you think they'll have bikes we can use?'

They piled out of the car and clustered in the tiled porch. Hubert tried one key after the other. Barbara repressed her irritation and looked around. Benches ran along both sides of the porch, with small stained-glass windows above them. In the corner beneath the right-hand bench was a pile of dead leaves, which had presumably lain there since the autumn. One of the windows faced west and the evening sun slanted through it, staining the opposite wall with the colours of the glass. As Barbara stared at the glowing window, the patterned glass resolved itself into a picture: a grey-bearded man in a white robe stood with his mouth open against an emerald green background; and above him hovered a black bird with what looked like a ruby in its beak.

'It's Elijah,' Richard said. 'We did him last term in Religious Studies. The raven's feeding him.'

He smiled up at her, his face alight with the pleasure of showing off. She patted his shoulder.

'What's the raven got for him? A berry or something?'

'I think it says "bread and flesh" in the Bible.'

'Flesh?' A wild vision of Old Testament cannibalism flashed through her mind. 'Oh, you mean meat.'

The lock clicked. 'That's it,' Hubert said.

He pushed open the door. The five of them, their eyes still dazzled by the sun, flooded into the darkened hall beyond.

'Yuch,' Kate said. 'It stinks.'

Richard held his nose between finger and thumb. He backed into the porch, where he pretended to be sick until Hubert told him not to be so childish.

Every house has its individual smell but this was worse than any that Barbara had previously encountered. Later, when she tried to analyse it, she decided that the more bearable elements were damp, stale tobacco, over-cooked cabbage, engine oil and coke fumes. At least one cat had sprayed against chairs and curtains, and the drop-pings of both rats and mice contributed to the atmos-phere. Far worse than these, however, and far stronger, was the sweet-and-sour stench of decay.

'It smells like someone's died here,' Peter said.

'Don't be silly,' Barbara snapped. 'Hubert, the first thing to do is open all the windows.'

Dark pine panelling stretched from floor to ceiling and carried on up the stairs. Apart from the open door the only source of natural light was a stained-glass window on the half-landing. The chequered black-and-white tiles felt gritty beneath Barbara's sandals. Against the wall to the left of the door was a refectory table, on which stood three milk bottles and an untidy heap of hymnals and prayer books. One of the bottles contained a third of a pint of what had once been milk. The Mollands' trunk, corded and labelled, was on the floor.

'I'll do the windows upstairs,' Kate volunteered. 'Can I choose my room?'

'Come on.' Richard, the smell temporarily forgotten, tugged at Peter's arm. 'After her, or she'll grab the best one.'

The children pounded upstairs, with Kate in the lead. Excitement buoyed them up. Barbara knew that for them the house was full of potential delights; the smell was an adult concern. Meanwhile, Hubert opened the nearest door, revealing a shabby drawing room crowded with furniture and dominated by an enormous and ornately carved wooden overmantel. His shoulders slumped forward. He looked very tired.

'I'll start with the kitchen,' Barbara said.

She set off down the hall and pushed her way through a green-baize door at the end. The smell grew stronger. Red quarry tiles replaced the chequer-board of the hall. There were small pantries on either side of the passage and, at the end, another door that opened into the kitchen. Barbara stood in the doorway and realized with dismay that she was going to have to spend the next four weeks cooking on an Aga.

Glass shattered upstairs.

'What was that?' Hubert shouted.

'A picture.' Kate's voice. 'I opened the window and it just blew off the wall.'

Hubert's feet thudded on the stairs. Barbara swore, quietly and viciously, and ran after him. By the time she reached the landing – more pine panelling relieved by monochrome engravings of the Holy Land – it was too late: the accident had already swollen to the proportions of a catastrophe. Towering over Kate, his cheeks pale with suppressed emotion, Hubert was engaged in passing judgement.

They were all in a large, high-ceilinged bedroom. The two sash windows were open to their fullest extent. One window looked south over the drive and the other west towards the unkempt garden that sloped down from the side of the house. Near the south-facing window a picture frame lay face down on the floor in front of a tall chest of drawers. Slivers of glass glinted on the carpet.

'You'll have to pay for it,' Hubert was saying. 'It was pure carelessness. We shall stop it out of your pocket money.'

Kate stood there, her arms folded and her mouth tight with rage. She was staring past her father at the sunlit garden below. Barbara bent down and examined the frame. The picture cord was brown with age and probably rotten.

'Well, have you anything to say?' Hubert demanded.

'If it was my fault,' Kate said carefully, 'I'm very sorry.'

Hubert looked down at his daughter. He was obviously wondering whether to accept the apology at its face value or to accuse her of insolence. Peter, who was standing by the door, shifted his weight from one foot to the other.

Barbara said quickly, 'We'd better find a dustpan and brush. Come on, we'll look downstairs.'

Apart from Hubert, the others followed her lead. The boys cantered ahead. Hubert stayed to gather up the glass.

As they went downstairs, Barbara said, 'Don't worry. I'll talk to him.'

'It's so unfair,' Kate muttered.

'He's very tired after all the driving.' In those days she still tried to keep up appearances with the children.

'You know what I think?' By now, Kate had passed the half-landing and was on the lower half of the stairs; fortunately she was almost out of Barbara's sight, so the latter could plausibly pretend not to hear the whispered words. 'He's an utter pig.'

Supper was very late on the first evening at Abbotsfield. While Hubert and the boys got the luggage into the house and upstairs, Barbara and Kate made the beds. The Timballs' blankets were stiff with dirt. The eiderdowns and pillows leaked feathers when you touched them. In the room that Richard had chosen, there were greasy finger marks on the door, overflowing ashtrays beside the bed and a pile of motorcycle magazines on the dressing table.

'Maybe the vicar's a secret rocker,' Richard said. The seaside battles of Mods and Rockers were much in the news that year.

'I expect the Timballs have a son,' Barbara said. 'Or perhaps a lodger. Take the ashtrays down to the kitchen.'

The dirt was everywhere. The curtains were thick with dust; brown stains ringed the lavatory pans; the door handles were sticky to the touch. In one of the kitchen cupboards Barbara found an open tin of baked beans crusted with mould. Vegetables rotted on a rack underneath the sink. She threw out the Timballs' rubbish recklessly. Soon the one dustbin was full. She packed the surplus into a cardboard box which Richard had found in an outhouse.

Hubert struggled to light the Aga, whose top was coated with an irregular layer of calcined food. Finally Barbara shooed him away to look at the church and did the job herself. The Aga was too important to be left to Hubert: it was necessary not only for cooking but also for hot water.

As she was preparing supper, the children came in from the garden.

'There's a tennis court,' Kate said. 'But the grass hasn't been cut for ages and we can't find the net.'

'How did you get so muddy?' Barbara asked Richard.

'We found a pond. It's right at the bottom of the garden, and it's got an old rowing boat on it.'

'I don't want you going near it until I've had a look at it.'

'Don't fuss, Mum.'

She waved the vegetable knife at him. 'You heard. And that applies to the rest of you, too.' She smiled at Peter and tried to draw him into the conversation. 'What did you think of the garden.'

'It's like a jungle,' he said.

Barbara wished she knew what he had seen at Carinish Court, and how he had interpreted it. He claimed he had left the car to relieve himself, which might explain the embarrassment he had shown when she and Ralph Salperton spotted him.

'The Timballs haven't got a television,' Kate said. 'I think this place is going to be boring.'

'We haven't got a television,' Richard said. 'Nor's Peter.'

Kate shrugged, implying that the homes of the Mollands and Redburns were therefore equally boring.

'I could do with some help,' Barbara said. 'Kate, you drain the potatoes. We'll eat in here tonight. You boys can lay the table.'

'What's for supper?' Richard said and then answered the question himself. 'Ugh. Salad and boiled spuds.'

The first evening at Abbotsfield had one more disaster in store for them.

Barbara had made the children go to bed after supper. She heard them scuffling and giggling overhead but she couldn't be bothered to read the riot act to them; they deserved a little latitude after being cooped up in the car all day. Hubert was investigating George Timball's study. Relieved to be alone, Barbara had her feet up in the drawing room. Her body was heavy with tiredness. She was sipping tea and wondering whether the water would be hot enough for her to have a bath before bed. She was also running over in her mind what had happened with Ralph Salperton.

Hubert poked his head round the door. 'Those children should be asleep.'

'Are they still awake?' Barbara swung her legs off the stool. 'I'll go and sort them out.'

'Don't bother. I'm going up anyway. I want to get my briefcase.'

'All right. Thanks.' Barbara sank back into her chair. She was fed up with the children and fed up with Hubert. Why couldn't they leave her alone for five minutes?

The stairs creaked under Hubert's weight. Against her will, Barbara found herself waiting for raised voices. She had been a fool to let Hubert go up. The scuffling stopped. The house was silent.

Hubert said in that slow, grating voice of his: 'Give that to me at once.'

The silence returned. Barbara's skin crawled with anxiety.

'Where did you find it?'

One of the children mumbled a reply.

'Get into bed. I shall want to see you both in the study after breakfast.'

He came downstairs and into the drawing room. He had forgotten the briefcase but he was carrying a small magazine. His face was pinched with shock.

'I found the boys sniggering over this. It's disgusting.'

For an instant Hubert showed her the cover. She just had time to read the title: *Health and Efficiency*. He knelt by the empty fireplace and began to shred the magazine into very small pieces.

He glanced over his shoulder. 'You realize what it is?'

'No – not really.'

The lie came automatically. Barbara had once examined a copy of *Health and Efficiency* in a newsagent's; she had chosen a moment when the shop was unattended. She remembered black-and-white photographs of fat, unlovely ladies with pendulous breasts and unconvincing simpers. It had amazed her that anyone could find such pictures erotic.

'It's sheer pornography,' Hubert said. 'Prurient, quite foul. God knows what effect it will have on them.'

'Where did it come from?' Barbara said.

'They said they found it among some motorcycle magazines.'

'Hubert, it was an accident. It's not the boys' fault.

Probably they didn't understand what they were seeing. We shouldn't make too much of it.'

'They're so young. It makes me wonder what we've done wrong.'

Hubert struck a match and soon the flames were climbing up the little mound in the grate. The paper curled and blackened. He crouched by the fireplace, staring at the pyre. His shoulders twitched, as if he were trying to relieve them of an intolerable burden. Barbara suspected he was praying for guidance.

'Smut,' he said savagely. 'Thank God Kate didn't see it.'

Ten

The office was in one of the seedier side streets running into Tottenham Court Road. The building that housed it was an angular construction of black glass above and smooth grey concrete below. It stood aloof from the rest of the street, a citadel of commerce protected by electronically controlled locks, security men and closed-circuit cameras.

Caring Hair Ltd had a suite on the top floor. The outer room contained a flourishing palm tree and a display of Scandinavian furniture in natural woods. Its sole occupant was the male secretary to whom Peter had talked on the phone. In the flesh, the secretary resembled a brooding stork.

'Mr Redburn?' The man's eyes slid over him and returned to the computer screen on the desk. 'Through that door, please.'

Peter knocked and went into the inner office. The tinted window framed a view of the Post Office Tower. Standing beside the desk was an unsmiling woman with green eyes and jade earrings. Ursula Salperton was much smaller than Peter had expected; James must have dwarfed her. For the first time it struck Peter as odd that after such an acrimonious divorce she had retained her former husband's surname.

'Mr Redburn?' She held out her hand and gave Peter's a limp-fingered shake.

'It's very kind of you to see me at such short notice.'

She sat down behind the desk and pointed him to the only other chair. 'I hope I won't regret it.' Her voice was throaty, and she had an unpleasantly metallic Thames Valley accent. 'You should thank Ginny, not me. I won't offer you coffee. I'm in a hurry.'

The chair sank alarmingly beneath Peter's weight. Low-slung, armless and instantly uncomfortable, it was made of tubular steel and olive-green leather. He realized, just too late to recover his balance without awkwardness, that it was also a rocking chair.

Ursula Salperton wore a severely cut navy-blue suit with faint chalk pinstripe and padded shoulders. Her long grey hair was confined to a neat bun at the back of the head. The face, which was heavily and expertly made up, had the vacant prettiness of an old-fashioned china doll's. It was as if the cosmetics had been carefully applied not to allure but to conceal.

'I expect Ginny has told you that I've been hired to help your ex-husband with his autobiography.'

'That's nothing to do with me. If James puts the boot in, my lawyers will handle it. I'm sure you'll pass the message on.'

'He doesn't know I'm here,' Peter said. 'I expect he'd sack me if he found out.'

'His childhood friend?'

'It would make the treachery even worse.'

'Treachery. That's a big word.'

'I imagine that's how he'd see it.'

Ursula took a cigarette. 'Of course he would. James judges everyone by their loyalty to him.'

'He doesn't apply the same standards to his own actions.'

'Most people don't.' Ursula struck a match. Before lighting the cigarette she said: 'I'm a busy woman. Either tell me what you want or get out.'

'I'd like some information about James.'

'Why ask me? He hasn't grown shy, has he? He used to love talking about himself.'

'Did Ginny mention I'm a writer, a novelist?'

Ursula said nothing. She had the knack of making even silence seem abrasive.

'James interests me – as a potential character, I mean. I'm thinking of using him in a novel. The real James, not the image he has of himself. And there's also the point that the better I know him, the better I can ghost his autobiography. So I want to understand him as well as I can.'

'Literary research, eh? You're hoping I'll cooperate to oblige Ginny? You're wasting your time. Good afternoon.'

'Wait a moment. I do have another reason.'

'I thought you might.'

'Have you ever heard of Richard Molland?'

She needed no time to think, which was instructive in itself. 'The cow's brother?'

'Kate's brother,' Peter said. 'Her twin.'

'Yes, I have. Not from James, though. Ginny told me about him.'

'He was my friend.'

'Tough luck.'

'I came across something the other day that suggested – just a hint, mind you – that James had something to do with what happened to Richard.' He hesitated. 'Ginny doesn't know. I don't want to tell her until I'm certain.'

'Are you saying James might have been responsible?'

Peter shrugged and waited. Ursula was interested now. He had banked on her continuing dislike of James – a reasonably safe bet, given the bitterness that had surrounded their divorce. Dislike thrived on nourishment.

'What makes you think I can help you?' As she spoke she exhaled, and the cigarette smoke floated over the desk like the words themselves made visible. 'It all happened twenty-five years ago, at least; that's long before I even knew James existed.'

'I know. But you were married to him for twelve years. It's an outside shot but I thought it was worth a try. Maybe James talks in his sleep, or maybe he got drunk one night and told you more than he realized. At the time you might not have realized its significance.'

'He never mentioned Richard Molland. I'm quite sure of that. What have you got to go on?'

'Very little. I found a sort of diary Richard kept. The last entry implied he was expecting to meet James.'

'As high priest or something?'

'Ginny told you about that?' High priest. Peter thought: His Holiness the Pontifex Maximus. Even now, Ursula's flippant reference to the short-lived state religion made him feel ill at ease. 'Did James ever talk about Emor?'

'What's that?'

'The game we used to play.'

'No.'

'But you knew about him being high priest. That was part of it.'

'Ginny happened to mention it when she was talking about Richard,' Ursula said. 'She didn't say what the game was called, okay? Why are you so interested?'

'In James? I don't like him any more than you do.'

'What's he done to you?'

'I told you: Richard was my friend.'

She stared across the desk. 'You want to get some dirt on James, and you won't say why. Suppose you find it: what would you do?'

'I'm not sure,' Peter said. 'Probably nothing. But I'd like to know.'

'The disinterested pursuit of knowledge. You want me to clap or something? From where I'm sitting, it looks more like attempted blackmail. Must be something pretty serious you've got in mind or it wouldn't be worth the effort. James hasn't got the mentality of a victim. Now, he's also a little shit, I don't deny that. He picked me up and used me, ripped me off and left. Put it this way: sometimes I almost feel sorry for that bitch he married. But why should I help you blackmail him?'

'I'm not asking you to. I don't want to blackmail him. If I found the right evidence, I might be tempted to expose him.'

'What as?'

'A murderer.'

The doll's face was as revealing as a deathmask. Only the eyes seemed alive. 'How would you do it? A full-page feature in the *News of the Stews*?'

Her calmness puzzled Peter. 'I don't know,' he said. 'This is all hypothetical.'

'Have you thought how the publicity would affect Ginny and Mary Salperton? Or don't you care?'

'You weren't exactly coy in the interview you gave the *Sun*.' The green eyes blinked at him. 'October nineteen eighty-eight,' he went on. 'The eleventh, I think it was. How did Ginny and her mother like that?'

'Accusing someone of being greedy and vindictive is one thing. Accusing them of murder is quite different.'

'I agree.' Peter changed his approach. 'The full-page feature was your idea. I'm more concerned with Ginny, with what's right for her. I know it would come as a shock — but if her brother is a murderer, don't you think she would rather know? Don't you think it would be safer for her?'

Ash fell from Ursula's cigarette and lay unbroken on the shining surface of the desk. Half a minute passed. Then with unexpected violence she swept the coil of ash on to the floor and stubbed out the cigarette.

'I don't want Ginny to get hurt,' she said.

'Nor do I.'

She examined her fingernails, which were short, square and unpainted. 'In a sense you're right: the only person who can really hurt her is James himself. And the more she knows about him, the less harm he could do her.'

'Why should he harm her?'

'He would if she got in his way.' She sat back in her chair and began to talk very quickly. 'You know what he did to me. I'd sweated blood over the Hair House. Then as soon as we floated it. I had to fight off a hostile takeover. If James had supported me, I'd have won. Do you know what his block of shares represented? An initial investment of less than two and a half thousand pounds. That's what he put into the company when I started. Twelve years later he sold out for nearly three and a half million.'

'He says that he needed the money, that he was advised to sell.'

'Then why didn't he wait a few months? I just needed time to raise the money. He wouldn't have lost out. No, of course he wouldn't wait: he wanted to twist the knife.'

'Because of that business with Kate?'

'Partly.'

'An expensive black eye.'

'I didn't mean to hit her. Not that she didn't deserve it: she started it, you know. Anyway, there were other reasons for twisting the knife, maybe more important ones. If you've got any sense, you'll be very careful.'

'Would you like to explain that?'

Ursula shrugged. 'When they were doing the casting for the first series of *Pemberley* they whittled down the shortlist for Darcy to two people. One of them was James. The other was a man called Hugo Mannering – not so good-looking but a much better actor, and his track record was more impressive too. One evening, Hugo was in Shepherd's Bush, waiting to cross the road. The pavement was very crowded. Someone jostled him, and he fell under a taxi.'

The phone on the desk began to buzz. Ursula ignored it. The office was very hot. After a while the silence returned.

'Was he killed?' Peter said.

'Not quite. After three months in hospital he was

almost as good as new. He even made an appearance in the second series of *Pemberley*. He played the impostor who pretended to be Darcy's cousin.'

'It might have been an accident.'

'James got drunk that same evening, which isn't something he does very often. At the time he hadn't heard about Hugo. The first he knew about it officially was when his agent phoned in the morning. I only made the connection afterwards.'

'It's not exactly evidence.'

'Who said it was? I nearly had a fatal accident myself. We used to have a cottage in Suffolk. It was in the back of beyond and it didn't even have a telephone. I was down there by myself one weekend. By that time James and I weren't spending much time together, not if we could avoid it. The bathroom was on the ground floor, and on my first evening I had to get up in the night. The stairs were very steep and the carpet was held on with those old-fashioned stair rods. One of the rods at the top had worked itself loose. I just broke a couple of ribs. I was lucky.'

She shook another cigarette out of the packet. Her hands were steady. Peter was not impressed by the story of the loose stair rod, which he thought revealed more about Ursula than about James.

'That's why you weren't surprised,' he said.

'What?'

'When I mentioned the possibility of murder. And that's all it is. A possibility.'

'That's all it ever will be. James is cunning. It took me a long while to realize that. Sometimes he seems rather stupid. In fact I think he is. But where his own interests are concerned he can be clever enough. And he's got one big advantage over the rest of us, though he tries to hide it as much as he can. He's so self-centred that other people don't count. They're not important. They don't have the same rights and privileges. In a way, everyone else doesn't really exist in the same way as he does. They – we – are boring black and white: he's glorious Technicolor. You see what I mean? It makes it so much easier for him to be ruthless.'

'You make him sound like a psychopath.'

'A label.' She dismissed it with a wave of the unlit cigarette. 'My mother would have said he was evil.'

The last three words produced a reverberation in Peter's memory.

'If you ask me,' Richard had said, 'it's quite simple: James is in league with the devil.'

When Peter got back to his flat, he examined his cuttings file for the Salpertons. One advantage of working in a public library had been unlimited access to newspapers, magazines and a photocopier.

The original purpose of the file had been to hold background research for *London*. Gradually, however, Peter had included more and more items that mentioned James and Ursula – and later Kate, of course. At first he had explained this to himself by the fact that one of the characters in *London*, John Humphrey Twistleton, was to be partly modelled on James. As the material mounted, it became increasingly evident that the Salpertons needed a file to themselves.

The incident at Daudet's took place at lunchtime on 18 August 1988. Daudet's was on the first floor of a discreet, eighteenth-century house in Old Compton Street. Peter had often passed it, but had never eaten there. It was too expensive.

By August of that year, James and Ursula were formally separated and waiting for the divorce to be finalized; James was already living with Kate, though this was not yet public knowledge. The accounts of what actually happened at Daudet's varied considerably. Mrs Salperton – James's mother, that is – was having lunch with Kate, her future daughter-in-law. All accounts agreed that Ursula had come into the restaurant while the others were actually eating. Ursula had never eaten there before. Coincidence or conspiracy? At an adjoining table were two freelance photographers armed with point-and-shoot cameras. Another coincidence?

The photographers knew who Ursula was. One of them had taken a picture of her only the previous week for an interview in *Tomorrow's Woman*. Peter guessed that long before Ursula arrived they had been watching Kate. Most men did.

At this point the confusion deepened – despite, or perhaps because of, the large number of witnesses. Did Kate really refer to Ursula as 'a sack of shit'? It seemed equally unlikely that Ursula had called Kate 'a money-grubbing cock-teaser' or that Mrs Salperton, whom Peter remembered as the acme of tremulous gentility, had used words which family newspapers can rarely bring themselves to print.

Some versions held that Ursula, whether by accident or design, had knocked into Kate's chair, causing Kate to drop a spoonful of raspberry bombe on herself. A second school of thought put the blame on Kate, who (it was said) had caught sight of Ursula and whispered to Mrs Salperton, 'Here comes Superbitch.' Another possibility was that Mrs Salperton had triggered the fracas by refusing to sit in the same restaurant as Ursula. Witnesses spoke of plates flying through the air, of Ursula pushing Kate (or vice versa) into the table, which then fell over, and of the head waiter thrusting the pudding trolley between the combatants in an attempt to separate them.

Only the photographs provided points of reference. Mrs Salperton stood beside an upturned table; one claw-like hand clutched her handbag, and the other was waving a table napkin like an ineffectual flag of truce. In another photograph, Kate was bending forwards with her hands over her face. A third captured Ursula, her mouth wide open in a shout and her hair in chaos, with a dark stain on the front of her dress. A fourth, snapped outside as Kate was leaving, revealed the impressive beginnings of her black eye.

Daudet's closed early. But the damage was done. The photographers sold their pictures. As it was August, news was thin on the ground so the story attained a prominence it might not otherwise have had.

James was always news, and the fact that Kate was his mistress gained piquancy from his role as an aspiring adulterer in the Trumper's advertisements. Ursula was well-known in her own right – her PR company had cultivated the image of her as one of the successful entrepreneurs of the decade. Even Kate was intrinsically newsworthy: at the time she worked as a presenter for Capital Radio; and, unlike Ursula, she photographed well.

By and large Ursula was presented as the villain of

the piece, which couldn't have helped during the takeover battle for the Hair House. She certainly made things worse for herself by her subsequent attack on James for selling his shares. As for Kate, the black eye was a blessing in disguise because it suggested that she, not Ursula, had been the victim; such is the power of visual imagery.

James came out of it surprisingly well. He might have lost a few of his more strait-laced admirers; but his defenders pointed out that he himself had not been concerned in the skirmish, that he was separated from Ursula, and that Kate was unmarried. James's engagement to Kate was announced shortly afterwards, a move which earned him both publicity and approval. A few cynics suggested that Ursula had done Kate a good turn: that the 'duel at Daudet's' had persuaded James to make an honest woman of her to minimize the damage.

To the disappointment of many, there were no legal proceedings. Daudet's wanted to smooth over the scandal as quickly as possible. Ursula had her hands full with the takeover. Neither she nor Kate could be assured of victory if one of them took the other to court for slander or assault. James was shrewd enough to broadcast his forgiveness of Ursula in the course of a prime-time television interview.

As Peter flicked through the cuttings, he tried to reach a verdict. Had Ursula or Kate started it? Which of them was the more likely to resort to violence?

On balance he was inclined to pin the blame on Ursula. Her professional success suggested an aggressive nature; you don't raise the annual turnover of your business from nothing to £43 million by being nice to people. In interviews she habitually attacked, never defended. When she lost control of the Hair House, she had immediately begun to build up another mail-order business, Caring Hair, in direct competition with her former company. During his conversation with her this afternoon he had noticed both her ability to nurse a grievance and the anger that bubbled to the surface whenever he provoked her.

Kate was very different. She liked things to be comfortable. He was certain that, given the choice, she would have preferred to be on terms of neutrality with James's first wife. It occurred to Peter that a dislike of confrontation was probably the reason why she had left him in the lurch in 1970.

It was true that Kate's behaviour at Abbotsfield had showed a streak of violence, a willingness to inflict pain. But you could hardly judge her – or indeed anyone else – on her actions as an adolescent. Her behaviour had not been unique. He, Richard, Ginny and James had been rocked by the same turbulence. 1964 was the first of the years of transition: the certainties of childhood had mysteriously vanished, and the comfortable inertia of maturity still seemed alien, unattainable and deeply unattractive.

In fact, like most teenagers, they had all been a little crazy.

When Kate found the dog-eared copy of *Health and Efficiency* on their first evening at Abbotsfield, Peter and Richard were in the bathroom. The door was open.

They were in their pyjamas and flicking water at each other with their toothbrushes. Peter happened to be facing the basin as he reloaded his brush. In the mirror he saw Kate slipping into Richard's bedroom, whose door was directly opposite the bathroom's. She was wearing a summer nightdress with a floral pattern. For an instant in the doorway the light from the bedroom outlined the shape of her body through the thin cotton.

Richard flicked water on his neck. 'What are you looking at, Pete?'

'What's Kate doing?' Peter muttered. 'She just went into your room.'

'Let's ambush her with the toothbrushes when she comes out.'

They waited on the landing, their backs pressed against the wall on either side of the door. Paper rustled inside. Richard frowned. He mouthed 'Emor' at Peter and burst into the room.

Kate was beside the dressing table with one of the Timballs' magazines open in front of her. She glanced up, her face flushed. 'I was looking for something to read.' She closed the magazine and tilted her chin at them.

'My room's private,' Richard said. 'I don't want you in here.'

'I see. You've got something to hide.'

He advanced towards her. 'What are you up to, anyway? You're not interested in motorbikes.'

'Who says?' Still holding the magazine, she backed away from her twin. 'Personally I've grown out of tricycles.'

Richard lunged at her. She evaded him and made a dash for the door.

'Stop her,' Richard hissed to Peter.

He caught Kate's arm. Its warmth and softness

surprised him. For a reason he did not understand, he knew that what he was doing was wrong. She hit him a stinging blow on the cheek with the magazine.

'Get your hands off me.' As she spoke, a smaller magazine fell out of the one she had used as a weapon. It fluttered to the floor. 'Let go.'

He relaxed his grip. She pushed him against the door jamb, wriggled past him and ran lightly down the passage to her room.

'What was all that about?' Peter said angrily; he was aware that his anger was faked, an emotional camouflage for guilt. 'Who does she think she is?'

Richard hushed him. He pointed downstairs. 'They'll hear us.'

'Are you going to let her get away with it?'

'Who cares? I don't want to read about motorbikes.'

His attention on Richard, Peter bent down and picked up the magazine that had fallen on the floor. 'What did you mean about Emor?'

'What? We'd better shut the door.'

Peter closed it softly. 'You said "Emor" just before we came in.'

'I thought she might be spying.'

'You've brought the Archives?'

'Only some of them. They're in my suitcase.' Richard looked both shame-faced and enthusiastic. 'This can be our summer palace, you see. I bet the court moved out of Rome in the hot weather. You know, like the viceroys in India used to move from Delhi to Simla in the hot season.'

'I didn't think you'd want to do Emor here.' What would Kate say if she found out? The prospect of bringing Emor to Abbotsfield embarrassed Peter, but he didn't want to show it; if he and Richard quarrelled, the next four weeks would be very lonely. 'I mean, it's not like being in Plumford. There're only the two of us.'

'We can keep in touch with them by post. Coleby could be a general on active service, and Joe could be a procurator or governor somewhere.'

But Peter wasn't listening. He was looking at the magazine.

'What's that?' Richard said.

Peter forced himself to grin. '*Health and Efficiency*.'

He knew – more or less – what *Health and Efficiency* was, though he had never succeeded in examining a copy. The magazine occasionally circulated at school but its circulation was usually confined to older boys. It contained dirty pictures of nude women. Judging by comments he had overheard, you were supposed to find the pictures both funny and exciting.

'Blimey,' Joe's elder brother had remarked on one occasion. 'I wouldn't mind sticking it into her.'

Presumably this copy belonged to the Timballs' hypothetical son or lodger – or even to the vicar himself. Surely *Health and Efficiency* wouldn't interest girls? Anyway, Kate was a clergyman's daughter. She wouldn't want to read something like that. Perhaps she hadn't known it was there.

Peter sat down on the bed and turned over the pages as casually as he could. He wished he were alone. The photographs neither amused nor excited him. His hands trembled, and he felt as though quite soon he might want to be sick. Were all women like that when they took their clothes off? These ones looked entirely different from his glimpse of Kate in the bathroom mirror, but perhaps she would grow like them eventually. What was it like having those huge balloons of flesh bouncing in front of you as you walked along? And where exactly did you stick it?

'It's disgusting.' Richard sat down beside him on the bed. 'I don't think we should be looking at this.'

Peter would have agreed if Richard hadn't spoken in the small, smug voice he reserved for God and similar subjects. 'Don't be such a baby.'

'It's a sin,' Richard said, edging closer. Suddenly he giggled. 'Look at that one. I bet they used trick photography.'

At that moment the door opened and Hubert Molland stalked into the bedroom.

As she had promised, Ursula phoned on Wednesday evening.

It was nearly seven o'clock, and Ginny was relaxing with a drink to the accompaniment of Sibelius's 'Finlandia'. She was weary, but a sense of achievement buoyed her up. She had bought at least seventy per cent of the Christmas presents she needed. The flat was clean and sweet-smelling. Best of all, she was alone. The pleasure the departure of Ralph gave her was almost worth the torment of having him to stay.

'Hullo, Tonic,' Ursula said; and both her hearty voice and the use of the nickname irritated Ginny. 'Reporting back as per instructions.'

'How did it go?'

'Well, he's not what I expected, I'll tell you that.'

'What did you expect?' Ginny said.

'I don't know. Someone suaver, I suppose – more like James. But he can stand up for himself, can't he? I slung a few rocks at him and he just slung them back.'

'Why did he want to talk to you?'

'It was about James, in a way. Look, I don't quite know how to put this. You remember telling me about what happened to Richard Molland?'

Ginny sat down heavily on the hall chair. 'I don't understand.'

'Peter thinks James might have been involved.'

'But Richard was alone.'

'As far as I can gather, Peter's found Richard's diary. And according to him, the last entry hints that Richard was expecting James to turn up.'

'It's absurd,' Ginny said in a high-pitched voice. Please God, she thought, make it absurd; just for me. Her face felt stiff with shock. 'James would have told someone if he'd been there.'

'Would he?'

'You don't agree?'

'James does what's good for James. At least, that's the way he's operated since I've known him.' A match rasped on the other end of the line. Ursula coughed. Then: 'I told Peter about Hugo Mannering, and about that time I fell down the stairs at the cottage.'

'You shouldn't have done that.'

'I know you think I'm imagining things. But what if I'm not?'

'There's not a shred of proof. And you're not exactly unbiased.'

'I'm as prejudiced as hell,' Ursula said. 'What's that got to do with it? The point is, Peter's dug up another little incident where there's not a shred of proof. But perhaps he'll find a few shreds if he digs hard enough. And if he does, I want to know. You should, too.'

'But – even if James was there – what about motive?' Please God, Ginny thought, please make her stop. 'Anyway, it's all academic. It happened too long ago.'

'It's amazing what people will remember when they try, especially if they do it together. The memories sort of bounce off one another.'

'Why's Peter doing this?'

'I'm not sure. I think he feels guilty about Richard. That's part of it. They were friends, weren't they?'

'Best friends.' Ginny frowned, trying to remember. 'At the beginning, in the first few days I knew them, Richard and Peter seemed very self-contained. James was almost jealous.'

'So what did he do? Muscle his way between them?'

'Something like that,' Ginny admitted; she hated having to think about it. 'Of course Kate was there too, which confused the issue.' She realized as she spoke that she was being selfish. The events at Abbotsfield had affected others. As Richard's mother, Barbara was more likely to be hurt than anyone if, after all these years, the whole, unpleasant business resurfaced. 'What happens if Peter does find something?'

'I'm not sure about that, either. In any case, forewarned is forearmed. He made the point that it would be safer if we all knew, assuming there's something to find out in the first place. Safer for you – he emphasized that. That's one reason why I liked him.'

Ginny fought back the panic that threatened to invade her. 'You didn't talk too much, did you?'

'What do you take me for? A blabbermouth?' Ursula chuckled, and suddenly Ginny disliked her intensely. 'But you can't put it off for ever. For one thing, it will change the way he thinks about James. So when are you going to tell him?'

On the evening of Wednesday 20 December, Peter drove back to Plumford in a rented Ford Escort. It was raining, and his mother's house was dank and unwelcoming. He wished he could have stayed in the flat. But there was too much to do in Plumford.

It took him more than an hour to unload the car, warm up the house and prepare a meal. He ate tinned soup, bread and fruit in front of the fire in the sitting room. Afterwards he sorted through the contents of a suitcase containing James's memorabilia up to the age of eighteen. He was due to arrive at Carinish Court on Saturday, and he had promised to bring a draft of the first chapter with him.

Peter was astonished by the tedium of the job. He had not expected the visible traces of James's childhood to be so boring. In the old days at Abbotsfield, James shed a certain glamour over everything he said and did. The glamour resisted attempts at definition, as perhaps glamour always does; and there was no trace of it in the team photographs, the school reports, the athletics medals and the theatre programmes. James's letters to his mother from school were all along the same lines: a resumé of his sporting career in that week, a remark about the weather, a pious wish that everyone was well at home, and the occasional plea for money.

Near the bottom of the suitcase Peter found a

postcard with a view of Lyme Regis on the back. He turned it over. It was addressed to James at his prep school.

Uncle Wilf much better. Looking forward to Sunday. Love, Mummy.

The shock made Peter drop the postcard on the hearthrug. The words weren't important – Uncle Wilf had been James's maternal great-uncle – but the handwriting was small, upright and instantly familiar. He picked up the postcard and carried it to the desk, where he compared the writing with that of M's letter to his father.

The writing on the postcard was the same as the writing of his father's lover.

'No,' Peter said aloud. 'No, it can't be.'

Johnny Redburn had cuckolded his best friend. Barring the possibility of an abortion, it followed that Peter had a half-brother or a half-sister.

Which of them was it? James or Ginny?

Eleven

Leo Quest glanced up from the *Times* crossword. 'What's wrong?' he said. He took another spoonful of muesli and scowled.

'Nothing,' Barbara said. 'Why do you ask?'

His jaws moving slowly, he stared at her across the breakfast bar. He swallowed with difficulty. 'Why do you think?'

'You tell me.'

'Now don't get cross, dear. You've hardly said two words to me since you got up.'

'I haven't had much opportunity, have I? You've been buried in that newspaper ever since I came down.'

'That's not the point.' Leo stirred the remaining muesli in his bowl, and the scrape of the spoon on the china made Barbara want to scream. 'I always look at the paper over breakfast. And you always talk while I do it. Doesn't matter whether I say anything or not.'

'It's not very polite.'

'You're trying to change the subject. What's wrong?'

'I haven't been sleeping well, that's all.'

'You had another of those pills last night?'

'Yes, I did.' She knew he disliked her taking sleeping tablets. 'Why not? I couldn't sleep.'

'All right, all right.' Leo dropped the spoon and pushed the bowl away from him. 'Why couldn't you sleep?'

'You should have more muesli than that,' Barbara said. 'It's good for you, darling. And if you had more muesli, you wouldn't need so much lunch.'

'Was something worrying you?'

Leo's black eyebrows arched in perfect semi-circles that made her think of the tops of question-marks. Everything about him was curved: his nose, his stomach, his plump little thighs. He perched on the chrome-legged stool like Humpty-Dumpty on his wall. Once aroused, his curiosity was terrible.

'Oh, you know,' she said. 'My mind wouldn't stop thinking.'

'What about?'

About the managing director and the Brighton hotel; Barbara remembered telling Peter about that in 1970 – she had been trying to reassure him. About Peter himself, and what he might have noticed at Abbotsfield, and what they had done together on a Saturday afternoon in May 1970.

'Kate?' Leo prompted. 'Was it what I said about problems between her and James?'

'No.' She tried to smile. 'Not this time. It was all Peter Redburn's fault. Him and James, with this wretched book.'

'What's that got to do with you?'

'Nothing at all,' she said more sharply than she had intended. 'But I suppose it's made me think about the past. I thought all that was over, but it isn't.'

'The past is a big subject,' Leo said. 'Would you like to be a little more precise?'

'I was thinking about Richard,' she lied, wondering why she had made such a point of stressing to Leo that, before him, there had only been Hubert Molland. Presumably she had been trying to flatter him. It was too late to tell him the truth now: he would feel their marriage had been built on a lie. If only she could be sure that Peter would keep his mouth shut.

'Richard?' Leo said gently and relentlessly.

As he spoke she realized that in a sense she had said no more than the truth: that Richard was bound up with all her lies and infidelities and always would be. The thought of Richard was the punishment for them; to some extent it was also the cause of what she had done with Peter. Her eyes smarted with tears. Leo's compassion was stronger than his curiosity. She made a conscious decision not to pull herself together.

Leo struggled off the stool, squeezed round the breakfast bar and put his arm round her shoulders. 'Now, look. We've been into this so many times. It wasn't your fault. There was nothing you could have done to stop it. You must just put it behind you.'

'I can't.' She pressed her head against his shoulder. As she wept, he patted her back and murmured word-lessly into her hair. She cried both for herself and for Richard, and also because it saved her from having to talk. She listened to the rumbling of Leo's stomach battling with the muesli. The rumbling made her cry harder. He ate the muesli for her sake. He was a good husband. She didn't want to hurt him. She would go mad if she lost him. The tears relaxed her.

She lifted her head and caught sight of the clock on the tiled wall above the dishwasher. 'Leo, you'll be late.'

'It doesn't matter.'

'But it does.' Barbara pushed herself away from him. 'Honestly, I feel much better.'

He padded across the kitchen to fetch her a box of paper handkerchiefs. His forehead was pink and wrinkled – like the twins had been when she first saw them in the hospital at Rosington.

'Are you sure?' he said.

'Of course I am. Off you go.' She blew her nose. 'It's Thursday. You've got the meeting with the section heads at ten.'

'They can wait.'

'There's no need. Really, I'm fine.' Barbara slipped off the stool. 'I'll get your coat.'

'You've got nothing to reproach yourself for,' Leo said with a hint of exasperation. 'Remember that.'

'You're right. Darling, I think your briefcase is still in the drawing room.'

She kissed him goodbye in the hall and stood in the doorway to wave. It was a relief to see him go. The trouble with Leo was that he gnawed at a problem like a dog with a bone; and he didn't stop gnawing until he was satisfied that the problem had been dealt with. Her own instinct, to continue the analogy, was to bury the problem in the hope that in time it would become less unpalatable, and perhaps even disintegrate altogether.

Leo turned to wave back, first at the bottom of the path and then at the corner where the road skirted the round pond. The Lavender Lane pond was far bigger than the one at Abbotsfield. One was a carefully maintained asset; the other had been an accidental eyesore.

Once Leo was out of sight, Barbara shut the door and went back to the silent kitchen. Maybe he was right, at least so far as Richard was concerned. It wasn't her fault. No one could say that she hadn't warned him about that bloody pond right from the start. What else could she have done? She had nothing to feel guilty about.

The silence in the kitchen grew so oppressive that Barbara snapped on the radio. Thank God the cleaning woman was coming this morning, and this afternoon she was due to play bridge. Card games were such a consolation. They kept the mind occupied.

Barbara had made a point of investigating the pond at the bottom of the Vicarage garden on the first morning at Abbotsfield.

It must have been the boys who woke her from a deep sleep as they clattered down the stairs. Wrenched awake, she looked at the alarm clock: five minutes past seven. The clock was familiar but its surroundings weren't. For an instant she hovered on the edge of panic. The memories of yesterday returned in a rush, and none of them was welcome: Ralph Salperton's hand slipping from her arm to her waist, and the feel of his fingers running down her thigh; the smell that greeted them when they opened the front door of the Vicarage; the crash of breaking glass upstairs; and Hubert kneeling by the fireplace and tearing *Health and Efficiency* into shreds.

Oh Christ, she thought, I don't want to get up.

Her mind ran on to the cleaning and the shopping that needed doing. She wanted to have a look at the garden, too – especially at the pond the boys had mentioned. She couldn't afford a lie-in.

Hubert was still asleep, his face turned away from her. Barbara slipped out of bed and carried her clothes into the bathroom to avoid waking him as she dressed. Kate's door was still closed. In the last six months Kate had begun to sleep as late as she was allowed.

Barbara went downstairs and coaxed the Aga back to life. Hubert liked a cooked breakfast; fortunately she had remembered to bring eggs with them and none of them had got broken on the journey from Plumford.

The kitchen overlooked the yard at the end of the house away from the garden. As she was filling the kettle, she caught a glimpse of the boys: they were exploring the outhouses that extended from the house along one side of the yard. The kitchen faced east so the room was full of light; and Barbara saw that it was even dirtier than she had thought. It was still cool but the sky was hazy with the promise of heat to come. Once the Aga got going, the kitchen would be intolerably hot.

The boys came back to the house just as the kettle was coming to the boil. Already their clothes were filthy.

'I'm starving,' Richard said. 'We found a loft full of rotten apples.'

'The floorboards are rotten too,' Peter said.

'But it's quite safe if you look where you're going.' Sometimes Richard could be very sensitive about her fears, far more so than Kate.

'Wash your hands,' she said. 'The corn flakes are in the cupboard.'

The boys chattered as they ate about the outbuildings and the garden. None of them brought up the subject of *Health and Efficiency*; Barbara guessed that they were both trying to forget their forthcoming interview with Hubert. She kept quiet about it. They would prefer to believe that she did not know.

Hubert came downstairs as the church clock was striking eight. The boys finished their tea in a hurry and stood up.

'We'll be outside,' Richard said.

Hubert looked at his watch. 'I want to see you two in the study in half an hour.'

The boys scuttled out of the kitchen. Hubert sat down at the table. Barbara gave him a cup of tea.

'Don't be too hard on them,' she said. 'I'm sure they didn't mean any harm.'

'They have to learn the difference between right and wrong.' A muscle twitched in Hubert's cheek. He glanced up at her. His eyes were still bloodshot from the driving. 'What do you think they really want to do this morning?'

'Explore the garden properly,' Barbara said. 'And then have a look round Abbotsfield.'

'Very well. I'll make them stay inside.' He looked round the room. 'They can do some cleaning in here. They might as well be some use to you. I'll tell them to start by scrubbing the kitchen floor.'

The boys would be more trouble to her than they were worth. But she was so relieved that Hubert wasn't going to beat them that she held her tongue.

'Extraordinary house,' Hubert said, evidently considering that the previous subject was closed. 'Have you noticed how impersonal it is? It's as if the Timballs just camp here.'

'I haven't had time to notice very much apart from

the dirt. There's no bacon I'm afraid. Would you like two eggs and fried bread?'

'Yes, please. Is Kate still asleep?'

'I assume so.'

'Rather late, isn't it?'

'Teenage girls need all the sleep they can get.'

Hubert drummed his fingers on the deal table. 'You know best in that department, I suppose.'

Barbara put two slices of bread into the fat that was sizzling in the frying pan. She smiled to herself.

After their interview with Hubert, the boys slunk back to the kitchen. Richard was flushed and Peter was pale. They avoided Barbara's eyes.

'Dad said we had to help you this morning,' Richard said. 'It's a sort of punishment for making a noise last night.'

'I see,' Barbara said, picking up her handbag. 'Well, I'd like you to scrub the floor and clean the sink and the draining-board. You'll find the cleaning things in the scullery. After that, you can do what you want as far as I'm concerned. I'm going shopping.'

Abbotsfield failed to impress her. It was too small to be a town and too big to be a village. The shops were even worse than Plumford's. Like the Vicarage, the place gave the impression that none of its inhabitants had much money to spare. On the main road opposite the church was a triangular patch of grass, bleached by the sun and speckled with dandelions and daisies. A path ran round the perimeter, linking a public lavatory to a broken wooden seat and a war memorial to the glorious dead. Half a dozen youths squatted and smoked on the steps of the memorial. They wore tight trousers and their hair needed washing. One of them let out a wolf-whistle as she passed.

Everywhere Barbara went, Mr Nimp the pink churchwarden had been before her.

'Ah, you're at the Vicarage,' the butcher told her, eyeing the front of her dress. 'Bert Nimp said you'd arrived. Bacon? Yes, of course. Mrs Timball always has back.'

'I'll have streaky,' Barbara said.

'A pound?'

'Half a pound.'

'You'll be wanting a joint for tomorrow. Mrs Timball usually has a nice bit of beef.'

'I'll have some lamb, please. What's the cheapest cut you've got?'

At the newsagent's Barbara learned that Mr Timball took *The Times*, not the *Daily Telegraph*; the woman behind the counter did not mention the motorcycle magazines or *Health and Efficiency*. The greengrocer, a stooping man with a crumpled face, told her that Mrs Timball owed him for five weeks' vegetables. He went on to hint that, as Barbara stood *in loco* Mrs Timball, she might like to pay the bill.

As she was leaving the greengrocer's, the air filled with the whines of high-pitched engines. It sounded as though a squadron of giant wasps were invading Abbotsfield.

'What on earth's that?' Barbara said.

A cavalcade of twenty or thirty motor scooters flooded down the road. The greengrocer stood in the doorway of his shop and stared after them.

'Mods. Heading for the coast and looking for a fight. It's insane, if you ask me, it shouldn't be allowed. They ought to put a stop to it.'

'I can never understand why there are so many Mods and so few Rockers.'

'They're all the same. Too much money, that's their trouble: they've had it easy. What they need's a dose of national service. The army would sort them out in no time.'

'Do they come here often?' What Barbara really wanted to know was whether the Mods and Rockers fought their battles in Abbotsfield itself.

'Too often for my liking, I'll tell you that. Most of them just pass through. This is a Bank Holiday weekend, so it'll probably be worse than usual. Riff-raff from Bristol.' The greengrocer looked sideways at her and added in a voice that was tinged with sly amusement: 'Mark you, we've got a few home-grown ones as well. As I daresay you'll be finding out.'

By the time Barbara had finished the shopping it was eleven o'clock. A string bag in each hand, she picked her way up the drive of the Vicarage. The Rover was no longer outside the front door; Hubert must have gone to fill it up with petrol.

The Timballs' smell washed over her as she opened the door. It was less powerful than yesterday, at least in the hall, but still impossible to ignore. She went through to the kitchen. Here the smell was much worse.

An unwashed cup and bowl stood in the sink, which suggested that Kate had woken up. Pencil-thin puddles filled many of the cracks between the quarry tiles; and between the puddles were parallel smears where the mop had combed the dirt rather than removed it. The mop itself, still in a bucket of dirty water, leant against the table. The boys had done their best.

Barbara put the kettle on to boil. If she were lucky she would be able to sit down for ten minutes before beginning to prepare lunch. While the water was heating she went back to the hall and into the drawing room, which was at the opposite end of the house from the kitchen.

French windows opened on to a gravelled path sprinkled with moss, chickweed and clumps of grass. Beyond the path, the ragged lawn sloped down to a belt of bushes at the far end. On the left were more bushes and small trees, part of the overgrown shrubbery that bordered the drive and the boundary wall along the lane. To the right was a lower lawn, a flat rectangle that might once have been a tennis court. She opened one of the windows. At the far end of the garden, Richard was shouting; he sounded very happy. It was time to take a look at that pond.

Barbara stepped on to the gravel and, at the same moment, the front-door bell rang. She swore under her breath and turned left, intending to walk round the corner of the house to the porch. The sensible thing would have been to go back through the drawing room into the hall, but Barbara had no desire to expose strangers to the smell of the house. The smell was a powerful, if irrational, source of shame. She feared that strangers would attribute it either to her domestic mismanagement, which would be bad enough, or to a lack of personal cleanliness, which would be even worse.

A small, stout man was standing in the porch. He wore a blazer, neatly pressed grey flannels and a pork-pie hat. While he waited, he examined the picture of the raven feeding Elijah in the stained-glass window.

'Hello,' Barbara said as she came up behind him. 'Can I help you?'

The man jumped. He turned round, raising his hat to expose a pink, shining scalp.

'Oh, it's Mr Nimp, isn't it?' Nimp the pink, Barbara thought, or pimp the nink. 'Were you looking for my husband?'

'Eh? Yes. That is — er, it is Mrs Molland, isn't it?' He blushed above his beard and held out his hand. 'Pleased to meet you.'

His hand was so soft and rubbery that Barbara wondered if there were any bones in it. The top of his head was on a level with her chin.

'You're the churchwarden, aren't you?' she said.

'One of them, yes. Mr Salperton's the other. Though by and large he tends to leave things to me.'

'I think my husband's looking for a petrol station. I'm sure he won't be long.' Barbara prayed that Mr Nimp wouldn't want to stay: she would have to offer him coffee, and he would smell the smell. 'May I take a message?'

'The thing is.' Mr Nimp sucked in his cheeks and stared at Elijah. 'I wouldn't want you to think I'm interfering.'

'I'm sure you're not,' Barbara said.

'We — that is, the wife and I — happened to notice a girl on the Triangle. You know the Triangle? The public garden with the war memorial?'

'Yes, I saw it this morning. A girl?'

Mr Nimp twitched. 'Yes. The point is, she was – ah – talking to some local youths.' The more he said, the faster the words spilled out. He spoke spasmodically in a high, wheezing voice; perhaps he suffered from asthma. 'Between ourselves, they're rather a rough crowd. Not at all nice. Most of them come from the council estate. They hang around there all the time. Smoking – even drinking, sometimes. I really wonder what the younger generation is coming to. No respect, you see, no sense of what's fitting. We've tried to stop them but to no avail. The parish council is powerless, and –'

'What was the girl like?'

'Fair-haired, wearing a sort of blue dress.' Mr Nimp rubbed his beard. His lips were moist, smooth and fleshy, like overripe soft fruit. 'Charming, I'm sure. "Not a local girl," I said to the wife – and, well, naturally we wondered. We thought in the circumstances Mr Molland would want to know. Just in case, that is. You can't be too careful with girls, can you? We've got one of our own, not that she's a girl now: she's married, flown the nest as it were; she lives in Bristol. Perhaps I'm barking up the wrong tree.'

'It sounds like Kate.' Barbara heard the distant wail of the whistle on the kettle. 'Well, thank you so much for warning us. I'll have a word with my daughter when she gets back.'

'If you like, I'll walk back with you to the Triangle and –'

'That's very kind. But I think I'll leave her to find her own way home.'

'I just thought I'd better let you know.' Mr Nimp stepped down from the porch and began to sidle down the drive. 'Children are such a worry, aren't they?'

'Yes, they are. Goodbye.'

Mr Nimp raised his hat. 'We'll see you tomorrow, I expect.'

She looked blankly at him.

'In church, I mean.'

Barbara made herself a cup of coffee and carried it into the garden. She picked her way across the rough grass to the tangle of bushes at the far end. Among the tangle were at least two apple trees with gnarled trunks, drooping branches and leaves that were spotted with disease; this had once been an orchard.

'The Lord High Admiral,' she heard Richard say, 'welcomes Your Majesty aboard.'

'Is everything prepared for the voyage?' Peter said.

They were playing that Roman game of theirs, which Barbara pretended not to know about. She peered through the undergrowth, looking for a path among the nettles and brambles.

'We could probably go overland,' Richard said in his normal voice. 'Hack our way through the jungle.'

'We shall go by sea. The imperial yacht awaits.'

'The boat's filling up again.'

'Roll up your jeans like me. We can take off our shoes and socks.'

'It might sink in the middle of the pond.'

'Are you afraid?' Peter said. 'Even admirals can be court-martialled.'

'Richard?' Barbara called. 'Where are you?'

An instant of silence preceded a burst of urgent whispering. The bushes rustled. Richard wriggled through the trailing branches of one of the apple trees. Despite the warmth of the day, he was wearing his school raincoat as a cloak fastened round the neck by the top button.

'I thought I told you not to go near that pond until I'd seen it,' she snapped.

'We weren't doing any harm,' he said; and she realized that she'd damaged his pride. 'Anyway, the water's less than a foot deep.'

'Well, now I'm here I'll have a look at it.'

Leaving her cup on the grass, Barbara followed Richard into the bushes. After she had negotiated the apple tree, the going became easier: a path zigzagged downwards.

'Watch out for rabbit-droppings,' Richard said. 'They're everywhere.'

The place smelled of decaying vegetable matter. The ground felt spongy underfoot and brambles snatched at her dress. A cloud of gnats hovered above a blackened tree stump. The sun barely penetrated here so it was much cooler than it had been on the lawn.

Suddenly the bushes dropped away and Barbara stepped into the sunlight. There was an unexpected sense of limitless space, as if she had emerged quite by chance on the roof of the world.

The pond opened out before her. It was an irregular semi-circle of murky water, much of it choked with waterlogged branches and leaves. She and Richard stood on the curving side where a narrow strip of ground was free of bushes; Peter was crouching beside a small, clinker-built dinghy. At its widest, the pond was no more than six yards across.

On the farther shore, which corresponded to the diameter of the semi-circle, was a mass of weathered concrete – a pillbox, Barbara guessed, left over from World War II. Beyond it was a sagging barbed-wire fence; and then the ground fell sharply away to the flatlands below. The air was very still. The sun sparkled on a moving ribbon of glass and metal: the main road to the south and west.

'Why doesn't the water just drain away?' she said, knowing that a request for information might help to soothe the hurt pride.

'It does,' Richard said. 'We think the pond's a sort of accidental overflow for the ditch along the lane. It probably gets a lot fuller in winter.'

'But the lane's miles away, isn't it?'

'No, it's not. We've explored.' Richard pointed into the bushes. 'The wall stops about there, and the ditch swings in. Look – you can see it. We reckon they must have dug out the earth where the pond is, and packed it round the other side of the pillbox. And over the years the water just filled the hole they'd left.' He added, in a self-consciously masculine way that made her want to laugh: 'You see, it's all to do with the lie of the land.'

'I see. And how do you know how deep it is?'

'We took soundings,' Peter said. 'I'll show you.'

He picked up a stick, clambered into the boat and leant over the water. His movements were quick and overconfident: he was showing off.

'Be careful,' Barbara said before she could stop herself.

Richard clicked his tongue against the roof of his mouth. 'It's quite safe.'

The tip of the stick sank into the water. Bubbles of gas rose to the surface. The stick touched bottom almost at once.

'It's the same everywhere,' Peter said. 'A few inches – a foot at the most.'

'It might be deeper in the middle,' Barbara pointed out.

'I don't think so,' Richard said. 'Not if you take into account the lie of the land.'

'What about the boat?'

'I think we can make it seaworthy.'

Peter scrambled on to the bank. 'The real problem's whether there's enough water to float it.'

Richard looked up at her, his face anxious. 'You don't mind, do you?' he murmured.

Of course she minded. Richard couldn't swim. She worried constantly when he was near water. On the other hand, the pond was shallow and he would be with Peter, who was quite a good swimmer. This part of the garden was ideal for them – away from the house, from Hubert and Kate: it was private. And if she forbade them to come here, Richard would lose face in front of Peter. He was thirteen, after all; she must learn not to be overprotective.

'As long as you're both sensible,' Barbara said. 'Don't damage the boat, because it isn't ours, and try not to get too dirty: that's all I ask. I don't see what harm it can do.'

Kate came into the kitchen as Barbara was peeling the potatoes for lunch.

'Would you give me a hand with these?' Barbara said.

'I'm busy.'

'So am I.' Kate edged towards the door to the hall.

'Come on. There's another knife in the drawer at the end of the table.'

'But there's such an awful smell in here. Anyway, why can't the boys help?'

'Don't worry – they will. They can do the washing-up. With two of us this won't take long.'

'Oh, Mum – must I?'

Barbara stared at her. Kate shrugged. She rummaged in the drawer for the knife, making far more noise than was necessary, and sat down opposite her mother, and as far as possible away from her. Barbara pushed a handful of potatoes across the table. For a moment they worked in silence.

'Where have you been?' Barbara asked.

'Here and there.'

'Have you had a look at the town?'

'You can hardly call it a town. It took me about five minutes to look round, and that was too long.' Kate dropped a peeled potato into the saucepan. 'Anyway, what's the point of looking in shops? I'm not going to have any money, am I?'

'We'll see.' Barbara wiped her forehead; the heat from the Aga was making her sweat. 'Just be patient until we know how much it will cost to repair the glass.'

'I bet the Timballs wouldn't even notice it's broken.'

'Of course they would, darling.' Privately Barbara agreed with her. She made an effort to divert the conversation from the pocket-money grievance. 'I'm surprised we didn't meet each other on the drive. You must have gone out as I was coming in.'

'There's a footpath.' Kate pointed the knife in the general direction of the kitchen yard. 'Over there, behind those sheds and things. It goes up to the main road.'

Barbara waited while she peeled another potato. 'Mr Nimp called.'

'Nimp the pink. He gives me the creeps.'

'That's unfair, darling. You don't know him at all.'

'I've heard things,' Kate said.

'From those boys on the war memorial?'

Kate dug her knife into a potato. 'You've been spying, haven't you? What is this? An inquisition?'

'Don't be silly.' Barbara wondered how long this tiresome teenage surliness would last, and whether Richard would develop it too; Kate's was making life increasingly uncomfortable for everyone. 'Mr Nimp happened to mention you were talking to them.'

'Why shouldn't I? I've got to talk to someone.'

'It's rather difficult. You know what your father's like, especially on locums. He doesn't want to upset anyone. I don't think those boys are quite suitable for you.'

'That's just snobbery,' Kate said. 'What's wrong with them?'

'I don't want to go into that just now,' Barbara said. 'Clergymen's families have to be very careful about who they mix with. People like to pick fault.'

'You should tell the Timballs that,' Kate snapped. 'I don't think they've been very careful with their son Frank.'

'What about him?'

Kate smirked. 'Oh, it's only gossip. Dad doesn't like us to pass on gossip.'

Barbara held on to her temper. 'To go back to those boys. I know it must seem unfair, but while we're in Abbotsfield it is important not to upset people like Mr Nimp.'

Kate flung down the knife and stood up. 'Mr Nimp? Damn Mr Nimp. You want to know what they say about him? He should be in prison. And you know why? He likes young girls. Girls like me.'

She ran out of the kitchen, into the hall and up the stairs. Barbara swore. The telephone in the study began to ring.

The study smelled of damp paper. One wall was lined with books. The window, which faced north, overlooked a high, red-brick wall; a tarmac path ran along the gap between house and wall from the kitchen yard to the garden. The phone was on top of a rolltop, desk in front of the window.

Barbara seized the heavy, black receiver. 'Yes,' she gasped, breathless with anger and exertion. 'Abbotsfield Vicarage.'

'Is that Mrs Molland?' a woman asked.

'Yes.'

'I'm Mary Salperton.' The voice on the other end sounded like the rustle of dead leaves. 'I believe you met my husband yesterday afternoon – at Carinish Court.'

'Yes, of course. He very kindly lent us some petrol.'

'We were wondering if you and your family would like to come over for lunch tomorrow?'

'Well –' In her mind Barbara balanced the possibility

that Ralph Salperton's hands would go once more a-roving against the pleasure of eating a Sunday lunch cooked by someone else in a civilized and sweet-smelling house. 'We'd love to, of course. But there are rather a lot of us. Besides my husband and myself, we've got two of our own children and my son's friend.'

'Peter Redburn?'

Barbara frowned. 'Yes, but –'

'You're wondering how we know. The Redburns are old friends of ours. Johnny was Ralph's best man, in fact. He dropped us a line to say that you were bringing Peter.'

It was odd, Barbara thought, that Lucasta Redburn hadn't mentioned the Salpertons to her.

'The more the merrier,' Mary Salperton went on. 'The children will keep one another company.'

'We met James yesterday. He was so helpful. You've got a daughter too, I gather?'

'Ginny – she's nearly fifteen. How old are yours?'

'Both thirteen – they're twins.'

'Splendid. They're all much of an age.' Mrs Salperton seemed to have taken Barbara's acceptance for granted. 'By the way, if it's a nice day the children might like to bring their bathing costumes. You and your husband as well, if you want.'

'You've got a swimming pool?' Barbara swallowed, and her envy tasted sour.

'Just a little one. It's Ralph's pride and joy. Shall we say twelve-thirty for one? Would that suit you?'

'Yes, I'm sure it would.'

'If there's any problem you can always ring me back – it's Abbotsfield three-two-one: easy to remember. But

219

if we don't hear from you, we'll expect you around twelve-thirty.'

They assured each other how much they were looking forward to meeting, and rang off. Barbara suspected that Hubert would object to the invitation with his usual argument that one should only accept hospitality one could afford to repay; secretly, though he would never admit it, he was shy. But she was confident that she could cope with him. She would hint that Mrs Salperton had already gone to a lot of trouble over lunch; and she would also stress that Peter's parents were old friends of the Salpertons, so in a sense the hospitality was being offered to the Redburns rather than to the Mollands.

'Who was that?' Kate shouted as Barbara came out of the study.

She was hanging over the banisters, her ill-temper apparently forgotten or at least temporarily set aside.

'Mrs Salperton from Carinish Court,' Barbara said. 'We're going to have lunch there tomorrow.'

'Really? Will that boy be there? What do you think I should wear?'

Barbara pushed open the green-baize door. 'We'll talk about it while you help me with the potatoes,' she said. 'And I expect you'd like to hear about the swimming pool too.'

The School-Boy Diary entry for Saturday I August 1964 was slightly longer than usual. *Emor. Ughish lunch. Found pond with boat – LUSH. Mr M in a fur and made us clean kitchen because of row last night. That boy from yesterday was spying on us.*

'Ughish', Peter remembered, was a private word whose use was confined to Richard and himself; it meant unpleasant or horrible. 'Lush', which derived from 'luscious', was widely used at Plumford Grammar School and perhaps in other schools. It was a term of the highest praise. 'Fur' came from furious or fury, and it could be used as a noun, an adjective ('furred') or even as an intransitive verb.

Both the language and the content of the entry suggested to Peter that he had been trying to cling to childhood. He hadn't described the *Health and Efficiency* episode, only the punishment that followed it. In the diary he also ignored – now and later – the feelings that Kate and Barbara Molland had aroused in him.

His entry corresponded to a few sentences in *The Secret History of Emor*. The sentences were undated but their contents tied them to 1 August. The passage was particularly interesting because it marked the point when Richard had begun to transform *The Secret History* from a continuous formal narrative, composed long after the events it described, into an almost daily journal of Emorian events.

The Court settled into the new summer palace at Campus Abbatis. Nearby was the island of Capri, where republican rebels had recently seized control of the citadel and put to the sword those of the islanders who remained loyal to the Crown. The Lord High Admiral, Gaius Marcus Mollandius, ordered a review of the fleet to celebrate the Emperor's arrival, but this was merely a brilliant ploy to deceive the rebels. Once at sea, Mollandius commanded the fleet to sail westwards. After a swift reconnaissance, he launched a daring and successful sea-borne assault on Capri. The Emperor, who insisted on fighting

incognito as an officer in the Imperial Marines, covered himself with
glory during the battle that followed the landings.

The farther shore of the pond was called Capri for the
rest of the summer. The citadel-pillbox, however, was
put to a variety of other uses, the most important of
which was its role as the Mithraeum or High Temple.

When they explored the pillbox just before lunch on
the first morning at Abbotsfield, Peter and Richard
immediately recognized its Emorian potential. It was a
hexagonal slab of concrete, half-buried in the spongy
earth that surrounded it. The ground must have subsided since the pillbox was built because the whole
structure tilted to the left. The roof and the walls were
fissured with cracks. On the side nearest the pond, a
narrow flight of steps led down to a wooden door that
hung askew on one hinge. Inside, it was very dark. The
only light came through the doorway and from the four
loopholes that commanded the hill. The floor, which
was covered with damp, dead leaves, was uneven, and
water had collected in a deep puddle just inside the door.
Their wet shoes got them into trouble at lunchtime.

In the afternoon – for the assault on the citadel –
they wore Wellington boots and brought Peter's torch
with them. In one corner of the pillbox they found a
broken beer bottle and an empty packet of Guards
cigarettes. There was also a deflated balloon, like an
empty sausage skin made of rubber.

Richard held it up. 'Funny sort of place to choose
for a party.'

They threw it away when they cleared out the glass,
the leaves and the cigarette packet. Almost a year later,

Peter realized that what they had found was not a balloon but a contraceptive sheath. The Mithraeum had once been someone's love nest, perhaps Frank Timball's.

The infuriatingly selective diary entry for the day contained one useful piece of information. *That boy from yesterday was spying on us*. It was the first written reference to James. The sighting was important because if James hadn't spied on them he might never have learned about Emor, and everything would have been very different.

Peter and Richard had poled the boat back from the pillbox to the side of the pond nearer the house. They were standing on the bank and discussing the grand assault on Capri that was to take place in the afternoon. The conversation grew quite heated – the Emperor and the Lord High Admiral each wanted the leading role in the invasion for himself.

'I still think,' Richard was saying, 'it would be better if the Admiral fought the duel with the republican leader.'

Peter shook his head. 'I tell you what, I'll tell the Senate to vote you a grant of fifty thousand sesterces after the victory.'

A branch cracked in the undergrowth between the pond and the lane.

'What was that?' Richard hissed.

For an instant Peter glimpsed the blond hair and long face of the boy from yesterday. He was crouching on the far side of the ditch that fed the pond. The face disappeared. Leaves rustled. Peter and Richard charged through the bushes and scrambled into the lane.

The boy was on a red bicycle and he was pedalling furiously downhill, away from Abbotsfield.

'It's a racer, isn't it?' Peter said. 'One of those twelve-gear jobs, I think.'

'How much do you think he heard?'

Peter shrugged. They stared at each other in dismay.

'A spy,' Richard said, instinctively trying to minimize the damage by restating it in Emorian terms. 'Probably from Parthia or Babylon.'

'Get the Secret Police to investigate,' the Emperor ordered. 'I will not tolerate spies. The punishment is death.'

Twelve

'Ginny? Is that you, dear?'

As usual Mary Salperton's voice was a rustling whisper, so thin and quiet that Ginny had to clamp the receiver against her ear. Her mother couldn't have chosen a worse time to phone. It was Thursday morning, and Ginny was trying to clear her desk before the Christmas holiday.

'It certainly is me. How are you?'

'Quite well, thank you. I'm not sure that the service is as good as last time but if anything the food is even better. There's a new manager, which might explain it. The views aren't so nice, either, but that's the weather, and there's not much we can do about that, is there? I can't recall such a mild winter. Is it still raining in London?'

'Most of the time. Anyway, what can I do for you?'

'Well, I knew I'd forgotten something as soon as I got here. I said as much to the man who drove me, when he was leaving, and he said it probably didn't matter. But last night I remembered just as I was going to sleep. And the man was wrong. It does matter. It was just as well I remembered, though I realize I must have missed the last day for posting. Still, better late than never. You don't mind, do you?'

'Mum, you're being elliptical again,' Ginny said. 'Mind what, exactly?'

'Finding my Christmas cards, dear. I forgot to bring them. The whole thing's rather mysterious: I was quite sure I'd put them in the little suitcase – the little red one, you know? – but they weren't there. And Christmas cards are not the sort of thing a chambermaid would want to steal, are they? In any case my chambermaid's a very nice girl. She comes from Morecambe and her parents run a bed-and-breakfast.'

'You could always buy some more cards,' Ginny suggested. 'Save the other ones for next year.'

'No, you don't understand. I've already written them, and addressed most of the envelopes. By next year people might have moved or died. Besides, I wrote little notes to some people, you know the way one does to friends you never write to except at Christmas, and they were all about the things I'd done this year, of course, not next year.'

'Okay, I'll post them for you. Where are they?'

Mary Salperton plunged into detailed directions. She always spoke so faintly that you had to strain to hear, which of course meant that you paid more attention to what she was saying than you might otherwise have done; and so feebly that you automatically became anxious for her, for the voice gave the misleading impression that she might not be strong enough to finish any sentence she began.

The letters were either in the buhl chest in her bedroom or in the bureau, which was in the sitting room. The key to the chest was hidden in the little china pot on the sitting-room mantelpiece, the pot with roses on it, not the one with shepherdesses. Unfortunately her address book was in her handbag here in the hotel.

Perhaps Ginny wouldn't mind phoning her and she would dictate the addresses for the envelopes that needed them. Obviously, with Christmas so close, time was of the essence; and did Ginny possibly think she could do it this evening, and post the cards immediately afterwards, preferably at a main post office?

'Yes, that's fine.' Ginny estimated the time it would take to drive to the flat in Putney, find the cards, get through to her mother (who would almost certainly be in the middle of dinner or a game of bridge), extract the addresses while listening to anecdotes about the addressees, lick the stamps and post the cards. 'Yes,' she repeated, 'that's fine.'

'Wonderful, dear. Such a relief. Now where was I? I had a little list but it seems to have disappeared. I know there was something else I wanted to ask you. Oh, I remember – about the Redburns. Did you see Peter? Did you go to the funeral?'

'Yes, I did.'

So that's why you phoned, Ginny thought. Suddenly she felt feverish – as though her eyes had grown too big for their sockets and her skin had been stripped of its top layers.

'I used to think Peter was such a peculiar little boy. Saturnine – is that the word I want? He always seemed to be on the alert for something, heaven knows what. So very different from poor Richard, who was really rather sweet, and not at all like Johnny, either. I expect he takes after Lucasta's side of the family.'

'We got on surprisingly well,' Ginny said. 'Have you talked to James lately?'

'Not since Saturday, or was it Friday?'

'He's asked Peter to help him with his book.'

'Oh dear. Is that wise? James was never any good at English. At school he had the most appalling reports imaginable. And I suppose Peter's an expert, as it were.'

In passing, Ginny registered the fact that her mother had been sufficiently interested in Peter both to notice he was a writer and to remember it. But why was she against his helping James?

'Anyway, I mustn't keep you,' Mary Salperton went on. 'I expect you're very busy. Am I right in thinking that Peter doesn't know?'

Ginny glanced over her shoulder. The only other person in the office was her assistant, who seemed safely absorbed in a problem of solid geometry: the task of wrapping a hexagonal box of chocolates in a rectangular sheet of paper.

'I certainly haven't told him,' she said.

'I'd be inclined to let sleeping dogs lie. But it's up to you.' Her mother sighed. 'I remembered something yesterday. I was in the bath, which I often find stimulates the memory. At one point, I thought Richard Molland might have known. It worried me dreadfully.'

'But how could he?'

'That weekend at Carinish Court – the one when Johnny came down with Lucasta. Do you remember the seat in the garden? The one underneath the oak? Johnny and I were sitting there, just talking. I remember feeling rather sad about everything. I mean you can't go back, can you? It never works, however much you want it to. And afterwards someone asked Richard what he'd been doing, and he blushed – he always seemed to blush when a grown-up asked him something – yes, he blushed and said he'd been climbing the oak tree. So he might have been up there while Johnny and I were talking, in which case he could have overheard.'

'It doesn't seem very likely. And if he did overhear you, it doesn't mean he understood what you were saying.'

'Yes, dear. That's what I told myself at the time. And of course, even if he had understood, he might not have told anyone. Still, it's worth bearing in mind, don't you agree?'

The warning was unmistakable, Ginny thought, even if the reason for it was obscure. She knew better than to ask directly: her mother would merely retreat further and further into a protective cloud of anecdotes, rhetorical questions and those bewilderingly abrupt transitions from one subject to the next. Before Ginny had time to approach the question in a subtler way, Mary Salperton decided that the conversation was over.

'Now I really must get ready for lunch. Are you sure you don't mind fetching the Christmas cards?'

'Quite sure.' Despite everything, Ginny meant what she said. 'I'll phone you this evening.'

The demands her mother made often irritated Ginny. So did the inconsequential chatter, the pretence of help-less old age and the regimented existence where every-thing had its place, from the key to the buhl cabinet to the angle of a napkin on a tea plate. But it would have been inaccurate and unfair to classify Mary Salperton as selfish: better to see her as presenting a post-dated bill for services rendered. Ginny remembered her child-hood as a series of battles between her parents, and her mother had fought many of them not for herself but for Ginny.

One of the worst battles had been over Ginny's education. It had been less of a battle than a ten-year war. Her mother was a woman of considerable intelligence whose schooling had taught her little more than how to dance, how to sew and the correct way of replying to invitations: she had been brought up to be an ornament. She once said to Ginny that in imperial China they would have restricted the growth of her feet with bandages to make her more beautiful in the eyes of potential husbands; in England they restricted the growth of her mind for the same purpose. By the time she had realized what had happened, it had been too late.

Ginny had learned about her mother not all at once but in a piecemeal fashion – from scraps of conversation collated over thirty years and cobbled together with speculation.

Mary had been unfortunate or perhaps foolish, depending on your point of view. John Redburn and Ralph Salperton both did their wartime service in the battalion commanded by her father. Both fell in love with her, a fact which by all accounts gave her much pleasure at the time. On the whole she had favoured Ralph: he was more amusing, better-looking, a better dancer and much wealthier; he also enjoyed the enthusiastic support of her parents. Johnny, on the other hand, who by the attraction of opposites was Ralph's best friend, was inclined to be serious. Mary enjoyed talking to him but sometimes found his relentlessly intellectual small talk a little wearing. He was a chemist's son – another point against him; her father referred to him as 'your temporary gentleman'. Johnny's hopes were pinned on his deferred place at London University and on the possibility of an academic career as a physicist.

Ralph could afford to marry her but Johnny couldn't: that had been the crucial difference between them. Timing was an important consideration. Mary couldn't wait to get away from her parents.

She blamed her mistake on her lack of education: unlike Johnny, she had not been taught to think or to make decisions. In consequence Mary brought Ginny up to believe in the importance of academic and professional qualifications for women. She was quietly determined that her daughter should have a wider range of choices than she had done. Even in the worst years, when she was drinking too much and leading an almost separate life from Ralph under the same roof, she never forgot what Ginny needed; and for that Ginny was grateful. It was Mary who in one sense was responsible for Ginny's going to Oxford.

'George Timball says you need Latin "O" level to get into Oxford,' she'd said.

She and Ginny were having tea on the terrace while Ralph swam up and down the little swimming pool a few yards away from their deckchairs; in those days Ralph made a practice of swimming fifty lengths a day. It was the first Saturday in August 1964, the day before Ginny met the Mollands and Peter Redburn.

'Then I won't get into Oxford,' Ginny had said, without raising her eyes from her book. 'You saw my Latin report.'

'I wonder if we could arrange some coaching. James says the locum used to teach classics.'

Ginny clicked her tongue and expelled her breath in surge of irritation. 'I don't want to spend the summer working.'

'It would only be for a few hours a week,' her mother said. 'I telephoned Mrs Molland this morning and invited them to lunch tomorrow. I'll ask him then.'

'Money down the drain,' Ralph said. He hauled himself out of the pool and held out a hand for his towel. 'What's the point? She'll only go and get married.'

'No, I won't,' Ginny muttered, perversely determined to thwart him and go to Oxford after all.

Mary passed him the towel. 'I'll use my money, dear. Don't worry.'

Ralph sniffed. 'Do as you please.' It was a sore point between them that Mary had an income of her own that she refused to let him touch. 'It's nothing to do with me.'

The Salpertons were regular churchgoers chiefly in the sense that they regularly put in an appearance in church at Easter and Christmas. They enlisted the rituals of the Church of England to add a fitting solemnity to their personal rites of passage: birth, marriage and death.

On Sunday 2 August Mary Salperton decided it would be both politic and polite for Ginny and herself to go to the ten-thirty Matins and Holy Communion. Ralph refused to come with them, and James wriggled out of it by claiming to feel unwell.

Ginny enjoyed some aspects of the trip to church – knowing that she was looking her best in a new summer dress; feeling adult because she was wearing a hat and carrying gloves; observing other members of the congregation; and relishing the sense that she was gracefully condescending to appear in a public place with the residents of Abbotsfield.

On the other hand, the services always bored her and today it was worse than usual. George Timball was a short, comfortable man who preached short, comfortable sermons. Hubert Molland, however, preached for fifteen minutes in a voice so harsh it was difficult to ignore. He took his text from the Gospel of the day, in which St Luke described how Jesus wept at the sight of Jerusalem.

For the days shall come upon thee, that thine enemies shall cast a trench about thee, and compass thee round, and keep thee in on every side, and shall lay thee even with the ground, and thy children within thee; and they shall not leave in thee one stone upon another; because thou knewest not the time of thy visitation.

Mr Molland described how Jesus's prophecy had been savagely fulfilled by the Romans, and went on to draw a parallel between Jerusalem in the first century and the soul of each member of the congregation before him. Ginny felt he was being offensively personal.

For her, the main interest of the service was the opportunity it offered for studying the newcomers in the Vicarage pew. Despite her dowdy clothes, Mrs Molland looked surprisingly young and attractive. The two boys and the girl interested Ginny less. They were only thirteen, mere children to someone who was nearly fifteen. Ginny took an instant dislike to the girl; she was obviously going to be very pretty.

Mr Nimp was taking the collection on that side of

the church. Ginny watched carefully to see what effect, if any, Kate Molland had on him. Perhaps it was her imagination but he seemed a little pinker than usual, a little more flurried in his movements. She wished Frank Timball were here. The widespread belief among Abbotsfield teenagers that Mr Nimp liked what Frank called 'young female flesh' derived solely from Frank's claim to have seen the churchwarden dallying with a schoolgirl on the Downs in Bristol.

After the service she and her mother met the Mollands and Peter Redburn in the churchyard. The vitality of Barbara Molland made Mary Salperton appear even less substantial than usual, as though the strong were feeding on the weak. The difference between them upset and angered Ginny; she also felt ashamed of her mother. In her mind she reacted by categorizing Mrs Molland as 'vulgar'. The children said nothing to one another.

Mary was silent during the journey home; she disliked talking while she was driving. The Jaguar nosed into the cobbled stableyard of Carinish Court. She braked in front of the coach house. A mottled cloud of grey and white pigeons shot into the air.

She clapped her gloved hands against the steering wheel. 'He'll do it.'

'Who?'

'Mr Molland. They're as poor as church mice. Did you notice their clothes?'

Ginny did her best to avoid their guests – without being actually rude about it, because Ralph was capable of telling her off in public.

Lunch was an ordeal because she was terribly afraid

that one or both of her parents would disgrace her before the visitors. Ralph was given to bursts of ill-temper and never allowed the presence of strangers to restrain him. Her mother consumed three dry martinis before the meal; during lunch she almost knocked over the gravy and her eyes looked like faded violets beneath half an inch of water.

'Quite a coincidence, eh?' Ralph said as he carved the chicken. 'Your knowing old Johnny, I mean. Do you see much of him?'

'He's not as much of a churchgoer as Mrs Redburn,' Hubert Molland said. 'He teaches Richard, of course.'

'Funny to think of Johnny as a beak. Dear God, if those boys only knew.' Ralph appeared to recollect that Molland was not only a clergyman but also a former schoolmaster. 'Still, we all had to sow a few wild oats, eh? Mrs Molland, a little breast for you?'

Mrs Molland coloured slightly and nodded.

'I've just written to your parents, young man,' Ralph said to Peter. 'Thought I'd ask them down for a week-end while you're here.'

That was the point when Mary Salperton almost knocked over the gravy boat. She was reaching for the potatoes as Ralph spoke. The long, thin jug wobbled on its saucer. A trickle of gravy ran down the side. No one except Ginny appeared to notice.

'I wish you'd talked to me first,' Mary said; unusually for her she showed her irritation. 'When?'

'Weekend of the fifteenth, I think.' Ralph's eyes snapped at her. 'Damn it, it's about time we saw them again. Haven't seen them – oh, must be for thirteen or fourteen years.'

'It's so easy to drift out of touch, isn't it?' Barbara Molland said. 'Especially if you have children to consider.'

Peter was listening to the adults, his eyes switching from one speaker to the next.

'We must decide what to do after lunch,' James said to Kate. 'We could go for a walk, or swim, or play tennis. Whatever you like. You choose.'

'I'd love a swim,' Kate said. 'We brought our costumes.'

'That's settled.' James sounded pleased. Ginny knew that this was because he was an indifferent tennis player but a very good swimmer. He looked at Peter and Richard. 'Okay by you?'

Peter agreed with enthusiasm.

Richard stared at the tablecloth. 'I don't like swimming much. I think I'll just watch.'

'You only don't like it because you can't swim,' Kate said.

Ginny thought: You bitch.

'Tell you what,' James said. 'I'll teach you.'

Richard looked up, and his face was full of hope. 'Could you?'

'It's easy. I taught several people at school. And our pool's very good for learning in – not too big.'

'That would be very kind of you,' Barbara Molland said. 'Are you sure you wouldn't mind?'

'Not at all.' He smiled at her, confident even then of his power to charm. 'I'd quite enjoy it, actually.'

'And how are you settling into the Vicarage?' Mary asked of no one in particular.

'Very well, thank you,' Mr Molland said. 'Aren't we, dear?'

'It's a little larger than we're used to,' Barbara said. 'Still, that means lots of room for the children.'

'In my opinion, that house needs a lot of money spent on it,' Ralph said. 'Ghastly old barracks, isn't it? George and Dorothy Timball don't use most of it, I gather. Far too big for them. They're by themselves now that Frank's gone.'

'Frank?'

'Their son. Between ourselves, he's been a bit of a disappointment to his parents. Rather wild, you know. He –'

'Ralph?' If the Mollands hadn't been there, Mary would have murmured, *'Pas devant les enfants.'* As it was she frowned: having caught everyone's attention, she was uncertain what to do with it. She added lamely, 'It doesn't matter.'

'Frank's all right,' Ginny said.

'Yes, dear, of course he is.' Mary smiled at Mrs Molland. 'I know Dorothy has found it terribly difficult to get domestic help lately. Do you have the same problem at Plumford?'

'Not really,' Barbara said. 'You see, we can't afford a cleaning woman.'

'Oh, we don't really need one,' Hubert Molland said.

At last the long, awkward meal came to an end. Afterwards the adults drank coffee in the drawing room and the four younger children, forbidden to swim until their lunch had had time to digest, wandered into the garden. Ginny tried to join the grown-ups but her mother signalled that her presence would not be welcome.

Ginny took her coffee outside and brooded on the

unfairness of life. No doubt her mother wanted to discuss the private tuition plan with Mr Molland and considered that Ginny was too young to hear the sordid financial details that the plan entailed. While she brooded, she sat on the seat under the oak tree and pretended to read *Mansfield Park*. She hoped that someone would come up and ask her what she was reading but no one did.

James was enjoying himself. Ginny suspected that he was lonely during the holidays: he had been at boarding school since the age of seven, so he had few local friends. She was slightly jealous of the ease with which he charmed and impressed the three children, though she had no desire to charm or impress them herself. Contrary to her expectations, he was not confining his attentions to the boys. It was the first time she had noticed his taking an overt interest in a girl. But Kate might have had something to do with that: Ginny had already characterized her as 'pushy'. What could you expect with a mother like that?

Occasionally she glimpsed the four children and heard their voices. Their laughter made her envious. Anyway, if they weren't such children they would know that there was nothing to laugh about.

Later, her mother came out on to the terrace and called her into the house.

'Ginny, Mr Molland has very kindly offered to give you a little coaching in Latin over the next few weeks.'

The adults waited for her to say something. In the end she muttered 'Thank you' at the carpet.

'Nothing too strenuous,' Mary went on. 'A couple of hours three times a week.'

'I thought the most useful thing would be to work through your set-books,' Mr Molland said. 'Your mother tells me you're doing book eight of the *Aeneid* and book five of the *Bellum Gallicum*.' His face glistened, and Ginny thought how ugly he was. 'And also perhaps we should try our hand at a few unseens and at the English-into-Latin sentences. It will be quite a treat for me. Do you like Latin?'

'Not particularly, I'm afraid.'

'Ginny takes after me.' For some reason Ralph was in a good humour. 'I never could see the point of learning dead languages.'

'Really?' Mr Molland was sitting bolt upright in his armchair. Round his neck was a red rim where the top of the dog collar had rubbed against the skin. 'Still, Latin has its uses. Especially if you want to go to Oxford.'

'We used to have a rhyme about it at school. "Latin is a language, as dead as dead can be. It killed the ancient Romans, and now it's killing me."' Ralph looked around, as if expecting applause.

'I suppose it gives you mental exercise,' Mary said. 'Rather like bridge does.'

'Oh, do you play bridge?' Mrs Molland said.

Dear God, Ginny thought, if she plays cards we won't get rid of them for the whole summer.

James appeared at the open French window. 'Can we swim yet?'

Ginny felt trapped. *Mansfield Park* was boring her. If she stayed in the drawing room, she would have to listen to the children's shouting and the splashes as they jumped into the pool. James would be showing off his racing dives, his crawl and his butterfly stroke. She hated them all, adults and children. None of them cared about her in the slightest. Abbotsfield in the summer holiday was the end of the world. She longed for something awful to happen, just to break the monotony.

What Peter remembered most about their first visit to Carinish Court was the almost unbearable excitement that gripped him from start to finish.

The Salpertons had everything – a huge house, a swimming pool, table tennis and a full-sized billiards table in the attics. The food was wonderful and you could eat as much as you liked. Everyone drank wine with lunch.

He never learned how many acres the Salpertons owned. Before they went swimming, James took them on a guided tour. The grounds of Carinish Court seemed limitless – far larger than Victoria Park in Plumford. Beyond the garden itself were fields – 'We let most of them to a local farmer,' James remarked – and even a small wood on the hill behind the house. James led them on an arc which began at the front of the house and after twenty minutes brought them to a cottage behind the kitchen garden. James asked them if they would like to see inside.

'There's a good view from the bedroom window. My mother says it's much better than any you get from the house.'

He lifted the Suffolk latch and opened the door. The cottage had been built against the west wall of the kitchen garden. It had only two rooms, one above the other. Downstairs was a living room-cum-kitchen with a flagged floor and a rusty iron range in the corner.

'Rather primitive,' James drawled. 'No mains water or electricity. No bathroom, either.'

Plaster had fallen off the walls, exposing the laths behind, and pale tendrils of honeysuckle had wriggled their way through the broken window. The cottage had its own garden, now overgrown with brambles, and at the bottom of the garden was an earth closet with a corrugated-iron roof.

'Our old gardener used to live here, believe it or not,' James said. 'But the new one bikes up from Abbotsfield so we've never bothered to have this place repaired.'

He led them up the narrow stairs. 'Keep your feet near the sides,' he said. 'Some of the treads are a bit rotten.' The stairs opened directly into what must have been the bedroom. James opened the small casement window – the glass was so dirty that it was impossible to see through it – and stood back to allow his visitors to enjoy the view.

None of them paid much attention to it because James pulled out a silver cigarette case.

'Turkish one side, Virginia the other,' he said.

Peter knew that was a quotation – from James Bond, perhaps, or Bulldog Drummond – but it still impressed him enormously. The Turkish cigarettes were oval and untipped. Kate and Peter both chose them. James nodded approvingly.

'They taste so much better, don't they? These are Sullivan Powells. What about you, Richard?'

'Not for me, thanks. I don't smoke.'

James raised his eyebrows and said nothing to such good effect that Richard blushed once more. He struck a match and lit the cigarettes. Then he bewildered Peter by saying to Richard: 'You're wise. I'll probably give up at the end of the summer.'

They sat and smoked in silence. For Peter the occasion had an almost sacramental quality: an outward sign of maturity. The Sullivan Powell was only the seventh cigarette he had smoked in his life. It was immeasurably superior to the previous six, which he had smoked with Joe at different times in the wasteland behind 29 Champney Road; it was also noticeably stronger. He wished he knew how to inhale properly.

Kate stubbed out her cigarette on the windowsill and said she had to go back to the house for a moment. Peter assumed from her sudden pallor that she needed the lavatory. His third cigarette had taken him the same way. James offered to go with her.

'No, don't bother. I know the way.'

She staggered down the stairs. They heard her running down the path.

James blew a smoke ring. 'Sorry about yesterday morning.'

'When you were watching us, you mean?' Richard said.

'I hope you didn't think I was eavesdropping. The thing is, I'd stopped for a fag. Frank and I often smoke in that old pillbox. Then I saw you were there, and I didn't want to disturb you, so I shot off.'

Richard dug his hands into the pockets of his trousers. 'But you must have been there for quite a while, and you must have known that we'd seen you.'

'Oh, don't be so stupid,' Peter said. 'It wasn't James's fault. It wasn't anyone's fault.'

'It looked like you were in the middle of a game.' James took a long pull on his cigarette. 'Seemed pretty interesting.'

He turned away to flick ash out of the window. His tone as much as his words managed to convey that he thought Emor had sounded fascinating and not at all childish.

Richard flushed. 'That's our business.'

James turned back. 'Sorry. Have I said something wrong?'

'Of course not,' Peter said. He wanted to make up for Richard's churlishness, partly because he admired James and partly because he hoped they would be invited back to Carinish Court. 'But it's not exactly a game. It's more complicated than that.'

'Tell me,' James said. And Peter did.

Ginny allowed herself to be bullied into joining the swimmers. 'The exercise will do you good,' her mother said. In fact Ginny was more than willing to be bullied. She was hot, and the water looked coolly inviting; and the only alternative to swimming seemed to be to listen to Mr Molland's views on the teaching of Latin.

For most of the time she lay on her back in the deep end and watched the others through her eyelashes. James surprised her. Apart from one racing dive and a showy dash to the end of the pool and back, he concentrated entirely on Richard. It was obvious that the poor boy was terrified of water.

James was very gentle. He showed Richard the mechanics of the breaststroke on the terrace and demonstrated them in the pool. Then he stood in the shallow end with one hand underneath Richard's stomach, and got him to work on the leg movements. Richard clung to a rung of the ladder, his back arched and his head lifted as far as possible away from the water. James maintained a flow of soothing comments.

'Kick a little harder. That's it, that's very good, keep it up. We'll save the arm movements till next time. Tell you what: I'll show you them again on dry land, and you can practise at home. Lie across a bed – that's what I used to do.'

Meanwhile Kate and Peter swam up and down on opposite sides of the pool. They were curiously sedate – conscious of the eyes of the adults, who had moved on to the terrace; and perhaps, Ginny thought, conscious of each other. Kate looked ridiculous – flaunting herself in a bathing costume that was a little too large for her and obviously second-hand, the material had a green and orange floral design; the bodice was boned, and there was a silly little skirt with a frill. She wore a dark-blue rubber bathing hat with a strap under the chin and pink flowers at the ears. Despite everything, there was no escaping the fact that Kate was very pretty.

Ginny got tired of watching them, especially Kate. She hauled herself out of the pool and lay on her towel in the sun until she was almost dry. She went upstairs to change.

Her bedroom was at the front of the house, looking east. She took her time over washing and dressing. Her door was open, and she heard the others come upstairs. Her mother's voice rustled up the stairwell.

'Use my room, dear, and have a shower if you want to.'

'That'd be lovely, Mrs Salperton. If you're sure it wouldn't be too much trouble.'

'The bathroom's through there. I'll get you a towel.'

Her mother's bedroom was directly beneath hers. Ginny heard Kate's footsteps below. Once she thought she heard the chink of china and it occurred to her that Kate was just the sort of person to enjoy prying in other people's houses. The pipes creaked in her own bathroom, which meant that Kate had started to run the shower.

Ginny lay on her bed and wished they would all go home. The Mollands were so dull, just like her parents, and they didn't even know it. Her eyes closed and for a few minutes she drifted into a fantasy in which she was riding on the back of Frank's motorbike with the wind chasing through her hair and her arms knotted round his waist.

The motorbike daydream was never dull but it did have the drawback of being fundamentally unsatisfying: Ginny was uncertain what she wanted to happen when the motorbike stopped. She swung her legs off the bed. She was thirsty, and soon her mother would be making tea. She tiptoed downstairs because she didn't want to meet Kate and be obliged to make conversation with her.

The door of her mother's bedroom was slightly ajar. A cheval glass on casters stood just within the room. It was the only piece of furniture that Ginny could see. Even at the time she realized what a fluke it was: had she been standing an inch or so back or forward, had the glass itself been tilted a few degrees higher or lower, she would have missed the reflection that moved in the mirror.

The glass was angled in such a way that Ginny could see the cupboard on the left of the double bed behind the door. Mary Salperton's crocodile-skin handbag was on top of the cupboard, and the bag was open. Kate, her back half-turned to the door, stooped over the cupboard and peered into the bag. Her hair gleamed from the shower, and she was wearing that childish dress with the puffed sleeves and the Peter Pan collar.

A small, white hand dipped into the bag and came out with a brown purse. Kate opened it and took out a folded wad of banknotes. Her fingers moved very quickly. The wad was a blur of colour: orange for ten-shilling notes, green for pounds and blue for fivers.

Kate returned the wad to the purse and the purse to the bag. The clasp clicked home. She folded the notes she had taken and lifted her dress. She tucked the money into the waistband of faded, navy-blue cotton knickers with a darn on the right buttock.

Thirteen

The whole business reminded Peter of one of the more baroque subplots of *Pemberley*, in which confusions of identity were commonplace and practically everyone had at least one illegitimate child.

The television series was set, rather imprecisely, in the years between the wars. It was true that in the first episode of the first series James returned home from the Western Front with his arm in a sling and his chest crammed with medal ribbons, which fixed the date at 1918 or early 1919. Apart from this, however, the scriptwriters skated to and fro over the history of two decades.

The first series was a relatively tame affair. Major Darcy struggled to keep his ancestral home in the family, fought off a predatory Fitzwilliam cousin who had designs on the estate, and contracted a secret marriage with a pretty nurse, who conveniently died in childbirth at the end of the final episode. In those early days, the ghost of Jane Austen exercised a restraining influence. A number of characters other than Darcy purported to be descended from the cast of *Pride and Prejudice*. One reviewer went so far as to label the series as 'a period soap for the intelligentsia'.

The storylines of the subsequent series grew wilder and wilder. Darcy plunged into the beds of strange women with the reckless abandon of a man who has something to prove. He survived numerous brushes with death. His relations – equally remarkable for their quantity, their variety and their habit of popping up out of the blue – could be relied upon to add to the excitements of his life: one joined the fascists; another was recruited at Cambridge by the Russians; one went bankrupt; another, a drug addict, had an unfortunate experience with a white-slaver; two allowed themselves to become unexpectedly pregnant; and, at least once a series, someone (usually but not always a cousin) tried to part Darcy from his one true love, which was of course the great house of Pemberley.

Another feature of the storylines was the bewildering frequency with which they compelled characters to adopt disguises. A black sheep from the colonies presented himself as a clergyman. A chorus girl of easy virtue turned out (just in time) to be Darcy's niece. The butler who behaved so sinisterly for most of the second series was really a detective sergeant from Scotland Yard, who had once been Darcy's batman.

In the night after Peter had discovered the identity of his father's lover, he dreamed about *Pemberley*. He invented an episode, perhaps a whole series. He, not James, was playing Darcy, and the crucial question he had to decide was whether his – that is, Darcy's – father had sired James or Ginny in an illicit liaison with a Russian princess. The answer eluded him in the dream as it had the evening before.

Johnny,
*   The doctor agrees, so there's no doubt any longer. Darling, it's good news, really. Perhaps it's the best thing that could*

*have happened. I don't think it will be a problem here – quite
the contrary in a way. As long as it doesn't look too obviously
like you, he'll be thrilled.*

*This had to end. We knew that from the beginning. We
never had a future. Can you imagine what it would be like, for
both of us (and both of them), if we did what you suggest?*

*Now you have given me something permanent to remember
you by. I am happy, I really am. Don't write again, please.
Too many people could be hurt, including you and me.
Goodbye, my love.*

M.

P. S. Johnny, please burn this.

After breakfast on Thursday morning Peter took himself in hand and approached the problem methodically. He could hardly ask Mary Salperton directly – he didn't even know where she was – but there might be other ways to arrive at the solution.

From his research, he already knew the birthdays of both Ginny and James: 13 November 1949 and 8 April 1951. If one of them were the child, and if the pregnancy had lasted for the usual term, his father must have been with Mary Salperton sometime in February 1949 or in July 1950. Peter realized that he could not be absolutely certain that Ginny or James was the child, in which case he had to face a second, though less likely set of possibilities: an abortion, whether planned or accidental, a stillbirth or an adoption.

Peter turned to his mother's account books, hoping to find circumstantial evidence of a meeting between his father and Mary Salperton: the purchase of a railway ticket, perhaps, or a cheque made out to a London hotel. He was dismayed to find out how many cheques were simply noted down as 'Cash' or 'To Self'; and the amounts of these varied wildly from month to month. The possibility of such a meeting remained, but it was neither more nor less likely than before.

Having drawn a blank, he fetched a roll of black plastic sacks from the kitchen and attacked his mother's desk. Most of its contents went into the sacks. He searched the rest of the ground floor. The narrow hall filled up with bags of rubbish. He moved upstairs and swept through the bedrooms. In other circumstances he would have enjoyed throwing away so much and so quickly. He was discarding those parts of his and his parents' lives that he no longer had any use for. It was as if he were remodelling himself. The process gave him a heady sense of personal power: he was shaping his past to conform to the future he had laid down for himself. A side-effect was that the more he threw away, the lighter he felt. The sensation was curiously physical. He might have been shedding surplus pounds of his own flesh.

He forced himself to work harder and faster. By midday he was up in the loft, his face coated with grime and streaked with sweat. He was panting and coughing, and in his ears was a hum like an untuned radio's. By three o'clock the landing and the stairs were choked with bulging sacks. Fine dust filled the house like a mist. Peter knew he was beaten.

The kitchen was less untidy than the rest of the house. Peter washed his hands and face in the sink while the kettle was boiling. He made himself a pot of tea and sat down at the table. What now? He didn't want to reveal his interest by asking direct questions. Ginny probably wouldn't know, and in any case he shied away from asking her – partly because he liked her. (Imagine it, he told himself: 'Do you happen to know if you're a bastard?'). James would be outraged.

Was it possible that one or both of them already knew? Apparently independently, Ginny and James had sought him out and drawn him into their lives. Perhaps they had wanted to investigate a possible threat to them or simply to meet their half-brother without the commitment that admitting the relationship would have entailed.

He tried to persuade himself that the illegitmate child was a side-issue, and that pursuing it was a waste of effort. It could have nothing to do with what had happened in the Mithraeum on the night of Sunday 23 August 1964. Nevertheless, such an intimate connection with the Salpertons fascinated him for its own sake; and he could not be sure that the knowledge would always be useless. Knowledge was power.

The doorbell rang as Peter was halfway through his second mug of tea. He picked his way down the hall. The panel of frosted glass was almost blotted out by the shadow of the man standing on the doorstep.

Peter kicked a sack out of the way and opened the door. 'Hello, Bill,' he said. 'I thought you might turn up.'

Coleby's red jowls twitched as though he had bitten into something unpleasant. 'And I thought you were going to phone me.'

'You'd better come in.' By force of habit Peter led the way into the sitting room.

'Having a bit of a clear-out?' Coleby said. 'Does that mean you've seen sense?'

'It means I'm having a bit of a clear-out.' Peter lifted a pile of James's memorabilia from an armchair. 'Do you want to sit down?'

A photograph fluttered to the ground.

'Well?' Coleby said, ignoring the chair. 'Have you made up your mind?'

'Yes. You can have this house for three hundred thousand.'

'Jesus. Are you insane? I said one-twenty.'

'And I'm saying three hundred.'

Coleby stared at the carpet, at the photograph. 'That bastard James Salperton.'

'What do you mean?'

Peter's voice was high and sharp. The photograph was a publicity shot from the early 1970s. The harsh lighting accentuated the bones and hollows of the face.

'The wife's in love with him, believe it or not,' Coleby said. It was impossible to know whether he was joking. The broad accent, as flat as the land it sprung from, was not designed to express nuances of meaning. 'God knows why, but there it is. I hate the little sod. What are you doing with a picture of him?'

'I'm helping him with a book.'

Coleby picked up the print and studied it. 'At first I thought it was a photo of you.'

'You think we're alike?'

'No, not really.' He tossed the print into the box. 'It was just for an instant. Something about the eyebrows, I think. How come you know him?'

'I used to know him a long time ago. Before he was famous.'

The small blue eyes were very bright in Coleby's face. 'That summer?'

Peter nodded.

'Was he in Emor too?' Coleby paused. Then – as if aware he had stumbled on something potentially useful but uncertain what it signified – he switched back to Number 29. 'I'll make it one-fifty, Peter, and that's your lot.'

'Did you find anything about Emor at your parents' house?'

'One-fifty?'

'Emor, Bill: let's talk about Emor first.'

Coleby drew a white envelope from the inside pocket of his overcoat. 'I couldn't find anything myself, so I asked my mother. And do you know, she had a whole drawerful of stuff. Photos. Locks of hair tied up in ribbons. A painting I did when I was at school; I must have been five or six. Came as quite a shock. I never realized she was sentimental.'

A fat envelope, Peter thought: more than one letter in it. 'May I see?'

'In a moment. One-fifty?'

'Tell me what's in it.'

'Sesterce notes. A set of instructions, written by you, on my duties as Minister of State for something or other. A sort of membership card for the casino. And a letter.'

'From Richard Molland?'

Coleby nodded. '"Campus Abbatis," it says at the

top. Very interesting, I'm sure. But what in God's name is a Mithraeum?'

The first exposure of the Mollands and Peter Redburn to Carinish Court affected the five of them in different ways and on different levels. The place was so far removed from their everyday experience that it had an almost magical effect: it enchanted them all, but with five different spells. For Barbara, the potency of the enchantment was heightened by the evil-smelling shabbiness of Abbotsfield Vicarage.

She drove back with Hubert and Kate immediately after tea. The boys walked; James had offered to show them a shortcut to the village – a path across the fields from Carinish Court. He said the distance by footpath was less than a mile. It surprised Barbara that Kate did not insist on going with them.

Kate was silent during the drive. She sat alone on the back seat of the Rover, hugging herself and staring out of the window. Barbara thought about Ralph Salperton. She was relieved that nothing unpleasant had happened. But mixed with the relief was a shred of doubt: perhaps he didn't really find her attractive.

When they got back to the Vicarage, Kate gazed round the dark hall and sighed.

'I'll be in my room,' she said.

Kate glanced back from the half-landing. She was smiling. The smile vanished when she saw that Barbara was watching.

Barbara knew she should be thinking about supper. Instead, she drifted into the drawing room. Carinish Court had given her an appetite for leisure, not food.

Yesterday she had noticed that the Timballs kept an assortment of games in a deal box with a cracked lid, which was wedged between the sofa and the wall. It was the obvious place to look for a pack of playing cards.

Hubert stood with one hand on the open door and watched. She tugged the sofa away from the wall and lifted the lid of the box with such careless force that it banged against the wall. He stirred behind her, and she guessed that the violent treatment of the Timballs' property was making him uneasy. She knelt down and rummaged impatiently through the top layer of the box's contents: Monopoly, Lexicon, Snakes and Ladders, a children's game called 'Journey through Fairyland', tiddlywinks and several hundred loose jigsaw pieces from different puzzles.

'The Salpertons' house is much larger than this.' Hubert paused to clear his throat. 'Yet they manage to keep it perfectly clean. It just shows, eh? It can be done.'

'Of course it can,' Barbara said, without looking round. 'All it takes is money.'

She tossed a pile of board games on to the seat of the sofa. Dust clouds silently exploded around the pile.

'What are you looking for?'

'Playing cards.'

Barbara saw a dog-eared pack at the bottom of the box. She ripped off the elastic band that secured it and began to count the cards.

'I doubt if you'll need those here, will you?'

'Mary Salperton says she often needs a fourth person for bridge. Besides, I can play patience.'

'I see. Well, you must please yourself, of course. What time are you planning to have supper?'

'In a while. No one's going to be very hungry. Not after that tea.' She spoke in the impatient but absent-minded voice that she often used on the children but only rarely on Hubert. 'Fifty-two, plus two jokers. That's a relief.' She picked up the board games. 'Oh, and there's another pack here.' The cards, still in their original box, had been wedged inside the Monopoly board. 'Would supper at half-past seven be all right?'

'Perfectly, thank you.' The front door opened, and the boys' voices filled the hall. Hubert turned. 'Wipe your feet.'

Barbara dropped the board games back into the box and allowed the lid to slam.

Hubert's mouth tightened. 'I shall be in the study,' he said. 'I think I saw a *Lewis and Short* in there.'

'A what?'

'A Latin dictionary. There may be other books. I shall have to do quite a lot of preparation.'

'Me, too,' Barbara said, thinking of supper.

'I meant preparations for teaching Ginny.'

'I know you did.'

His face twitched with disapproval. He left the room without another word. In the hall the boys were on the mat, wiping their feet with military precision. 'Leftus, rightus,' murmured Richard in time with their feet, 'leftus, rightus.'

'Good walk?' Barbara said.

'Fine.' Richard came to a standstill. 'It can't be more than about half a mile.' He looked at Peter. 'I'm going in the garden,' he went on, and Barbara realized that the boys were in the middle of a quarrel. 'You can come if you want to.'

'Rather a waste of time to wipe your feet,' she said.

Richard shrugged. His face was grim and for an instant very like his father's. The two boys crossed the drawing room and went out through the French windows.

Barbara put the two packs of cards on the mantelpiece and went into the hall. The smell swept out to envelop her as soon as she opened the green-baize door. Damn supper. She would open two tins of kidney soup and give them a loaf of bread to hack at. They could count themselves lucky.

In the kitchen she opened the window and the back door. Later, she knew, the moths would fly in, attracted by the light. Their clumsy wings and erratic movements made her shudder, but this evening the need for sweet-smelling air outweighed everything else.

She fed the Aga with coke. The saucepans were in one of the cupboards underneath the window. She wanted one with a lid for the soup.

Dorothy Timball did not waste time on her saucepans, which were discoloured with food stains both inside and out. Barbara crouched in front of the cupboard and reached for an aluminium one at the back. It was larger than she wanted but it looked cleaner than the rest. She lifted it on to the draining board and tugged at the lid, which had stuck. With a jerk she pulled it free.

The stench rose up and choked her. It was worse than anything she had ever smelled before: like a blow in the face. Barbara glimpsed a domed layer of something grey-green and furry at the bottom of the pan. Sharp white bones poked through the surface, and – in her dreams, at least, when she saw the pan again – insects, pale and tiny, scurried among them. It seemed to her that the thing was breathing.

Barbara retched. She threw the pan and the obscenity it contained through the open window. She shut her eyes and vomited the Salpertons' food and drink into the kitchen sink.

'The Romans had all sorts of gods, didn't they?' James said. 'People like Mars and Venus.' He was leaning on the balustrade that separated the terrace from the drive. 'Do you know much about them?'

A wedge of light spilled across the terrace from the French windows. Otherwise it was very dark. James's face was a grey, formless blur against the mass of trees on the other side of the drive.

'Why do you want to know?' Ginny said, wondering why he had come outside to join her.

'Keep your voice down.'

'They can't hear us. Not with the telly on.'

Ginny guessed that neither of their parents would be watching the television. Under cover of its chatter they pursued their private interests. Ralph was assembling an Airfix model of the *Mayflower*, his hands manipulating the tube of glue and the tiny plastic pieces with extra-ordinary delicacy. By now Mary would be on her second brandy and her third game of patience.

James edged closer to her. 'All right, I'll tell you. Peter and Richard have got a kind of game they play. It's called Emor – that's Rome backwards, it's based on

Rome. They've been doing it for years. By the sound of it, they've got just about everything: armies, navies, ministries, money, laws, a court, even a casino. It's hard to describe – it's like a proper government would be. Peter says they've got tons of documents to go with it. And they take it in turns to be emperor and chancellor and so on.'

'Is that girl in it?'

'Kate? I don't think so.'

'You quite liked her, didn't you?'

'Me? Don't be stupid. She just tagged along this afternoon. I couldn't very well tell her to go away.'

She's a thief, Ginny almost said. But she doubted if anyone would believe her, and even if they did they'd somehow find a way of blaming her. What was the point of telling them? Her mother was notoriously vague about the money in her purse, a characteristic which Ginny herself had found convenient on more than one occasion. Besides, it was pleasant to hug the knowledge to herself for a while. She was the only person who knew what Kate was really like. Maybe she would tell Frank when she saw him.

'They didn't want to talk about Emor in front of her,' James went on. 'That's why I walked back to Abbotsfield with Peter and Richard. They made me swear not to tell anyone, anyone at all.'

'You're telling me.'

'You can keep a secret,' he said. The compliment made Ginny's cheeks glow, even though she knew that James's compliments usually had a purpose. 'Anyway, they have sort of hereditary posts as well. Like Richard's almost always the Lord High Admiral because his grandpa was in the navy. But as far as I can tell they haven't got any sort of religion.'

Ginny snorted. 'I expect they get enough of that at home.'

'Peter asked if I wanted to join in.' James hesitated, and a defensive note entered his voice. 'Well, why not? It's so boring here. I've got to have something to do and at least they're the same age as me. We're not even going away this year. And if I did join in, I thought it would be good to have something of my own. Otherwise they'll just push me around all the time. You see? I could be high priest or something.'

'His Holiness the Pontifex Maximus,' Ginny said in a deep voice. 'Or perhaps you could be a blind soothsayer in a cave. You could prophesy doom like the witches in *Macbeth*.'

'Come off it,' James said. 'I was asking for your help.'

She considered walking away but decided against it. Even this childish nonsense was better than gawping at the television or struggling with *Mansfield Park*. A memory stirred. The urge to show off was temporarily stronger than the urge to seem adult.

'How about Mithras?' she said.

'Who?'

'He was a god of war, I think. Something to do with soldiers. A secret cult. Don't you remember, he came into *Puck of Pook's Hill*?'

'That was a fairy story,' said James in disgust. 'Mum used to read it when we were kids.'

'Yes, but there was a lot of history too. You know, Romans and so on. And Kipling put a poem about Mithras at the end of one of the chapters.' In her mind she saw a blur of italic type on a right-hand page, and glimpsed a faded orange binding. Two lines of the poem, never consciously memorized, tramped through her head like a file of marching soldiers. She licked her lips and whispered them aloud. '"Mithras, God of the Midnight, here where the great Bull dies, Look on thy children in darkness. Oh take our sacrifice . . ."'

'They had blood sacrifices?'

'I expect so,' Ginny said. 'A lot of those religions did.'

'Can't you remember any more?'

'No. Only something about "Mithras, also a soldier . . ." I suppose we could look it up.'

'Could you find out more about it?'

She shrugged in the darkness.

'Please, Ginny. You're so good at that sort of thing.'

The second compliment was as worthless as the first. But in the summer of 1964 she had needed flattery as a plant needs water.

'All right,' she'd said. 'If you really want.'

Fab day at Carinish Court. James may join Emor. Mrs M taught me how to play Bezique – good.

Before supper Peter argued with Richard about the wisdom of admitting James to Emor. They poled the boat over to Capri and sat on top of the pillbox in the evening sunshine. The advantages were so obvious that it astonished Peter that Richard should hesitate.

'Emor won't be the same if we let James in,' Richard said, over and over again. 'He won't understand it like we do.'

Peter had the sense to conceal his admiration for

James. Instead he outlined the importance of being friends with him as a means of access to the delights of Carinish Court. He also argued that James knew too much about Emor to be left out: otherwise they would have to risk his talking about it.

'I knew we shouldn't have told him,' Richard said.

'We had to. He already knew, because of watching us yesterday. Anyway, you told him as much as I did.'

That was true. On the walk back to Abbotsfield, Richard had been unable to resist the temptation to correct and amplify what Peter was saying. James's attitude had encouraged them both: he played to perfection the part of an admiring tourist in a strange and fascinating country.

'Listen,' Peter said. 'It'll be much more fun with three. And if James joins, we can do Emor at Carinish Court. Think of all the things we can do there.'

'All right then. I suppose we haven't any choice.'

'It'll be better, you'll see.' Now he had gained the point, Peter felt guilty. 'We can do lots more with three.' Instinctively he changed the subject: 'How do you think I should die tomorrow?'

At this stage of Emor, each emperor reigned for a week, and the crown changed hands on Mondays.

'Babylonian guerrillas,' suggested Richard. 'They're trying to steal the Great Seal so they can set up their own empire in the east.'

The Great Seal was always in the possession of the current emperor; it was in fact the one item in the imperial regalia. The seal was a plastic screwtop from a bottle of cheap wine. Moulded in relief on its face was a shield with three wavy lines across it. Richard had found the top in one of the churchyard litter bins last term. For a week they had sealed all imperial documents with it; but the results were so messy and fragile that the seal was now used largely as a badge of office.

'A gang of them break into the imperial villa as I'm having breakfast,' Peter said, wondering what precisely a guerrilla was. 'I kill most of them, but then I'm stabbed in the back and one of them, the ringleader, escapes with the Great Seal. And you're just coming in for a privy council meeting –'

'And I ride after him and avenge the Emperor's death with his blood and save the Great Seal.'

A handbell tinkled in the distance.

'Come on.' Richard slithered off the roof of the pillbox. 'Supper's ready.'

In *The Secret History of Emor*, Sunday 2 August was dismissed in a sentence: *At a meeting of the Privy Council, the Emperor and the Chancellor of the Exchequer considered the application of one Jacobus Salpertonius to join the Imperial Court, and decided in favour.*

Supper was a brief and silent meal. Peter hated kidney soup and needed all his willpower to force himself to eat it.

'I think I've found the source of that smell,' Mrs Molland said. 'There were some chicken bones rotting in a saucepan.'

'Oh, *Mum*,' Kate said, screwing up her face. 'Must you?'

Afterwards Mr Molland said he was going to work in the study. Richard and Peter washed up, while Kate cleared the table and Barbara made coffee. Kate went upstairs to read, managing to suggest that the company of the two boys would be intolerable to any civilized person. The others went into the drawing room. Richard found a copy of *The Thirty-nine Steps* in the bookcase and settled down to read it.

Mrs Molland raised her eyebrows at Peter. 'Would you like a game of cards?'

'Okay. If you want.'

'Richard?'

'I'd rather read.'

'Just the two of us, then.'

Peter wished Richard were playing. Cards on Sunday seemed almost wicked, especially with a clergyman's wife. He remembered his mother talking in an undertone to his father: 'Mrs Molland's a good deal too fond of playing bridge. It's not really suitable. People are beginning to talk.'

'What games do you know?' she asked.

'Pontoon. Poker and rummy. Knock-out whist.'

'So you understand about suits and tricks and so on? Good. Why don't we try bezique? It's a bit like whist and rummy combined.'

He nodded, registering her urgency without understanding it.

'We'll need both packs,' she said, 'But we don't use all the cards – only sixty-four of them. Come and sit here and I'll explain. It sounds more complicated than it is.'

Barbara Molland sat in a low armchair with a wicker back and arms. Peter sat opposite on a stool, and between them she placed a low round table whose legs were wooden but whose top was a dented brass tray.

'Play as you learn, that's the best method.' She sorted

the two packs, discarded the lower-value cards and shuffled the remainder with a speed that bewildered him.

'Will you teach me how to shuffle like that?' he said.

'Later.' She grinned at him. 'Impressive, isn't it? It makes your opponents think you're a better player than you are. Now, we begin with eight cards each.'

Peter had a good brain for cards and he learned quickly. They played several games, scoring all but the first. Mrs Molland won the second and third but Peter overhauled her on the fourth with a double bezique, which scored 500 points.

'I'm glad we're not playing for money,' she said. 'Another?'

Peter's problems began during the fifth game. He felt increasingly hot and excited, which affected his concentration. He was aware of everything – the rustle as Richard turned a page, the creaks of wickerwork, the irregularity of his breathing, the slight greasiness of the cards, the coolness of the brass tray and, above all, the nearness of Mrs Molland.

She was leaning forward, her legs slightly apart, and he could see the insides of her thighs: not far, just an inch or two above the knees. He tried to keep his eyes on the cards: he didn't want to look. The crotch of his trousers was tight and uncomfortable. He knew what was going on down there, but he was not sure why it was happening to him. His two great fears were that he was abnormal and that someone might notice.

Was he in some terrible way unique? While they were changing after the swim, Peter had observed that James was hairier and generally better developed than he was. He wondered if James had ever felt like this, and whether he knew the explanation. But it was not the sort of question you could ask anyone, because the subject was shameful, ignorance was childish, and the answer might label you as a freak before all the world.

'You're not concentrating properly,' Barbara said at the end of the fifth game, and Peter felt several degrees warmer. 'Let's give this a rest. Isn't it about time you two went up to bed?'

Peter contrived to stand up and leave the room without betraying himself. As they went upstairs, Richard chattered about *The Thirty-nine Steps*. He had obviously noticed nothing. Peter's panic subsided.

There was a line of light under Kate's door. Peter and Richard did not linger in the bathroom. Peter scuttled down the landing to his bedroom, towards the reassuring normality of the Letts School-Boy Diary and an Agatha Christie detective novel.

Behind him, Richard said, 'What time's James coming tomorrow?'

'About ten, I think.'

'I wish he wasn't.'

Monday 3 August 1964 was a bank holiday, and on bank holidays Ralph Salperton refused to put his nose outside Carinish Court.

'All those damned trippers cluttering up the road,' he would say. 'Dropping their rubbish and playing their bloody transistors at full blast. Why can't they stay at home?'

Ginny had her own reasons for remembering the events of that particular day. In the morning she played a set of tennis with her father. As usual she lost. Even so, he was in a bad temper because the news had been full of stories of clashes between the Mods and the Rockers.

Ralph was convinced that these teenage gang fights at seaside resorts were aimed in some unfathomably sinister way at him and at all he believed himself to represent. This was not unexpected: in those days he tended to take the news personally. His range of sympathy was global in its extent. When the National Guard had been busy quelling the race riots in New York the preceding week, Ralph had lent them his full emotional support.

'Of course they need rifles and armoured cars,' he'd roared across the breakfast table at at Mary, James and Ginny. 'They've got to defend themselves, haven't they? Give those niggers an inch and they'd take a mile. I'd have sent in tanks as well.'

The Mods and Rockers had a disruptive effect on their game. Every now and then Ralph would stop playing and cock his head to listen to the snarl of engines on the main road.

'More of those bloody hooligans.' He made a back-hand slash with his racket, as if trying to swat them. 'Did you know they had to fly a contingent of police down to Hastings yesterday? It's unbelievable.'

Throughout the morning he quoted statistics with ghoulish relish: the number of arrests, the number of knife wounds, the numbers of the injured, the cost of police operations to maintain law and order.

Ginny did not attempt to argue with him. Like every other teenager she knew, she found the Mods and Rockers frightening but romantic. At her school – the

Girls' High in Paulstock – you supported one or the other, just as you made a choice between the Beatles and the Rolling Stones, or (if you liked to be thought sexually precocious) claimed to have a preference for boys who were roundheads or boys who were cavaliers.

Mods were more dashing and they had an air of sophistication, but their scooters were not impressive; Rockers had a darker glamour, a compound of dirt, leather, speed and large motorbikes. At school, Ginny always favoured the Rockers – because there were fewer of them, she said, and therefore they had more need of her.

At lunchtime she asked her father if she could use the study.

'Why?'

'I've got some schoolwork to do. Some Roman history.'

'Why can't you do it in your bedroom?'

'Because I need to look at the encyclopaedia.'

Ralph pushed back his chair. 'All right. But don't leave a mess or I'll be down on you like a ton of bricks.'

The study was a small, cold room at the front of the house. The children were forbidden to go there without asking permission. Ralph used it once or twice a week for something he referred to as 'business'; and it was also the place from which he conducted his genealogical researches when he could find the time.

One wall was lined with books. The majority had come from Ginny's maternal grandparents, and few of them were more recent than the 1930s. The memoirs of obscure soldiers rubbed shoulders with long Victorian novels by ladies with improbable names. There were regimental histories and elderly Wisdens, Edwardian directories and leather-bound editions of the better-known British poets of the nineteenth century. Finally, and most usefully, there was the eleventh edition of the *Encyclopaedia Britannica*.

Its twenty-nine volumes were deployed along the bottom shelf of the bookcase. She pulled out volume XVIII, MED TO MUM, and carried it to the table. The article on Mithras filled the double columns of several closely printed pages.

Mithras, a Persian god of light, whose worship, the latest one of importance to be brought from the Orient to Rome, spread throughout the empire and became the greatest antagonist of Christianity . . . The Mithras legend has been lost . . . it is impossible to know otherwise than very imperfectly the inner life of Mithraism.

As she struggled through the article, Ginny made notes for James on a sheet of paper torn from an exercise book. Mithraism was well-established in the Roman Empire by the end of the second century AD. The cult spread with traders and the army, and it was democratic in the sense that a slave could be the equal of a senator. The authorities favoured it because it identified itself with the imperial house and supported the divine right of the monarchy.

Mithraism became the chief rival of Christianity, which it much resembled. Its temples, often situated in artificial grottos and wholly or partly underground, were known as Mithraea.

The followers of Mithras believed in purity and abstinence. Initiates could ascend through seven degrees –

starting with Corax, the Raven, who was the servant of the sun, and moving up to the highest degree of all, that of Pater. The degree ceremony was called the *Sacramentum*; and it was preceded by an oath of silence, prolonged abstinence and severe deprivations. The preliminary ordeals varied: sometimes the participants' eyes were bandaged with the intestines of fowls, and candidates had to leap across water or witness a simulated murder. No women were allowed to join.

An eternal flame burned on the altar of a Mithraeum. Priests made libations and sacrificed animals. In return for moral purity, worshippers were offered the hope of an afterlife. A day of judgement would come, when the dead would arise and Mithras would sacrifice the bull; and the righteous would drink the bull's fat mixed with consecrated wine and become immortal, while the unjust would be destroyed by a fire sent from heaven.

Ginny found the whole thing disgusting. Still, her notes would preserve her reputation for erudition. She closed the book and returned it to its place on the shelf.

Her mother was arranging flowers in the hall.

'Where's James?' Ginny said.

'He went back to the Vicarage.'

'Typical. Do you know when he'll be back?'

'I said I'd drive over and collect him at four-thirty.' Her mother yawned. 'Mrs Molland asked me to tea. Do you want to come?'

'Not particularly.'

'It's up to you.' Mary Salperton stuffed the rest of the flowers into the tall blue vase. 'I think I shall go and lie down.'

Ginny wandered into the garden for want of anything

better to do. James's absence irritated her: she was doing him a favour, and the least he could have done was be on hand to accept it. She walked past the swimming pool, through the gap in the box hedge and down the lawn in the direction of the oak tree. Everywhere she looked, she saw the prospect of endless boredom. Her legs felt heavy and the grass seemed painfully bright. She veered towards the darker green of the shrubbery that masked the drive. It was then that she saw the blood.

The flecks of red stood out vividly on the grass. Bull's blood, she thought, fertilizing the earth. Probably someone had shot a rabbit, which had lived to run away but only to bleed to death in peace. She felt indignant on the rabbit's behalf.

'Ginny . ...'

The whisper came from the rhododendrons. She swung round and stared into the mass of leaves.

'Who is it?' she gasped.

A branch was pulled aside. She glimpsed a man in black. He was kneeling on the ground. He stretched a hand towards her.

For an instant she thought he was wearing a shiny red bandana across the bottom of his face, like an outlaw from the Wild West. But it wasn't a mask. It was fresh blood.

Fourteen

For a day or two Ginny was very happy.

'I knew one of you'd come if I waited long enough,' Frank Timball said as he knelt before her in the shrubbery with the blood smeared down his face. 'You or James.'

It was a miracle. From all the people in the world he had chosen her when he needed help. And James, of course; but James wasn't here.

'Mustn't be seen,' Frank muttered. 'Will you hide me?'

Ginny would have done anything for him. For the time being, the urgent need to make decisions on his behalf overrode her curiosity and her concern – and even the shock his appearance had given her.

The obvious place to conceal him was the cottage behind the kitchen garden. How to get him there was the first difficulty she had to face. Crossing the lawn was impossible because it was in full view of the windows of the house. They had to creep through the shrubbery, which arched round at the bottom of the drive and followed the line of the boundary wall.

Ginny worried about the blood. The exertion re-opened a wound in Frank's scalp, and one of the slashes on his cheek was still bleeding. They left a trail that anyone could follow. Another problem was the motor-bike – Frank's Triumph Bonneville, which was lying on its side in the bushes just inside the drive. It was too heavy for her to move by herself.

Frank was very weak and also he had twisted his ankle. He limped along, panting, with his arm and much of his weight across Ginny's shoulders. She had never been so close to him before. When his head lolled against her bare arm, she felt the prickle of stubble. He smelled of leather and oil, sweat and sea air. Frank wasn't large but his body was compact and well-muscled.

The hedge of the lower paddock joined the wall at right angles, with a five-bar gate where they met. After she and Frank had passed the gate, the going became easier. They staggered along in the lee of the hedge until they reached a second, smaller gate that led to the garden of the cottage.

The enclosed garden was a haven after the openness of the field. It was warm and windless. Nothing moved and nothing made a sound – apart from the buzzing of a bee that was investigating the tangle of dog roses on the left of the door.

Ginny raised the latch with her elbow and kicked open the door. Once inside, Frank let go of her with a sigh. For a few seconds he leaned on the wall, pressing his cheek against it. He frowned, as if his weakness puzzled him, and slid to the floor. Flakes of plaster lodged in his hair and pattered on to the shoulders of his jacket. She helped prop him into a sitting position.

'You'd be safer upstairs.'

'Later,' he said. 'I've dripped blood on your dress.'

'It doesn't matter.'

'They'll notice.'

'I'll say I cut myself.'

'But you haven't.'

'I shall have by the time anyone sees me,' she said. 'I think you need a doctor.'

'No.' He tried to get up. 'Don't you dare, Ginny, do you hear? You don't understand.'

She pressed him back. 'But we can't just let you bleed to death.'

'It's not as bad as it looks. Scalp wounds always bleed a lot.' He touched his cheek with thick, very dirty fingers and winced. 'The cuts aren't that deep.'

'Don't touch them,' Ginny said. 'Look, I'm going to clean the wounds with antiseptic. I'll get some plasters and a bandage as well.' She stood up and put her hands on her hips. 'And blankets, cushions, food and water. Anything else you can think of?'

'Cigarettes and matches,' he said. 'You're incredible. Don't you even want to know what happened?'

'Of course I do.' She crouched beside him. 'If you feel strong enough to tell me.'

'We went to Weston-super-Mare yesterday.' He swallowed, and his lips trembled. 'A whole lot of us from Bristol. And we met even more of them and they were looking for us. So there was a fight on the beach, quite a small one. But one of the Mods got hurt, I think – a broken bottle or something. So there was another fight this morning, and everything got a bit vicious. You know? Bottles and razors and knives. The police turned up and that made it worse.' Frank was over three years older than Ginny but at present he looked younger than James. 'I think I might have killed someone. Tall bloke, with carrot-coloured hair.'

In the silence Ginny noticed that blood had dried on

the right sleeve and shoulder of Frank's black leather jacket. She wondered how you removed blood from leather. Would it simply wash off? What Frank was saying was quite unreal. Killers belonged to newspapers and wars and detective novels.

'If you have killed someone, it'll be on the news tonight.' Ginny thought that her calm was magnificent but simulated; like Frank, she was playing a game. 'But why don't you know?'

'Everything happened so fast.' He rubbed his forehead, and she longed to smooth away the creases. 'This bloke came at me with a cutthroat razor. I got it off him in the end, and I was so angry that I just slashed at him. At his throat. A lot of blood. Then the cops were coming so I ran back to the bike. I wrapped a scarf round my face and just made for Abbotsfield. Nowhere else to go.' His skin, where she could see it, was very pale, and by now the words were coming in short gasps. 'That old pillbox? You know? Thought I could hide up for a while. Kids playing there, so I came on here. Ginny, they'll be after me. I've got to hide.'

'Did they get the number of the bike?'

'I don't think so.' He said nothing for a moment, and when he spoke again his voice was even weaker. 'The blood must have covered most of my face. But they'll be looking for someone with razor slashes. And my fingerprints must be on the razor. Oh Christ.'

His face crumpled. She shook his arm. 'Could someone give your name to the police? Someone you were with?'

'They just know me as Frank. I met them in Bristol.'

'Do they know where you live, who your father is?'

'Don't be stupid.' The dark eyes gleamed. 'Tell them my dad's a vicar? Come off it.' The amusement faded from his face, and he added dully, 'It's not the sort of thing you boast about, not in that company.'

'You'll have to grow a beard,' Ginny said, remembering the stubble. 'That would hide the cuts. You can stay here for a few days.'

'Someone might find me, and then you'd be for it.'

'The only person who comes here is James. He was here yesterday, with those kids from the Vicarage.'

'Then you'd better tell him.'

'No.'

'Why not? Don't you trust him?'

She shrugged. Two's company, she thought; three's none.

'He won't talk,' Frank said. 'And if he knows, it'll make your life much simpler. You'll need help to move the Triumph.'

'All right,' she said reluctantly. She didn't care how complicated or dangerous her life became. She agreed not for her sake but for Frank's.

It was Hubert who suggested asking Mary Salperton to tea.

He would have preferred to even the honours of hospitality by inviting the whole family to lunch or even dinner. But Barbara was firm. Her housekeeping allowance wouldn't run to it; and she refused to contemplate the dismal prospect of cooking a formal meal in the Timballs' kitchen and serving it in their dining room.

With Hubert standing over her, Barbara spent much of Monday in the drawing room. She moved some of the furniture back against the walls and rearranged the rest; she cleaned, dusted and polished. Hubert found some yellow roses in the garden. Their leaves were spotted with blight and the petals fell when you touched them, but they made a splash of colour against the darkness of the overmantel. Fortunately, her worst worry had vanished with the removal of the chicken bones: by now the Vicarage smell was barely noticeable.

Hubert had intended to join them but a telephone call after lunch disrupted his plans. A parishioner was dying in Paulstock Hospital, and her family required the consolations of religion. Barbara tried to suppress a callous hope that the parishioner would need a lot of consolation and would postpone her death until she had got it.

'How nice you've made everything look,' Mary Salperton said as soon as she came into the drawing room, trailing scarves and clouds of perfume. She floated across to the window and glanced at the garden. The four children were playing French cricket among the clumps of grass and thistles on the old tennis court. 'I haven't seen it like this for years.'

'Perhaps Mrs Timball hasn't much time for house-keeping.' Barbara gave the sentence an ambiguous inflection so that it was not quite a statement and not quite a question but something between the two.

'Dorothy was always rather slapdash, but it's got worse in the last year or so. People say it's Frank's fault. Well, they would, wouldn't they? He's such a marvellous scapegoat. Not that he hasn't upset his parents – of course he has – but one can't blame him for everything. So unfair, don't you think?'

Barbara seized on the point that really interested her. 'But what's Frank done?'

'He's a bit of a rebel, I suppose.' As she was speaking, Mary Salperton glided across the room. 'He's eighteen now – you'd think he'd have grown out of it but he's exactly the same as he was two years ago.' She subsided on to the sofa. 'And it's not that he's a fool. Far from it: nine "O" levels, was it, or ten? But he didn't like the sixth form so he got himself deliberately expelled. I believe he turned up drunk one morning. The poor Timballs couldn't even hush it up. He was at Paulstock Grammar School, you see, so everyone knew.'

'Does he live off his parents?'

'Oh no – to do him justice he already had a job lined up for himself. He's some sort of trainee mechanic at Abbotsfield Motors; that's the garage on the main road. Nevertheless he's been very trying – he rides around on a great big motorbike and wears a leather jacket. Ralph says he's one of these Rockers. It's true that he's got some very rowdy friends. There are some very unpleasant youths who come from the council estate. You've probably noticed them – they tend to congregate by the war memorial on the Triangle. Did you hear about the Christmas carols?'

If Hubert had been here, this conversation could not have taken place. As it was, Barbara sat down in the wicker chair and said, 'No. What happened?'

'It was in March. I think they were celebrating Frank's eighteenth birthday. Frank and four or five others were thrown out of the pub at closing time. I believe the police had to be called, all the way from Paulstock. Afterwards they went on the rampage. They went round almost every house in Abbotsfield, singing carols. Oh, and Mr Nimp had a window smashed. Childish, I know, but everyone got very cross. The police weren't any use because they'd gone back to Paulstock, and by the time they'd got back here it was all over. So frustrating for them.'

'Did you have any trouble at Carinish Court?'

'We were spared, mercifully. I suppose we were too far away, otherwise Frank could hardly have resisted paying us a visit. He and Ralph don't get on. But they came here, not that George and Dorothy will admit it. They claim they were asleep and heard nothing. One can sympathize. There's not a lot they can do, is there? Frank may be under age but they can't *make* him be sensible. He doesn't even live here any more. He's got a bedsitter at the garage. Heaven knows what he gets up to there.'

'We found a magazine upstairs,' Barbara said, wondering whether she would need to be more explicit. 'I expect that was his.'

Mrs Salperton opened her crocodile-skin handbag and took out a cigarette case. 'It's all right for me to smoke, isn't it? You don't, do you?'

'As a matter of fact, I do smoke – just occasionally.' Before Christ had waylaid Hubert, Barbara used to smoke ten cigarettes a day. Now she was lucky to smoke as many a month. It was a question of how many pennies a week she could squeeze out of the housekeeping. She never smoked in Hubert's presence because he considered cigarettes to be an unnecessary luxury.

Mary leaned forward to offer the case and simultaneously returned to the subject of the magazine.

'Something rather vulgar, perhaps? Yes, that would have been Frank.' She lit their cigarettes and exhaled thoughtfully. 'He probably left it here on purpose. I'm not saying he's malicious, though some people do. It's just that he's got a peculiar sense of humour. For instance he started a ridiculous rumour about poor Mr Nimp.'

Barbara's cigarette tasted heavenly. 'The churchwarden? I think Kate mentioned something about that.'

'Well, one assumes it's a rumour. Personally I think Frank was just getting his own back. I know one shouldn't gossip, but I've always thought that Albert Nimp started that story about Mad Margaret – you won't know her, of course: she lives in Paulstock and goes in for temporary husbands. How she manages with all those children underfoot I just don't know. I wouldn't have thought she had time for anything else. Anyway, they say that Frank's responsible for the latest addition to her family. It seems rather far-fetched to me. She's terribly ugly, poor thing, and she smells, too. Is that a car I hear?'

The Rover's engine had a distinctive cough in first gear.

'It's Hubert,' Barbara said. She exchanged a glance of perfect complicity with her guest. 'I'd better make the tea.'

Frank was trouble, everyone knew that. His parents called him 'Francis', but no one else did because he wouldn't let them. He wasn't good-looking but he stood out in a crowd: Ginny thought he looked like a cross between a cherub and the devil. In her mind she filed him in a holy of holies whose other inhabitants were

Heathcliff, Mr Rochester, Lord Byron, James Dean, Sean Connery and Mick Jagger.

She was happy to be Frank's slave and protector. She cut her finger with the vegetable knife to explain his blood on her dress. She fed him and bathed his wounds. She knew that she would steal and lie for him with a clear conscience. She would be his spy in the outside world, constantly alert for information about the bank holiday battle at Weston-super-Mare. The parallel with Flora Macdonald and the Young Pretender did not escape her.

Ginny reluctantly told James about Frank when he got back from Abbotsfield on Monday evening. He wanted to go and see Frank straight away, but she wouldn't let him. After dinner, while Ralph was building the *Mayflower* and Mary was playing patience, they manoeuvred the Triumph Bonneville across the lawn and up the paddock to the cottage. They hid the motorbike in the earth closet at the bottom of the garden.

To Ginny's relief Frank was still in the cottage; to James's disappointment he was fast asleep. He lay in James's sleeping bag on a pile of blankets. In the torchlight he looked very young and defenceless. The sight of him made Ginny want to cry.

'If you wake him, I'll kill you,' she whispered to James.

That night her nerves were tight with anxiety. There was so much to worry about on Frank's behalf. Before she fell asleep she had mapped out at least half a dozen avenues that would lead him directly to disaster. Her fears co-existed with her happiness and by a strange emotional alchemy nourished it. When she woke up on

Tuesday morning she pinched herself to prove that the events of the day before were more than a glorious dream.

Frank slept for sixteen hours. On Tuesday morning he was almost his old self when she and James arrived. His injuries had responded quickly to Ginny's first aid, which had been painfully acquired during her time with the Girl Guides and never previously used.

'Any news?' was the first thing he said when he saw them.

'They mentioned fighting at Weston,' Ginny said. 'But no one's dead.'

'Thank God.'

'Fifteen people in hospital, though,' James said. 'Including a couple of cops. I forget how many arrests.'

'Shit.' Frank rubbed the stubble on his chin. 'I'd better carry on with the beard.'

'How long will it take?' James asked.

'Three or four days to get a reasonable covering. Luckily I haven't shaved since Saturday.' He added, without smiling – it was often difficult to know whether Frank was joking or being serious, 'Like Esau, I'm a hairy man. It's just as well. Could you bring me a mirror some time?'

They established a routine. During the day Frank spent much of his time outside, hidden between the earth closet and the high brick wall of the kitchen garden. After nightfall he moved upstairs. At a pinch it would be possible to escape by the window if Ralph or someone paid a surprise visit to the cottage. Both Ginny and James would happily have spent all day with him; but he refused to allow them to stay with him for long.

'It's too risky,' he said. 'Not just for you, for me as well. If I'm caught I can always say I nicked this stuff from the house. You know nothing about my being here. Okay?'

Ginny feared that the real reason might be that large doses of her company bored him. If Frank were caught, she wanted to share his punishment. The prospect of being a martyr was not unappealing.

'What's that you're reading?' he asked when Ginny brought him his lunch on Tuesday.

She was alone because James was down at Abbotsfield. The lunch – bottles of beer and water, beef sandwiches and two apples – was in a basket. Ginny had concealed the food with a cardigan and *Mansfield Park*.

'Jane Austen,' she said, hoping he would be impressed.

'Can I borrow it?' he said unexpectedly. 'I've got to do something. Have you got any Dickens?'

'There's a complete set in the study.'

'Be a love and see if you can find *Bleak House*. I've never read it. And can you bring me a newspaper? Where's James got to?'

'He's playing with those kids at the Vicarage,' she said, annoyed that Frank had bothered to ask. 'They've got some silly game.' She smiled in what she hoped was an amused, adult way. 'They pretend they're Romans or something. It's not just a game, actually – more like a secret world.'

'Like the Brontë children?'

At that stage Ginny hadn't come across the Brontës' Angria. 'Something like that,' she said.

'When's he coming back?'

'Probably about five.' Ginny turned away. 'I'd better go. I'll see you later.'

'Okay. And Ginny?'

She looked back at him. He was lying on a blanket and propped against the wall, with a cigarette in the corner of his mouth and *Mansfield Park* beside him.

'Thank you,' he said. 'And next time you come, could you bring a bottle-opener for the beer?'

Emor was always changing; but in the last few weeks of its existence the pace of change accelerated. This was due to James.

His presence altered the balance of power. Emor belonged to Peter and Richard. At Plumford, the others who took part followed their lead. Under their direction Emor had developed steadily and – given the premises on which it was founded – almost predictably.

Peter and Richard rarely disagreed about fundamental policies. In the day-to-day running of the empire they intrigued interminably against each other and constructed temporary alliances with the others. But they settled the important issues – such as the mechanics of the imperial succession, the gens system and major innovations like the Sinking Fund – between themselves. Each tacitly recognized the other as his equal partner in an unofficial but omnipotent duumvirate. In private they negotiated, often bitterly, but the negotiations generally resulted in compromises that were acceptable to them both. In public they presented a united front. All this changed for ever when James was formally admitted to the imperial court at Campus Abbatis on the morning of Wednesday 5 August.

Unlike Joe and Coleby and the rest, James wanted a share of the real power in Emor. He never said as much: he merely assumed it as a right. Since the very beginning of Emor, it had been one against one, Peter against Richard. With the advent of James, the duumvirate became a triumvirate, and the balance was lost; as a matter of simple arithmetic, it was always two against one.

'I've got a suggestion to make,' James said on Wednesday morning.

They were sitting in the pillbox, which on that occasion was functioning as the Imperial Privy Council Chamber. He and Peter were smoking Sullivan Powells.

'You may speak, Mr Secretary,' Richard said. He was emperor that week. James had been appointed Secretary of State for the Interior and Chief of the Secret Police.

'I think we need a state religion,' James said. 'People always have a religion, don't they, so why shouldn't we?'

Richard shrugged. 'We've never had one before.'

'It could be quite interesting,' James went on. 'The Romans had military cults, you know.'

'What did they do exactly?' Peter asked.

'Blood sacrifices, secret rituals, stuff like that.'

'If we do have a religion I think it should be Christianity,' Richard said firmly. 'After all, Constantine the Great was a Christian.'

'That's no reason why we should be.' Peter was reluctant to give Richard such a marvellous opportunity to use his tiresome religious expertise. 'A bit boring, isn't it?'

'Take Mithras, for example.' James's air of knowledge greatly impressed Peter. 'They had initiation ceremonies for each of the seven grades – sort of ordeals for the candidates. It was very popular with the army.'

'Paganism,' Richard said. 'It would be blasphemy.'

'Don't be stupid.' Peter tried to blow a smoke ring, and failed. 'We're talking about Emor, not real life. It can't be blasphemous if we say it isn't.'

'I'll forbid it.'

'Religious persecution?'

'I know what we could do,' James said. 'It needn't be the state religion. We could make it voluntary. A private thing, like the casino.' He turned to Peter. 'What do you think?'

'I'm in favour. Seems a great idea.'

James rewarded him with a smile.

'I still think it would be wrong,' Richard said. 'It's a matter of conscience.'

'You and your conscience,' Peter jeered. 'Well, you can do what you like. It's your conscience, after all – not mine and James's.'

Richard stared at the ground.

'You know something?' James said. 'This place would be just right for the Mithraeum.'

The Emperor Gaius Marcus Mollandius Maximus was disturbed by rumours that the Cult of Mithras was gaining a foothold in the capital and in the Army. It was introduced by Babylonian prisoners of war. Senior Court Officials, including the Chancellor of the Exchequer and the new Minister for the Interior, fell under its sinister sway. The People of Emor petitioned the Emperor to ban it, but he reluctantly refused to do so because he believed in religious toleration.

When Peter read *The Secret History of Emor*, he realized that James's strategy had never varied. Divide and rule. James wanted to dominate Emor, and in the beginning the simplest way for him to do this was to make Peter his ally. That explained the Sullivan Powells, the confidential conversations and the impression James gave that he and Peter were special friends. Without Peter's help he could never have forced Richard to cooperate.

The introduction of Mithras marked Peter's first major betrayal of Richard. At the time it seemed insignificant, hardly a betrayal at all. Even then, however, Peter must have felt slightly uneasy about it. Wednesday's entry in the School-Boy Diary showed that, after James had gone back to Carinish Court, Peter had allowed Richard to win 75,000 sesterces at poker dice.

Mrs Molland, Kate, Richard and Peter went to Carinish Court on Thursday afternoon. Mr Salperton collected them in the Jaguar. The grown-ups played bridge with a friend of the Salpertons. Ginny appeared only briefly, at teatime.

While the adults played cards, James took the other three children up to the wood on the ridge behind the house. The day was overcast and no one felt like swimming. Kate's presence made it impossible for them to discuss Emor. James divided them into two teams – himself and Kate, Peter and Richard – and each team took it in turns to hunt the other. Peter was in a bad temper because he would have liked to be with James.

His mood improved after tea, when James beckoned him out to the terrace, away from all the others, and gave him a long white envelope.

'Read it when you get back,' he said. 'It's the Laws of Mithras. There's something I need you to do.'

Peter had lost this document – almost certainly he had thrown it away before leaving Abbotsfield. As far as he remembered, the Laws had been typed on a thick sheet of white paper. They were prefaced by an oath of secrecy and a passage of rhyming mumbo-jumbo. Peter later realized the latter had been adapted from *Puck of Pook's Hill*. The Laws themselves were really an outline of the initiation ceremonies, which had been reduced from the original seven to two: the Raven and the Father.

The Raven required a candidate to punt across the 'Great Water' at midnight; to enter the Mithraeum and recite a portion of the Kiplingesque mumbo-jumbo; and finally to light a candle – one of those nightlights that burn for eight hours. If the candle was still burning at daybreak, it was to be taken as a sign that Mithras had accepted the candidate as a Raven.

Peter remembered much less about the ritual for the Father. This degree was reserved for His Holiness the Pontifex Maximus – in other words for James, since the high priesthood was a hereditary privilege of the Gens Salpertonia. Among other things, it involved fasting for twenty-four hours, swimming half a mile, and pouring a libation in the Mithraeum at midnight. At the time Peter accepted the conditions without question. It did occur to him, however, that the half-mile swim was another way of ensuring that only James could be the Pontifex Maximus; Peter had never succeeded in swimming that far.

The envelope also contained a note in which James said that he planned to initiate himself as a Raven during the night; he wanted Peter to visit the Mithraeum as soon as possible after daybreak to confirm that the candle was burning. This, of course, had to be kept secret from Richard, who was not privy to the mysteries of Mithras.

For Peter, James's daring was a sign that he belonged to a superior order of beings. The initiation ceremony was fraught with danger: it required James to leave the house at night and walk or cycle from Carinish Court to Abbotsfield.

On Friday morning Peter went to the Mithraeum before seven o'clock. Sure enough, the candle was burning, and on the saucer beneath it was the oval butt of a Sullivan Powell. James was a Raven.

Later the same morning James cycled over to the Vicarage. He was very pleased with himself. He drew Peter aside and said that tonight he would initiate himself as the Father; he hinted at the necessity for a blood sacrifice, and asked Peter to visit the Mithraeum in the morning.

'Are you going to light another candle?' Peter asked.

'No – that's just for Ravens. I'll take an electric torch and leave it switched on when I go. If it's there, you'll know I've succeeded.'

'The batteries will be flat.'

'What does it matter?' James said. 'It's the thought that counts.'

When Mrs Molland offered biscuits and drinks at elevenses, he ostentatiously declined both. 'I'm fasting, you see,' he whispered to Peter.

On the whole, Friday was a disappointment for Peter. The Vicarage could not compare with Carinish Court.

Once again, the presence of Kate stifled Emor. To make matters worse, James paid Kate more attention than Peter thought was strictly necessary. He heard them laughing together in the loft where the apples were stored, and he felt excluded.

Early on Saturday morning, Peter got dressed, let himself out of the house and walked down the garden. The dew glistened on his Wellington boots. He poled across the Great Water to the Mithraeum.

A bottle lay half-submerged in the puddle inside the doorway. It had once contained Cockburn's port. Beside the puddle was a handful of black feathers, the sight of which made Peter shiver. The torch – a large, shockproof cylinder covered with rubber – stood with its bulb pointing upwards on the sill of the embrasure furthest from the door. Peter later verified that it was switched on and that the batteries were flat, as he had predicted.

What drew his attention, however, was not the torch but the saucer on the sill beside it. A candle flickered in the saucer and around it was coiled a crude wreath of seven wilting dandelions. The wick had burned very low. As Peter watched, the flame flared into a ragged sheet of orange rimmed with oily smoke.

Another candle meant another Raven.

Common sense rescued him. James must have lit the candle as part of his own ritual or simply for illumination. The idea of a second Raven was absurd. Peter himself was going to be the second Raven; there were no other candidates. The wick arched itself and fell into the molten wax, which hissed as it drowned the flame.

When the candle died, the Mithraeum seemed darker

and colder. Peter stumbled up the steps and into the daylight. The boat swayed beneath his weight as he clambered in, and the sudden movement almost over-balanced him.

'Calm down,' he said aloud. 'There's no hurry.'

He poled across the pond as quickly as he could. Maybe Richard's right, he thought: Mithras is blasphemy. Will Jesus send us all to hell? He walked along the path through the bushes, wriggled through the drooping branches of the apple tree and came out on to the sunlit lawn.

Kate stood there, as if waiting for him. He was astonished to see her out of bed so early. The sun dazzled him. He could not see her face clearly but he thought she was smiling.

On Saturday afternoon Barbara went to Bristol in Ralph Salperton's Jaguar.

She had no choice in the matter – the Salpertons changed their plans without consulting her. The original idea had been to use two cars: Mary would drive one and Ralph the other. (From the first, Hubert had announced his intention of staying at Abbotsfield to write tomorrow's sermon. He would never allow Barbara to drive his father's car.)

At the last moment, however, Mrs Salperton developed migraine, or so she said. Ginny had already decided that she didn't really want to see a silly old film about the Beatles because she was only interested in the Rolling Stones; anyway, Bristol was boring. The first that Barbara knew of this was when Ralph and James arrived at the Vicarage after lunch.

'We can all squeeze into one car,' Ralph said. 'You and I in the front, kids in the back.'

He gave her no opportunity to refuse. Nor did Hubert – he was obviously keen to have the house to himself; the composition of sermons was an anxious process for him. In any case it would have been cruel to deprive the children of such a treat. She knew that there was a quarrel in progress between Kate and James on the one side and Peter and Richard on the other. An outing would take their minds off it.

The comfort of the Jaguar soothed her. Ralph would hardly start pawing her in front of an audience of four children. To her delight, he asked if she would like to drive on the way back.

'Are you sure you wouldn't mind?'

'Of course not. You'd enjoy it. I bet you're a natural driver.' He changed down and overtook a lorry; the acceleration pressed her into the seat. 'She handles beautifully.'

When they reached the cinema, Ralph gave James a £5 note and told him to get on with it. Barbara tried to protest.

'This is our treat,' he said. 'What would you like to do?'

'Aren't we going to see the film too?' Barbara said in surprise.

'Do you really want to?' He gestured at the queue. 'The average age must be about fifteen. All they want to do is screech at four long-haired layabouts. I don't know about you but it's not my idea of fun.'

'Well – what do you suggest?'

'How about a walk around Bristol? You don't know

the city at all, do you? Then we could have tea somewhere and come back for the kids.'

She agreed to the proposal for several reasons: she
had no desire to see *A Hard Day's Night*; she rarely had
a chance to look in the windows of city shops; Ralph
Salperton – apart from that first evening – had been
consistently courteous and unthreatening, so much so
that she was beginning to wonder if she had misinter-
preted the pass he had made at her; and finally, and
perhaps most powerfully, she thought that she deserved
a bit of a holiday.

It was a wonderful afternoon. Ralph never touched
her. Instead he showed his admiration by opening doors
for her, by walking protectively between her and the
road, and by complimenting her on her appearance
in such an oblique way that the compliments were a
pleasure not an embarrassment.

They had tea on the terrace of a hotel in Clifton.
After they had finished eating, there was one, slightly
awkward moment.

Ralph lit their cigarettes. 'Had a letter from Johnny
Redburn yesterday,' he said. 'They're coming down for
a couple of nights next weekend. Why don't you all
come over for the day on Saturday? Perhaps we could
go out in the evening.'

'I'd love to.' Barbara hesitated. 'I shall have to see
what Hubert thinks, of course – Saturday can be difficult
for him.'

'Why?'

'The sermon has to be written.'

'See if you can get him to do it on Friday. All work

and no play makes Jack a dull boy. I say, I haven't had such a nice afternoon in years.'

Barbara was immediately cautious. 'I've enjoyed it too.'

'People think my life must be all roses,' he said. 'You know, they see the car, the house and so on, and they draw the obvious conclusion. But it's misleading.'

'I'm sorry to hear that. Should we be getting back to the cinema?'

'Yes, of course.' Ralph crooked his finger at the waitress. 'Perhaps I shouldn't be telling you this. Did you know you're very easy to talk to? You've probably gathered that Mary isn't a well woman. Sometimes she's not easy to live with.'

'Oh dear,' Barbara said, wondering if he meant that he and Mary slept in separate rooms. Aware that 'Oh dear' sounded inadequate, she added, 'I *am* sorry.'

'Well, I mustn't bore you with my little difficulties. I just wanted to explain why this has been such a treat for me.' He smiled at her. 'Enough of me. Let's go and collect the kids.' He laid the car keys beside her plate, 'You can drive.'

During this period, the Emperor became increasingly disturbed by the rapid growth of the Cult of Mithras among all classes of society. In normal circumstances he would have ordered the Secret Police to investigate. However, he did not trust their loyalty because the Chief of the Secret Police, Jacobus Salpertonius, was the Pontifex Maximus of the new religion. The Chancellor, Petronius Redburnus, was also worried, even though he was himself a disciple of Mithras. This Redburnus was a good soldier and a capable administrator, but he was not a man of the same calibre as his father or great-uncle. He sought a private audience with the Emperor. He said that he had learned that the Pontifex Maximus had just initiated a woman into the cult, which was contrary to the laws of Emor. And the woman concerned was none other than the Emperor's sister.

A Hard Day's Night left Peter dazed with pleasure. Afterwards the problems flooded back.

'Was the candle still alight?' Kate had said on the lawn at Abbotsfield. 'Yes? So I'm a Raven.'

James had initiated Kate into the Cult of Mithras without consulting anybody. When Richard and Peter taxed him with this, he defended himself by saying that Mithras was separate from Emor and that he, as Pontifex Maximus, had a perfect right to admit whom he chose.

Neither Peter nor Richard was satisfied but they had little chance to discuss the matter – either with each other or with James – during the day. Most of Saturday was spent in a state of armed and silent neutrality that stopped just short of an open quarrel. James and Kate made things worse by laughing together over private jokes. But James confused the issue at the cinema: he went out of his way to sit next to Peter and talked with the utmost friendliness about the Beatles.

At bedtime Richard summoned Peter to his room for a conference.

'I think we should expel James from Emor,' Richard said. He was sitting cross-legged in his pyjamas with his back against the headboard of the bed. 'He's gone too far.'

'But we can't do that. He knows too much.'

'So what?'

'If we chuck him out, he'll tell everyone. Think what that would mean.' Peter did not mention the other likely consequence: that James would bar them from Carinish Court.

'He's probably told Kate already.'

'We don't know that.' Peter wondered if Richard were right. If Kate did know, and if she felt vengeful towards them, it was more than probable that she would tell all her friends in Plumford. The friends would tell their brothers and soon everyone would be laughing at them. Emor wouldn't be a secret any more.

'If I were you,' Richard said, 'I'd resign from the cult in protest.'

Peter shrugged. 'I'll think about it.'

'Are you a full member yet?'

'I'm sorry,' Peter said. 'You know I can't talk about that. I'm under oath.'

The decision could not be deferred for long. James had given Peter a brown paper bag when they got back from Bristol. The bag contained a candle, a box of matches and a cigarette.

'Tonight's the night,' James had murmured. 'Don't let me down. Kate will check that the candle's still alight in the morning.'

Peter knew that if he refused to go through with the ceremony Richard would be delighted; on the other hand Kate and James would think him a coward, the risk of publicity would increase, and James would construe the refusal as a declaration of war. He thought how difficult it would be to stay awake and how Mr and Mrs Molland might hear him leaving the house. He thought about the Mithraeum at midnight: a cold, dark pit populated in all probability by the ghosts of soldiers and evil spirits.

'Don't do it.' Richard's face was unhappy. 'Pete, it's wrong. I know it is.'

'That's a matter of opinion. How do you know Christianity is right? Ever seen a miracle? I haven't.'

'My father has.'

'What's that got to do with it? For all I know he imagined it, or made it up.'

'Don't be stupid,' Richard shouted. He remembered they were supposed to be in their separate rooms and dropped his voice to a whisper. 'Are you saying my father's a liar?'

Peter had already realized his mistake. 'Of course not. All I'm saying is that it was his miracle, not yours: you didn't actually see it, did you?'

'No, but –'

'So how can you be sure that Christianity is true?'

'It's obvious,' Richard said. 'Anyway, Mithras hasn't given you a miracle, has he?'

'He doesn't have to. This is Emor, remember?'

'But God's important everywhere,' Richard said in his smug, hotline-to-heaven voice. 'If you ask me, it's quite simple: James is in league with the devil.'

'You can't be sure. Not without a miracle.'

'The air we breathe is a miracle. So's the water we drink. God does miracles every day. That's more than Mithras does.'

'For all you know, it's Mithras who's doing the miracles. Anyway, they don't count. I'm talking about real miracles, like loaves and fishes and raising the dead.'

'Jesus could do all that.'

'So they say. But if Mithras did that sort of miracle, you'd have to believe in him, wouldn't you?'

'Yes,' Richard said unwillingly. 'But he won't – a false god can't do proper miracles. Everyone knows that. False gods are just agents of the devil. You *must* resign. Please.'

'I'm going to bed.' Peter avoided Richard's eyes. 'I'll see you in the morning.'

At that point Peter was still undecided. If anything, Richard's bossy piety had tipped the balance in Mithras's favour. But the conversation had also made Peter more afraid. Anything might be lurking in the darkness of the Mithraeum: god or devil.

He shut Richard's door softly behind him and tiptoed down the landing towards his own room. Someone whispered his name. He swung round.

Kate was standing in the doorway of her room. She raised a finger to her lips. A long dressing gown concealed her body. She smiled and beckoned him towards her.

He followed her into the corner bedroom where the picture had fallen from the wall on the day they arrived. He had not been there since the first evening. He stood just inside the doorway. The room seemed to be full of her and intensely feminine.

'James told me about tonight,' she whispered. 'Do you want to borrow an alarm clock?'

He nodded, not trusting himself to speak. She had hardly spoken to him all day – all week, come to that. Suddenly and miraculously everything had changed. A miracle from Mithras.

'Use the back stairs – they don't creak so much and

they're further away from my parents' room. I oiled the hinges and bolts of the side door.' She picked up a clock from her bedside table. 'Put it under your pillow. That's what I did.'

'Okay.'

'Are you scared?' Kate was now so close that Peter fancied he could feel the warmth radiating from her. She looked up at him and he knew that he had never seen anyone look at him like this in his entire life. 'I was terrified.'

He could not imagine her being scared of anything.

'I wondered – would you like me to come with you? It's much nicer if someone else is there.'

Fifteen

'Do you think David will like it?' Barbara Quest said.

'Sure to,' Ginny lied. 'He's fanatical about coffee.'

The Christmas present sat between them on the sofa. Barbara had wrapped it in several sheets of silver paper, across which the words 'Merry Christmas' were repeated endlessly in a pink Gothic script entwined with stylized wreaths of holly. She frowned at the parcel. Her expression suggested that choosing a present for her stepson had been a nerve-racking business.

'The man in John Lewis said it was one of the best filter machines on the market. We use ours all the time.'

'It looks enormous in that box.'

'Exactly. Not the sort of thing one can send in the post, and anyway I've left it much too late. Of course we could have taken it down ourselves after Christmas, but it wouldn't have been the same, would it?'

'No, it's nice to have your presents on the day itself. I left yours and Leo's in the hall, by the way.'

Ginny wondered what lay in store for her in the Harrods carrier bag propped up against the sofa. Barbara chose presents for other people as though she were buying for herself, and her tastes did not accord with Ginny's.

'His father's got him a book.' Barbara eyed the lines of Christmas cards that dangled from the picture rail on the fireplace wall. She stood up and straightened one of them. 'Another book,' she said. 'He's got no imagination.'

'It's probably something David wants. Leo's very good at that.'

Unlike Barbara. David loved strong, black coffee. Unfortunately he disliked unnecessary technology and believed that perfect coffee was merely a matter of combining freshly ground beans with an earthenware jug and boiling water.

'I'll make some tea, shall I?'

Barbara drifted towards the door. Her movements lacked their usual briskness. The lines on her face were deeper than usual and the skin beneath her eyes was puffy. Above the neck she looked almost as old as she really was. Below it, two decades dropped away from her age: she wore tight designer jeans and a blue jersey with a chain of red lozenges emblazoned across the chest. She glanced out of the window.

'I thought Kate would have been here by now. She's late.'

'I didn't realize you were expecting her.' Ginny injected enthusiasm into her voice. She would not have come if she had known that Kate was planning to visit her mother. 'How nice. I haven't seen her for ages.'

'Didn't I mention it? James has got one of those men-only dinners at his club, so she said she'd come over and bring their Christmas presents. It's a pity we can't all be together for Christmas itself, but there it is.'

Ginny guessed that this was a dig at her and David as well. 'When are they going to Carinish Court?'

'Tomorrow morning.' Barbara paused, her hand on the door. 'I believe it's going to be a working Christmas.

301

Apparently Peter Redburn will be there for a day or two.'

'Really? I didn't know.'

'I thought you'd seen him recently.'

'We had lunch together on Tuesday.' Suddenly Ginny was afraid. Had Barbara guessed what Peter was doing? Was that why she looked such a wreck? 'Have you met him yourself?'

'Oh no.' Barbara laughed: a tinkling, artificial sound that affected Ginny like the scrape of fingernails on an enamel bath. 'I doubt if we shall. We've got nothing to say to each other, have we? By the way, you're welcome to stay to dinner if you like. I'm sure Kate would love to see you.'

'I'd better not, thanks. I've got to spend the evening packing and wrapping.'

Barbara slipped out of the room to make the tea. It seemed to Ginny that their conversation had turned into a verbal fencing match, with each of them trying to discover what the other knew and each of them concealing her motives. It was depressing to discover that Barbara, who usually appeared so enviably uncomplicated, could be as devious as herself.

Ginny stared through the window, her mood colouring what she saw. Lavender Lane was looking scruffy, the roofs and the road greasy with rain and the pavements and lawns littered with dead leaves. She thought how pretentious the houses were, with their mock half-timbering, their fussy brickwork and their thickly leaded windows.

Barbara had irritated her this afternoon: not just the concealed curiosity about Peter, but also the invitation to dinner and the hint that she and Leo were not looking forward to the prospect of spending Christmas by themselves. In her own way, Barbara was as bad as Mary or even Ralph: they all wanted Ginny to cherish them; and they all made Ginny feel guilty when she refused. She had already given up several precious hours by coming here to exchange presents this afternoon. Presents, she thought sourly, that none of us wants.

Underneath the irritation was a layer of anxiety. Something was wrong with Barbara. Irrationally, Ginny wanted to blame Peter for it. Why couldn't he leave the past alone? But if anyone was to blame it was she herself. Exactly a week before she had gone to Lucasta Redburn's funeral and later to 29 Champney Road.

She got up and walked restlessly across the room to a shelved alcove on the right of the piano. Above the shelves hung a small oil painting of a blackened frying pan in which two eggs sizzled and bubbled. Barbara had draped a branch of holly along the top of the frame. The yolks looked like yellow eyes in a dark, impish face. The painting was more vivid and more alive than anything else in this bland, comfortable house. David had given it to Leo on his father's last birthday; and Barbara had hung it in the part of the drawing room where you were least likely to notice it. As always, the picture made Ginny hungry for David.

The doorbell rang. Ginny moved away from the alcove. A moment later Kate came into the room, followed by her mother with the tea. Kate and Ginny murmured their pleasure at seeing each other again.

'Don't come too close to me,' Kate said. 'I've got an awful cold.'

'Kate came by tube,' Barbara said in a voice that suggested the achievement was something to marvel at.

'It's very quick. Faster than getting a taxi, and so much cheaper.'

Kate was wearing a loose black suit with a high-necked white shirt beneath the jacket and the minimum of make-up. She should have looked dowdy. Instead she made her mother look gaudy and Ginny feel under-dressed.

'But, darling, you must get a taxi when you go home.' Barbara shuddered. 'Public transport is so unsafe late at night.'

'I'm afraid I can't stay long.'

'But what about dinner? I thought –'

'I'm sorry,' Kate said. 'I suddenly realized on my way here: I'm running out of time. You don't mind, do you?'

'If you can't manage it, that's all there is to say.'

'Your first Christmas at Carinish Court,' Ginny said. 'I expect you're looking forward to it.'

'James certainly is.' Kate sat down. 'Which reminds me – we wondered if you'd all like to come down for lunch on the day after Boxing Day. Wednesday, that is. You and David, Mummy and Leo – a sort of family housewarming.'

'We'd love to,' Barbara said. 'Just for the lunch, is it?'

'I wish we could put you up but the house isn't really habitable yet. Everything's in chaos.'

'Yes, of course. Perhaps Leo and I could find a hotel for the night. There used to be one in Abbotsfield, didn't there, on the main street?'

Kate nodded. 'The White Boar – it's a lot smarter than it was. Four-posters and window boxes: that sort of thing. If you want I'll phone them tomorrow and see if they've got a room.'

'At this time of year they may be fully booked. Still, it's worth a try.'

'I honestly don't think you'd like to stay in the house,' Kate said. 'Not just yet. Poor old Peter's going to have to camp out in James's old room. He'll probably end up in a sleeping bag.'

'Oh.' Barbara busied herself with the teapot. 'I didn't realize that Peter would still be there.'

'Almost certainly, I should think. James is hoping he'll stay until the new year.'

'I see. Well, as I say, we'd love to come, naturally; but I shall have to check with Leo. He may have to go into the office. In fact, I'm almost sure he said something about it this morning. Why don't I phone you, darling – tomorrow evening, perhaps?'

'What about you, Ginny?'

'I don't know what David's got planned,' she said. 'And do you know that we're seeing Ralph over Christmas?'

Ginny deliberately left vague the length of time that Ralph would be with them.

'That might be a bit of a problem.' Kate stretched out a long leg and looked at it with apparent fascination. 'I don't think James is intending to invite his father. It's rather awkward, I'm afraid.'

'It is rather, isn't it?' Ginny felt a rush of dislike for her brother and Kate, who seemed so effortlessly to ignore their responsibilities, and a corresponding surge of affection for Ralph, whom nobody wanted, least of all herself. 'Will my mother be coming?'

'I doubt it. James said he'd ask her but you know what Mary's like when she's enjoying herself. It would take an act of God to drag her away from Lake Windermere. And of course it would be a long journey for her, and we'd have the same problem about her staying overnight.'

'Perhaps we could all come another time,' Barbara said. 'I'd like to see Carinish Court in the summer. That's how I remember it. The sun always seemed to be shining.' She handed round cups of tea. 'Now, would anyone like a biscuit?'

Kate shook her head and sneezed.

The choice of Kate's Emorian name had been a sly joke.

James had asked Ginny for suggestions. He told her a good deal about the affairs of Emor – he had to, because he needed her help. She had realized that he was pumping her so that he could appear knowledge-able before the others. James had always been like that: he had no interest in information for its own sake, but he hated to seem ignorant. Therefore he was capable of working surprisingly hard to give the impression of knowing a little more than everyone else.

One Sunday evening on the terrace, he'd told her that he was arranging for Kate to join Emor. 'It's not easy, either. Richard hates the idea.'

'Then why bother?' Ginny had said. 'I thought you didn't like her.'

'I don't, really. But it's more fun with four. Anyway – it upsets the others.'

This was before Ginny had seen much of James

and Kate together, before she realized that they were fascinated with each other. She thought that James wanted Kate in the game just as a way of making clear to Peter and Richard that he was now the leader.

'How will you manage it?'

'I've already got Kate into Mithras,' he said. 'I can handle Peter, I've seen to that. Tomorrow I'll be emperor so I'll just issue a decree about it. Richard'll moan but there's nothing he can do.'

'He could resign.'

'He won't do that. He'd never leave Emor. The thing is, Kate wants a good Roman name.'

'What wrong with Caterina?'

'She wants the sort of name an empress would have, a real one. Have you got any ideas?'

'Julia? Augusta?'

'Sounds a bit stodgy. I think she'd like a name that people don't use today.'

'Let me think about it.'

Ginny remembered the conversation, and remembered that it took place on Sunday 9 August, because immediately afterwards she slipped through the darkness to the cottage behind the kitchen garden.

The cottage was empty. She knew that as soon as she lifted the latch.

'Frank,' she whispered without hope. 'It's me.'

The beam from the torch darted round the kitchen. Ginny gasped when the windowpane reflected the light back to her. In the room upstairs she found his bedding, neatly folded, a tobacco tin full of cigarette butts, and her copy of *Mansfield Park*. Tucked inside the book was a pencilled note. All it said was *Thanks*.

Ginny knelt down and hugged the bedding. It smelled of Frank. She cried for a few minutes. She had known that Frank planned to slip back to the bedsitter above the garage when his beard was well enough established. She told herself that she would see him again – they could hardly avoid meeting in a place the size of Abbotsfield. At least he had taken *Bleak House* with him, which she interpreted as a sign that their new intimacy would continue. There was also the consolation that he hadn't said goodbye to James.

The following morning Ginny went to the Vicarage for a Latin lesson. She pretended to loathe these sessions with Hubert Molland but secretly quite enjoyed them. He was a methodical and unemotional teacher, an approach that suited her temperament.

She asked him near the end of the lesson if the empresses of Rome had been as cruel as the emperors. The question arose naturally from the unseen they had been translating, which concerned the activities of Nero. Mr Molland said that some of the empresses were even worse than their husbands, and reeled off a selection of names: Agrippina, Messalina, Poppaea.

Messalina sounded suitably sinister – a name full of hisses. After the lesson, Ginny looked her up in Mr Timball's copy of *Chambers's Biographical Dictionary*.

'MESSALINA, Valeria . . . infamous for avarice, lust and cruelty . . .' A woman who indulged in bigamy, had her rivals killed and was herself executed on the orders of her understandably irritated husband, the Emperor Claudius.

Ginny suggested the name to James as they were cycling back to lunch at Carinish Court. 'Imposing, isn't it? And the full name could be Valeria Messalina Mollandia.'

James liked it. So, apparently, did Kate. He told her and the other children about it in the afternoon, when the three of them came over for a swim. After tea, James and Kate disappeared for nearly half an hour. Ginny played snooker with Peter and Richard, neither of whom was very talkative. Nor was Ginny. She was missing Frank.

The new Emperor, who took the title of Jacobus I, was besotted with one Valeria Messalina, a distant relative of the Gens Mollandia. On the first day of his reign he introduced her to the Court and loaded her with honours. He also decreed that the Cult of Mithras should henceforward be the state religion. The salary of the Pontifex Maximus was fixed at 100,000 Sesterces per reign. This was a larger amount than any other salary, except the Emperor's. Petronius Redburnus, who was once again appointed Chancellor of the Exchequer, agreed to everything the Emperor suggested. He was a weak man, an unworthy descendant of the great family whose name he bore. Only Gaius Marcus Mollandius remained true to the old ways. Nicknamed 'Verus' by the people, he was a nephew of the previous Emperor and had come to Court only recently. Jacobus I secretly hated him, but was forced to make him Lord High Admiral because of his popularity with the Plebs. When Mollandius refused to join the blasphemous new religion, the Emperor ordered him to be tried for treason. The Plebs rioted when they heard the news. The Emperor sent out the Praetorian Guard and the Cohortes Urbanae, who crushed the revolt with great brutality.

According to the School-Boy Diary, the trial was originally fixed for Tuesday but had to be postponed until Wednesday. On Tuesday the Mollands and the Salpertons took a picnic and went first to the ruins of Glastonbury Abbey and then to Wells Cathedral. Peter remembered little of the day, apart from the wasp incident.

This occurred during their picnic lunch, which they ate on Glastonbury Tor. Hubert Molland was the victim. He was eating a ham-and-tomato sandwich at the time. The wasp must have landed on the sandwich and Mr Molland ate it by mistake. He squawked and spat out everything he could – a mouthful of sandwich, his false teeth and the crushed body of the wasp. His eyes bulged. He wrapped his handkerchief round the teeth, stood up and walked away from everyone. No one else moved. Barbara Molland asked Ralph Salperton to pass the salt. Peter had not realized Mr Molland wore false teeth. The picnic continued as though nothing had happened.

What struck Peter most forcibly about the wasp incident was how it illustrated a fundamental difference between his parents' marriage and the Mollands'. Had the wasp stung John Redburn, especially in so sensitive a place, Lucasta would have fussed over him for days. She would have probably insisted on taking him immediately to the nearest hospital. Mrs Molland, on the other hand, had asked Mr Salperton for the salt. It was very puzzling. Peter had previously assumed that all marriages were conducted along essentially the same lines as his parents'.

A few minutes later Mr Molland returned. He sat down without a word and poured himself some orange squash.

'Better now?' Barbara said.

Mr Molland swallowed. 'Yes, thank you.'

*

On Wednesday morning Richard went on trial in the Mithraeum. James was the judge; Kate prosecuted; Peter acted as the jury; and the prisoner defended himself. James and Kate made it clear from the start that they considered the proceedings to be a formality. Kate pressed for Richard to be exiled to Capri, which in effect would have meant that he was banished from Emor for the rest of the reign. His only hope of saving himself from this fate was to join the state religion.

Richard refused. He said that liberty of conscience was an important principle of the constitution, and that the Emperor had no right to act unconstitutionally.

'Let's see this document,' James said.

'It's at Plumford. I call Petronius Redburnus as my witness.'

Emor had never had a written constitution. That was not the real issue. As all four of them knew, the important question was whether or not Peter would come out in support of Richard. James raised his eyebrows and smiled encouragingly at Peter. Richard's face was hot and angry.

'Well?' Kate glanced from Peter to James, who switched his smile to her.

The timing of her glance and his smile was their one mistake. Peter felt excluded at the precise moment when his loyalty was wavering between them and Richard.

'That's right,' he said. 'Article Three guarantees liberty of conscience. Therefore the defendant cannot be guilty.'

Kate was furious but James made the best of it. No Emperor wishes to lose two-thirds of his subjects.

'All right,' he said to Richard. 'So there's no case to answer. The High Court clears you.'

'Thank you.'

'However, there's no reason why you shouldn't recognize that Mithraism is the state religion, is there? It's a pure formality. You don't have to be a member to do that.'

Richard hesitated.

'Put it this way,' James went on. 'If we don't interfere with your liberty of conscience, you shouldn't interfere with ours. It's logical.'

'Okay. But I still say there's only one god: the god of the Christians.'

'That's what you think.' James smiled, this time at Richard. 'But I think we should all agree to keep an open mind about religion.'

'What do you mean?'

'You never know – Mithras might prove you wrong.'

James was very cool towards Richard and Peter for the rest of his reign.

It was not an easy time for Peter. He wanted Kate and James to like him. His lie about the constitution had prevented the trial from ending with an open breach, but it had left no one satisfied.

Emor was changing beyond recognition. Kate's influence even affected the casino, which Peter had always thought of as his own preserve. She introduced bezique and suggested that they should gamble for real money. Peter agreed, simply to please her. She refused to accept that ten per cent of all winnings should go to the proprietor.

When they played for sesterces he usually won, but with real money at stake his luck deserted him. He soon lost the rest of the pocket money he had brought with him and was reduced to borrowing from Richard. He hoped that his parents would tip him when they came to stay at Carinish Court. He was almost looking forward to their visit. The weekend, however, was even harder to bear than the week that preceded it.

'It was quite a shock, I can tell you,' Ralph Salperton whispered. 'I had no idea.'

'He looks much worse than he was,' Barbara said, moving along the terrace away from Kate, Peter and James, who were playing tag in the swimming pool. 'Even a few weeks has made a difference.'

'He saw a chap in Harley Street last week. Apparently there's nothing they can do. Makes you sick, doesn't it? Six months, the chap reckoned. Maybe less.'

'It seems so unfair,' Barbara said. Unfair to John Redburn, and also unfair to her. She wondered why it had to happen to one of the few mildly amusing men in Plumford. Occasionally she'd caught him looking at her in a way that suggested he found her attractive.

'Poor old Johnny.' Ralph offered her a cigarette. 'I was hoping I'd get some tennis in while he was here. He used to have a beautiful serve. But as soon as I saw him last night I realized that was out. I had to help him down from the train. Why, he looks thirty years older than he is.'

For a moment they smoked in silence, staring across the lawn. John Redburn and Mary Salperton were sitting on the bench beneath the oak tree.

'He's only a month or two older than I am,' Ralph murmured with barely concealed outrage. 'You just wouldn't believe it, would you? Mary's very cut up about it, naturally.'

'I didn't realize she knew him that well.'

'Oh yes. Almost as well as me. Her father was our CO in the war. I think Johnny was a bit sweet on her at one time.'

'What about Lucasta?' Barbara asked. 'Was she part of the same crowd?'

Ralph shook his head. 'Mary and I didn't meet her until just before Johnny's wedding. That was in nineteen forty-eight, I think, the year after we got married. If you ask me he made a mistake. She gives me the creeps. She broods over Johnny like a bloody hen.'

Barbara glanced involuntarily over her shoulder, half expecting to see Mrs Redburn standing there. Lucasta had gone into Abbotsfield to do some shopping; and Hubert, who was revising tomorrow's sermon at the Vicarage, had agreed to drive her back to Carinish Court in time for lunch.

'Sorry.' Ralph reddened beneath his tan. 'I wasn't thinking. Perhaps she's a friend of yours.'

'I wouldn't say that,' Barbara said.

'Didn't think she would be. Ghastly woman. I've no idea why Johnny married her.'

'Does Peter know about his father?'

'They haven't told him yet. I mean, what can you say? Better to let the poor little beggar have his fun while he can.'

'Will John be able to go out tonight?'

Ralph and Mary had planned to take their grown-up

guests to a cocktail party in Paulstock, and bring them back to Carinish Court for a cold supper.

'He's determined to go,' Ralph said. 'That's old Johnny for you: he's a fighter. Lucasta wanted him to stay here but he wasn't having any. I bet she tried to keep him from coming down here.'

'Is he in a lot of pain?'

Ralph nodded. 'It's all so depressing, isn't it?' He cocked his head. 'Someone's coming.'

'Hubert's early.'

'No, it's not the Rover.'

Ralph strode along the terrace to the balustrade that separated it from the drive. Barbara followed him. The sound of the engine grew louder and louder. James swam to the ladder and hauled himself out of the pool.

'Well, I'm damned,' Ralph muttered under his breath. 'Of all the sheer, bloody impudence.'

The motorbike braked sharply, throwing up a spray of gravel, and came to a halt beside the balustrade. The rider wore a black leather jacket and tight jeans. He left the engine running and sat back, folding his arms.

'What are you doing here?' Ralph said.

'Hello.' The young man grinned. 'Is Ginny around?'

His self-confidence and his accent confirmed what Barbara had already suspected: here at last was Frank Timball. He looked like a gipsy in need of a shave.

'No, she's not.' Ralph frowned. 'Why do you want to see her?'

'I wanted to return a book she lent me.' Frank unzipped his jacket and held up a plump red volume. '*Bleak House*,' he explained, looking at Barbara; and his face was full of amusement. 'Do tell Ginny I enjoyed it. Hello, James.'

James had come silently along the terrace and was now at Barbara's elbow. He was smiling at Frank.

Frank held out the book. James leaned over the rail of the balustrade and took it from him.

'Everything okay?' Frank said.

James nodded.

'Well, goodbye,' Ralph said. 'You know the way out.'

Frank revved the engine. He fluttered his fingers at his audience of three and swung the bike round in a wide turn that sent the gravel spurting once again. James left the book on the step of the French windows and dived into the swimming pool.

Ralph stared at the drive. 'That boy needs a good hiding. Do you know who he is? George Timball's son. And I'd like to know why Ginny's been lending him books.'

The roar of the engine diminished in volume. It merged with the sound of a second engine. Gradually the latter grew louder, drowning the motorbike. Gears grated. The engine coughed.

'Hubert and Lucasta,' Barbara said brightly.

Saw Dad and Mum at CC, said the School-Boy Diary entry for Saturday 15 August. *Dad gave me £1! Good swim. Fairly sunny.*

True to form, Peter had censored the events of the day before he recorded them for posterity. His father had slipped him the pound note soon after Peter arrived at Carinish Court with the Mollands.

'Don't tell your mother,' John Redburn said, his voice

hoarser than ever. 'This is between ourselves, old man.'

Before she went shopping, his mother had pecked him on the cheek and asked Mrs Molland if he had been a good boy. Peter felt uneasy, remembering the games of bezique on Sunday evening and what he had seen Mr Salperton do to Mrs Molland on their first evening at Abbotsfield. But Mrs Molland merely laughed and said that he had been the perfect guest.

Peter would have suspected that his father was dying even if he hadn't overheard Mr Salperton and Mrs Molland talking about it on the terrace before lunch. After the fortnight's gap, Peter saw his father almost with the eyes of a stranger. John Redburn looked awful, as though he were already dead. His face was like a cracked wax mask.

Peter didn't know what to feel. He guessed that deep sorrow was in order when your father was dying. But his father's apparent cheerfulness and his unexpected generosity made it difficult to be gloomy. Moreover, Peter could not imagine life without his father, so the thought of his dying was in a sense an abstraction that corresponded to nothing he had known before. He was ambivalent about his parents' failure officially to break the news to him. This made him feel both relieved and insulted. In sum, his emotions had more to do with anger and confusion than with sorrow.

In the meantime life carried on as though nothing had happened, as though the closeness of death were no more than one of those minor social embarrassments to which well-brought-up people are taught to turn a blind eye. 'Don't stare,' Lucasta Redburn would say when she caught Peter looking at a man with one leg or a woman with a moustache. 'It's bad manners.' Perhaps adults had access to a secret code of conduct that governed how they should behave in all such situations: when someone was dying or had bitten a wasp.

Peter spent Saturday morning in a daze. He was not unhappy. He thought less about his father than he did about the choice between climbing the oak tree with Richard and playing water-tag with James and Kate.

Lunch was on the lavish scale that Peter had come to expect from the Salpertons, but he enjoyed it less than usual. His mother said little to anyone apart from Hubert Molland, with whom she briefly discussed the new organist at St Clement's in Plumford and the language of *The New English Bible*. She refused to take wine with the meal and asked for small helpings of everything; it was as if she were determined to accept as little hospitality as possible. Square and upright in her chair, she waited for lunch to finish with the air of an early Christian martyr waiting for the lions to work up an appetite. Only her eyes were restless: they moved to and fro between her husband and her son.

Conversation proceeded by fits and starts. The younger members of the party said very little. Mr Molland never talked much in company, and Mrs Salperton's mind appeared to be elsewhere. Ralph did most of the talking, seconded by Mrs Molland and from time to time by Peter's father.

Mrs Salperton knocked over her wine glass as she was clearing the table between the courses. A streak of purple stained the brilliant white of the tablecloth.

'For God's sake!' Ralph snapped.

Mary Salperton blinked at him. A hush settled over

318

the room. John Redburn coughed and Hubert Molland sucked in his breath.

'Sorry, padre,' Ralph said gruffly. 'Nothing personal. Ginny – fetch a cloth, will you? Don't want to mark the table. Nice bit of mahogany. Used to be my grandfather's.'

'Try salt,' Mrs Molland advised. 'It soaks up the wine.'

'Not always,' John Redburn said, so quietly that only Peter heard him. 'Sometimes it just fixes the stain. Use white wine, if I were you. Acts as a solvent.'

'Wonderful to see you all here,' Ralph said as Ginny returned with two cloths. He raised his voice, as though deafness were another of John Redburn's afflictions: 'Mustn't leave it so long next time – eh, Johnny?'

A short silence followed this burst of unwarranted optimism. Ginny and Mary Salperton dabbed at the wine. Ralph concentrated on dividing a block of ice cream into twelve equal portions. He marked out each of the cuts he intended to make on the top of the block. Peter wondered why Mr Salperton didn't use a ruler since precision was so important to him, and who would get the twelfth slice.

'Last time Johnny was here we made him work for his keep,' Ralph went on. 'Maybe that's why he wasn't keen to come back.' He chuckled and cut the first slice of ice cream. 'Remember, Johnny? What an evening that was.'

'Just a very small piece for me.' Lucasta Redburn rubbed her hands together. 'If it's not too much trouble.'

'Oh. Right you are.' He glanced at her with venom

in his eyes. 'I bet you were glad you didn't come with Johnny last time.' He looked round the table. 'It wasn't much fun for anyone. I pranged the car. A complete write-off. Not my fault, mark you – we were coming round a corner when we met a tractor on the wrong side of the road. I slammed on the brakes, of course, but the car went into a skid. It was pitch dark – I couldn't see a thing – the car went into a ditch and turned on its side. Johnny was okay, just a few cuts and scratches. So was the tractor driver. But I finished up with a broken leg and concussion. Poor old Johnny had to break the news to Mary and cart me off in an ambulance to Paulstock Hospital.'

'How awful,' Mrs Molland said. 'Were you in hospital for long?'

'A week or so, I think. Then I was hopping around on crutches. What a palaver that was. And all I saw of Johnny after the accident was about ten minutes' worth at visiting time.'

He passed the bowls of ice cream down the table. By this time, Ginny and her mother had sat down, leaving the wine stain to its own devices.

'It seemed like an act of God,' Mrs Salperton said suddenly.

'What on earth do you mean?' Ralph said.

'The accident.' She poured herself another glass of wine. 'As if God were punishing you for something.'

'Rubbish. Now there's fruit salad, too. Just help your-selves, everybody. Don't hold back.'

'I don't think I want any pudding,' Mrs Salperton said.

Peter stared at the rectangle of ice cream in his bowl.

It was already beginning to melt. He thought about the idea of God punishing people while they were alive. He wondered if God would punish a person by hurting someone else, whom the first person loved. Richard would know; there was sure to be something about it in the Bible. The idea gathered momentum in his mind.

Suppose he were responsible for his father's illness? It might be God's revenge for his joining the Cult of Mithras.

Ginny saw the book after lunch. It was on the plant stand on the left of the French windows. She recognized it immediately by its size, its faded red binding and the gilt lettering on the spine.

She pounced on it. 'Where did this come from?'

'*Bleak House?*' James said. 'Frank brought it back just before lunch.'

'He was here?' Ginny could hardly believe her bad luck. She had spent the latter part of the morning up in the woods behind the house.

'Not for long.' James winked at her; Kate, Richard and Peter were behind him so they saw nothing of that. 'Dad was there.'

'Did Frank leave a message?'

'Just to tell you he enjoyed it.'

'I'll put it back in the study,' Ginny said.

She walked across the drawing room. The hall was empty. She riffled through the pages, hoping against hope that Frank had left a note for her or even marked a few passages in the book. Nothing there. She closed the book and kissed it. A floorboard creaked behind her.

Kate was standing in the doorway. 'Excuse me,' she said, smiling.

Ginny wished she could die.

'Good book?' Kate said.

Ginny wanted to slap her. What stopped her was a vision of Kate whispering her news to everyone in the house: 'I saw Ginny kissing the book that Frank brought back.'

'You're not going to tell anyone about this,' she said.

Kate opened her eyes very widely. 'Tell them what?'

Ginny ignored the question. 'You're not going to tell anyone because if you do, I've got something to tell them too.'

'I don't know what you mean.'

'I saw you in my mother's room a couple of weeks ago.'

Kate's face lost its colour. Her freckles, which were not usually visible, made pale orange islands on her skin.

'How much did you steal from her handbag?' Ginny said.

'Nothing. It's a lie.'

'A few pounds? More? Do you want me to tell everyone?'

Kate pushed past her and walked quickly down the hall to the downstairs lavatory. The door slammed. The bolt clicked home.

Ginny moved towards the stairs, clutching the book to her chest. The study door opened.

'I want a word with you, young lady,' Ralph said. 'What do you think you're doing with that book?'

'I—I wanted something to read.'

'And who said you could lend it to Frank Timball?'

'No one. I thought you wouldn't mind.'

'You thought wrong. Have you been seeing him behind my back?'

'No. Of course I haven't.'

Ralph came towards her. His lips were pressed together. Ginny was terrified that he would insist on knowing the exact circumstances of her lending the book. She cast about for a convincing lie. Her mind went blank.

'Ralph?' Barbara Molland was coming down the hall from the kitchen with a tray of glasses in her hands. 'Mary said these go in the dining room. Where do you want me to put them?'

'The sideboard, please.' Ralph turned away from Ginny. His voice had become warm and gentle. 'Here, let me show you.'

'Please God,' Peter prayed silently as he stood on the terrace after lunch. Behind him, James was offering to give Richard a swimming lesson later on in the afternoon, and Richard was refusing. 'Please God, if you make my father better I swear I will give up Mithras, and I won't swear or smoke cigarettes or laugh at dirty jokes. Through Jesus Christ Our Lord. Amen.'

That seemed to cover it. Peter was pleasantly aware of his generosity: for the sake of his father, he was offering God quite a bargain. He repeated the prayer several times during the afternoon and the early evening. He spent most of this time with Richard. They played snooker and table tennis in the attics. Neither of them said very much.

'Do you know where James and Kate are?' Richard muttered as they were coming down the stairs at teatime.

'Search me.'

'I think they're up to something.'

Peter virtuously stifled his jealousy. He began to recite to himself the prayer to the god of the Christians.

'Do you know what I saw them doing yesterday?' Richard whispered. 'They were in the Mithraeum together. They were *snogging*.'

This information shocked Peter far more than his father's condition. He abandoned the prayer in mid-sentence. The thought of Kate and James touching each other and kissing made him feel physically sick.

'You're imagining it,' Peter said. 'James wouldn't do something like that.'

The grown-ups left for Paulstock at six o'clock.

'Supper's laid out in the kitchen,' Mrs Salperton said to Ginny. 'Don't wait for us if you're hungry. If you need us, the phone number's on the hall table.'

'Don't fuss, Mary,' Ralph said. 'We're late enough already.'

Time passed very slowly that evening. James said that with luck their parents wouldn't be back until ten; they were going to the Morgans', whose parties always lasted for ages. The five of them picked at the sandwiches Mrs Salperton had left. Later they watched television. Peter thought about his father and about what Richard had told him. He studied Kate and James but could see nothing different in their faces.

It grew darker, but no one switched on the lights or drew the curtains. The drawing room became a place of shadows dominated by the grey, flickering light from the television.

'I'm bored,' James said. 'Let's play Murder in the Dark.'

The suggestion surprised Peter a little. Murder was the sort of game you played at children's parties. He would have expected James to consider it beneath him.

'Yes, let's,' Kate said.

'There's not enough of you to do it properly,' Ginny said.

'We can manage if you play as well.' James got up and switched on the overhead lights. Everyone blinked. 'Go on, Ginny. Be a sport.'

She shrugged. 'All right. If we must.'

'We'll draw lots, then,' James said. 'Come on.' He turned off the television and picked up one of his mother's packs of cards. 'We need five cards. The jack is the murderer, the ace is the detective.'

'What's the forfeit?' Kate asked. 'The one we used to have was "Kneel to the wittiest, bow to the prettiest, and kiss the one you love the best."'

'Ugh,' Richard said.

James grinned at her. 'Suits me.' He shuffled the cards and dealt one to each person.

Richard held up the ace of spades. 'I'm the detective.'

James collected the cards and returned them to the pack. 'Right – this is the way we play it. The mains switch is in the hall, so Richard will wait there. Count to a hundred, okay, and then turn out the lights. The rest of us separate. Once the lights go out, the murderer can creep up on his victim at any moment and tap his shoulder three times. Whoever's killed has to scream, and that's the signal for Richard to turn on the lights again. Then he studies the corpse and asks us all questions. Only the murderer can tell lies, of course. And then the detective can make his accusation. He only has one try. If he's right, the murderer has to say so and pay the forfeit; and if he's wrong, the murderer goes free.'

When Richard began counting, Peter ran upstairs. He turned on lights as he went. No one seemed to be coming after him, but in a house like this it was difficult to be sure. Carinish Court was so large and so rambling that the pursuit could go on for hours. He pushed away the fear that James and Kate might take advantage of the darkness to do some more snogging and concentrated on the practical task before him.

As he wasn't the murderer, Peter's strategy was simple: keep on the move. One stretch of the landing ran between the main staircase and the back stairs to the kitchen. Once there he would be able to hear anyone who came up either of the staircases; and the other staircase would provide an escape route. If necessary he could even retreat to the attics. He would work on the assumption that anyone who moved was the murderer.

The lights went out almost as soon as he reached his destination; Richard must have counted quickly. Peter shut his eyes, which made the darkness more tolerable. Creaks and scuffles rose up the stairwell. Peter hated this part of the game: waiting for the three taps on the shoulder, waiting for the scream.

'Please God,' he gabbled under his breath, 'if you make my father better I swear I will give up Mithras, and I won't swear or smoke cigarettes or laugh at dirty jokes. Through Jesus Christ Our Lord. Amen.'

The minutes slipped by. Peter repeated the prayer. On one occasion he thought that he heard a door close and someone coming up the back stairs.

When it came, the scream was terrible. Peter knew at once that something was wrong, that the wrong person had been killed.

He felt his way along the wall towards the head of the main staircase. The lights had not come on. Below him he heard stealthy movements and ragged breathing.

Suddenly there was a click, and light flooded through the house.

'Who's dead?' Ginny asked. It sounded as if she were in the hall.

No one answered her. Peter started to run down the stairs. A car was coming up the drive.

'Who's dead?' she repeated, and this time her voice was high with panic or anger. 'Do you know who screamed?'

'I screamed,' Richard said.

'But you can't be dead,' Ginny told him crossly. 'You're the detective.'

Sixteen

'Not here,' Kate had said. 'You mustn't come here.'

What was wrong with his going to Montpelier Square? Why did she want to see him in the first place? Was it important that James shouldn't know?

Peter had phoned the Salpertons' flat at lunchtime, just after his return to London; he intended to report that he had written the first draft of chapter one and to confirm the arrangements for tomorrow. Kate had answered, which had thrown him because he'd been expecting to talk to James. The first and only thing she'd wanted to know was whether he was free to meet her this evening. She said nothing about Christmas or James or the book.

'Yes,' Peter had said. 'What time shall I come?'

'Can you manage six o'clock?'

'Any time. Right, I'll be there. But —'

'Not here,' she'd interrupted. 'You mustn't come here.'

Peter's tension crept higher and higher all afternoon. His flat was cold but at times he felt unbearably hot, as if the excitement were making him feverish. He packed his bags for Carinish Court and wrapped the presents he had bought for James and Kate: a bottle of vintage champagne as a token of appreciation for their hospitality, an anthology of theatrical anecdotes for James, and a tiny silver brooch for Kate. He worried about the brooch, which he'd bought on impulse at an antique shop in Plumford. It showed a swallow in flight. Would Kate like it? Would she think he had spent too much or too little? Would she think he was presuming?

The feeling that he was either too hot or too cold persisted after he left the flat and took the Jubilee Line to central London. Peter was early for the meeting – much too early – so he got off the train at Bond Street and walked in time-killing zigzags that gradually took him southwards.

The streets were crowded. Today was the Friday before Christmas. The decorations glittered; Oxford Street and Regent Street churned with people. Everyone moved with an urgency that verged on hysteria: hurrying to their homes for the Christmas holiday; shopping for presents with last-minute abandon; pouring into pubs and winebars to celebrate with colleagues their temporary release from drudgery.

If London were a body, he thought as he waited in the rain to cross Piccadilly, it would be running a high temperature.

At last the lights changed. The pedestrians threaded their way through the temporarily frozen river of traffic. Peter walked quickly, fighting the temptation to run, down the slope of St James's Street. According to Kate, Green Place was a cul-de-sac on the right-hand side; the club was at the end, its garden backing on to the Park.

The premises of the Royal Commonwealth Institute trailed round three sides of a cramped forecourt. The RCI was a charitable organization that helped to pay its bills by allowing its members to use the headquarters as a club. The hall was full of middle-aged women talking in loud voices and middle-aged men looking at their watches. According to the clock behind the porter's desk it was 5.49. Peter surrendered his coat and asked for Mrs Kate Salperton. The porter directed him to the Mortbank Room on the second floor. Peter mounted a broad staircase with a scrolled, wrought-iron handrail. The soles of his shoes slapped on the stone treads.

The Mortbank room had the cubic capacity of a small house and the privileged tranquillity of a private chapel. It was furnished as a drawing room. Tables, chairs and sofas had been arranged in archipelagos on the blue-green sea of the carpet. No one looked up as Peter came in. Perched in an armchair by the glowing, simulated coals of the electric fire was an Indian gentleman with a shock of white hair; he was reading the *Illustrated London News*, which he held six inches away from his eyes. Flanked by their handbags, two ladies sat on a distant sofa and conversed in whispers. The only other person in the room was Kate.

She was stooping over a table covered with newspapers and magazines. Her hair gleamed in the light from a nearby standard lamp. Her black clothes and bowed head gave Peter the impression that she was in mourning.

She turned. Her face brightened as she saw him. She put her hands on his shoulders and kissed his cheek.

'Thank you for coming,' she murmured.

'A pleasure.' Peter hesitated, then blurted out, 'Are you all right?'

Kate shrugged. 'What do you want to do? If you

want a drink, we could go down to the bar. But it's packed out this evening. Everyone's celebrating.'

'Whatever you want.'

'Then let's stay here for a while.'

She led him to a sofa between two full-length windows curtained in faded green velvet. They sat down, a yard apart. The elderly Indian turned over a page. The two ladies continued to whisper.

Kate blew her nose. 'I've got a cold. A real stinker. Where have you been? I tried to phone you yesterday.'

'I had to go to Plumford.'

'About your mother's house?'

Peter nodded.

'Have you managed to sell it?'

'We agreed a price yesterday.' He remembered with difficulty, because it seemed so long ago, how Coleby's heavy features had twisted with surprise and reluctance as they shook hands on the deal. 'I got what I wanted: a quarter of a million.'

'I'm glad for you.' Kate was silent for a moment. He waited for her to continue. She stirred beside him, as if shaking off an unpleasant memory. 'You look tired.'

'I was up for most of last night. I wrote the first four thousand words of James's autobiography.'

'That will please him.'

'I hope so. To me it seems incredibly boring.'

Kate teased the strap of her handbag through her fingers. 'He's having dinner at his club tonight. At least that's what he said.'

The Indian turned another page. The two women shuffled towards the door, still whispering.

Peter frowned. 'You don't believe him?'

'I'm not sure. I'm not sure of anything any more.'

'Does he know you're meeting me?'

'No. And he mustn't. That's why I asked you to come here. If you'd come to the flat, one of the neighbours might have noticed, or James might have come home unexpectedly. You won't tell him, will you?'

'Not if you don't want me to. But what's it all about?'

She dropped the strap on her lap and leaned back. 'I need to talk to someone. You don't mind?'

'Of course I don't. It's a surprise that you chose me – a nice surprise, I mean.'

'You underrate yourself.' She glanced at him. 'You always did.'

'But why me? I would have thought there were dozens of people you could talk to.'

'There's talking and talking. It's taken this to make me realize how few friends I have. I thought perhaps I could talk to my mother. I went to see her this afternoon. Ginny was there for some of the time, which didn't help – she doesn't like me, did you know that? I wish she did. Anyway, to go back to my mother: I love her dearly but she's not the sort of person you can confide in. It would just make her unhappy. She doesn't want to know, not really, and I think she's got her own problems.'

Peter's mind whirled with shock, delight and anxiety. He took refuge in formality: 'If there's anything I can do, you have only to say.'

'Thank you. I knew that when I saw you on Tuesday.' Kate ran the tip of her tongue along her lips. 'You're being very patient with me. I just want you to listen. To tell me I'm not being stupid.'

'Something's wrong between you and James? I wondered about that the other night.'

'It's not what you think. He's not seeing someone else, or not that I know of. Oh, it's true we're not exactly happy.'

'I'm sorry.'

She shook her head, rejecting his sympathy. 'That's not the problem. I'm used to it. I'm used to him watching every penny I spend. I'm used to having to pretend we're the perfect couple. Do you remember what Ralph was like, when we were children? A sort of household tyrant that everyone went in fear of? James is just like his father. He's a little more subtle about it, that's all.' She bit her lower lip, and Peter realized that her eyes were bright with tears. 'I don't like it, you understand, but I can live with it.'

'Then what is it?'

'Two things happened yesterday. Actually, I blame you for one of them.' She looked at him and lifted the corners of her mouth in a way that made the words not an accusation but a compliment. 'I'll show you.'

Kate pushed the baggy left-hand sleeve of her jacket up to her elbow. She unbuttoned the white cuff of the shirt underneath and slowly folded it six inches above the wrist.

Her forearm was rounded, lightly tanned and speckled with tiny golden hairs. With her right hand she pointed out the line of four dark-blue bruises.

Peter said, 'But Kate . . .'

She turned the arm so he could see the paler, smoother

skin on the other side. Here was another bruise – darker and larger than the others. Along part of its edge ran a sickle-shaped line of dried blood.

Kate touched the scratch and glanced at Peter. 'That's where he dug in his thumbnail.'

On the threshold Barbara paused to listen. Leo was humming, which made up her mind for her. She went into the drawing room. He did not look up. She eyed him covertly as she drew the curtains and lit the gas fire. If she were going to do it at all, it might as well be now.

The omens were good. He was in the wing armchair he used when he wanted to relax. His short legs stuck out from his tubby body and rested on an upholstered footstool. He had undone the buttons of his waistcoat and the waistband of his trousers. On the table beside him was his second glass of a wine he particularly liked – an underpriced Italian Chardonnay which he looked upon as a personal discovery. The air smelled faintly of the liver casserole that was approaching perfection in the kitchen; Leo had a weakness for liver casserole. Pencil in hand, he was engrossed in a bookseller's catalogue. In front of him stretched ten days of interrupted leisure. And of course he was humming.

Barbara opened her mouth, closed it and decided that before she did anything else she would rearrange the family cards on the mantelpiece.

Leo's humming infuriated Barbara. It reassured her too, because it meant that he was happy. It consisted of the same handful of funereal notes, repeated endlessly with minuscule variations of pitch and pace. Once she had asked him what, if anything, the tune was supposed to be; and he, surprised that she had needed to ask, had said it was the opening bars of Dvorak's New World Symphony.

The humming stopped. Leo looked up over his glasses.

'It's a pity Kate couldn't stay,' he said. 'But I must say it's rather nice to be on our own.'

'Yes. That's what I was thinking. Just the two of us.'

He pushed the glasses back up his nose and turned a page of the catalogue. 'Are you planning to tell me?' he asked. 'Or do you think you'd rather spend the rest of the evening fiddling with the Christmas cards?'

'Tell you? What do you mean?'

'Only you know that, my love. Come on, it'll make you feel better.'

One of the cards toppled over and fluttered down to the hearth. She made as if to pick it up.

'Leave it for a moment.' Leo swung his legs off the footstool and, having marked his place with the pencil, put the catalogue on the table. 'Come and sit here and tell me all about it.'

She did as she was ordered. Her knees felt weak. She knew that it would be easy to cry.

'I lied to you,' she said. 'I'm sorry.'

'About Peter Redburn?'

She nodded.

'Is that the real reason why you don't want to go Carinish Court? Because he might be there?'

'Yes. It wasn't all a lie. I meant what I said the other day – about him reminding me of Richard. But it wasn't all the truth, either. You see, before we got married

I told you that the only other person had been Hubert. I – I didn't want to put you off.'

He sat back, sipped his wine and waited. She glanced up at him through her eyelashes, wishing that he would say something, wishing that she had never started.

'The first one was a man I used to work for. That was before I met Hubert. He was married. I wasn't in love with him or anything like that.' Now she was fully launched, Barbara forgot the little speech she had so carefully prepared. 'He was a bit like you, actually, but not so kind. And then, just once – it was an accident, really, I didn't even enjoy it: there was Peter himself. Kate had just left him – I told you about that, didn't I? Well, I was trying to comfort him, that's all it was. It happened a few weeks before I left Hubert. For some reason I told Peter about the man I used to work for. I think I was trying to make him feel less guilty. I've been so worried you'd find out. I can't tell you how worried.'

'But why?' Leo said.

'Don't you see? It would be so embarrassing to meet Peter. He's got quite the wrong idea about me.' The more she said, the more foolish she sounded; but she pressed on: 'And of course I was afraid he'd let something slip, and you'd realize I'd lied to you and . . .'

On cue, the tears rolled down her cheeks.

'. . . you'd hate me for ever.'

Leo shuffled his bottom forward to the edge of the chair and put his arms around her. 'You're very silly.' He rubbed his cheek, which at this time of day was uncomfortably rough with bristles, against hers. 'I guessed there might have been other people. From the first.'

Outraged, she stopped crying for a moment. 'How?'

'By the things you suggested we did, and by your description of Hubert. The two didn't tally.'

'You never said.' Memories surged through her mind, and she knew that she was blushing.

'What did it matter?' He hummed three notes deep in his throat. 'You could say that I was their beneficiary.'

'You brute,' she said. 'I've been worrying myself sick for days.'

He lifted his head and smiled at her. 'Is the casserole all right? It's not burning, is it?'

Barbara kissed him and, glad of the excuse, rushed into the kitchen. She was still crying, but this time the tears were tears of relief.

Nothing was wrong with the casserole. She suspected that Leo had pretended to smell burning as a way of bringing the conversation to an end. As she was sliding the dish back into the oven, she realized that there was one thing she had forgotten to mention to him. She decided to leave it, at least for the time being.

Leo wanted to relax. In any case, she couldn't face screwing herself up to a confessional pitch twice in the same evening. Dinner was nearly ready. Besides, when she came to think about it, what was the point of telling him? It added nothing of importance to what he already knew. If the news had any effect at all, it would simply upset him: it was too close to home; he would wonder why she had left it out and whether she were telling the whole truth; he might also wonder if its omission meant that it had some special significance for her that the others lacked.

Which was nonsense, of course. She poured herself

half a glass of wine and carried it into the sitting room. There had never been anything significant about Ralph Salperton.

'Has it happened before?' Peter asked.

'Once or twice,' Kate said. 'Usually it's verbal or he punishes me in other ways, like not giving me enough money or making me look stupid in public. This is the first time he's actually marked me.'

From the other side of the Mortbank Room came a long sigh. The elderly Indian by the fire stood up and shuffled over to the table where the magazines were kept. This brought him within earshot of Peter and Kate. The Indian returned the *Illustrated London News* to its place, sighed again and shuffled to the door.

Peter watched the man's movements, willing him to hurry. As the door closed, he said: 'So why does James do it?'

Kate blew her nose. 'He likes to be in control. He likes to feel that he's the boss. He's got this idea in his mind of how his life ought to be, and when life doesn't measure up to the idea he takes it out on people. On me.'

'Surely he can't blame you for everything that goes wrong for him?'

'Can't he? Why not? I'm nearer than anyone else, and more dependent on him. I'm the natural victim. If he hasn't got a reason to attack me, he just makes one up. He's says I'm not appreciating him enough or I ironed the wrong shirt or whatever comes into his mind.' She hesitated, and then went on in a rush: 'Yesterday it was because of you.'

'I saw you on Tuesday – three days ago. Why the delay?'

'He likes to think about his injuries.' Kate shivered. 'It's as if he needs to whip himself up. He gets jealous very easily. Sometimes I've only to smile at another man and that's enough.'

'You don't have to put up with it. You could leave him.'

'I'm scared.'

'He couldn't hurt you.'

'Couldn't he? He once said that if I tried to leave him he'd disfigure my face so no one else would ever have me.'

Peter glanced at her. The threat shocked him more than anything else had done. Kate's face was perfect: to mar it would be a form of sacrilege. For his own sake as much as hers, he tried to put what James had said in a different, less menacing perspective. 'It's easy to say that sort of thing in the heat of the moment.'

'He means it. Oh God, I suppose I'd better tell you. Have you ever heard of someone called Hugo Mannering?'

The conversation had reached a watershed. Until now it had confined itself to a domestic quarrel – unpleasant, certainly, and even violent, but not so very different in essence from a million other conjugal conflicts. With Mannering, however, they had come without warning to the borders of a darker landscape, a place without maps.

'The man who almost got the part of Darcy. Yes, I know about his' – Peter's fingers sketched inverted commas around the next word – 'accident.'

'How?'

'Ursula told me.'

Kate swung to face him. 'You've seen her? When?'

'On Wednesday. Does that make you angry?'

The strain ebbed from her face. 'I'm sorry,' she said. 'I was surprised. No, it's more than that – Ursula hates me, doesn't she, and I was afraid of what she might have told you.'

'You had no need to be,' Peter said – roughly, for he felt as if Kate had thrown doubt on his loyalty to her. 'Ursula also believes that James tried to kill her. It was while they were still married. She claims that he arranged an accident for her on the stairs at their cottage.'

'It wouldn't surprise me.'

'Tell me, how do you know about Mannering? That must have happened long before you met James again.'

'It was mentioned in one of the anonymous letters,' Kate said. 'But why did you go and see Ursula? You don't know her, do you?'

'I've never met her before. I wanted to ask her what she thought of James. What's this about anonymous letters?'

'I get them every now and then, ever since I married James. Not many – four altogether. They're always the same – The message is pricked with a pin. Usually they're very short – things like *Your husband nearly killed Hugo Mannering to get the part of Darcy.*'

'Have you told the police?'

'What's the point? Ursula must write them. It's rather sad. She's still in love with him, I think.' Kate saw the next question in Peter's face. 'No, James doesn't know about the letters. Things are bad enough between them

340

as it is. But you still haven't told me why you went to see her.'

'And you haven't told me the second thing that happened yesterday.'

'Two questions,' Kate said. 'Maybe one answer.'

She opened her bag and took out a small brown envelope, which she gave to Peter. It was addressed to Kate at Montpelier Square, but the address was typewritten and the envelope was unstamped. Inside was a single sheet of paper torn from a short-hand pad. At first Peter thought it was blank. Then he saw the pinpricks that filled the first two lines of the page. They were so small as to be almost invisible in the dimly lit room. He stood up and held the paper against a table lamp. The letters were unnaturally regular, as if the writer had used a stencil.

Ask James what happened to your brother.

'Is that why you went to see Ursula? Is that why you're helping with James's book? Is that why you're coming to Carinish Court for Christmas?'

With each question Kate's voice became higher and higher, louder and louder. Her face had lost its natural colouring, and her pupils were tiny. The vast, blue-green emptiness of the Mortbank Room made her small and vulnerable: a child once more, lost in an adult world.

Peter took a step towards her. 'Yes,' he said. 'I think James may have killed Richard.'

Richard, too, had been lost in a world that was beyond his understanding.

At the time Richard's behaviour irritated and embarrassed Peter. He remembered thinking – as he came down the stairs at Carinish Court on that Saturday evening in the middle of August – that Richard was becoming more and more tiresome. The detective in Murder in the Dark is never murdered, and therefore never screams. But Richard had screamed, presumably because he was afraid of the dark; or perhaps the creeping footsteps around him had temporarily destroyed his self-control.

By now the car on the drive had reached the house. Its engine died. Doors slammed. The kindest thing to do, Peter felt, was to pretend that nothing out of the way had happened: that the game had ended before its natural conclusion simply because the grown-ups had at last come back from their party.

Almost immediately, Peter's attention was diverted from Richard. John Redburn appeared in the doorway. His eyes were closed. Peter had never before seen a man in such naked pain; it hurt to look at him. Hubert Molland and Ralph Salperton were holding his arms, almost carrying him. They brought him into the house and took him upstairs. Behind them stalked Lucasta Redburn. As she passed Peter in the hall, she did not speak to him or even throw him a glance.

'It's nothing to worry about, Peter.' Barbara Molland patted Peter's arm. 'Your father got a little tired. The party went on much longer than anyone expected. He'll be as right as rain in the morning.'

As right as rain? What a stupid thing to say, Peter thought. Rain was wrong – everyone complained like anything when it rained. He felt sick when he thought of those unanswered prayers to the god of the Christians. How stupid he had been. How childish. He was aware that Kate and James were whispering to each other.

'Would you like some coffee?' Mary Salperton said, her eyes wandering up the stairs. 'Oh, and there are sandwiches, aren't there? I almost forgot.'

'We've had ours,' Ginny said.

'That's very kind of you,' Barbara said, 'but I really think we should be getting home. Hubert will have to be up early.'

The two women exchanged glances.

'Of course,' Mrs Salperton said. 'I must admit I don't feel hungry myself. The Morgans' snacks were quite substantial.'

Five minutes later Peter and the Mollands were in the Rover. No one spoke on the way back to Abbotsfield. Mrs Molland packed the children off to bed as soon as they reached the Vicarage. Richard and Kate went into their bedrooms, leaving Peter to use the bathroom before them. He noticed that they avoided looking at him.

When he came out of the bathroom, Richard was waiting for him on the landing. He beckoned Peter into his room.

'What is it?' Peter said. 'Can't it wait till morning?'

That night he didn't want to talk to anyone. He wanted to burrow under his eiderdown and fall asleep as quickly as possible.

Richard shook his head. 'This is important.' He stood aside to let Peter into the room. He shut the door and pointed at the bed.

'What are you on about?'

'On the pillow, you fool,' Richard snapped.

Peter stared. In the middle of the pillow was a black feather. The tips curled at the edges. It was a glossy black, as if it had been freshly plucked from a living bird.

'Do you –' Richard swallowed. 'Do you think it could be a raven's feather?'

'Well, it's black and I suppose ravens are black,' Peter said. 'Where did you get it from?'

'Nowhere. I just found it on my pillow.'

'But how did it get there?'

'That's what I'd like to know. It wasn't on the pillow before we went to Carinish Court this morning. I'm sure of that, because I was up here just before we left. I'd have noticed it. Dad locked all the doors and windows when we went out – he always does. When we got back, I was the first person to come upstairs.'

'Maybe someone broke in.'

Peter meant to mock, but Richard took the suggestion seriously. 'To leave a feather on my pillow?' he said. 'Who?'

'How should I know? It wasn't me.'

'I never said it was.' Richard lowered his voice. 'But it must be someone who knows about Mithras.'

'That means James or Kate. Or maybe Ginny.'

'She wouldn't do something like this. Anyway, she was at Carinish Court. And so were James and Kate.'

'One of them could have biked over this afternoon. We don't know where they were all the time.'

'But how did they get in?'

'Perhaps Kate left a window open.'

'Perhaps.' Richard sat down on the end of the bed and stared at the feather. 'She'd never admit it.'

'The feather must have got there somehow. Kate and James are the most likely people, aren't they? It's just a joke, Richard – can't you see? A message from Mithras.'

'I could believe that if it weren't for the other thing. There's no explanation for that.'

'I wish you'd talk sense.'

Richard glanced at him. 'That isn't the first feather. It's the second. I found the first on the floor at Carinish Court.' He winced at the memory. 'When Ginny switched the lights back on, after I yelled out.'

Peter lost his temper. Richard's problems seemed insignificant beside his own. Hubert Molland wasn't dying. He asked, with malice in his voice, 'By the way, why did you scream?'

'It's not what you think. I wasn't scared of the dark. If I tell you, will you promise not to tell anyone?'

'All right.'

'On your blood oath as an Emorian gentleman?'

'I said all right.'

'I counted a hundred. I didn't know where any of you were, though I could hear people moving around. Then I went in the cupboard and switched out the lights. And when I came out, someone grabbed me.'

'You're making it up.'

'I am not. Someone really strong. An arm went over my mouth and another arm round my chest. I tried to bite the arm but nothing happened. I couldn't speak, I couldn't move, I could hardly breathe. Something brushed my cheek and it felt like the wing of a bird. And a voice said over and over again, "A raven for Mithras, a raven for Mithras."'

He glanced at the feather and stopped. Peter waited.

Despite himself he was impressed. Richard's hands were shaking. The fear was real, if nothing else.

'Then, just before the arms let go of me, the voice said, "The first feather. Look on the floor." And when I was free I just screamed. You'd have screamed, wouldn't you? Anyone would have screamed. A bit later, Ginny switched on the lights. I looked down at my feet and I saw the feather.'

Peter sat down beside Richard. He felt very old and very wise. 'Look – someone was playing a game on you, trying to frighten you. It must have been James.'

Richard shook his head. 'It was someone bigger. Anyway, James couldn't have sneaked back without my seeing him. Nor could you or Kate or Ginny. There wasn't time.'

'Okay. So James got a friend to hide in the house and pounce on you. What was the voice like?'

'Just a whisper. You know – hoarse. I couldn't even tell if it was a man or a woman. But it can't have been a friend of James's. Don't you remember – we drew lots for the detective and the murderer? James couldn't have known I'd get the ace.' Richard felt in his pocket and took out a feather – more battered than the one on the pillow but in other respects its twin. 'It's no use. I've got to face facts.'

'How do you mean?'

'Like my father did.'

'You're crazy,' Peter said. Really he wondered if he himself were going mad; either that or he was dreaming or running a temperature. He got up and stumbled towards the door. 'I've got to go to bed. I'll see you in the morning.'

He went along the landing to his own room, switched on the light and shut the door behind him. Was Mithras real? Had the god somehow come to life again because they had brought him into Emor? He picked up his pyjamas, which were folded on top of the pillow. A black feather was lying underneath them. It twitched in the draught as though it were a living thing.

'Oh Christ,' Peter said.

He put a hand over his mouth and shut his eyes. It was no use calling on Christ. The god of the Christians wouldn't help him, any more than he would help John Redburn get better. Either Christ didn't exist or Christ had abandoned them to another god.

Peter groaned. He slumped to his knees and rested his forehead on the bed, his eyes still closed so that he wouldn't see the feather. In his mind he saw his father's face and tried to feel his pain. The pain was more real than any god could ever be.

'Dear Mithras,' he muttered. It was worth trying. But how were you supposed to pray to Mithras? The rituals in the Mithraeum – which really consisted of no more than the Raven initiation ceremony – gave Peter no guidance. How did you talk to Mithras on personal terms?

'Dear Mithras, forgive me my sins and make my father get well. Through the raven and the blood of the bull, amen.'

After that he felt better, as if he had transferred the responsibility for his father's pain to someone else. He had done what he could. If Mithras existed, he might help; if not the prayer had done no harm.

He pulled off his clothes and dropped them on the

floor. Before he got into the bed he shook his pillow out of the window. He could not bring himself to touch the feather.

In the morning his father phoned the Vicarage, just as Peter and the Mollands were getting ready for church.

'Hello, old son,' John Redburn said, and his voice sounded much stronger. 'How are you? I thought I'd give you a ring before we leave. Sorry I was such a wet blanket last night.'

The Imperial Propaganda Office put it about that the Emperor Jacobus I was killed while fighting the Babylonians on the Eastern Front. This was untrue. In fact he died of drink whilst in the arms of his concubine. The People of Emor were astounded to learn that Jacobus had willed the throne to this same concubine, Valeria Messalina Mollandia, and such a flagrant contravention of tradition and decency led to riots in Emor and all the major cities of the empire. The Pontifex Maximus, a cousin of Jacobus I, used his religious position to sway the army in her favour. Petronius Redburnus, who held the key position of the Exchequer, also supported her bid for power. Messalina bribed the secret police, who crushed all who spoke against her. It is said that she personally crucified three Senators who dared to oppose her. Thus she terrorized the Senate into approving the late emperor's will, and became the first Empress Regnant of Emor. It was a sad day for the empire. The Court was given over to all sorts of lewd lasciviousness. Only Gaius Marcus Mollandius had the strength of will to resist the new regime. He remained at Court as Lord High Admiral and Director of Foreign Trade and Commerce. Secretly he became the head of an organization which aimed to overthrow Messalina and restore the old monarchy. To add to his problems, Mollandius was assailed at this time by grave religious doubts. The god Mithras had shown him

personally several examples of his supernatural powers. (The first of
these, a miraculous visitation, in fact took place during the reign of
Jacobus, but the signs and portents mainly occurred during the opening
years of Messalina's reign.) But was Mithras a god or a devil?

Kate became Empress of Emor on Monday 17 August.

The 'signs and portents' continued for the whole of
that week. Almost every day Richard found a black
feather: in the pages of a book he was reading, in his
Wellington boot, on his dressing table. Once he heard
a voice whispering at his bedroom window as he lay
drifting towards sleep: 'Mithras needs another raven.'
On another occasion the water in the glass by his bed
changed during the day into a small deposit of what
looked like dried blood.

Richard believed – unwillingly but with increasing
conviction – that Mithras was making a bid to convert
him, just as Christ had converted his father by appearing
miraculously in a railway carriage. With such an example
before him, divine intervention in his own life seemed
strange but by no means impossible. He explained to
Peter that obviously Christ must be real as well; otherwise Hubert Molland would not have seen him. Therefore, he argued, Mithras was either the same as Christ,
or the devil in disguise. This uncertainty was now the
only reason he gave for his reluctance to join the cult
of Mithras.

Peter suspected that there was another reason for
Richard's hesitation, a reason that had nothing to do
with theology. To accept Mithras would be to accept
what James and Kate had done to Emor. Richard
devised a plan that would allow him to capitulate to

Mithras on his own terms. He explained some of this to Peter on the evening of Saturday 22 August.

In its original form, the plan came to this. On Sunday night, Richard would undergo the Raven Ceremony – with certain Christian modifications that were designed to cover the possibility that Mithras was really Satan in disguise. Peter was due to become emperor on Monday. Richard wanted him to cancel the edict that had made the worship of Mithras the state religion of Emor. If James and Kate disagreed, Richard urged Peter to split the empire.

'There's no point,' Peter said. 'We'll be going home next week.'

'So will Kate. I don't want her in Emor when we get back. I want this settled now. I want them to realize who's in control.'

'Does it matter?'

'Of course it does. Think what the others will say next term if we have to have an empress and all this Mithras business.'

'We might not do Emor next term.'

'Don't be stupid. It's up to you. If you want to help the counter-revolution, that's fine. If not, you'll have to take the consequences.'

Richard's determination was impressive but Peter didn't take it too seriously; melodramatic statements and strategies were part and parcel of Emor. However, he did wonder if this time Richard had something in reserve, a secret weapon in the armoury of the counter-revolutionaries.

Richard thought that Emor would last for ever and ever. Peter knew that it would end, perhaps with the summer. Richard believed in God, whether Christ or Mithras. Perhaps he was naturally religious. Peter wasn't. He had flirted with both gods when he needed them but, as the crisis had passed, so had his taste for religion. His father was going to get better.

The miracles puzzled Peter, and he was relieved that they were happening to Richard and (apart from the single feather under his pyjamas) not to him. However, he thought about them surprisingly little during the last week at Abbotsfield. What was the point? They were inexplicable, like so much else that had happened to him this summer. Besides, he had other things on his mind. His main concerns were to stay friends with everyone – Richard, Kate and James – and to spend as much time as possible at Carinish Court. As a result he was completely unprepared for the events of Sunday 23 August.

Kate held out her hand to Peter. He took it. She drew him back to the sofa. This time they sat so close that their bodies were almost touching, as if they were children huddling together for security. She kept hold of his hand.

The Mortbank Room was full of shadows. Peter heard a distant roar, like the wind blowing through the leaves and branches of a great tree; the Christmas celebrations were continuing below them. He felt the throbbing of a pulse against a fingertip, and he didn't know if it were Kate's pulse or his or even both pulses beating together.

'It doesn't seem possible,' Kate whispered. 'Oh God. Poor Richard.'

Her hand twitched in his. The pulse stopped.

'We don't know he was murdered,' Peter said. 'Not for sure.'

'What made you start thinking about it again? It's all so long ago.'

'When I was clearing out my mother's house I found a box of Emor papers your mother gave me. One of them I'd never seen before. Richard wrote it at Abbotsfield. It's called *The Secret History of Emor*, and it's almost like a diary. He must have written the last few lines just before he went to the Mithraeum. You remember he was going to be initiated as a Raven that night. Because of the miracles.'

Kate frowned. 'The miracles?'

Peter realized that she was struggling to remember about Mithras and the miracles. In the last week his memories of that summer had become so vivid that he found it difficult to grasp that hers were still buried beneath the intervening events of twenty-five years.

'Oh I remember,' she said. 'The feathers and the other tricks.'

'Tricks?'

'Didn't you know? James arranged them all. He was obsessed about getting Richard to become a Raven. All part of wanting to be the boss, I suppose. He hasn't changed.'

'But how did he do it?'

'Frank Timball helped him. You remember? The vicar's son, with the motorbike? Ginny was in love with him. I think Frank must have been a little in love with James. Mary told me that he's gay now. Anyway, it began with that game of Murder. James fiddled the cards beforehand so Richard would get the ace. Frank was hiding in the study. When the lights went out, he grabbed Richard.'

'What about the feathers and things at the Vicarage?'

'Frank had a key. It was easy.'

Peter felt a sense of loss. The age of miracles was over. He said, 'Richard was expecting to meet James in the Mithraeum.'

'What were they going to do?'

'It's hard to tell exactly. The *Secret History* puts everything in Emorian terms. I think Richard was planning some sort of blackmail. He was very upset about Emor.'

'About James and me being in it? I know. I feel bad about that.'

'So do I.'

Kate squeezed his hand. 'We couldn't have known what would happen. What was Richard going to do?'

'I think he wanted to humiliate James. Give him a state trial or something – you, too. He wanted Emor to be his again. That's what really upset him, the fact that Emor was out of his control.'

'Was that all?'

'No.' *The Court was given over to all sorts of lewd lasciviousness.* Peter looked at the carpet. 'He'd seen you and James kissing. Hell, it was an awkward age for all of us. He thought it was – well, evil, I suppose. Utterly wrong.'

'He didn't want to grow up.'

'Maybe. I made it worse for him. In his eyes I was a traitor. I've got a letter he wrote to Bill Coleby – do you remember him at Plumford? He was in Emor at school. Richard must have posted it on the way to the Mithraeum. He said he was going to seize the throne and exile me for ever from Emor. And he mentioned you and James: he said you were sinful people and he was going to make you both wish that you'd never been born.'

'I suppose he meant he'd tell my father about James kissing me.' Kate shivered.

Peter thought about how Hubert Molland had reacted to the broken glass of the picture frame and understood the shiver. 'But it doesn't explain everything,' he said. 'James wouldn't have suffered. Only you.'

'I think I can guess what he had in store for James. I – I don't know if I should tell you this.'

The answer leaped at Peter. 'Is it something to do with my father?'

Kate let go of his hand. 'How do you know? Surely Richard didn't tell you?'

'I found a letter Mary Salperton wrote to him.' Peter struggled to assess the implications. 'Who told you about it?'

'Richard. He was trying to make me see the error of my ways. He went on and on about how wicked James was and about how I still had time to save my soul. And I laughed at him. You know how funny he could be when he was being pious. I couldn't help laughing. And he said, "James is a bastard, do you know that? We shouldn't have anything to do with him." He'd overheard your father talking to Mary, I think. He heard enough to realize that they'd had an affair, and that James was your father's son.'

'And my brother,' Peter said. 'I didn't know for sure. Ginny might have been the bastard, you see. Are you certain it was James?'

'Richard was.'

'It's the motive, don't you see?'

'Hush,' Kate murmured. 'Someone might hear.'

'Think how it would have affected someone as conceited as James,' Peter said in a rush. 'How he'd hate it if everyone knew. It'd be bad enough now but then it would have been even worse. In nineteen sixty-four people were still ashamed of bastards, especially in places like Abbotsfield. And especially someone like Ralph, with his family history. Have you told James about it?'

'Of course not. I thought it was better forgotten. I thought it didn't matter any more.'

'Thank God for that.'

'What do you mean?'

'He killed Richard to shut his mouth,' Peter said. 'That's what I mean. And since then he's tried to kill other people. What makes you think he'd stop at you?'

'Or you.'

'I don't follow.'

Kate swept the hair from her forehead. 'Perhaps I'm being paranoid. I know he needs you to help him with his book. But suppose there was another reason why he suddenly wanted to see you again: to find out if you knew anything about his mother's affair with your father. Perhaps he was scared you'd tell Ginny, and Ginny would tell Ursula. It would destroy him. It would destroy the picture he's got of himself – do you see? And if he discovers that you've been asking questions about that summer, he's going to suspect something's up, isn't he?'

'Calm down. He doesn't know a thing. He can't do.'

'And now of course he's got another reason to hate you. Peter . . .' – Kate took his hand again – '. . . please don't come down to Carinish Court. I'm scared. Make some excuse. He's dangerous.'

Peter gripped her hand. He noticed what a woman would have noticed long before: that this evening she wasn't wearing a wedding ring.

'What's the other reason?' he said.

'He's jealous of you, and this time it's different. I'm sure he's guessed how I feel.'

Seventeen

'Must we have turkey?'

'Yes,' said Ginny. 'It just wouldn't be Christmas without the turkey.'

David Quest's swarthy cheeks bulged, and he made his eyes pop out in mock dismay. 'It was worth a try.'

He collected their pudding bowls and took them into the kitchen. Ginny noticed that there was a hole in the seat of his jeans. The shoulders of his baggy jersey were streaked with white, as if he had incautiously propped himself up against a freshly painted wall. David's attraction for her, like God's, was wholly mysterious. He had spilled a drop of wine on the unvarnished pine surface of the table. Ginny's finger shaped the stain into a heart.

David came back with the cheeseboard and a bowl of fruit. His mind was still on the turkey. 'We could easily stick it in the freezer,' he said. 'There's still time. Or perhaps we could give it to a poor but worthy woman with a family of hungry mouths to feed. Isn't that what you Christians like to do? Don't you think that Ralph would much rather we had a brace of pheasants?'

Ginny soaked up the heart with her paper napkin. 'I'm quite sure he wouldn't. Did you remember the crackers?'

'Yes. They were amazingly expensive.' David pretended that the palm of his left hand was a sheet of paper, and with his right index finger he scribbled a series of ticks against the items on an invisible list. 'And I also remembered the mince pies, the chestnuts for the stuffing, and the little coloured balls and strips of tinsel to go on the tree.'

Ginny frowned at his levity, which she considered misplaced. 'I brought the Christmas pudding. Have you any brandy to pour over it?'

'I have got everything.' David reached for the wine bottle. 'Don't worry. I'm the perfect host.'

'You must let me know how much it all cost.'

He refilled her glass. 'No, I mustn't. This is my pleasure. I sold a couple of pictures on Thursday.'

'You didn't!'

'Don't sound so surprised. And you'll never guess how much I got for the pair. Nine hundred quid.'

They were both a little drunk. Ginny had driven down to Bristol during the morning, expecting to seize a sandwich and then spend Saturday afternoon rushing round the shops to buy all the things that David had forgotten. Instead she had found a three-course lunch waiting for her. By now they were halfway down the second bottle of Rioja. As far as she could tell David hadn't forgotten anything. It was most disconcerting.

'Do you want to go to Paris in the New Year? Ursula said we could stay at her house.'

'With or without Ursula?'

'Without her.'

'Okay.'

The wine made her careless. 'You don't like her very much, do you? I hadn't realized that before.'

'I wouldn't say I don't like her. Not exactly.'

David began to peel an apple with a penknife. She

watched, half-hypnotized by the deftness of his fingers. Usually he left an unbroken coil of peel on the plate. Perhaps it was a private superstition. It occurred to her how little she knew of him, of Ursula, of anyone.

When he had reached the halfway point in his peeling, she said, 'Ursula can seem a little – I don't know – overwhelming.'

'It's not that,' he said. 'There's something sour about her. And she gives the impression that she's the only friend you've got. I think I'm probably jealous. Talking of friends, have you seen anything of Peter?'

'Not since he took me out to lunch on Tuesday. He's going down to Carinish Court for Christmas. Which reminds me, Kate asked us over for lunch on Wednesday. A sort of family housewarming, I think.' She glanced at David. 'I said no because they're not asking Ralph. In fact I implied he'd still be with us. I suppose we could go if you want to meet Peter.'

The penknife stopped moving. 'But you'd rather not?'

Ginny nodded. The sky was the colour of ashes and the shadows were already invading David's living room.

'Has something happened? You're not quite so enthusiastic about him as you were last weekend.'

'Peter frightens me a bit.' Put into words, it at once sounded not so much frightening as ridiculous. 'He's so interested in the past, in Abbotsfield. Obsessed, even. It's as if he's trying to expiate something and doesn't quite know how to do it. He even went to see Ursula.'

'About Abbotsfield? But she wasn't there.'

'I know. Apparently he was trying to find out from her what James was like when they were married. And whether Ursula could tell him if James was involved in what happened to Kate's brother.'

The knife sliced across the strip of peel. David swore at it.

'Don't get tangled up in that, love,' he said. 'It was a long time ago.'

'That's what my mother says. Let sleeping dogs lie.' Suddenly Ginny was angry. 'Typical. You know what really concerns her? She thinks Richard Molland may have known about her and John Redburn.'

'That's neither here nor there, surely?'

Ginny focused with difficulty on her glass. She was surprised to see that it was empty again. The anger receded, leaving sadness behind. I've never told anyone this,' she said. 'And I wouldn't be telling you if I weren't drunk. But I know for a fact James wasn't in his bed that night.'

'The night it happened?'

'Yes. Sunday the twenty-third of August nineteen sixty-four.' The date rolled off her tongue. 'I couldn't sleep. It was very bright – there was a full moon, I think. I don't know what time it was but I got up and had a look in James's room. His bed was empty.'

'Why?'

'You mean why was it empty?'

'No. I mean why did you look?'

'I never told you about Frank, did I? Our local vicar's son.' Of course she hadn't: she hugged her humiliations to herself. 'He was three years older than me and I thought he was God Almighty for at least eighteen months. He was in trouble with the police that summer, and we helped him. Afterwards, James used to sneak out with him at night. He'd climb out of his window, and off they'd go on Frank's motorbike. God, I was jealous. I saw them once, running across the lawn together.'

'Here,' David said. He pushed a clean paper napkin towards her.

She realized that she was crying. 'This is stupid. I thought I heard them outside, you see, and I had to go and check. It was like having to pick a scab – I couldn't stop myself.'

'You still care, don't you?'

'Not any more. I was jealous of my brother. And do you know what? Frank's gay. I never even suspected it. Maybe Frank didn't, either. He was always going out with village girls. I suppose he was trying to prove something. They said he got someone pregnant. But the last my mother heard he was living in Islington with an architect. A man, I mean.'

'There's nothing wrong with falling in love with someone who's not in love with you. You assumed that James was with Frank that night?'

'Well, of course. What else was there to think? It was only when Ursula told me about Peter that I began to wonder. Maybe James wasn't with Frank. Maybe –'

'Ginny,' David interrupted. 'Just stop it, will you? It's over. Water under the bridge.'

'Stop being so bloody reasonable,' Ginny shouted. 'You're just like your father.'

'To go back to Frank –'

'You look a bit like him. Same size, same colouring. I expect he's podgy, too. Sometimes I think that's why I –' She broke off, flushing.

David nodded, as if agreeing with the words she

hadn't said. 'Quite possibly. I believe it's a common pattern – that people tend to fancy one particular type. But there's one big difference between me and Frank. I happen to love you.'

All the Salpertons, even Ralph, went to church on Sunday 23 August 1964. They were obliged to pay their respects to God because the Mollands had invited them to the Vicarage for drinks after the service. Ginny complained about this as they drove to Abbotsfield.

'I know it's tiresome,' Mary Salperton said. 'But one could hardly drink the Mollands' sherry without putting in an appearance at church. It wouldn't be tactful. Besides it's their last Sunday. They're going home on Tuesday.'

'Good.'

'Don't be silly, dear.'

'If you don't stop whining, madam,' Ralph snapped, 'you won't be getting any pocket money this week.'

Ginny knew that Frank would not be in church but she prayed in vain for a glimpse of him as they drove into Abbotsfield. During the service she noticed the glances that Kate and James exchanged. Ralph bellowed the responses and the hymns with a vigour that was all the more apparent for his inability to sing in tune; he called it 'giving a lead to the villagers', and this assumption of quasi-feudal responsibility made Ginny squirm with embarrassment. Mr Nimp, his face gleaming with sweat even in the cool of the church, took the collection. You dirty old man, Ginny thought.

Afterwards the Mollands and the Salpertons trooped down the churchyard, across the lane and up the sun-baked mud of the Vicarage drive. Everyone moved slowly, as if debilitated not only by the warmth of the day but also by a summer that had dragged on too long. As they went into the shabby drawing room, they disturbed a bluebottle; it droned in long, lethargic loops from wall to wall and slipped through the open window.

The refreshments had already been laid out on a round table with a pitted brass top. Ginny examined them without enthusiasm: cheese straws, Ritz crackers, salted nuts; South African sherry and orange squash. They did things very differently at Carinish Court. This, Ginny thought, must be how poor people live.

Prompted by their mother, Kate and Richard handed round the snacks. Mr and Mrs Molland poured the drinks with a clumsiness that hinted at lack of practice. Ginny overheard a snatch of their conversation.

'We shall have to put the furniture back before we go,' Hubert murmured. 'We must leave everything just as we found it.'

'You must be joking,' Barbara said. 'Even the dust and the dirt?'

Hubert opened his mouth to say something but shut it when he realized that Ginny's parents had moved within earshot. He handed Mary Salperton a very small glass of sherry.

'Let me top you up,' Barbara said. 'You've barely got a thimbleful.'

Mary held out her glass. 'We're having a few people round for bridge after dinner,' she said. 'We'd be delighted if you both could come.'

Ginny knew this was a half-truth. Her mother had originally asked the Morgans for the evening; but yesterday evening Mrs Morgan had phoned to say that her husband was in bed with influenza. It was Ralph who had suggested asking the Mollands in their place. Mary had reluctantly agreed to give it a try, though she thought that Hubert might disapprove of card-playing on Sunday; and in any case, she said, his presence at a bridge-table would almost certainly be more of a liability than an asset.

'It's very kind of you.' Mr Molland backed away. 'But I'm afraid we can't spare the time. Packing and so forth.'

'Nonsense, Hubert,' Mrs Molland said. 'We've got plenty of time.'

'And then there's the children. I don't like the thought of leaving them on their own.'

'In that case you can stay here and babysit. I'll go by myself.'

'But how will you get there?'

'No problem there, old chap,' Ralph said. 'I'll fetch her and bring her back.' He smiled at Hubert. 'Door-to-door service. I promise we'll take good care of her.'

'I really don't think we should trespass on your good nature,' Hubert said.

'Not at all – it's my pleasure.'

'Good,' Mary Salperton said. 'Well, that's settled. Would half-past eight suit you?'

Barbara nodded. She picked up a glass of sherry from the tray and drank most of it in one swallow.

Hubert turned away to pour himself some orange squash.

Mary said in an undertone, 'I do hope we haven't upset him.'

Barbara looked at her and winked.

During the sherry party, as so often that summer, Ginny did not know what to do with herself. She swung between the two groups, adults and children, partially accepted by both but belonging to neither. Her self-awareness crippled her, forcing her into the role of observer. People talked in front of her as though she were not there or, at best, a household pet with limited powers of understanding. Perhaps they saw right through her and knew how little she counted in the scheme of things.

Holding a glass of orange squash in one hand and a Ritz cracker in the other, she drifted away from the adults towards the open French windows. Kate, James, Richard and Peter were already in the garden. None of them spared her a glance. She guessed they were playing the Emor game.

Richard was talking earnestly to James, who listened with his head thrown back and his lips twisted with amusement. As Ginny watched, Richard broke away and walked slowly down the garden towards the clump of trees at the end.

'Well, young lady,' Hubert said behind her. 'How do you feel about Latin now?'

Ginny jumped, almost spilling her orange squash. Mr Molland towered over her. For the first time she noticed how worried he looked. His forehead was seamed with horizontal creases like a monkey's, and two vertical lines, much deeper than the others, rose from the bridge of the nose.

'I don't know,' she said. 'It's hard for me to judge.'

'If you work at school as you have with me, I don't think you'll have much trouble with "O" level.'

'Really?'

'I'm quite sure. I've known far worse candidates pass.'

Pleased, embarrassed and, above all, surprised, Ginny mumbled, 'Thank you for all you've done.'

'What I'd advise you to do is concentrate on your English–Latin sentences. That's your –'

A shout from Richard interrupted him. He came running up the garden towards the other children.

'Did you see it?' he said.

'See what?' Kate said.

'The raven.' Richard pointed down the garden in a direction that was roughly parallel to the lane down the hill. 'It flew that way. You must have seen it.'

'Afraid not,' James drawled.

Hubert Molland cleared his throat. 'Are you sure it was a raven?'

'Of course I am. It was huge.'

'I wouldn't have thought ravens are commonly found in Somerset. In the north, yes.'

'They've got them in the Tower of London,' James said with the air of one trying to be helpful. 'They get two-and-fourpence worth of horseflesh every day and they have a special yeoman quarter-master to look after them.'

'They're in captivity, so that's rather different. In the wild you'd expect to find them in mountains and moors and so on.'

'But it was a raven.' Richard held his arms wide. 'Its wingspan was that big.'

'Well, I suppose it's just possible,' Hubert Molland conceded. 'But it's more likely to have been another member of the crow family. Some of them are very large. Take the carrion crow, for example, or the rook.'

Richard stared at his father and shook his head. Mr Molland turned to Ginny and took refuge in the past.

'An interesting bird, the raven,' he said. 'In Christian art it was often a symbol of God's providence. But otherwise it was generally considered a bird of ill omen. There's a Roman legend that a raven pulled off Cicero's bedclothes on the day he was murdered.'

'Hubert,' Barbara called from inside, 'do we have any more sherry? This bottle's getting rather low.'

Mr Molland ducked back into the drawing room.

'You imagined it,' Peter said.

'It was a raven.' Richard looked in turn at each of them, silently appealing for support. 'I know it was.'

James smiled at him. 'You know what I think? You've got ravens on the brain.'

Once the Salpertons had left, everyone became a little nastier.

'Thank God that's over,' Barbara said as the Salpertons disappeared round the bend in the drive.

Hubert Molland muttered something to her. Peter was too far away to hear but he assumed the remark was a reproof.

Spots of red glowed on Barbara's cheeks. 'I thought they'd never go.'

'I thought you liked them,' Kate said.

'I do.' Barbara led the way back to the house, adding over her shoulder: 'But someone's got to see to lunch. Assuming you don't want charred beef and burned potatoes.'

'I feel sick.'

'You probably ate too many cheese straws.'

'I didn't eat anything. I just feel a bit sick.'

'Well, go and lie down.'

Kate shook her head.

'Then you can collect the glasses. The boys will help you.'

In fact the roast beef was excellent. Peter gorged himself. He and Richard benefited from Kate's not being hungry. Apart from the food, however, it was not an enjoyable meal.

'Take your elbows off the table,' Mr Molland snapped at Richard; and then, to Kate: 'Can't you sit up properly?'

'I've got stomach-ache,' Kate said. 'It hurts to sit up.'

'If it hurts so much you'd better go to bed.'

Kate straightened herself. 'It's not that bad.'

For a moment the only sound was the scrape of cutlery.

'Peter,' Hubert Molland said, 'do you mind not making quite so much noise with your knife and fork?'

'Sorry.' Peter felt the rebuke all the more because, with the exception of the *Health and Efficiency* episode at the beginning of their stay at Abbotsfield, Mr Molland had never told him off – and, indeed, had rarely spoken to him on any subject.

During lunch, Mrs Molland complained about all the things that had to be done before they left Abbotsfield on Tuesday.

'In that case,' Mr Molland said, 'perhaps it would be wiser if you didn't go out this evening.'

'Oh, I shall go. Mary's depending on me. Kate, I wish

you'd sort out your room this afternoon. It's like a pigsty.'

'There's no point in tidying it if we're leaving in a couple of days.'

'You'll do as your mother says,' Hubert said. 'Is that clear?'

After the washing-up, Barbara and Kate went upstairs. Kate said she still had stomach-ache and wanted to lie down; her mother, who had suddenly become sympathetic, said that aspirins might help. Neither of them mentioned the pigsty. Hubert went to the study. Peter and Richard wandered into the garden. Barbara had told them to set up the deckchairs.

It was an effort to do anything. The afternoon was warm and very still. The sky was a blue haze, streaked with wispy clouds; and the sunlight, despite the heat, was too weak to cast strong shadows. The garden smelled like a compost heap.

Peter's clothes felt clammy against his skin. He was conscious that he had eaten too much for lunch, and the memory of the rich, heavy food revolted him. He wished that James had asked them up to Carinish Court for the afternoon as well as for tomorrow morning. He would have liked to swim. He wanted to get away from the Mollands. For the first time that summer he felt seriously homesick for Plumford, and even for 29 Champney Road.

'I did see a raven.' Richard kicked a tussock of grass. 'I'm certain. It was a portent.'

Peter cast his eyes upwards. 'Maybe you did. Maybe you didn't. I don't care.'

'I think it's a good omen for tonight. Dad said the raven was a symbol of God's providence.'

'Well, that's all right, then.' Peter yawned. 'I'm bored.'

'We could go over to Capri and have a conference,' Richard suggested.

'What about?'

'Tonight, of course. It's the start of the counter-revolution.'

Peter tried to flare his nostrils; he had observed James doing this to show disdain. 'It's too hot,' he said.

'Suit yourself. Well, I suppose we'd better get the deckchairs. Then I'm going to read.'

They didn't want to be together but neither of them wanted to be alone. They walked slowly round the house to the yard beyond the kitchen; a dusty collection of garden furniture was housed in one of the sheds. The frames of the deckchairs were rickety with age and mistreatment, and their sun-bleached fabric was liable to rip if you sat down incautiously. Peter and Richard set them up in a ragged line on the old tennis court, which was the flattest part of the garden.

They chose to sit at opposite ends of the line, separated by three empty chairs. For nearly an hour both of them read, or at least pretended to do so. Richard, who had spent much of August working his way through the Timballs' extensive collection of John Buchan thrillers, was reading *Mr Standfast*. Peter was trying to finish a book that Ginny had lent him – Mary Renault's *The King Must Die*; he hoped to take it over to Carinish Court in the morning.

A shadow fell across the pages of the book. He glanced up. To his surprise, Kate was standing beside him. She looked paler than usual but she was smiling.

'Are you okay?' he blurted out.

'I'm fine now. Just bored. Do you want to play cards or something?'

Richard was within earshot but Kate's stance and her tone of voice excluded him from the invitation; this pleased Peter.

'Yes, all right – what shall we play?'

'Bezique?'

He nodded.

'Shall we go inside?' she said. 'It's so damned hot.'

Richard clicked his tongue against the roof of his mouth, perhaps to express his disapproval of Kate's swearing.

'Yes, let's,' Peter agreed. 'It really is bloody hot out here.'

He followed Kate through the French windows into the drawing room. She collected the cards from the mantelpiece.

'We'd better go upstairs,' she said. 'Dad doesn't like us playing cards on Sunday.'

'What about your mother?'

'Mum doesn't mind. Anyway, she's lying down. We'll use my room, shall we?'

Without another word they crept upstairs. No one had actually forbidden the boys to go into Kate's bedroom but Peter guessed that it was not a practice that Mr and Mrs Molland would encourage.

Kate closed her bedroom door as quietly as possible. The room was certainly more untidy than it had been on the night of Peter's initiation as a Raven. The bed was unmade. Last week's *New Musical Express* lay open on the floor. He delicately averted his eyes from the stack of clothes on the armchair: he feared he might see something he shouldn't.

Among the litter of objects on top of the chest of drawers Peter caught sight of a bundle of Emorian currency and the Great Seal itself. The lack of concealment shocked him. Secrecy had always been such a fundamental principle of Emor.

Kate swept the clothes from the armchair to the floor. Underneath the clothes was a paper bag containing a long-playing record.

'What's the record?' Peter asked.

'*A Hard Day's Night*.' She picked it up and put it in her suitcase. Without looking at Peter, she went on: 'Don't tell anyone, will you? I'm not meant to buy pop music. Dad would go crazy if he found out.'

'I can keep my mouth shut.'

'Don't even tell Richard, okay? You know what he's like. He might say something without meaning to.'

'No problem.'

Kate smiled at him. 'You can have the armchair, I'll have the stool, and we'll use the bed for a table. Do you want to gamble?'

'The trouble is, I haven't got any real money left. All I've got is sesterces.'

'Not sesterces. Emor's so childish.'

'It is a bit, I suppose.'

'I'm thinking of giving it up.'

'Me too.'

'I just can't understand why the others get so excited by it.' She sat down and began to sort out the cards. 'Well, what do you want to do?'

'I could give you an IOU for real money,' Peter offered. 'If I lose, that is.'

'All right,' Kate said. 'But it's up to you. If you want, we'll play for love.'

'I want to ask you something,' Richard murmured as they went upstairs to bed that night. 'It's important.'

Peter sighed. 'All right.'

'Come in my room. Can I borrow your torch, by the way? For my initiation as a Raven.'

Peter fetched his torch. He assumed that Richard wanted company on his trip to the Mithraeum. Peter didn't want to go but he couldn't think of an acceptable way of refusing.

Richard was waiting in his doorway. Further along the landing, Kate's door was closed; she had gone to bed early. Peter handed Richard the torch and pushed past him into the bedroom. Richard closed the door. The curtains, which had already been drawn across the open window, billowed into the room. A wind had sprung up since the afternoon. According to the weather forecast on the radio, they were due to have rain in the night.

Peter leaned against the wall and crossed his arms. 'What do you want to talk about?'

Richard dug a hand in his pocket and took out the Great Seal.

'What are you doing with that?' Peter said.

'Do you know where it was? Kate had just left it on her chest of drawers.' Richard spoke in a whisper but his voice hissed with anger. 'Anyone could have found it.'

'You mean you searched her room?'

'While she was having a bath. It's just as well, isn't it? She can't even be trusted with the Great Seal.'

'Does it matter? It's only a bottle top. They wouldn't have known what it was.'

'Of course it matters. It's the Great Seal. Besides, she'd left a small fortune in sesterces beside it.' Richard looked challengingly at Peter. 'That would have made up my mind if I hadn't already decided.'

'Yes, but why've you got the seal? You're not going to be emperor tomorrow. I am. And in the meantime the seal belongs to Kate.'

'You just don't understand, do you?' Richard shook his head, as if astonished by Peter's obtuseness. 'This is the counter-revolution. I've already set up a provisional government. I'm making the laws.'

'Oh, don't be stupid.'

'You're the one who's being stupid. I'm giving you one last chance, Peter. I'm going to deal with Kate and James. By tomorrow, they'll be exiled for ever from Emor.'

'Great,' Peter said. 'What makes you think they'll agree? They may decide to exile you instead.'

Richard smiled, drawing his lips against his teeth. 'They won't. I promise you that. I've made plans, you see.'

'And if they do go,' Peter went on, 'which I doubt, they'll tell everyone about Emor, won't they? Is that what you want?'

'I told you. I've got plans. They'll keep their mouths shut for ever if necessary.'

'What plans?'

'That's my secret. For the time being, anyway. First I want to know if you'll join the counter-revolution. I'll give you a post in the provisional government.'

'Look, I'm due to be emperor tomorrow –'

'Not now you aren't.' Richard's fingers closed over the Great Seal. 'But maybe you will if you join the counter-revolution. Yes, I'll definitely think about it. But first I need to be sure of your loyalty.'

'Let me get this straight,' Peter said. 'If you're so against James and Kate, why are you becoming a Raven?'

'That's different. That's nothing to do with Emor.'

'Of course it is.'

'It was. Times change. I've already written a decree to separate the cult of Mithras from the state of Emor. I'm sacking the Pontifex Maximus, too. There won't be another one. We won't have religion in Emor again. Are you with me or against me?'

'You're mad. You can't just seize control like that.'

'Why not? I've thought it out very carefully. All I need to know is whether you're a friend or an enemy.'

Peter hesitated. He felt angry with Richard for putting him in this awkward position. 'What happens if I'm an enemy?' he said.

'I don't want to, but if necessary I'll exile you from the empire like the others.'

'You can't do that.' Peter stared at Richard in astonishment. 'You can't have Emor without me.'

'Yes I can. And maybe it'd be better that way. But it's your choice. So now you'd better make up your mind.'

Richard's determination and his air of certainty were

both impressive. The weight of habit was also on his side: Emor belonged to Richard and Peter. On the other hand, Peter wanted to go swimming at Carinish Court tomorrow. James had suggested that they write to each other next term, and had even hinted that Peter might be invited to stay during the Christmas holidays. Nor did he want to upset Kate, especially after her friendliness this afternoon: greatly daring, he had asked her round to Champney Road to listen to *A Hard Day's Night* on the Redburns' record player. Finally, and perhaps most powerfully, he hated the idea of Richard's dictating terms to him. Petronius Redburnus had always been a leader of men, not a follower.

Peter drew himself up and looked down his nose at Richard. He tried once more to flare his nostrils, which had the effect of making the tip of his nose twitch like a rabbit's.

'I don't really understand why you're getting so worked up,' he said in a careful imitation of James's drawl at its most patrician. 'Don't you think that Emor's rather childish?'

Mollandius devised a three-pronged strategy for the coup d'état. Before the Provisional Government, with himself as Prime Minister, could openly take the reins of power, he needed a) to destroy the power of the new members of the Court, b) to form alliances with influential Emorians who were not at the Summer Palace, and c) to win the support of the Chancellor, Petronius Redburnus. Firstly, his secret agents brought him information about the sordid private lives of the Empress and the Pontifex Maximus. (They were tainted with barbarian blood and lacked the nobility of true-born Emorians.) Mollandius intended to use this information to persuade them to resign from Emor.

By a stroke of good fortune, one of his agents was able to bring Mollandius the Great Seal of Emor, which the Empress Messalina had left unguarded in her chamber. It so happened that at midnight Mollandius was due to initiate himself to the Raven degree. Accordingly, he arranged to meet the Pontifex Maximus at the Mithraeum for a private conference. Secondly, before he left for the Mithraeum, Mollandius wrote a despatch to Guillielmus Colbiensus, a general who was then waging a war against Tunisian rebels. He explained to Colbiensus that the Summer Palace at Campus Abbatis was in turmoil and told him that the counter-revolutionary Provisional Government had seized the Great Seal and was on the verge of restoring control. He offered Colbiensus high rank in the new government in return for his support. Mollandius knew that Colbiensus would be able to win over the other Emorians who were not at the Summer Palace. Thirdly, Mollandius attempted to persuade his old friend Redburnus to join him in the Provisional Government. The two gens had always been closely allied, and Mollandius hoped that Redburnus would accompany him to the Mithraeum and help him confront the evil Salpertonius. Here, however, to his great sorrow, he failed. Redburnus had been corrupted by the Empress and the Pontifex Maximus. He was no longer capable of listening to reason and no longer worthy of Emorian citizenship. Mollandius, another Captain of the Gate, realized that he alone stood between the Empire of Emor and the barbarian forces of darkness.

'Don't you think that Emor's rather childish?'

Those words were Peter's last and worst betrayal of Richard. Even at the time he had regretted them, though anger and pride prevented him from retracting them. A few hours later, of course, it was too late.

The Secret History of Emor showed him Richard's side of the affair. Richard had seen himself as the champion of the true Emorians, gallantly attempting to stem the barbarian tide. Interpreted in another way, the last pages of *The Secret History* recorded a doomed attempt to stop time itself: Richard had tried to defend not Emor but his own identity as a child. In a sense he had succeeded, though not in a way he would have chosen.

The reference to the 'Captain of the Gate' mystified Peter, until he remembered how Macaulay's *Lays of Ancient Rome* had been drummed into them at school. On Friday night – when he got back to the flat after meeting Kate at the Royal Commonwealth Institute – he tracked down the quotation in an anthology of narrative verse. Horatius had volunteered to defend the bridge that led across the Tiber to Rome against the invading army of Lars Porsena.

> *Then out spake brave Horatius,*
> *The Captain of the gate:*
> *'To every man upon this earth*
> *Death cometh soon or late:*
> *And how can man die better*
> *Than facing fearful odds,*
> *For the ashes of his fathers*
> *And the temples of his Gods?'*

Horatius, however, had had an advantage denied to Richard: friends on either side of him.

This is a wonderful evening, Barbara thought as Ralph helped her into her coat, and I wish it could last for ever.

Hubert had hardly said a word to her since lunchtime. She had felt his disapproval all afternoon. By coming alone to Carinish Court she had abandoned, if only for a few precious hours, her God-given role of wife and mother; by playing bridge on Sunday evening, she had asserted the rarely exercised right to make her own decisions. At last she was having a holiday.

Events had conspired to increase her enjoyment. She deserved a treat after the strain of entertaining the Salpertons after church; Hubert was incapable of appreciating the sheer humiliation of having to offer them such penny-pinching hospitality. As Ralph was driving her to Carinish Court, he complimented her on her dress. She had already met the Salpertons' friends – two couples and an elderly widow, who had motored over together from Paulstock – at the Morgans' party, and they were charming. Ralph and Mary went out of their way to make Barbara feel at home.

Even the cards had been kind to her. It was nonsense to say that bridge was purely a game of skill, and tonight she had been unusually lucky. Everyone drank a good deal, for Ralph was a very attentive host, and by the end of the evening Barbara had reached an enjoyable plateau of alcoholic euphoria. No doubt this had affected her standard of play but as they were all in the same condition it didn't matter.

The other guests had already left. Ralph opened the front door. The gravel sparkled in the moonlight as though covered with hoarfrost.

'A full moon,' he said. 'They say it's going to rain.'

Mary kissed Barbara on the cheek. 'You'll come over to say goodbye before you go, won't you?'

'Of course,' Barbara said, wondering what Hubert's reaction would be. Damn Hubert. 'Thank you for everything.'

Ralph opened the passenger door of the car.

'I think I'll go straight to bed,' Mary called to him. 'I'm shattered.'

'Right-ho.' He handed Barbara into the Jaguar. 'I'll try not to disturb you when I come in.'

The car moved slowly down the drive. Barbara relaxed into her seat, determined to make the most of her last few moments of freedom. The car even smelled of luxury: a blend of leather, polish and Turkish tobacco.

'It's been a wonderful evening,' Ralph said.

She laughed. 'You read my thoughts.'

'And it's a lovely night.' He braked at the end of the drive. 'You're not in a hurry, are you? The view from Paulstock Hill is quite spectacular by moonlight.'

'I'm not sure –'

'It won't take us five minutes. Honestly.'

'All right, then.'

The Jaguar turned right, away from Abbotsfield, and purred up the long hill. Ralph offered her a cigarette and asked her to light one for him. It seemed a dreadfully intimate thing to do for a man who was not your husband. As she passed him the lighted cigarette, their hands touched. She shivered.

'Are you cold?' he said. 'There's a flask in the glove compartment. Have a nip. It'll warm you up.'

They reached the top of the hill. He pulled into a lay-by, a dog leg that had once been part of the main road and was now separated from it by a hedge, and switched off the engine. It was as if he had switched on the silence of the night; the only sounds were their breathing and the bleat of a sheep in distress.

'There's the view,' he said.

Barbara glanced out of her window, away from the road. On this side of the lay-by the ground dropped sharply away. In the nearer distance she saw a cluster of yellow lights, which she presumed belonged to Abbotsfield. Solitary sparks marked farms and cottages. Otherwise the world was reduced to a monochrome vision of silver fields and black shadows.

Ralph leaned across her, opened the glove compartment and took out a silver flask. He uncapped it and offered it to her. 'Here. It's brandy.'

In her nervousness she swallowed too much and began to cough. Ralph patted her gently and inefficiently on the back. She gave him the flask. His arm remained across her shoulders.

'Ralph?' she said, trying to pull away.

The arm tightened its grip. Suddenly his mouth was on hers. Barbara struggled. Her right arm was pinned against her. She couldn't fend him off with her left because she was still holding the cigarette. His tongue parted her lips and ran along her teeth.

She jerked her head aside. 'Ralph, you mustn't. Don't spoil it.'

His lips returned. She opened her mouth to protest and his tongue slipped between her teeth and touched hers. She felt warm and alive. Well, why not? she thought. Why shouldn't I have a bit of fun?

It was Ralph who ended the kiss. He pulled his head gently away. 'First things first, eh?'

He tucked the flask on the dashboard, took her cigarette and dropped it with his own through the window. When they started kissing again, his right hand caressed her breast.

'Not here, Ralph. Someone might come.'

His hand ran up her leg. 'There's an old cottage in the garden,' he whispered urgently, though they were in no hurry and there was no one to hear. 'We could go there if you like. Take the rugs from the car.'

She said nothing in the comfortable knowledge that Ralph would take her silence for assent. He squeezed her leg, straightened himself and started the engine. Barbara smoothed her dress.

'Have another drink,' he said.

They drove down the hill with the wind whistling through the open window. Ralph braked at the entrance to Carinish Court. But instead of swinging into the drive, he stopped altogether.

'Well, I'm damned,' he said sharply.

Barbara looked up, the flask still in her hand. Standing between the stone piers, trapped in the beam of the headlights, were two motionless figures on either side of a motorbike. One was dark, the other fair: Frank Timball and James Salperton.

Ralph poked his head out of the window. 'What the hell do you two think you're up to?'

'Just – just going for a walk, Dad.'

The sound of James's voice broke the paralysis that held her. Barbara began to shake. Brandy dripped on her dress.

'At this time?' Ralph bellowed. 'Are you insane?'

'Take me home,' Barbara muttered.

A drop of rain fell on the windscreen. Then another.

'What?' Ralph said, the anger still in his voice but now directed at her.

'Take me home,' she repeated. 'I'll walk if you want. I want to go home.'

'Don't be so bloody stupid,' Ralph said. 'It's beginning to rain. James, I'll see you in the study in about ten minutes. As for you, Frank, I want you off the premises.'

Ralph drove her back to Abbotsfield in silence. He didn't touch her. The rain fell more and more heavily. Barbara bit her lip to stop herself from crying. It was so bloody unfair.

He dropped her at the bottom of the Vicarage drive. He couldn't even be bothered to take her up to the door.

'Goodbye,' she said. 'Thank you for the lift.'

He grunted. 'You little fool – you lost your head. They couldn't have seen you, you know. Not with the headlights in their eyes.'

'I – I changed my mind.'

'Well, that's your look-out. You bloody cock-teaser.'

Barbara stumbled up the drive and let herself into the house. Apart from the light in the hall, everywhere was in darkness. She glanced at her watch. It was nearly one o'clock.

It seemed to her that as usual she had had the worst of both worlds. To all intents and purposes she had surrendered her virtue and got nothing in return. She collected what was left of the sherry from the kitchen and went upstairs to the bathroom.

For nearly an hour she lay in the bath, drinking sherry from the toothglass. The rain pattered on the window. When at last the bottle was empty, she clambered out of the bath, wrapped herself in a towel and opened the bathroom door. She knew that Hubert would be sleeping the sleep of the just and snoring gently. It was surprisingly difficult to walk along the landing in a straight line. Twice she found it necessary to fend herself off the wall.

For that reason, and also because she was still furious with herself and all the world besides, she did not bother to look in on the children. Usually she liked to put her head inside their rooms and listen: just to make sure they were still breathing.

Eighteen

The crack of iron on iron filled the church. Peter spun round, his hands clenching in the pockets of his raincoat.

Someone had lifted the latch on the door behind him. That was all. The hinges creaked and the heavy door swung inwards. Nothing to feel nervous about. He had every right to be here.

An old man slipped inside, preceded by a draught of damp December air. He was bald, small and very thin, and he bent forward from the waist as though there were an invisible burden on his shoulders. In his hand was a cloth cap. A tweed overcoat enveloped him like a small tent from neck to knees. He glanced at Peter and turned to examine the postcards and pamphlets on the table by the door.

Peter's heel clattered on a central-heating grating in the tiled floor as he moved to the west end of the nave. For a moment he stood there and made an effort to visualize how the church had looked when he'd last seen it. He wished very much that he could find something to recognize: something in the present that would bring the past into focus.

Nothing stirred in his memory except a phrase they had sometimes used: 'the temple of the god of the Christians'. It astonished him how little he remembered. He must have sat through a service here at least once a

Sunday. He had visited the church at other times, too; he remembered carrying piles of green hymnals and purple prayer books from the Vicarage and arranging them on the table by the south door.

Perhaps it had been foolish to come. He was here on impulse, largely because he had time to kill after a leisurely lunch at the White Boar. The drive from London had not been as bad as he had expected: by leaving early he had avoided the worst of the holiday traffic. He was due to reach Carinish Court at about four o'clock, and it was now barely two-thirty.

From the noticeboard in the porch, Peter had learned that the church was dedicated to St Thomas Becket, another fact that he had entirely forgotten, and that Abbotsfield was now one of five combined parishes whose spiritual needs were the responsibility of something called a team ministry.

He concentrated on the present. The high altar had a disused look, as if the receding waters of liturgical fashion had left it stranded. They had installed another altar between the choir stalls in the chancel and the pews in the nave. Christmas was coming: an exhibition of Nativity paintings by children at the local primary school filled the south aisle; and directly opposite the door, in the north-west corner of the nave, was a crib scene with crude, papier-mâché adults and animals, a plastic doll for Jesus and real straw.

He suspected that he was being observed. What did ordinary visitors do? Peter strolled down the nave, glancing at the indifferent stained-glass in the windows. The church was a Victorian building constructed from – or at least faced with – local stone. Its tower was asymmetrically positioned at the south-west corner, above the porch. The architecture was budget gothic; perhaps the architect had been restrained by shortage of money or had lacked the courage of his Puginesque convictions.

A brass plaque caught his eye: *In Loving Memory of Charles Wilberforce Curran, Esquire, of Carinish Court.* Peter skirted the altar rails and walked back along the south aisle of the nave. He stopped and, under the pretext of examining a painting of three, stick-like shepherds beneath a star like a golden jellyfish, glanced towards the door. The old man was watching him quite openly.

As Peter approached, the man coughed. The sound reverberated among the dark-stained pine timbers of the roof. Dark-stained pine, Peter thought: like the panelling in the Vicarage. He fumbled in his pocket for a coin to put in the box by the door.

'Good morning,' the old man wheezed. His wispy beard needed combing and clipping. The food-stains on the lapels suggested that he was in the habit of breakfasting in his overcoat. 'Enjoying our lovely church?'

'Yes, indeed. It's nice to find a church that's open. These days so many churches lock their doors.'

'What's that?'

Peter raised his voice. 'These days so many churches lock their doors.'

'No need to shout. I'm not deaf. If I had my way, I'd lock the church when it's not in use. We lost a pair of candlesticks from the high altar last summer. The police say we'll need a miracle to get them back. Beyond belief, isn't it? Still, I always say that forewarned is forearmed. We do what we can. Or at least some of us do.'

Peter slipped fifty pence in the box.

'Just passing through, are you?'

'Yes.' Peter changed his mind and decided to prolong the conversation. 'That is, I'm on my way to Carinish Court. Do you know it?'

'Of course I do.' A watery gleam appeared in the old man's eyes. 'The Salpertons' place. I know it like the back of my hand – and them. Are you a journalist, then?'

'No – a friend.'

The gleam faded. Peter wondered if the man had hoped that his specialized knowledge of James might have commercial value.

'Mr Salperton's come down for Christmas? And his good lady?'

Peter nodded.

'I remember him when he was just a boy. Give him my regards, won't you? Tell him Bert was asking after him, eh?'

'I will,' Peter said. 'Well, goodbye.'

He turned up the collar of his coat and went back into the rain. It was not until he was walking through the churchyard to the gate on to the lane that his mind made the connection. Bert, a scruffy, skinny man, perhaps in his late seventies. Could he once have been a plump and dapper churchwarden with a taste for gossip and a rumoured penchant for little girls? Albert Nimp. Nimp the pink, they used to call him. Pimp the nink.

On the other side of the lane was the redbrick wall

of the Vicarage garden. But both the Vicarage and its garden had vanished. In their place were a dozen houses, arranged with careful irregularity in a cul-de-sac: bright, convenient modern homes, with integral garages, satellite dishes and double-glazed mock-Georgian windows. The drive had been widened into an access road, and it now continued down the slope of what had once been the lawn. Even the trees had gone. The new owners had planted laburnums and fast-growing firs, magnolias and flowering cherries. A sign on the corner said VICARAGE CLOSE.

The only thing that Peter recognized was the pillar box at the junction of the lane and the main road. On the Sunday night Richard must have gone there on his way to the Mithraeum to post the last despatch of Emor, the letter to Bill Coleby.

From the Summer Palace of Campus Abbatis . . .

Peter followed the lane down the hill. A pavement had replaced the drainage ditch that used to feed the pond. In his memory the wall of the Vicarage garden had stopped at the point where, on the other side, the remains of the orchard began. Now the wall gave way not to the bushes which had sheltered James when he spied on Emor but to a new, shoulder-high fence topped with a trellis. Further down the hill were the rust-red roofs of more houses, a tide of tiles spreading towards the flat farmland below.

He walked on until the fence swung away from the lane. At the corner, he parted a leafless curtain of Virginia creeper and peered through the trellis. The back garden of the house at the end of the cul-de-sac was repressively neat. Its salient features were a pyramidal rockery and the sort of wooden shed you can assemble yourself from a kit. A small conservatory projected from the back of the house. The trees, the bushes and the pond had all disappeared; and so, too, had the Mithraeum.

Nothing was left. Nothing was the same. Even the view had changed. The present retained not the slightest trace of the past. Here, just after dawn on his last morning at Abbotsfield – yes, precisely here: between the rockery and the garden shed – Peter had seen the raven on the water.

The conservatory door opened. Yapping hysterically, an adolescent labrador bounded down the garden and threw himself at the fence. A large, grey-haired woman was standing in the doorway. She tapped the palm of her hand with a heavy rolling-pin.

'May I help you?' she asked.

'No,' Peter said. 'I don't think you can.'

According to the ever-reliable Letts School-Boy Diary, dawn was just before six o'clock, British summer time, or five o'clock by Greenwich Mean Time. On the morning of Monday 24 August 1964 Peter woke up suddenly. His head felt heavy and he was mysteriously apprehensive, as though today were the start of a new term.

His room, which faced east, was full of light. He scrambled out of bed, driven by an urgency whose cause he did not remember until his feet touched the floor.

He had to go to the Mithraeum. A candle should be burning. Richard should now be a Raven.

Beneath the urgency lay guilt: Richard had gone alone

to the Mithraeum because of their quarrel last night. Peter pulled a jersey over his pyjamas and opened his bedroom door. He tiptoed along the landing to Richard's room. He wanted to make amends for the quarrel without actually admitting he had been in the wrong. If Richard were awake they could go together.

The door was closed. Peter opened it and put his head inside the room. The bed was empty. The sheets and blankets were still tucked in. The eiderdown lay in a heap on the floor. Either Richard hadn't slept in the bed or he had already made it.

Peter crept downstairs. The side door was unlocked and unbolted. If Richard had made the bed, Peter thought, he would have put the eiderdown on top; therefore the door must be unlocked because he hadn't come back from the Mithraeum last night.

Panic welled up. It just didn't make sense. What was Richard doing? Peter didn't bother to fetch his Wellington boots from the kitchen. He opened the door and stepped outside.

It was much colder than he had expected. The rain and the time of the morning combined to intensify the colours. The green of the grass was bright to the point of virulence. The silver disc of the full moon shared the blue-green sky with a fat sun like an immense blood orange. Streaks of red and purple clouds lingered above the eastern horizon.

Peter would have liked to shout Richard's name, but he dared not run the risk of waking Mr and Mrs Molland. He jogged down the lawn. For a second he hesitated before plunging under the branch of the apple tree and into the tangle of dripping bushes that masked the pond. He was tempted to go back to the house for his boots. Panic drove him on – that and the sense that his feet couldn't possibly get much wetter and colder than they already were.

The path through the bushes was muddy with rain. Branches slapped against his legs, soaking the bottoms of his pyjama trousers. A nettle stung his left foot.

'Richard?' Peter whispered as loudly as he dared. 'Richard? Where are you?'

Sobbing for breath, he emerged on the bank of the pond. Before him was the Mithraeum; and beyond it the slope of the hill carried the eyes down to the mist-covered fields on the plain beneath.

'This is the sort of place where Satan brought Christ and tempted him,' Richard had said one day. 'Here are all the kingdoms of the world.'

There was nothing to worry about: the boat was moored on the farther shore near the steps down to the pillbox.

'Richard,' Peter called. 'It's me.'

As he spoke, his eyes drifted away from the boat and the Mithraeum. The pond seemed larger than usual, as if swollen by the rain: more like a real lake. Its surface had a silvery sheen to it. In the centre of the pond floated a great, black bird.

The raven on the water. Richard's raven. Richard the Raven. No, it wasn't a bird.

Peter whimpered through closed lips – a soft, high-pitched noise that came of its own accord from the back of his throat. Part of him, however, was still capable of thinking lucidly. As he stood there – for perhaps a couple of seconds – an orderly procession of ideas flashed through his mind. In the night it had rained: Richard would have worn his navy-blue school mackintosh. When it was waterlogged, navy-blue became indistinguishable from black. Probably Richard would have worn the coat anyway, whatever the weather. It would have pleased his sense of occasion. Not as a raincoat, of course, but as a cape fastened round the neck by the top button: the uniform of an officer in the Praetorian Guard.

Peter turned and ran back through the bushes. A bramble slashed his cheek. He dived under the branch of the apple tree. Missing his footing, he stumbled and fell full-length on the long, wet grass of the lawn.

'Help!'

The cry emerged as little better than a whisper. Sobbing with frustration, he picked himself up and ran on. Why didn't someone come? Why was the lawn so long and so steep? Why did everything hurt so much?

He threw open the side door and pounded up the stairs. He hammered on the Mollands' door. Someone was snoring inside. No one answered but the snoring stopped. He twisted the handle and went in.

'Please,' he said. 'You've got to come. It's Richard.'

'What?' Hubert Molland sat up. He wore blue-and-red striped pyjamas and his teeth were in a glass of water beside the bed. 'What's that?'

'It's Richard. He's in the pond. I think he's been there for hours.'

Barbara stirred and opened her eyes.

Mr Molland threw off the bedclothes and plunged out of bed.

'Hubert, what's happening?'

He pushed Peter aside and ran out of the room.

'Richard?' Barbara Molland said. 'For God's sake, Peter, what's happened to him?'

'He's' – Peter swallowed – 'in the pond.'

'Oh, my God.'

He followed Mrs Molland. Their bare feet thudded on the stairs and slapped across the tiles of the hall. Hubert had chosen the shortest route: through the drawing room and into the garden by the French windows. They were just in time to catch a glimpse of him as he crashed into the orchard.

At the window Barbara glanced back at Peter. 'You stay here. Don't you dare move.'

He was glad of the excuse – indeed, he almost wished she had ordered him back to bed. He watched her running down the lawn, with her pink floral nightdress billowing behind her. Should he perhaps pray? He abandoned the idea because he could not decide whom to pray to or what to say. Anyway, what was the use? Richard must have been almost six hours in that pond. They were too late. There was no point in bothering any more.

He sat down in the wicker chair, wrapping his arms round his legs in an effort to make himself warm, and stared out of the window. Tears pricked behind his eyelids but he found it impossible to cry. Mrs Molland had disappeared into the bushes. They had abandoned him. He was cold and wet. No one cared. He felt very sorry for himself.

'Peter!'

He sprang up. Mrs Molland was standing by the

apple tree. She carried the body of a black bird in her arms. A wing tip touched the ground. No, not a bird.

'It's all right, Peter,' she shouted. 'It's only his mac.'

She started to walk slowly up the lawn. He ran down to meet her.

'I thought it was –'

'I know,' she said gently. 'So did I for a moment. But look – it's only his coat.'

She held it out to him, as if sensing that he needed to touch it before he could be sure that Richard was not concealed in its dripping folds. The water made the raincoat very heavy. They were standing about twenty yards from the apple tree. Hubert Molland was still crashing through the undergrowth: it sounded as if he were taking the overland route to the Mithraeum.

'The top button's gone,' Peter said.

'Has it?' She put an arm round his shoulders. 'Come on. You need a hot bath and some warm clothes.'

'I mean, he was probably wearing it as a cloak.'

'Playing some game or other. You're shivering.'

'Don't you see? The button must have come off as he was poling the boat across the pond.'

'Very possibly. Back to the house, young man. Don't worry – Mr Molland will find him. He's probably gone for a walk.'

'But you don't understand,' Peter said. 'Why did he just leave it there? Why didn't he pick it up?'

'Well, it might have been dark and –'

'There was a moon.'

'Maybe the clouds covered it. It rained during the night, you know.'

'But he had a torch. He borrowed mine.'

Her arm tightened across his shoulders. 'Did you know he was going out at night?'

'Of course not.' Peter instinctively tried to minimize his part in what had happened.

'Why did you think he wanted the torch?'

'I thought he just wanted to read in bed.'

'Oh *no*.'

He glanced at Barbara, wondering what he had said to upset her. She was no longer looking at him but at the house. Kate had come through the French windows and was walking slowly down the lawn. She wore a thin nightdress of plain sky-blue cotton. Unlike the rest of them she had found the time to put on her Wellington boots.

'Darling, you might as well go back to bed,' Barbara said. 'Richard seems to have gone for an early-morning walk. That's all.'

Kate ignored her mother. She was staring at something behind them and slightly to their left. Her mouth opened. She shook her head.

Peter looked over his shoulder. Mr Molland was backing out of the bushes. The water from the pond had plastered his pyjama trousers against his long, thin legs. He turned to face them. He was cradling Richard in his arms.

Richard's head lolled against his father's shoulder. He was wearing jeans, a brown polo-neck jersey and Wellingtons. His clothes looked dry. His face was curiously flushed – purple, tinged with blue, which made his hair seem even fairer than usual. There were rings of pink froth around the lips and the nostrils.

'It's all right, my son.' Hubert Molland brushed his

lips against Richard's hair. He seemed oblivious of the three of them standing on the lawn. 'Everything's going to be fine.'

Peter stared down at his own feet, which were smeared with mud and pink with cold. He would have liked to cover his ears as well as avert his eyes.

'For Christ's sake,' Barbara screamed.

'There, there, my little one,' Mr Molland mumbled in a harsh, sing-song voice. 'Daddy's here.'

He walked steadily towards the house. Barbara ran after him. Kate looked at Peter and licked her lips with the tip of her tongue. She turned to follow her parents.

Peter trailed after the Mollands. On the back of Kate's nightdress was a bright red stain about the size and shape of an egg.

He knew it was blood. What else could it be? Richard's blood.

With the car keys in his hand Peter turned out of the lane and walked along the main street of Abbotsfield. The rain had at last stopped. The labrador was still barking, though with less conviction now the intruder's head had vanished.

Peter had left the Ford Escort in the car park of the White Boar. He glanced at his watch. It was after three o'clock. He could have a cup of tea at the hotel and then drive on to Carinish Court.

As he walked, he thought about the blood. He was glad that he hadn't mentioned it to anyone – the Mollands or the doctor or the police. At the time, both the shock and the medication had urged him to take the line of least resistance.

397

The shock and the medication were also responsible for the fact that his memories of the day were patchy and chronologically jumbled. Afterwards – over a period of years – he had tried to impose a logical sequence on them. As a result, he was now uncertain about the status of some of the memories: had they really happened or had he, at some later date, willed them into existence to fill the gaps? He remembered some events – the conversation with the policewoman, for example – so vividly that they must have had a firm basis in reality; but others – like the tea and toast on the scratched tin tray from the kitchen – might well be later inventions.

As far as he remembered, no one had actually said outright that Richard was dead – no one, that is, apart from the policewoman who talked to him just before he left. Peter had simply assumed his death as soon as he had seen Mr Molland cuddling Richard as though he were a baby.

At the hotel he decided against having tea. Since lunchtime the drinkers had overflowed from the bars to the lounge and the hall. The Abbotsfield Rugby Club had arrived.

Instead Peter sat in the car. On balance, he thought, it had been a mistake to return to Abbotsfield.

When they had reached the Vicarage with Richard's body, Mrs Molland had ordered Peter and Kate to go to bed. 'Keep warm,' she kept saying. 'You must keep warm.'

His bedroom was bright with sunshine. Peter stripped off his pyjamas. He pulled on a jersey, jeans and two pairs of socks, and got into bed. His teeth were chattering but the chattering stopped as he grew warmer. He heard movements in the house and cars in the drive. The sounds didn't interest him: his mind was too numb for speculation. When he tried to read *The King Must Die*, he couldn't remember who the characters were or what they were doing. He stayed in bed until the doctor came; he didn't know what else to do.

The doctor was a brusque, grey-haired man who smelled of used ashtrays. He gave Peter a cursory check-up and told him to swallow two pills. Peter presumed they were tranquillizers.

After the doctor's visit, Mrs Molland brought him a tray of tea and toast. 'Everything all right?' she said. The skin below her eyes was pink and swollen. He sat up and she put the tray on the bed. Tea slopped over the rim of the mug. 'Never mind,' she said, and left the room.

A little later, she came back with the two plain-clothes policemen. They were kind to him in their own impersonal way. He hadn't actually found the body, of course, so he was not an important witness. They merely wanted to establish that he and Richard used to play in the pillbox. One of them, whose beaked nose was disconcertingly out of line with the rest of his features, asked if he or Richard had ever been out at night before. Peter said no. Saying yes would make things worse. Besides, if he said yes, they would want to know why. That would mean telling them about Emor and the reason for Richard's visit to the Mithraeum.

Towards the end of the morning, the policewoman appeared. She said that she had come to help him pack his clothes.

'What's going to happen to me?' he asked.

'Haven't they told you?' The WPC was young, dark and rather pretty. 'Typical men. You're going home, lovey, that's all.'

'But – won't there be more questions and things?'

'Maybe. Nothing very important. There's no reason to keep you here.' She glanced at him; her expression was openly calculating, as though she were estimating the weight of the fat lady at a fair. 'You'd only be in the way. It's best to get you home to your parents.'

'How shall I go? By train?' What he really wanted to know was whether they were sending him by himself. The prospect of being alone among strangers scared him.

'Mrs Salperton's come to drive you up to London,' the policewoman said. 'She's a friend of your parents, isn't she?'

Peter nodded.

'And your mum's coming up to town by train and she'll meet you at Liverpool Street Station.' She held up a couple of books, the Mary Renault and a P. G. Wodehouse novel, which he had left on the bedside table. 'Are these yours? Shall I pack them?'

'No – the Renault one belongs to Ginny Salperton. The Wodehouse is Richard's. What – what happened to him?'

'Just one of those accidents, I'm afraid. Try not to think about it, lovey.'

'I want to know,' Peter said. 'I've got to.'

Again that assessing glance. 'Well, during the night he decided to go down to the pillbox. We don't know why. Any suggestions?'

'I haven't the foggiest.'

She shrugged. 'Maybe he couldn't sleep, and it seemed like a bit of an adventure, a bit of a lark. We found a torch down there, and he'd lit a candle. One of those nightlights – you know? It was still burning.'

'He was actually in the – the pillbox?'

'Just inside the entrance. It looks like he tripped at the top of the steps. Knocked himself out. He would have been okay if there hadn't been a puddle at the bottom.'

Peter frowned. 'You mean –'

'Yes,' the policewoman said. 'It looks like he drowned.'

'But there was only an inch or two of water.'

'That's all you need.'

'So there wasn't any blood?'

'No.' She looked puzzled. 'Why do you ask?'

'I just wondered,' he muttered. 'It's funny – Richard couldn't swim.' He knew what he'd said was irrelevant; but in his mind he saw the raven on the water and the egg-shaped bloodstain on Kate's nightdress. 'I thought he'd fallen in the pond, you see. But he hadn't, had he? It was only his coat.'

She gave his shoulder a squeeze.

'Do you think he knew what was happening?' he said.

'That's the one big consolation, lovey. He can't have felt anything. After that blow on the head he probably went out like a light.'

The policewoman took him downstairs; she carried his suitcase for him, which made him feel like an invalid. Mary Salperton and Hubert Molland were waiting in the hall. Neither Barbara nor Kate had come to see him off; the policewoman told him that they were resting in their rooms. Mr Molland shook hands with him but said nothing.

Mrs Salperton had brought the Jaguar right up to the porch. As Peter climbed in, he glimpsed white, vacant faces near the bottom of the drive and the back of a uniformed police officer. There were more people on the lane. He recognized among them several of the boys who used to hang around the war memorial on the Triangle. Mr Nimp was there, too, standing by the gate to the churchyard. The bystanders peered and pointed at the car. Peter felt a brief glow of self-importance.

As the Jaguar rolled past him, Mr Nimp doffed his pork-pie hat and waved.

It was nearly three-thirty. Peter was cold and thirsty. It wouldn't matter if he got to Carinish Court a little early. He started the engine.

He was still grateful to that policewoman, whose name he had never known. She had given him both kindness and information. Thanks to her, he had realized that the mysterious bloodstain could have nothing to do with Richard's death. She had saved him from more than worry: he now knew that she had also prevented him from making a fool of himself. The real explanation of the stain had emerged a few months later when his friend Joe passed on to him a selection of interesting biological facts and rumours. Among them was a garbled account of the phenomenon of menstruation.

Traffic was heavy on the main street. Unlike Plumford, Abbotsfield did not have a by-pass. As Peter waited for a gap in the flow, he looked across the road. Mr Nimp's house had vanished, along with its neighbours. In their place was a supermarket.

A tractor appeared, delaying the cars behind it and giving the Escort a chance to escape. Peter turned right and drove out of Abbotsfield. The outskirts stretched further north than they had done in the 1960s. In the interim Abbotsfield had acquired an industrial estate and a wealth of new housing. It had never been a beautiful village: now it was an ugly little town.

The road ran into open country. Less than a mile later, just before the hill, Peter slowed for the entrance to Carinish Court. The pineapples still stood on their pillars, whose stonework had been cleaned and re-pointed. The pillars looked smaller and less intimidatingly grand than he remembered. The wrought-iron gates were new. They had been closed when Peter passed them on his way to Abbotsfield; now they were standing open.

He drove slowly up the winding drive. The passage of heavy vehicles had left ruts in the gravel and churned the grass verges into mud. Most of the trees and bushes had lost their leaves. There were fewer trees on the right: the elms must have fallen victim to disease, and perhaps the gales had culled the rest. Through the bare branches on the left, he caught a glimpse of the oak tree on the lawn, the one that Richard had climbed, and the wall of the kitchen garden.

The Escort rolled across the open space in front of the house. Peter braked and switched off the engine. The doll's-house façade reared up in front of him. Its perfect regularity was marred by the strip of corrugated iron that covered the study window. Two of the first-floor window frames were new, and all the woodwork needed painting. A stack of concrete blocks masked the balustrade that divided the drive from the terrace. There was a heap of wet sand on the left of the front door.

I'm coming home, he thought with a stab of surprise; and he smiled at his own folly.

The sense of homecoming caught him off guard. He had expected many things, most of them disappointing, from Carinish Court; but not that. He had thought that the house and grounds would seem smaller; that in winter they would be far less attractive than they had been in summer; that memories of Richard would haunt him; that the years of neglect and the renovations of the last few months would have left their scars; and that an adult would measure the place with a different yardstick from that of a child whose only point of reference was 29 Champney Road.

To some extent he had been right. The reality reflected all his fears. The net result, however, was not disappointing but endearing. The passage of time had diminished Carinish Court to lifesize; this made it no less desirable. As always, he envied James.

The front door opened. Peter glanced up.

Kate waved to him and walked down the steps. She was wearing denim dungarees and had a blue quilted jacket draped round her shoulders; she looked too young to vote. As Peter opened the car door, he realized that he had been fooling himself. He wasn't coming home to Carinish Court, much as he coveted the place. He was coming home to Kate.

404

He scrambled out of the car and walked towards her. She smiled at him and held out her hand. He took it, a little hurt that she hadn't offered to kiss him; but perhaps she was afraid of giving him her cold.

'James is watching,' she hissed. 'Please be careful.'

'This was my room,' James said, resting Peter's bag on the wooden blanket box at the end of the high single bed. 'Do you remember?'

'Very well.' He remembered the contents rather than the room itself: the Fidelity record player, the Philips tape recorder, the shelf full of the expensive Airfix models that Ralph Salperton made. 'You used to climb out of that window, didn't you? Your secret exit.'

'Christ, yes. Down the drainpipe to the end of the terrace. And at night-time, too. I must have been mad.'

Peter looked out of the window. It was already beginning to get dark. The bedroom, which was above part of the drawing room, faced south. Immediately below was the terrace and the swimming pool. The pool was sheeted over with blue plastic, and the ragged box hedges around the sides away from the house were now nearly six feet high. Beyond the pool, the lawn stretched past the oak tree to the shrubbery that screened the main road. The grass was smeared with dark drifts of dead leaves. It was almost as unkempt as the lawn at Abbotsfield had been.

The room was very cold. He rested his hand on a new, unpainted radiator beneath the window. It was off.

James joined him by the window. He was dressed for the country in a baggy Guernsey above green corduroy trousers. 'The garden needs a hell of a lot of work,' he said. 'We'll need to reline the pool. It hasn't been used for years.'

'You sound almost cheerful about it.'

'In a way I'm looking forward to it. This place has a lot of happy memories, and I'd like to see it looking straight again.'

'That's understandable.' Peter thought of his distaste for 29 Champney Road. 'You were lucky to grow up here.'

'I know.' James turned away. 'Your bathroom's through that door. I should warn you, things are still rather primitive. We haven't really sorted out the central heating yet.'

'I hope my coming hasn't put you out too much.'

'Not at all.' James smiled. 'The boot's on the other foot. I'm extraordinarily grateful to you. It's not just the book, either. It's a pleasure to have you. Kate feels the same.'

For an instant Peter was almost taken in – by the smile, the welcoming words and, most of all, the tone of voice. He reminded himself of the five bruises on Kate's arm.

'Do you want to put your car under cover?' James went on. 'I need to put ours away as well. There's just time before tea. And I can show you what I'm planning to do with the stableyard.'

They went down the uncarpeted stairs. Some of the treads were new.

'Woodworm,' James said. 'The whole place was riddled with it. The carpenters are still working in the attics.'

'By the way, I stopped off in Abbotsfield before I

came here,' Peter said. 'There was an old man in the church who sent his regards to you. Said his name was Bert.'

'Bert Nimp? Dreadful little man.'

'I wondered if it was him. He's changed, hasn't he?'

James opened the front door. 'Not in some ways. He's as nosy as ever. I bet he makes an excuse to come up here in the next few days. He likes to keep tabs on me and Kate. Just doing his job.'

'At his age? What does he do?'

'He's the Abbotsfield correspondent of the *Paulstock Guardian*. It gives him a licence to pry.'

'He's a journalist, you mean?'

'That makes him sound misleadingly professional.' James grinned. 'He's just a gossip who occasionally gets paid for it. You remember where the yard is? If you drive the car round, I'll go on and open the gates.'

Peter gave James a moment's start and then followed the drive round the north end of the house. The black gates to the stableyard were beyond the kitchen wing.

The Escort bumped across cobbles with dead and dying weeds growing in the cracks. Once the yard had been full of pigeons. Peter edged the car alongside a beige Range Rover. On his left were two of the kitchen windows. Kate had the lights on. He saw her for a moment – reaching up to take a plate from the top shelf of the dresser; her hair glowed like gold. The doors of the coachhouse stood open.

James was waiting by the Range Rover. He pointed at the coachhouse. 'You can drive straight in,' he shouted.

The Escort's engine sounded very loud in the enclosed space. The builders had stacked scaffolding and planks along one wall of the coachhouse and parked a cement mixer and a couple of wheelbarrows against another; and still there would have been room for a small lorry. Peter climbed out of the car. The building was lit by a single unshaded bulb. Above his head were dusty rafters. The flagged floor was gritty with sand.

'My idea's that we turn this into staff accommodation,' James said. 'Just the coachhouse, that is. There's room to stick in another floor. Ideal for a married couple.'

'What else are you going to do?'

'We'll probably keep a couple of looseboxes. The others can be storerooms or something. And we'll convert the open barn into garages. Hang on a moment. I'll just put the Range Rover under cover.'

Left to himself, Peter glanced at the kitchen windows. Kate was no longer in sight. He wandered across the yard and into the open barn, which was directly opposite the kitchen. If they cleared out the rubbish, they would have enough space for three or four cars.

The Range Rover's engine fired, and its headlights cut across the yard and lit the interior of the coachhouse. James began to manoeuvre expertly, if noisily, in the limited space available. Perhaps he was sufficiently adolescent to want to show off his driving skills.

Determined not to be impressed, Peter turned his back on the yard and examined the rubbish in the barn. There was enough light to identify most of the larger objects heaped against the rear wall, despite the film of dirt that covered them: a lawn mower of antique design; a leather sofa that was in the process of disgorging its horsehair stuffing; a cast-iron garden table; a two-light casement window frame without any glass in it; an immense scythe entangled with a cartwheel that had lost most of its spokes; and, propped against a tall cupboard without a door, a row of rusting, six-inch spikes that might once have lined the top of a gate.

Did the Salpertons never throw anything away? He saw a stack of yellowing newspapers on one of the cupboard shelves and wondered how old they were. He stretched out his hand towards the pile.

The engine note changed: the roar modulated into a whine as the revs increased. Peter glanced over his shoulder.

Time dissolved and reformed itself on a different scale. He would not have believed that a couple of seconds could be so crowded with sensations.

The Range Rover backed towards him at speed. He saw dazzling blocks of colour: the red tail-lights and the white reversing ones. The kitchen door was ajar and Kate stood on the step. Her mouth gaped. White teeth. Shouting or screaming? Kate darling. Poor Kate. The barn filled with noise. It grew darker. Dead leaves swirled in the air. They danced in the blue-grey fumes from the exhaust.

He jumped to his right. He knew that he had leaped too late. He saw his body with a prophetic clarity. It was as though his consciousness had already parted company with it. He saw flesh and bone crushed between the wall and the Range Rover. He saw his body impaled on the spikes.

And this, he thought, is death.

Nineteen

'My dear chap,' James said. 'You were quite safe. I could see you all the time.'

'Sorry.' Peter gripped the arm of the sofa and pulled himself up. The Range Rover had stopped at least four feet away from him. 'I suppose I overreacted.'

Kate ran into the barn. 'Are you all right?'

'Really, I'm fine.' Peter forced a smile.

She rounded on James. 'What the hell were you doing? Why were you going so fast?'

'It didn't seem fast to me, darling. You forget: I've been driving around this yard since I was fifteen.'

'But you could have killed him.'

'Rubbish, darling.' His voice was amused and a little scornful. 'I knew that Peter was there. You don't think I'd reverse without looking where I was going, do you?'

Peter was trying to brush the dirt off his trousers. The handle of the lawn mower had grazed his left cheek. His hands were trembling.

'It was all my fault,' he muttered. 'I panicked. But there's no harm done.'

'You see,' James said to Kate. 'He's quite undamaged.'

She ignored him. 'Are you really okay?' she said to Peter. 'Would you like a drink or something?'

'I'd prefer to wash my hands and have a cup of tea.' Peter was surprised that his voice sounded so normal. What he really wanted was a hot bath and a large whisky.

'Right.' James locked the Range Rover. 'Tea in the drawing room?' he said to Kate. 'I'll remind Peter where the lavatory is.'

James closed and bolted the gates of the stableyard. They went into the house by the back door, which opened on to a small scullery. Beyond the scullery was the kitchen itself. It was large, clean and well-equipped by the standards of twenty years before.

'I put the champagne you brought in the fridge,' Kate said to Peter. Her cold sounded much worse than it had been yesterday. She pushed back her hair in a weary gesture that reminded him of Barbara Molland in the kitchen at Abbotsfield Vicarage. 'I thought perhaps we could have it this evening.'

'Super idea,' James said. 'This way, Peter.'

The cloakroom was off the hall, between the stairs and the door to the study. The walls were unpainted plaster: pink and almost silken to the touch. The lavatory was old – probably Victorian, with a massive wooden seat – but the washbasin was new, as was the plumbing.

As he washed his hands he glanced at himself in the mirror. The graze, a red smudge along the cheekbone, was barely visible. His face looked tired but otherwise quite normal: not the face of a man who has just escaped death. The very idea seemed bizarre and fanciful. True, Kate was scared of James; and perhaps she had good reason to be. But there was a wide gap between a bullying husband and a man who was prepared to kill on impulse. And of course James had stopped well clear of where Peter had been standing.

On the other hand, James might have suddenly

noticed that Kate was watching and lost his nerve at the last possible moment.

Kate was alone in the drawing room. She was sitting on a low stool and staring at the pale flames of a newly lit fire. The curtains had already been drawn across the windows. The room gave an impression of harmony – the accidental harmony that unrelated fabrics and pieces of furniture sometimes achieve if they are left to grow old and shabby together; the effect would have been welcoming if only the temperature had been a little higher. Peter noticed that *The Babylon Baby* was on a table at the end of the sofa. Kate stood up and came towards him.

'James has gone to get some logs.' Her fingertips touched his arm. She glanced at the door, which was still a few inches ajar. 'He won't be long.' She positioned herself so that she could cover the hall and lowered her voice to a whisper. 'Peter, you've got to make some excuse and leave.'

He shook his head.

'You must. Please, Peter – for my sake.'

'If you ask me, James was just showing off his driving. I honestly don't think he meant to –'

'You didn't see his face when he got out of the Range Rover. Thank God I opened the door. I think that's the only reason he braked.'

'I can't believe he'd run such a risk.'

'He's done it before, hasn't he?'

Kate stared at him, her face pinched with fear. Peter didn't want to believe her. But if they were right about James, he wasn't afraid of taking risks or acting on impulse. Success in the past must have boosted his confidence and perhaps had made him reckless. Nothing had ever gone seriously wrong for him. Richard was dead; by falling under a taxi Hugo Mannering had lost the part of Darcy; it was true that Ursula had got off lightly with two broken ribs, but James had lost nothing by trying to kill her. They seemed to be three unconnected accidents, and no one could prove otherwise.

'In any case why should he do it?' Peter said. 'He can't know about Richard's letter and *The Secret History*.' He hesitated, not wanting to appear presumptuous. 'And it can't be because of us. We've done nothing.'

'Except meet last night.'

'He can't have found out about that. He was at a dinner.'

'So he said. Anyway, he might have had me followed.' Her eyes widened. She shot away from the door and sat down beside the teatray, which was on a table to the right of the fireplace. 'The tea's Assam. Trumper's, of course: James gets an unlimited supply. Would you like milk or sugar?'

'A dash of milk, please.'

Peter sat down in a low armchair with a deep seat. A moment later, James shouldered open the door. He dumped the basket of logs on the hearth and grunted with relief.

'Wood fires are very picturesque but by God they mean a lot of work.' He tossed a log on to the flames and turned to Peter. 'How are you feeling now?'

'Never better.'

'That's a relief. I'd hate to lose my ghost.'

James sprawled on the long sofa and flashed the

smile at Kate as he stirred his tea. Kate smiled back. The strain between them seemed to have vanished. Everything was perfect: the perfect married couple at home with their old friend, the perfect ghost.

'How's your cold?' James said.

'Congealing. I can't smell a thing, and I think I'm losing my sense of taste.' She blew her nose. 'By the way, did you remember to unload the word-processor?'

He nodded. 'Sorry – I should have mentioned: I put it in the dining room. You don't mind if we eat in the kitchen while Peter's here, do you? I'm sure he won't mind.'

'If anything it makes life easier. Less fetching and carrying. And it's warmer, too.'

At that moment the phone began to ring.

'I'll get it.' James went into the hall, leaving the door ajar. Peter and Kate glanced at each other. 'Hello,' they heard him say with professional warmth. 'How nice to hear from you again. How are you?'

'The study's uninhabitable at the moment,' Kate said in a loud, cold-sodden voice. 'The builders took out the old window frame on the day the suppliers were meant to deliver the new one. But the new window never turned up, so we'll be stuck with corrugated iron and plywood until the middle of January.'

Peter made an effort to follow her lead. 'From what I remember, the dining room's a nicer room to work in.'

'It'll certainly give you more space to spread yourselves. Caliban takes up quite a lot of room, what with the printer and everything.'

They ran out of conversation. Kate blew her nose

again. In the hall, James was saying goodbye. He grinned at Peter when he came back into the room.

'What did I tell you?' he said. 'That was Bert Nimp.'

'What did he want?' Kate asked.

'In theory he wants an interview for a feature he's planning: how Darcy spends his Christmas, that sort of thing. In practice, of course, he just wants to satisfy his curiosity. I said he could come over tomorrow morning.'

Kate raised her eyebrows. 'I'd have expected him to want to go to church.'

'He will – he said he'd go to the eight o'clock communion, instead.' James chuckled, and imitated Mr Nimp's high, wheezing voice with unexpected accuracy. '"An early start is a small sacrifice for me to make. I can't tell you how much I'm looking forward to renewing our acquaintanceship, Mr Salperton."'

'Why do you bother?' Peter said.

James shrugged. 'It's all publicity. And there's a lot to be said for keeping the locals happy. After all, this is my home now.'

My home? Not Kate's as well?

'He'll come over at about eleven.' James glanced at Kate. 'I said we'd give him coffee. Is that all right, darling?'

'Of course. He won't want to see me, will he?'

'Not if you don't want to.' James finished his tea and passed his cup to Kate. 'I suppose we should discuss the book.'

'I've done the first chapter,' Peter said.

'Kate told me. That's quick work. Incidentally, I'm sorry I wasn't in when you phoned last night.'

Peter wondered if there had been a slight hesitation before the word 'phoned'. 'It's a little over four thousand words. Only a first draft, of course.'

'So what's the drill? Do you want me to read what you've done and suggest revisions before we move on?'

'It's up to you, really. If you want we could get chapter one exactly as you'd like it before we do anything else.'

'But you wouldn't advise it?'

'I think it would be better to carry on.' Peter put down his teacup. 'By all means read what I've done and comment on it. But I'm not sure we can afford the luxury of producing a clean copy at this stage. Not with this deadline hanging over us.'

Kate's teaspoon chinked against her cup. Deadline, Peter thought, had been an unfortunate word to choose.

'I take your point,' James said. 'You think we should incorporate all the revisions once we've finished the first draft?'

'It'll save time in the long run. It shouldn't take too long if we use the word-processor for the rest of the book.'

'I can't wait to read what you've written.' Yet again James smiled – this time at them both, as if inviting them to share the anticipation he felt. 'I imagine it'll be rather like catching a glimpse of one's reflection in a shop window. You know the feeling: is this really me?'

The remark was an unusually perceptive one for James; perhaps he had borrowed it from someone else. But his pleasure at the prospect of a prolonged bout of narcissism was entirely characteristic.

'Do you mind if I make a start after tea?' he went on. 'Where's the manuscript?'

'Upstairs.' Peter made a move to stand up, but James waved him back to his chair.

'No hurry. Let's finish our tea.'

'I hate these winter afternoons,' Kate said with sudden violence. 'It gets dark so quickly.'

'I used to like the long, dark evenings.' James grinned. 'Just right for playing Murder.'

When the phone began to ring, Ginny Salperton was sitting very, very still.

She welcomed the interruption. She was in bed, with her back against the wall and David's blue towelling robe draped round her shoulders. She hadn't moved for fifteen minutes, and every muscle in her body seemed to ache with the strain. The Rioja they had drunk with lunch had left her with a dry mouth and a headache. It was only five o'clock but she would have liked to curl up and go to sleep.

David put down his sketchbook and looked round the room for the cordless phone.

'I think it's under the bed,' she said. 'Have I got to stay like this for much longer?'

'Relax. You're all in. We'll carry on tomorrow.'

She stretched her arms and then slithered down the bed. She closed her eyes.

David answered the phone. 'Yes, she's here. One moment.'

Ginny sat up. He passed her the handset.

'Hello,' she said.

'Ginny? Is that you? It's me.' Ralph's voice was faint and barely recognizable.

'What's wrong?'

'Damn silly. Tripped on that mat in the hall. Think I've broken something.'

The phone was in the hall of Wistaria Cottage. In one way he had been lucky. Had he fallen elsewhere, he might have lain there undisturbed until she had come to collect him on Christmas Day.

'Have you rung for an ambulance?'

He grunted, perhaps with pain. Then: 'Thought I might as well let you know while I was waiting. Your friend's number on the pad. Door's on the chain. They'll have to break in.' The voice rose in volume and pitch. 'Oh Christ, Ginny, it hurts.'

'Don't worry, Ralph.' She swung her legs off the bed and thought what a stupid thing to say: *Don't worry*. The dressing gown fell from her shoulders. 'I'll be over right away. As soon as I can. I promise.'

'Come soon,' he said, and put down the phone.

'He's hurt himself,' Ginny said to David. Frantically she broke the connection and punched in Ralph's number. 'Damn it, I'm getting the engaged signal. He must have dropped the phone. I've got to go.'

David scooped up her clothes from the chair and passed them to her. 'I'll drive you.'

'You don't have to,' she said, aware that she sounded ungracious.

'I'm less drunk than you are.'

In the end he did more than drive her. He phoned directory enquiries for the numbers of Ralph's next-door neighbour and Paulstock Hospital. By the time

Ginny was ready to leave, he had despatched the neighbour to Ralph's house and checked that an ambulance was on the way. He took the car keys from her handbag and led the way downstairs.

'Don't you worry, either,' he said as he started the car.

'I feel so guilty.'

'Don't be absurd.'

'If I'd asked him to stay with me over Christmas, this wouldn't have happened.'

'Will you marry me?'

'What?'

David edged out into the traffic. 'I asked if you'd marry me.'

'What a bloody stupid time to choose.'

'We want the A37, don't we?'

'Yes.'

Ginny thought of Ralph lying helpless in the tiny hallway of the cottage. Stupidity wasn't one of David's drawbacks. Like God's, his sense of timing was uncanny. He jumped a red light and cut into another lane. Horns blared behind them.

'Of course I'll marry you,' she said. 'Can't you drive any faster?'

Peter thought that James was trying to get him drunk.

He wasn't sure. The suspicion crept over him during dinner. James had given him more than his fair share of the champagne beforehand, and during the meal he kept topping up Peter's glass with burgundy. Afterwards he offered brandy, which Peter refused.

It was a long evening. James professed to be

delighted with what Peter had written. He suggested a few alterations and additions, none of them substantial. After dinner he and Peter went to the dining room and set up the word-processor and the tape recorder. Later they sorted through the material for the next section. James had already made some tapes to complement what he referred to as the 'documentary evidence'.

Kate was left to clear away the meal. She brought their coffee to the dining room but at James's suggestion had hers elsewhere.

'You don't mind, do you, darling?' James said without looking at her. 'We've such a lot to get through.'

'No, of course not.' At the doorway she paused. 'Have we any matches?'

He looked up. 'Matches? Why do you need matches?'

'For the gas fire upstairs. The automatic ignition doesn't seem to be working.'

'Oh, I see. I'll find you some before we go to bed.'

James bent his head over Peter's manuscript and pencilled a note in the margin. Kate, her face expressionless, glanced at Peter. She shut the door behind her very quietly.

It was cold in the dining room. Peter found it difficult to concentrate. At Montpelier Square, Peter remembered, James had not been particularly generous with the drinks. It seemed that he rationed even the matches. Did James want to get him drunk? If so, why? To make him vulnerable?

The phone rang while they were working. Kate answered it and called James out to the hall. He was away for only a moment. When he returned he was frowning.

'That was Ginny,' he said. 'Apparently Ralph managed to break his hip this afternoon.'

'How did it happen?' Peter asked.

'He slipped in the hall of his cottage. He's in Paulstock Hospital now.'

Peter muttered the conventional regrets. Then: 'Will you go and see him tomorrow? I suppose it's too late to go tonight.'

'Well, I offered to go, naturally.' James sat down. 'But Ginny says he doesn't want to see me. You know what old people can be like. They get their quirks and fancies. It's not a rational thing so it's useless to argue with them.'

Peter said nothing. It seemed entirely reasonable that Ralph should not want to see a man who had cheated him and who in normal circumstances treated him as something to be ashamed of. He wondered if there might be another reason: perhaps Ralph had guessed that James was not his son.

'Still, what can one do?' James opened a box file full of theatre programmes. 'Where were we? Nineteen seventy-four?'

Apart from a short break when James fetched another jersey from upstairs and Peter went to the lavatory, they stayed in the dining room for several hours. Peter transferred some of the new material on the tapes to the word-processor, editing and expanding it as he went. He found the work absorbing. Reconstructing James's life offered him a temporary escape from his own.

It was nearly midnight when James called a halt. They joined Kate in the drawing room. She was sitting with her feet up on the sofa, glancing through a swatch of curtain fabrics. The television was on, and the fire was now throwing out a strong, steady heat.

'It's sweltering in here,' James said. 'Do you really need such an enormous fire?'

'I was cold.'

'It is chilly.' Peter held out his hands to the fire. 'I know it's a mild winter but it's very dank.'

'Damn,' James said. 'I haven't shut the gates.'

'Need you bother?' Kate said. 'It's still raining.'

'I think I shall. We don't want any undesirables.'

'Have you had problems with security?' Peter asked.

'A few. We're quite isolated here. Ralph had a couple of burglaries, and he used to get the odd courting couple in the drive. Occasionally a motorbike belts up and down just for the hell of it. It's not going to get any better once people realize I live here.'

'The price of fame,' Kate said. 'James is thinking about installing electronic locks and an entry phone.'

'Well, it's not a bad idea. Either of you fancy a stroll down the drive?'

Kate and Peter shook their heads.

'I can't say I blame you. Filthy weather.' James fetched a Barbour jacket from the cupboard by the stairs, the cupboard where Mithras had ambushed Richard. He came back into the drawing room and lobbed a box of matches on to the sofa. 'There's a whole packet of them in there,' he said. 'Next to the firelighters. I won't be a moment. See if Peter wants some tea or a nightcap.'

The front door slammed. Peter sat down in a chair. Kate stretched out her hand to the television and turned up the volume.

'We've got five to ten minutes,' she murmured. 'Probably nearer five. Sometimes I wonder if he's got the house wired for sound. Don't laugh. I know I'm being paranoid.'

'I hope you are. What was all that about the matches?'

'He doesn't approve of my having a gas fire. It's one of those Calor Gas things. I had to buy it second-hand with my own money. He thinks fires in bedrooms are effete.'

'It wasn't exactly warm in the dining room, either.'

'There's no reason for it to be cold. Apart from his meanness, I mean. I'm pretty sure the central heating's working perfectly. But he won't use it. He claims it needs to be tested first.'

'You must be joking.'

'I wish I were.' Kate lowered her voice still further. 'You haven't changed your mind about going?'

'I'll go with you,' Peter said. 'Not otherwise.'

'Lock your door tonight, won't you?'

'But surely –'

'I wouldn't hear him, you see. I'm in the room that Ginny used to have, and he's on the other side of the house, in what used to be his father's room. We haven't slept together for months.'

The surprise must have shown on his face.

'Not what you'd expect from the perfect couple, is it?' she went on. 'I suppose it's all part of the problem. James is practically impotent.'

Despite his tiredness, Peter found it hard to sleep. The mattress sagged in the middle. The pillow was lumpy. His feet were cold. Worst of all, he was scared.

He had come up to his room soon after James had returned from locking the gates. A few minutes later, the others came up to bed: separately – first Kate, then James. Peter hadn't been able to lock his door because there wasn't a key. Instead he had jammed a chair against the handle. The chair would not make an effective barrier but he hoped that it would deter anyone who wanted to enter the room without making a noise.

The curtains were open but it was very dark. He had forgotten how black the night could be in the country. At intervals he slipped into a doze; but for what seemed like hours he lay awake and listened to the wind soughing in the trees and the rustle of the rain on the window.

The familiar thoughts rattled through his mind like clockwork trains on a circular track. At one moment the chair seemed a pathetically inadequate precaution, at another a childishly unnecessary one. He had so few facts to go on. Almost everything depended on hearsay, circumstantial evidence and the ranking of possibilities in the order of probability.

The accidents suffered by Hugo Mannering and Ursula Salperton might be no more sinister than they had seemed on the surface. It was a matter of interpretation; and Ursula, who hated James and had every reason to slander him, had done most of the interpreting. Similarly, the incident with the Range Rover might have been as innocuous as James claimed.

Peter was on firmer ground with James's behaviour to Kate. He had seen the bruises with his own eyes. He had no reason to doubt what Kate had told him about

James's threats of violence, his meanness and his domestic tyrannies; and some of what she had said was confirmed by his own observations. But it proved only that he was a bad husband: it did not make him a murderer.

Richard's death, however, belonged to a different category. *The Secret History* and the letter to Coleby made it clear that Richard had been expecting to meet James in the Mithraeum, and that he had intended to blackmail him out of Emor. Whether or not he had turned up, James had subsequently concealed the proposed meeting, though that was not necessarily a sign of guilt. Two small facts, however, if taken together, suggested that James had been at the Mithraeum that night: the raincoat and the nightlight.

Peter was sure that Richard would have stopped to pick up the raincoat if he had been alone. But if he had seen someone waiting for him, he would probably have left it until later. In the circumstances, he might well have considered it undignified to fish the raincoat out of the pond before the eyes of his greatest enemy. At the time he had been a counter-revolutionary Emorian nobleman, buoyed up by the importance of his mission, and the meeting in front of him would have taken precedence over everything else.

Nor was it possible that an outsider had been waiting for him. According to the policewoman, Richard had lit the nightlight; it was inconceivable that he would have gone ahead with the Mithraic initiation in front of a stranger.

Then what? Either James had already left when Richard fell down the steps, or he had still been there.

The first alternative was the less likely of the two: Richard had no reason to linger in the Mithraeum by himself; and blackmailers do not usually die completely accidental deaths just after they have blackmailed their victims. The second alternative did not rule out the possibility that Richard had fallen by accident; but it was surely more probable that James had pushed him, perhaps in a fit of rage; and in either case James had left him unconscious at the bottom of the steps with his face in a puddle of water.

It seemed equally certain that James had the strongest of motives: his vanity coupled with Richard's threat to expose him as a bastard. James's later career – from Hugo Mannering's accident to the bruises on Kate's arm – suggested that he was still capable of resorting to violence when he felt that his interests were threatened.

Was the chair a wise precaution or a foolish indulgence? Peter realized that his speculations had reached full circle. He made an effort to distract himself by thinking of Kate. His skin had tingled when she brushed his arm with her fingertips in the drawing room. This evening she had looked so fragile beside James. He tried to visualize her face but it kept turning into Richard's, which was strange because usually he found it hard to remember what Richard had looked like. The face became Kate's again, then Richard's; and then it darkened into a black silhouette on a silver plate. The outlines swirled and the silver rippled. Suddenly he saw the raven on the water.

A sound – on the landing outside his room? On the stairs? – jerked him back to consciousness. His muscles stiffened. James and Kate should have been asleep for hours. Peter lay without moving for at least a moment. His breathing was fast and shallow. He heard only the wind, the rain and the ticking of his watch on the bedside table. Gradually his thoughts began to run wild. He slid into a doze.

Seconds, minutes, even hours might have passed.

A faint, metallic rasp brought him awake again. He was sure that it had come from somewhere in or near the room. Was someone trying the door? He listened with all his concentration.

A creak. Once more his muscles tightened. It might have been the door handle or an unoiled hinge. Sweat broke out on his forehead.

It was hard to breathe. He felt as though a weight were pressing against his diaphragm. He had to do something. But if he moved, he would make a noise, alert the intruder. Besides, he couldn't move. The darkness pinned him down.

Why had James mentioned Murder in the Dark at teatime?

As the minutes slipped away, his fear ebbed a little. The sounds might be the product of his imagination. Or perhaps a draught was reponsible. Or the timbers settling as the temperature changed.

A soft thud destroyed these comforting speculations. The door hitting the chair? Fear paralysed him. Someone must be there. The long intervals between one noise and another suggested a stealthy malevolence with an infinite capacity for taking pains.

At last there came another creak – so distant that it might have come from the stairs. Peter waited.

His breathing returned to normal. He sat up in bed

and switched the light on. The glare made him blink. His door was shut.

'Is anyone there?' he whispered.

All he could hear was the wind in the trees and the ticking of his watch.

Twenty

Breakfast on Christmas Eve was not a comfortable meal.

Peter felt the strain in the atmosphere as soon as he came into the kitchen. It was nearly nine o'clock – in the latter part of the night he had fallen into a heavy but unsatisfying sleep. Kate was laying the table; James was slicing bread; and they had their backs to each other. As Peter came in, they turned towards him with a speed that suggested they were relieved to have a third person in the room.

'Good morning,' James said, glancing at his watch. He was wearing a dark-blue workman's jacket and faded jeans with a hole in one knee. He still contrived to look distinguished. 'How did you sleep?'

'Wonderfully, thank you,' Peter lied. 'I hope I'm not late.'

'It doesn't matter.' James nodded across the room. 'Kate slept in as well.'

'There's tea in the pot.' Kate wasn't wearing make-up, which accentuated her chapped nostrils and the dark smudges under her eyes. 'Or do you prefer coffee at this time?'

'Tea, please. Don't bother. I'll help myself.'

'I'm having a boiled egg,' she went on, passing him a cup and saucer. 'Shall I do one for you? James has already had breakfast.'

'Yes, please.'

'There's cereal on the counter.'

'Would you like some toast?' James said loudly, as if making a bid to win Peter's attention away from Kate. 'White bread or granary?'

Once the decisions had been made, Peter sat down and poured himself some tea. The breakfast service was made of delicately painted blue and orange china. It was a pleasure to use: a far cry from the chipped willow pattern he had at the flat.

'I've got a bit of a problem, actually,' James said in the same loud voice. 'The roof's leaking. The first thing I saw when I woke up was a great big patch of damp on the bedroom ceiling. It's a new ceiling, too.'

Peter tried to look suitably shocked. 'That's sounds serious.'

James pushed two slices of bread into the toaster with rather more force than was strictly necessary. 'In this weather it could be a major disaster.'

'Have you found out where the water's coming from?'

'The leak's above one of the dormer windows in the attic. It must have been coming in for a day or two. There's a puddle on the floor. I just hope the water isn't getting into the walls. I bet the builders dislodged a slate or two when they were doing the guttering. Typical British workmanship.'

'How long do like your egg to have?' Kate asked.

Peter smiled at her. 'Three and a half minutes, please.'

'I got on the phone to our builder straight away. He was most unhelpful. Said he couldn't come over till the day after Boxing Day.'

'You can't really blame him,' Kate said, addressing herself to Peter. 'After all, it's both Sunday and Christmas Eve. He's probably got better things to do.'

'I'm afraid I don't agree,' James said. 'The leak could well be his responsibility. If he's not careful, I shall think very seriously about finding someone else to finish off the house.'

'*Is* there someone else? I thought you said he was the only reliable builder in the area.'

James scowled at her.

Peter coughed. 'Surely someone must be willing to come out?'

'You'd think so, wouldn't you?' James said, temporarily distracted from Kate. 'But I've combed through the Yellow Pages. Either they don't answer or they say no. One bloke said he'd come but he wanted to charge me an exorbitant fee for the privilege. No wonder this country's an economic shambles.'

'So what will you do?'

'I can't just leave it for three days, not with the rain that's forecast. I shall have to sort something out myself. It's a damned nuisance but there you are. At least it's not actually raining at the moment.' James paused and cocked his head at Peter. 'I don't suppose you're any good at DIY?'

There was a crash of breaking china behind them. They swung round. Kate had dropped an eggcup. She stared at the fragments on the floor. The stem, which had landed upright, had snapped halfway between the cup and the base; and the cup itself had broken into three blue-and-orange pieces.

'Oh my *God*,' James said.

'No,' Peter said. 'Afraid not. I was never much of a handyman. I'm all thumbs.'

'I'm sorry.' Kate was still staring at the floor. 'It just slipped.'

'That breakfast set was my grandmother's,' James said. 'It's survived intact for sixty or seventy years. And now this.'

He knelt down and picked up the pieces, one by one. Kate backed away from him. The heavy taupe jersey she wore stretched halfway down her thighs; it made her look tiny, like a child in her mother's clothes.

'You could probably mend it,' Peter said.

'Perhaps. It wouldn't be the same.' As he stood up, James glanced at the saucepan boiling away on the hob. 'I imagine that egg has had a lot more than three and a half minutes.'

Peter got up and switched off the toaster. The bread had just begun to burn. James put the fragments of china in a saucer, which he placed on the dresser. Kate found another eggcup for Peter's egg.

The yolk was hard. While he ate Peter thought about the noises he had heard in the night and wondered what had happened to Kate. She looked as if she hadn't slept. The desire to help was so strong it made him physically uncomfortable. He had to find a way to talk to her. The only sensible solution was for them both to leave, and damn the consequences.

James was still talking about the leak in the roof. He was thinking aloud: about the old tin bath in the open barn, which if it were watertight might come in useful for catching the drips; about the incompetence and ingratitude of builders; about the possibility of claiming from his insurance company; and about the terrible consequences that might ensue if the water were left to find its own level inside the house.

Peter realized that for the first time James was treating him as a member of the family: he was still polite but he wasn't bothering to use the charm. Perhaps charm was wasted on employees. Towards the end of the meal, even the politeness was fraying: James hinted that Peter's inadequacies as a handyman were a sad disappointment to him, and made it quite plain, without actually saying so in as many words, that he expected Peter to spend Christmas Eve working on the book.

After breakfast, Peter offered to help with the washing-up; but James despatched him to the dining room.

'I'll call you if I need a hand upstairs,' he said, as though Peter had just asked if he could help him with the roof.

'I should warn you I've got a terrible head for heights.'

'Oh really?' James managed to imply that this was another of Peter's inadequacies. 'If I'm not down by ten to eleven, could you give me a shout? I'll need to get changed before Bert Nimp arrives.'

In the dining room, Peter switched on the word-processor and skimmed through what he had written yesterday. The words blurred on the screen. He wanted to talk to Kate, and he could think of nothing else. Through the open door he heard James moving about in the hall and on the stairs; it would be better to wait until he was safely up in the attic.

For over an hour Peter copied out old reviews: pure

padding, but who cared? Then he wound back the tape in the recorder to the beginning of an anecdote about David Niven. He might as well transcribe it while he was waiting. James had recorded the anecdote last night. It was neither sensational nor amusing: it was designed solely to make the point that David Niven and James Salperton had been sufficiently well-acquainted to share a taxi.

He smelled coffee and heard footsteps. Kate was standing in the doorway behind him. She had the pot in one hand and a cup and saucer in the other. He switched off the tape recorder.

'I thought he was here for a moment,' she whispered.

'Kate,' Peter said; and her name seemed the most wonderful word in the world. 'Someone tried my door in the middle of the night.'

'It wasn't me.'

They looked at each other.

'He made the coffee himself,' Kate went on. 'Usually he never does anything like that. He came all the way down from the attic. When he went back upstairs, I poured it away and made another pot.'

'I can't see him slipping us a dose of weed-killer.' Fear made Peter flippant. 'Someone might notice.'

'I feel sick all the time. Sick in my stomach.'

'Kate. Kate, dearest.'

She touched his shoulder, mutely accepting his right to use the endearment. Her unhappiness had made him miserable: now it also made him furious.

'This has gone on for long enough,' he said. 'We've got to get out of here. I'll look after you, I promise.'

'Don't let him get you up on the roof, will you?'

'Of course I won't. Will you come away with me? Nothing's keeping you here. We'd survive.'

'You don't know James. You don't know what he's capable of. I can't live like this for the rest of my life. So scared.'

She swayed on her feet. A drop of coffee spurted from the spout of the jug. Peter leapt up and put his arm around her.

'Come on. Something's happened, hasn't it? Tell me.'

He took the jug and the cup from her and put them on the table.

'Shut the door,' she said.

Afterwards she nestled against him and murmured something into his shoulder.

'What? I couldn't hear you.'

She raised her head and stared into his eyes. 'Last night,' she said. 'After you'd gone to bed – James tried to kill me.'

'Bloody stupid place to spend Christmas Eve,' Ralph mumbled. 'God knows how long I'll be here.'

He was in a large ward whose walls and ceiling were draped with Christmas decorations. Each bed had its own cluster of visitors. A colour television chattered quietly to itself at the far end of the room, near the window that overlooked the car park. Somewhere on the premises a brass band was playing carols.

'Mark you, there've been a few changes since I was here before,' Ralph went on. It wasn't easy to understand what he was saying, partly because his teeth were in a glass on the bedside table and partly because the painkillers slurred his speech. 'That was with a broken leg. The ward sister had a bloody great big moustache. In those days it was like being back in the army. No television, no anything. Just sit up straight, take your medicine and be grateful for it.'

'So it's more easy-going?' David said.

'Only in some ways. Not in others.' Ralph glared at him as if he held David personally responsible for the hospital's deficiencies. 'They won't let me smoke. Haven't had a ciggie since I came.'

'We brought you a few things from the cottage,' Ginny said. 'Do tell us if there's anything else you want.'

Ralph had been eyeing the carrier bag ever since they had come through the door. She put it on the bed and he pawed through the contents with the indecent haste of a child opening a Christmas stocking. His shaving things. Dressing gown and clean pyjamas. A jar of the powerful anchovy paste that he smeared in large quantities over his toast. A couple of newspapers. A box of chocolate fudge. Two Christmas cards from neighbours who had suddenly remembered his existence.

'You forgot the pot for my teeth,' he said. 'Don't like seeing them in a glass.'

'I'll bring it this evening.'

The strain of emptying the carrier bag seemed to have exhausted him. He sank back against the pillows. His face was grey, his cheeks sprinkled with silver stubble. He muttered something. His eyelids drooped.

'What was that?' Ginny said.

'Has James been to see me?'

'No. You said you didn't want him to come.'

'Did I? Well, I don't mind if he comes. It's up to him.'

'All right. I'll tell him.'

436

'Did you manage to lock up the house? A lot of thieves around at this time of year.'

Ginny glanced at David. Ralph had asked the same question twice before, once last night and again as soon as they had arrived this morning.

'Yes,' she said. 'The ambulance men didn't have to break the door down. Your neighbour had a key. The chain came off but David put it back again last night.'

'David? Who's he?'

David came closer to the bed. 'I'm David. David Quest.'

Ralph looked incuriously at him.

'You were going to have Christmas lunch at my flat,' David said. 'You, me and Ginny. Remember?'

'Turkey,' Ralph said. 'Crackers.'

'Cranberry sauce,' David said. 'Christmas pudding with brandy butter. We'll have to postpone it till next Christmas.'

'Mustn't forget the crackers. We always used to have crackers.'

'David and I,' Ginny said, enunciating the words very clearly, 'are going to get married.'

'Good,' Ralph said. 'A woman needs a husband.' The eyes closed. 'I think I'll have a bit of shut-eye now.'

Kate's body trembled in Peter's arms. He lowered his head and smelled the sweetness of her newly washed hair.

'I just wasn't expecting it,' she said. 'When I went upstairs I was worrying about you, hoping you'd locked your door. James turned out the lights in the hall. I heard him coming up behind me. I hurried a bit – didn't

437

want to have to talk to him. My door was closed. I didn't think anything of it at the time. But I'm almost sure I left it open. I just had my hand on the knob when all the lights on the landing went out. I was half-expecting that, of course. James hates wasting electricity. So I went inside and found the light switch. But it didn't work. He must have planned it so carefully, put in a dud light bulb or something.'

She rubbed her head against Peter's shoulder. The trembling continued. He tightened his arms around her.

'It was completely dark. He knew I'd be carrying the matches, he knows I can't smell anything with this cold. I tried to get out a match. It was the obvious thing to do, just what he planned me to do. But I was carrying your book as well and that made me fumble. Somehow I managed to drop the matches. Thank God.'

Peter felt her horror as his own. He tried to speak but the words wouldn't come. Murder, he thought: Murder in the Dark.

Kate put her arms round his waist and hugged him, as if to stop herself shaking. 'I bent down. I found some matches, but not the box. Then I heard something, something that wasn't the wind and the rain. A sort of hissing. Very faint, very steady. I wouldn't have heard it if I hadn't dropped the matches.'

Her hand moved down his spine. She shuddered. For an instant Peter felt incongruously joyful: Kate had come to him in her trouble; he was holding her in his arms.

'And I thought I heard his footsteps, too. Not outside but in his room, as if he were pacing up and down. Waiting. And I crawled across the floor to the lamp by the bed. Christ, it took ages. I kept bumping into things. And all the time the hissing went on and on and on. I found the lamp and turned it on. And just as I pushed the switch I thought that maybe there'd be an electrical spark but there wasn't. And then –'

'Hush now,' Peter said. 'It's all right now.'

It was all terribly wrong. So wrong that it could never be put right again.

'You know what he'd done? There's a rubber hose that goes from the valve on the gas cylinder to the ignition mechanism. It's held in place by a clip at either end, those ones with screws in.'

'Jubilee clips?'

'He'd just unscrewed one of them and pulled off the hose and turned on the gas at the cylinder.'

Peter closed his eyes. His mind filled with the glare and boom of a gas explosion in the confined space of a bedroom. A second-hand Calor Gas stove that was known to have a faulty ignition mechanism. A terrible domestic accident. An independent witness in the shape of Peter Redburn, an old friend of the family. Big black headlines in the tabloid newspapers. Old photographs of Kate at the wedding, and new ones of James looking harrowed by the tragic loss of his beloved wife. No doubt the insurance company would have paid for the cost of restoring the damaged room.

'I turned off the gas and opened the windows as far as they'd go. I locked the door. I couldn't sleep. I sat in my bathroom with the light on. And in the morning I had to nerve myself to go downstairs.'

'You should have come to me.'

She pulled a few inches away from him. 'Do you

think I didn't want to? But I didn't dare. *He* was waiting in the darkness. I thought I heard him moving. And I'd asked you to lock your door.'

Murder, Peter thought once again: Murder in the Dark.

'There's nothing we can do,' she said in a dull voice. 'Just wait for the next time.'

She was right. If he and Kate ran away together, they would still have to wait for the next time. They would spend the rest of their lives waiting. There was no alternative. Nothing they could say would impress a policeman or a lawyer. James must know that. It wasn't easy for ordinary people to disappear. James had money, determination and the confidence to kill. Ursula had said, 'James judges everyone by their loyalty to him.' Even if they were lucky, and James failed to find them, they would live under a sentence of death; and that would be no life at all.

'I can't bear it,' Kate said. 'Truly I can't. Darling, there isn't any way out.'

The blood pounded in Peter's ears. It was difficult to think in a connected way because of the pounding. Kate had called him 'Darling'. James had nearly succeeded in killing her. The raven on the water. Richard might still have been alive if Peter had not let him down. Treachery: 'That's a big word,' Ursula had said. The eternal blood friendship between the Gens Mollandia and the Gens Redburna. The motto of the Emperor's Luck Casino – and, indeed, of Petronius Redburnus: 'The gods help those who help themselves.'

'What is it?' Kate said, her voice high with desperation. 'Peter, what is it?'

He looked down at her. A terrible pity filled him;

that anyone should be so beautiful, so vulnerable, so unlucky as to be married to James Salperton. Her need for protection overrode everything else, even his fear. He kissed her forehead. The touch of her skin made the blood pound faster. He unclasped her arms and stepped away from her.

'What are you going to do?' she said.

He tried to smile. 'Don't worry.' His voice came out in a croak: like a raven's. 'Just stay there.'

'But Peter –'

He opened the door, slipped into the hall and shut the door behind him. He climbed the stairs. The house seemed very quiet. His feet fell into the rhythm of the drumming in his head. Up and up he went until he reached the top landing that ran from the main staircase to the head of the back stairs down to the kitchen wing. The door to the attics was open.

At the top of the stairs was a small landing. The pale yellow of the new floorboards glowed against the darkness of the old ones. Two doors, both ajar, faced each other. Peter pushed open the left-hand door and looked into a huge room that filled more than half of the roofspace of the main house. This had once been the games room. The billiards table was still there, shrouded with dustsheets. Otherwise it was empty.

He crossed the landing. The opposite door gave on to a narrow, badly lit corridor with three much smaller rooms, all along the left-hand side, opening on to it. The first one was empty.

James was in the second room. The single dormer window, which faced west towards the massive, flat-topped cedar of Lebanon on the lawn, was made up of two casements divided by a central mullion. Both casements were fully open. James was crouching on the sill. He had his back to the garden. Most of his body was outside the window. His left arm was hooked round the mullion. His face, his right arm and most of his shoulders were above the top of the window. On the floor below the window was the tin bath. It was surrounded by a damp patch that marked where the puddle of rainwater had been. A plastic bucket half-filled with wet rags stood beside it, and a long-handled broom rested against the wall.

Peter crept towards the window. His foot knocked against an empty paint tin. The tin rolled across the floor.

'Who's that?' James said. 'Kate?'

'It's me, Peter.'

James's flushed face appeared at the top of the window. 'I was right,' he said. 'A couple of slates had slipped down into the gutter. The gutter was blocked, which wasn't helping. The water was forcing itself up under the slates, as well as coming through the hole.'

Peter's hands were shaking so he put them behind his back. 'Can you fix it?'

'I've pushed back one of the slates and wedged it into position. It should at least help. The second one's more of a problem. I can't get a good grip on it – my hand's too big. Why don't you try? Your hands are much smaller than mine, aren't they?'

Peter moved closer to the window. The pounding in his brain had become a steady roar, like surf breaking on a shingle beach. Downstairs the phone began to ring.

'God, you're as white as a sheet,' James said. His

nostrils flared. 'Never mind – leave it. I forgot you're afraid of heights.'

The sneer registered in Peter's mind. He was grateful for it.

'We all have our problems,' he said softly.

'I'll give it one more try, I think, and if that fails, maybe you'd get me the toolbox in the coachhouse. A bit of leverage with a chisel might do the trick.'

As he was speaking, James was moving up to the gutter again. There was so much noise in Peter's head that he could hardly make out what James was saying.

He picked up the broom. The wooden handle felt rough and slightly warm. In the early days of Emor, he and Richard had used a broom to simulate the trident of the *retiarius* in their gladiatorial duels. *Ave Imperator*, the gladiators chanted, *morituri te salutant*. He hoisted the broom into the air and steadied the end with the brush between his arm and his body.

'I'm not in the least afraid of heights,' Peter shouted.

James stopped. His body swayed. The change of direction had thrown him off-balance. His left hand slipped a few inches down the mullion. The knuckles whitened with strain. His face, now frowning, appeared again below the top of the window.

'Well, in that case perhaps you wouldn't mind –'

Peter charged forwards. Not a trident: a lance. He rammed the handle of the broom between James's legs. The tip jarred against the crotch.

James screamed. His body arched away from the pain. His hands flashed downwards in an attempt to protect himself. He looked like an actor: a man pretending to be in agony.

443

The first blow for Richard. Peter pulled back the broom, ready to lunge again. *The second for Kate. The third for me.*

But once was enough. James fell backwards. His fingers stretched for handholds that were no longer within reach. One moment he was there, the next he had gone. It was as simple as that.

Peter heard a thud, then a scrape. The roof was steeply pitched and the slates were slippery with rain. James screamed again. The scream hung in the air.

Before it stopped, Peter dropped the broom. He clamped his hands over his ears.

The phone rang on and on.

Ginny glanced at her watch. It was nearly eleven. Maybe the three of them had gone to church in Abbotsfield. It was just possible, she supposed, that James had felt obliged to advertise his piety to the locals.

Four people were now hovering nearby, waiting to use the single payphone that the hospital authorities had provided. Every seat was taken in the reception area. The flower stall was doing a brisk trade. A posse of children had clustered round the Christmas tree just inside the doors. David caught her eye and smiled.

Five more rings, she thought, and I'll give up.

On the fourth ring the phone was answered.

'Hello,' Kate said.

'Kate, it's Ginny. I'm ringing from Paulstock Hospital.'

A pause. 'How's – how's Ralph.'

'A bit dopey. Is James around?'

'He's up on the roof,' Kate said. 'Mending a leak or something. May I take a message?'

'If you wouldn't mind. It's only to say that Ralph would like to see him after all. Between four and six this afternoon would be the best time, I gather. He's in ward seven.'

'Ward seven, between four and six,' Kate repeated. 'Right, I'll tell him.'

On impulse Ginny added: 'Do try and persuade him to come. They can't go on quarrelling for ever.'

'I'll do my best. Must dash. Bye.'

Kate put the phone down. Ginny shrugged and returned the receiver to its rest.

'How did it go?' David said when she rejoined him.

'Kate answered. She said she'd pass the message on. Frankly she didn't sound very interested.'

'Do you think James will come?'

'Probably. She was very brusque with me.'

'Did you manage to tell her we were getting married?'

Ginny shook her head. 'There wasn't time.'

'Don't leave it too long,' David said. 'The more people you tell, the less likely you are to change your mind.'

After a while the nausea passed.

Peter listened to the silence. The phone had stopped ringing. The blood no longer roared in his head. The top branches of the cedar swayed gently in the wind. He felt empty, yet the thought of food was repulsive; it was as though he hadn't eaten for so long that he had lost the habit of hunger.

His mind stirred. The lethargy lifted a little. He wondered what they would do to him. He must invent a motive for killing James that didn't involve Kate. He wasn't mad, so they would put him in jail. Perhaps they would let him write. Would Kate want to visit him? Perhaps she wouldn't want to. Would he even want her to come? The questions seemed as unreal as the prospect of prison itself.

James was a killer, Peter told himself; he killed Richard; he deserved to die; he had to die that Kate might live. I had no choice.

The words were just words. He said aloud, 'I love Kate', but even those words had lost their magic; they were merely a statement of fact, as unremarkable as the greyness of the sky. Had he killed for the sake of words like that? He wished – with a mild regret that he knew might later harden into remorse – that he had never come upstairs. He wished that James were still alive.

He bent down and picked up the broom. Would such a rough surface take fingerprints? He had touched nothing else, not even a door knob. He wiped the handle with one of the damp cloths and propped the broom against the wall. Even as he did so, he knew the effort was useless. He couldn't lie to Kate. He couldn't pretend to her that the fall had been accidental. When she asked what had happened, he would tell her.

He walked slowly down the attic stairs, along the landing and down the main stairs. Everything was the same as it had been a few minutes before. As he reached the hall he felt a draught of cooler air and heard a door close. Kate had just come through the half-glazed door to the garden. His stomach lurched at the sight of her.

She must already know, he thought. How she must hate me.

Kate darted forward and clung to him. The warmth of her body surprised him. Tears pricked in his eyes.

At least Kate was alive. Those words still had meaning.

'I thought it was you,' she said, and she dug her fingers into his back. 'Oh God, I thought it was you who fell.'

'Is he –?'

Peter stopped. What was the point of asking? James must have fallen thirty or forty feet; he must have landed on the flagstone path that ran along the west side of the house from the terrace to the kitchen wing.

She nodded. 'Poor James,' she said with a curious lack of emphasis. 'What a terrible accident.'

Their eyes met.

'I must tell you –'

She covered his mouth with her hand. 'An accident,' she repeated. 'You were –'

The doorbell rang.

Kate wrenched herself away from him. Her mouth was slightly open.

'Don't – don't answer it,' Peter said.

'If we don't he'll come looking for us. He'll walk round the entire house and look in all the windows. He's that sort of man.'

Peter belatedly realized who the visitor must be. Nimp the pink. Pimp the nink.

Suddenly Kate smiled. His astonishment was so intense that it stabbed like a knife through the anaesthetic of shock.

'Just follow my lead, my love,' she whispered. 'Trust me. It's going to be all right.'

Bewildered, he moved aside to allow her to pass him on her way to the front door. He felt incapable of deciding anything himself. She unlocked the door and opened it.

'Mr Nimp,' she said; and Peter knew by the sound of her voice that she was smiling.

Mr Nimp raised his hat. They shook hands. He advanced into the hall, plucking with arthritic fingers at the buttons of his tent-like overcoat. He wore bicycle clips around the cuffs of his trousers. He came to a halt at the foot of the stairs and peered at Peter, who was standing by the door of the dining room.

'This is Peter Redburn,' Kate said. 'The novelist, you know.'

'We've already met,' Mr Nimp wheezed, holding out his hand. 'I didn't quite catch – ?'

Kate raised her voice. 'Peter Redburn. The novelist.'

'The novelist, yes,' Mr Nimp said. 'We met in church yesterday.'

She took his hat and waited for him to remove the tweed coat. Underneath it was a dark-blue pinstripe suit; like the coat, it dated back to an era when Mr Nimp had filled a greater volume of space than he did at present. Peter smelled the hospital tang of mothballs. It reminded him of the clothes that he had found embalmed in the loft of 29 Champney Road.

'James is mending a leak in the roof,' Kate said. 'Come and wait in the drawing room and I'll let him know you're here.'

With a flick of the eyes she indicated that Peter should come with them. She allowed the two of them to precede her. Though the fire was out, the drawing room was warmer than the hall.

'You know what men are like when they're doing things like that,' she said in a clear, carrying voice. 'They lose all sense of time.'

'I hope I haven't called at an inconvenient moment.'

'Of course not. James's so much looking forward to seeing you. Look, I won't be a moment. Do sit down. I'll go and find James, and I'll fetch the coffee too. I've just made a pot.'

She slipped out of the room, leaving the door open. Mr Nimp, who was still wearing his bicycle clips, lowered himself into a wing armchair. Peter sat down on the sofa. The pot of coffee was on the dining-room table, he thought; and James's body must be more or less outside the dining-room window.

Mr Nimp and Peter spoke at once.

'A novelist, eh? That must be –'

'I didn't realize –'

'Please.' Mr Nimp waved his hand. 'After you.'

'I didn't realize –' Peter had been on the verge of adding, *You were Nimp the pink*. 'That is, I didn't realize you were a journalist until James told me. But I gather you're also an old friend.'

'Oh yes. I've known the Salpertons for over thirty years.'

'So is this visit for pleasure or for business?'

'Both, really. You live in London, do you?'

The conversation staggered on. It consisted largely of Peter's answers to Mr Nimp's questions. Suddenly Peter stopped in midsentence. There were voices outside.

James was talking.

'Anything wrong?' Mr Nimp asked, his eyes bright with interest.

Peter shook his head. It sounded as though James were at the other end of the hall or on the stairs – too

449

far away for Peter to be able to distinguish most of the words.

However, he recognized two of them: *Niven; taxi.*

'There he is,' Mr Nimp said.

'All right, darling,' Kate said loudly. 'I'll tell them.'

A moment later she came back into the drawing room with a coffee tray in her hands. She flashed a smile at Peter from the doorway.

'I expect you heard most of that,' she said to Mr Nimp. 'I met James in the hall and told him you'd arrived. He asked if you'd bear with him for another five minutes. He's nearly finished, and then he'll need to wash and change.'

'Tricky things, roofs,' Mr Nimp said. 'He'll want to finish before it starts raining again, I daresay.'

For five minutes they sipped lukewarm coffee and chatted about roofs, the unseasonably mild and wet weather, Ralph Salperton's accident and Mr Nimp's plan for a feature entitled 'A Celebrity Christmas'. This time Mr Nimp did most of the talking, replying to questions that Kate threw at him. Peter sat silently on the sofa and tried to conceal the shaking of his hands.

Kate broke into Mr Nimp's flow. 'What was that?' She glanced at Peter. 'That shout – was it in the house or outside?'

Peter frowned. His head throbbed. *Just follow my lead, my love.* But where was she leading them? *Trust me.*

'Outside, wasn't it?' He turned to Mr Nimp. 'What did you think?'

Mr Nimp moistened his lips. The tip of his tongue was still pink. 'To be honest I'm not sure where it came from.'

Kate stood up. 'I'd better go and see. I thought it came from outside.'

'You may well be right,' Mr Nimp said. 'On reflection, I think it did.'

Kate crossed the room and opened the French windows. Peter and Mr Nimp followed her on to the terrace. She turned right and walked quickly to the corner of the house.

And then – at long last – she began to scream.

Twenty-one

'I didn't know what to do,' Barbara said to Ginny; but her eyes followed the three men walking slowly down the sun-drenched lawn of the house in Lavender Lane. 'The poor lamb's had so much to bear. But Leo thought she should know.'

'I'm sure he was right.'

Ginny looked gaunt and tired, which puzzled Barbara. With all that money just falling into her lap, and David as well, she should have been on top of the world.

'Anyway, she insisted on coming back,' Barbara said. 'I must admit I was glad.'

'When's the funeral?'

'On Tuesday.' Barbara glanced at her watch. 'They're late. They said they'd be here by twelve-thirty. Not that it matters: everything's cold, so we can eat whenever we want.'

'Is there anything I can do to help?'

'It's all done.' Barbara waved a hand at the trestle table, covered with a white cloth, on the other side of the patio. 'I thought we'd eat out here. It's such a lovely day it seems a shame to be indoors.'

'It's very brave of you to have us all for lunch.'

'You and David were coming anyway, and Leo said that if I cancelled I'd just sit around and mope. Besides, I like family parties. The more the merrier.'

Simultaneously they picked up their wine glasses

from the wrought-iron table between them; their eyes returned to the men.

Leo was a little in front of Ralph and David. David looked ridiculous in a baggy white polo shirt and army combat trousers. As Barbara watched, her husband reached the three pear trees, heavy with yellow fruit, at the bottom of the garden. Ralph paused to light a cigarette. He dropped his lighter. David picked it up. Despite the warmth, Ralph was wearing grey flannel trousers, a striped tie and blazer with brass buttons and shiny patches at the elbows. Leo raised his arm, showing a dark smudge of sweat beneath his armpit, and waved to Barbara and Ginny on the patio.

'It doesn't feel like September, does it?' Barbara said. 'More like June or July.'

The patio was sheltered from the sun by clematis and vines but most of the garden trembled in the heat. On the wall behind the pear trees, the Virginia creeper, whose leaves were changing colour, gave off a glare that hurt the eyes. The trees and beech hedges separating the Quests' garden from their neighbours' gave an impression of rural seclusion. Only the smells and sounds belonged to a suburban Sunday: the barbecue next door, the chatter of a television, the splashes and shrieks of children in a swimming pool.

'You don't mind our bringing Ralph?' Ginny said.

'Of course not, darling. Why should I?'

Barbara did mind; but less so than she had anticipated when Leo had told her that David had asked if he and Ginny might bring Ralph to lunch. It was the first time Barbara had met him since the wedding of Kate and James; and she hadn't held a proper conversation with him since Abbotsfield. Seeing him now, she found it difficult to imagine his making a pass at her, and quite impossible to imagine her responding to it. When he had shaken hands with her a few minutes before, he had looked at her with the eyes of a stranger.

Ginny put down her glass. 'He's got very dependent on us since he came out of hospital.'

'I'm sure it's only temporary. Why, he's walking very well now. Soon he won't need a stick at all.'

'It's not that.'

'But he can't stay with you for ever.'

'He'd like to, given a choice.' Ginny stared at him. 'It's odd but he's really taken to David. Follows him around like a dog.'

'And what does David say?'

'He doesn't mind. He's got a nicer nature than me. He says that as long as he's got a studio with a bolt on the inside of the door, I can do what I want.'

'But – but you don't mean you're thinking of letting Ralph live with you? Permanently?'

'What else can we do with him? He's terrified of being on his own in case he gets mugged or has another fall.'

'Well, there's all sorts of sheltered housing –'

'That scares him too: living with people he doesn't know. No, we think we'll find a house with a granny flat. In Richmond, maybe, or Barnes.'

'Well, you know best. At least money isn't a problem.'

'No,' Ginny said. 'Money isn't a problem for any of us.'

'I only meant, you can afford to make all three of you comfortable –'

The doorbell rang. Relieved to be interrupted,

Barbara went into the kitchen. She wondered why Ginny was being so foolish about Ralph and so absurdly prickly about the money. A period of mourning was fair enough; but surely after nine months she should be able to settle down and count her blessings?

She almost ran through the house and opened the front door. Kate, with Peter just behind her, was standing on the doorstep. In the drive behind them was the silver Mercedes that had once belonged to James.

'Darling, how lovely to see you.'

Barbara swept Kate into her arms. It was only then that she realized quite how much she had missed her daughter. Kate and Peter had been in Ireland for just over three weeks, staying in a cottage without a telephone. In that time Barbara had had two postcards and one phone call.

Kate pulled away from her. 'How are you?'

'A little shocked.' Barbara inclined her cheek for Peter to kiss. 'Silly of me, but there you are.'

'It's not silly at all. It was bound to be a shock. But what exactly happened? Your letter didn't say.'

'A chest infection that turned to pneumonia. Leo's been marvellous. So helpful. I don't know what I would have done without him.'

'I wish we'd been here.'

'Well, you're here now, that's the main thing. Come along to the garden.'

Barbara led the way down the hall. It was wonderful to see Kate looking so well. And Peter too, of course. The troubles of the last nine months had finally come to an end.

'The others are already here,' she said. 'I hope

you don't mind: Ginny and David brought Ralph with them.'

'I don't mind if he doesn't,' Kate said.

Barbara paused at the end of the hall. 'There's one other thing – before we join the others. It turns out that your father never bothered to change his will. Not that he had much to leave. Still, it's rather embarrassing. I'm the only beneficiary.'

Ginny was the main beneficiary of Ursula Salperton's will, though not the only one. Ursula's death – on New Year's Eve, exactly a week after James's – took everyone by surprise.

The worst thing about it, from Ginny's point of the view, was the fact that she hadn't even tried to get in touch with Ursula after James's death. No one had. Ursula must have learned the news from a report in the press or on television.

She killed herself in the Manhattan apartment – put a gun in her mouth and pulled the trigger. She left a little note: *I can't go on. Sorry about the mess.* The media speculated that after James's death, she could not bear to live, that she needed him alive so that she could love or hate him. Ginny thought that the media were probably right.

The speculation was fuelled by the terms of her will. She left the Beak Street flat and £10,000 a year to the people who ran the Italian restaurant on the ground floor. Both the flat and the annuity were conditional on their agreeing to look after Ursula's three cats. The cats were to be inspected by a vet, whom Ursula specified, every two months. When the last of the cats had ceased to exist, so would the annuity.

She left £500,000 to the RSPCA and £500,000 to Hugo Mannering. Mannering, the man who might have been Darcy, said in an interview that he was immensely grateful and totally mystified; as far as he could recall, he had never met Ursula Salperton.

The rest of Ursula's not inconsiderable estate would eventually come to Ginny.

'Peter Redburn?' Ralph said as he shook hands. 'You're old Johnny's son, aren't you?'

His stick, which he had propped against the wrought-iron table, began to slide. Ginny caught it before it fell, and gave it back to Ralph.

'And you've married Kate now? Poor James. Well, well. Who'd have thought it?'

'It was Peter who helped to write the book about James,' Ginny reminded him.

Ralph picked up his glass. 'You showed it to me. Afraid I didn't read it. I don't have time for reading.'

The Man Who Was Darcy – the title was the publishers' choice – had eventually been published in June. Ginny suspected that Peter was responsible for the whole book; but the first third was written in the first person, ostensibly by James. It had sold well enough to make a brief appearance among the bestsellers. James's death had been good for business. The viewing figures for the last series of *Pemberley* had been thirty per cent higher than those of the previous ones.

'Poor old Johnny,' Ralph said. 'He was a good sort. One of the best. He was my best man, you know.'

Ginny glanced at Peter. His face wore an expression of polite interest. Nothing more. Since James's

457

death, they had met infrequently and neither of them had mentioned Peter's interest in their shared past. David said that Peter no longer had a reason to be interested. As for the other matter, perhaps Mary Salperton had been right all along: it was best to let sleeping dogs lie.

'I remember my father saying how much he enjoyed staying with you,' Peter said.

'I think lunch is nearly ready,' Ginny said. 'Shall we sit down?'

Barbara and Kate were bringing trays of food, crockery and cutlery from the kitchen; Leo and David were setting up chairs around the patio.

'At Carinish Court?' Ralph brightened. 'Let me see. He stayed with us twice, I think. Once with your mother. That was just before – that was with your mother. And once he came by himself. Had an interview for a job in our part of the world. Not that we saw much of each other. That was the time I smashed my leg.'

'Your leg?' Peter moved a little closer. 'That rings a bell. Was it in a car accident?'

'Where do you want us to sit?' Ginny said to Barbara, who was bringing a bowl of rice salad from the kitchen.

'Anywhere you like.' Barbara put down the bowl on the table. 'I thought we could just help ourselves and eat on our laps.'

'That's right.' Ralph nodded happily: he was safe in the past, or rather in the version of it he chose to remember. 'Your father was actually with me in the car. Just as well, as it turned out. It was pitch dark, as I remember. We came round a corner and there was a tractor slap in the middle of the road.'

'If you want to sit down,' Ginny said to Ralph, 'I'll bring you some food.'

'In a moment. Don't fuss.' Ralph's eyes, gleaming like the Ancient Mariner's, were still on Peter. 'I slammed on the brakes, of course, but it was too late. Car went into a skid – there was a lot of ice about that winter – and we ended up in the ditch. What a business. The car a complete write-off. Your father covered in bruises. And I had a broken leg and concussion.'

Leo bustled up to them with a wine bottle and a handful of glasses. 'Drink, Peter? There you are. What about you, Ginny? A refill? Ralph?'

Ralph held out his glass. Usually he drank very little; but he was now accepting his third glass. Probably the heat was making him thirsty, Ginny thought, and the wine was making him talkative.

'Come along, everyone,' Barbara said.

Ralph allowed Ginny to settle him in a chair. She joined the others at the table. Around the centrepiece of Coronation Chicken was arranged an array of salads.

Kate passed her a plate. 'We've hardly had time to say hello. How are you?'

She was wearing a blue dress that picked up the colour of her eyes. Ginny had last seen her at James's funeral, looking drab and washed-out. Now she gave off the sort of glow that health, money and happiness bring.

'I'm fine – how are you?' Ginny wondered if Peter were happy as well. 'Sorry about your father.'

'It was very sudden, by all accounts.' Kate's eyes drifted across the patio to Ralph. 'I wish I'd seen something of him before he died. Still, it can't be helped.'

'Darling, you mustn't blame yourself,' Barbara said

behind her. 'It was his fault, after all. Who'd like some garlic bread?'

Ginny filled plates for her father and herself. As she carried them towards him she saw that Peter Redburn had settled himself in the chair beside Ralph. Ralph waved his glass at Ginny. Between them, the wine and the company had made him more sociable than she had seen him for years.

'What's this about Hubert Molland? Peter tells me he's dead.'

It was impossible to mistake the satisfaction in his voice: Hubert was dead but Ralph was alive.

'Yes, he died last week,' Ginny said. 'I told you.'

'Did you? Oh well. Haven't seen him for years. He wasn't at James's wedding, was he? I can't have met him since that summer they came to Abbotsfield. Sometime in the early sixties.' He rounded on Peter. 'You were with them, weren't you? That's why your parents came down.'

'That's right,' Peter said softly. 'It was nineteen sixty-four.'

'Ah yes.'

Ralph drained his glass. Barbara came over to them with a freshly opened bottle. 'We were talking about that summer you came to Abbotsfield,' he said. 'Remember?'

'Very well.' The neck of the bottle chinked against the rim of the glass. 'Has everyone got all they want?'

'Thank you.' Ralph chuckled and raised his glass to Barbara in a toast. 'You remember how we caught James? The young scamp.'

'No,' Barbara said. 'I don't think I do.'

'You must. You'd been over at our place for the

evening, and I was driving you back. You were by yourself, weren't you? I expect Hubert had to write a sermon or something. Anyway, it was a super night. Bags of moonlight. Must have been well after midnight. And there was James as bold as brass with the vicar's son – what was his name? – at the end of the drive. What *was* his name, Ginny?'

'Frank Timball.'

'That's it. He had a motorbike, and he and James had gone joyriding off to Paulstock. Typical James. He was only about twelve.'

'Thirteen,' Ginny said.

'Thirteen, yes. Proper chip off the old block, eh? I gave him a thrashing of course, but I don't suppose it did him any good. *Surely* you remember, Barbara?'

'No,' she said. 'No, I don't think I do. Excuse me.'

Barbara went into the kitchen. A moment later, Ginny slipped after her. She was staring blankly at the open refrigerator.

'I'm sorry about Ralph,' Ginny said. 'I'd have stopped him if I'd known how to do it.'

'It doesn't matter.'

'He didn't realize, I'm sure. He's probably forgotten.'

'About Richard, you mean?'

'What else? His memory's getting very selective. He only remembers what he wants to remember. The nice bits.'

Barbara closed the fridge door. She had evidently forgotten why she had opened it in the first place. 'It must have been the same night.' Her eyes widened. '*Peter.*'

He was standing at the back door. 'Sorry to startle you. Ralph wondered if you had any tomato ketchup.'

'Ketchup?'

'He acquired a taste for it in hospital,' Ginny said. When she and James were children, Ralph said ketchup was vulgar and refused to allow it in the house. 'He has it with everything now.'

'In the cupboard underneath the microwave.' Barbara picked up the bottle of wine she had brought into the kitchen. 'I'll just see if anyone needs a refill.'

She went back to the heat of the garden. Peter glanced at Ginny as he crossed the room to the cupboard. She fancied that he was willing her to speak, to make the first move. For an instant she was tempted to forget her resolution and talk to him. Then it was too late: there were footsteps outside.

Kate came into the kitchen. 'We need some cloths, I'm afraid. Ralph's had a little accident.'

To Barbara's relief, Ginny, David and Ralph left immediately after lunch.

'He's a bit tired,' Ginny whispered to Barbara as Ralph, leaning on David's arm, walked down the path to the car. 'I think we'd better get him home.'

Ralph had spilled a plateful of Coronation Chicken over his trousers. Later he had managed to break a glass. Towards the end of the meal the vivacity had slowly drained away, leaving him flushed and bewildered.

Barbara shut the door and went back to the kitchen. Leo was making the coffee while Kate and Peter cleared away.

'What will you do after the funeral?' Leo asked. 'Go back to Ireland for a while?'

'It's hardly worth it,' Kate said. 'We'd like to settle down. It's about time Peter did some writing.'

'Have you decided where?' Barbara asked.

She knew that within reason money was no object. Kate had inherited everything that James had owned.

'Not yet.'

'But you're going to keep the flat?'

'Probably. I like Montpelier Square. And the flat's exactly what we need. It seems a pity to get rid of it just because . . .'

'I'm sure James would have liked the thought of your living there.'

'And we want a place in the country, too. Somewhere with a bit of space. Actually, Carinish Court would be ideal.'

'It's a lovely house, darling. But wouldn't people talk? They might think you and Peter a bit callous.'

'But that's silly. They wouldn't be so stupid, surely?'

'How about you two?' Leo said. 'How would you feel about the associations?'

'I honestly don't know,' Kate said.

'What do you think, Peter?'

He shrugged. 'I'd be inclined to sell it.' He glanced at Kate. 'But I'm open to persuasion.'

Kate nodded. 'Which is why we're going down there this afternoon.'

'You're going to spend the night there?' Barbara said, surprised.

'Well, it's the only way to find out if there are . . . associations. Yes, we thought we'd go down for twenty-four hours – come back tomorrow afternoon, ready for the funeral on Tuesday.'

'Shall we have our coffee outside?' Leo said.

'You go on,' Barbara said. 'I want to get something to show you.' She fetched a shoebox from Leo's study and brought it outside. She handed it to Kate. 'I wondered if you'd like that. Leo found it when he was going through your father's flat. It was at the bottom of his wardrobe.'

Kate removed the lid. Peter leaned over to see what was inside.

Barbara blinked back tears. 'You wouldn't have thought he was sentimental, would you?'

Kate lifted out the contents, one by one, and arranged them on the table beside her chair. A tin containing baby teeth – both hers and Richard's because there were too many for one child's mouth. A snapshot taken at Rosington School of Barbara with a twin on each knee. A Matchbox D-type Jaguar with chipped paint and only three wheels. A tiny rag doll, no more than three inches high, wearing tartan trousers, an orange jersey and a silly little pillbox hat made of plastic. A postcard that Richard had sent them when he was eight.

Peter stretched out his hand and picked up the doll. 'What's this?'

'I think his name was Angus,' Barbara said. 'He used to live on Kate's windowsill.'

'Did he?' Kate said. 'I don't remember. What's it got on its head?'

Peter took off the hat. 'It looks like the top of a bottle.'

'Oh look,' said Kate. She held up a little sandal. 'Whose was this?'

'I don't know.' Barbara felt the first tear rolling down her cheek. 'Yours or Richard's, I suppose. Damn, I don't mean to be so silly.'

Between themselves they always referred to it as the accident.

Peter sometimes wondered if Kate genuinely believed it had been an accident. In her case there was some excuse. She had no way of knowing what had really happened. She had a right to believe what she wanted.

Whatever the case, he admired her presence of mind enormously. As soon as the doorbell rang, she had grasped that Albert Nimp could be converted from a drawback to an advantage. She had needed to bend the truth a little to do so; but if she genuinely believed it was an accident her conduct was at least defensible. Without cost to anyone, it saved the living from a great deal of trouble. She and Peter had an alibi for the time of James's death; they were spared the raised eyebrows, the tabloid innuendos and the unnecessary attention of the police. In return Mr Nimp was given a rare treat by the small deception his unacknowledged deafness had unwittingly assisted. Personally it was a triumph for him; professionally it was a scoop; and he sold his exclusive reminiscences of James as a boy and James as a corpse to one of the Sunday newspapers.

Kate's innocent little ploy also made things easier for the police. The case was entirely straightforward. James Salperton was, perhaps rashly, trying to mend the roof after failing to persuade several local builders to come out on Christmas Eve. His wife, his friend and Mr

Nimp were all downstairs in the drawing room. Both Mr Nimp and Peter Redburn had heard him talking to his wife in the hall only a few minutes before. All three of them had heard the shout that James Salperton gave as he fell to his death. All three of them went out to the body, and the three of them subsequently stayed together until the police arrived.

Nor was it possible that an intruder had been involved. The house was locked up as tight as a drum; and everyone who had known Mr Salperton at all well could testify to the importance he attached to domestic security. The only recent fingerprints in the attics were those of the builders and James Salperton himself. The autopsy revealed nothing that was not consistent with the obvious explanation of an accidental fall.

The eight months before their marriage were a dreary time for Peter. Kate thought it better that they shouldn't meet too often. James's death, followed by Ursula's suicide and her eccentric will, had aroused a lot of interest; and *Pemberley* kept James's name fresh in the public's memory.

Peter almost enjoyed working on the book. This was partly because it gave him something to do, and partly because it made his memories of James easier to handle. Whether he wrote in the first person as James or in the third as James's biographer, the effect was the same: James was reduced to the level of a character in a book. *The Man Who Was Darcy* was Peter's creation. It was possible to imagine loving or hating or killing James Salperton only in fictional terms.

He cherished the memory of what Kate had done because it proved she loved him as nothing else could

466

ever do. Had she not intervened, he would probably have blurted out the truth to anyone available.

'I killed James Salperton.'

'How did you think it went?' Barbara asked as the Mercedes skirted the pond in Lavender Lane.

'Very well,' Leo said. 'All things considered.'

'I thought the chicken was a bit on the tough side.'

'It was beautiful.'

'And Ralph was a bit of a trial. Poor Ginny. Did she tell you he may come to live with them?'

'David told me.'

'I must say, I think it's most unwise.'

Leo shut the front door and put an arm round her shoulders. 'I just hope our children look after us in the same way.'

Barbara repressed a shiver at the prospect of an old age like Ralph's. 'Kate seems happy, doesn't she?'

'I shouldn't be surprised if Peter's just what she needs.'

They walked down the hall towards the kitchen. Barbara began to load the coffee cups into the dishwasher.

'I wonder if they'll live at Carinish Court,' she said.

'I don't think Peter wants to.'

'How do you know?'

'Just an impression. Anyway, I imagine his feelings won't have much to do with it.'

'What do you mean?'

'You can tell who wears the trousers, can't you? Wherever they live, it'll be Kate's decision.'

*

The fine weather had brought out the traffic. By the time they reached the M4 it was after four o'clock.

Peter was driving. Kate was looking through the invoices the Abbotsfield builder had sent to Montpelier Square while they were in Ireland. They had exchanged barely a word since they left Edgware. The silence had grown between them.

'It won't hurt if we just have a look at it, darling,' Kate said suddenly.

'It's up to you,' he said.

'What is it? You were fine this morning, and now you've gone all peculiar. Is it the idea of Carinish Court? We don't have to live there if you don't want to.'

'No, it's not that.' Peter pushed the speed up to seventy m.p.h. and pulled out of the inner lane to overtake a lorry. 'James wasn't my brother after all. He wasn't a bastard.'

'Peter . . .' Kate sucked in her breath. 'Let's try and forget it. I thought we had. In Ireland we –'

'Listen. Ralph was talking about the time he broke his leg. That was the time my father was there, when he and Mary Salperton must have made love. Ralph said he skidded *on ice*.'

'What's that got to do with anything?'

'James's birthday was in April, so he must have been conceived in the summer. If anyone's the bastard it's Ginny: she was born in November.'

Another silence stretched like a desert between them. Peter felt the first nibbles of panic.

Kate stirred in her seat. 'Well, all I can say is that Richard told me it was James.'

'Are you sure?'

'Of course I am. I suppose he must have misheard what Mary and your father were saying. He was up a tree at the time, wasn't he?'

If Ginny were the bastard, Peter thought, it removed the greater part of James's motive for killing Richard.

'Anyway, what does it matter if Richard got it wrong?' Kate went on. 'James wouldn't have known.'

'Ralph said something else. On the night of Richard's death he and your mother saw James with Frank Timball in the drive at Carinish Court. They'd been for a ride on Frank's motorbike.'

'When was this?'

' "Well after midnight," he said. It doesn't give James an alibi for midnight itself, but it's odd, don't you think? If he'd just killed Richard, you wouldn't expect him to go joyriding with Frank immediately afterwards.'

'It's not impossible, knowing James. Or they might have seen him on a completely different night. It's a long time ago. Anyway, what are you trying to say?'

'That maybe I got it wrong.' He glanced quickly at Kate. 'Maybe Richard's death was an accident after all. Tell me – why do you think Ursula left half a million in her will to Hugo Mannering?'

'God knows.'

'A sort of apology? She wasn't quite sane where James was concerned. She killed herself when he died. She attacked you in public. I wonder if it was she who pushed Hugo. For James's sake, of course, to make sure he got the part of Darcy.'

'It's plausible, I suppose. Darling, why don't we give this a rest?'

'No,' Peter said. 'Not yet.'

He swung into the outside lane to overtake a saloon car towing a small caravan. The road began to swoop down a long, curving hill.

'It's all over,' Kate said. 'I hate to see you worrying about it. We know that James tried to kill us both. That's what's important. There's no sense in regretting the accident. He got what he deserved.'

Did James deserve it? Everything rested on Kate's word. She might have made the five bruises on her arm herself; it was she who said that James had tried to kill Peter in the open barn; someone tried his door that night but it could have been Kate herself; as for the gas leak – had it ever existed outside her imagination?

'Anyway,' Kate said. 'It was an accident. *Wasn't it?*'

If it wasn't an accident, James had been murdered: and Peter had killed him.

And Richard's death – was that an accident too? What if James had told Kate about the midnight meeting with Richard? What if she had gone in his place? She was a Raven: her presence would have surprised Richard but it wouldn't have prevented him from lighting the candle or saying what he wanted to say. He was planning to blackmail Kate as well as James.

'*You get out of Emor or I'll tell Dad about you and James snogging.*'

Had that been the trigger? Perhaps money was involved as well, another lever for blackmail. Kate was never short of money at Abbotsfield, even though her father had docked her pocket money to pay for mending the picture frame. They hadn't gambled for real money until the second half of the holiday.

And then . . . ?

Angus's plastic hat. A bottle-top with a shield moulded in relief on its face; and on the shield were three wavy lines; and between the lines were minute red and blue fragments of something brittle and powdery. Sealing wax.

The Great Seal of Emor?

'Will you slow down?' Kate said. 'You're going so fast.'

Peter glanced at the speedometer. The needle flickered between seventy-five and eighty m.p.h. He increased the pressure on the accelerator.

Richard had taken the Great Seal from Kate's room. Kate couldn't have known that Richard had shown it to Peter. And Richard would have enjoyed producing it with a conjurer's flourish at the Mithraeum.

'By the authority vested in me by the Great Seal –'

A fight? A push? Perhaps an accidental fall. Perhaps Kate had stood there with the seal in her hand, looking down at him; his unconscious body must have been visible in the candlelight. The fall might have been accidental. But the fall hadn't killed him. Richard hadn't died at once. The raven had drowned in the water.

'Pull over,' Kate screamed.

He glanced at her. Her face was almost ugly with fear. 'I can't,' he said, which was true – the middle lane was blocked by a line of cars. And bearing down behind them was a double-decker bus, the sort that ply long distance between the cities.

'We're going to have an accident.'

'*An accident* . . . The coach behind them filled the rear-view mirror. The driver sounded his horn.

James's accident: she'd known from the start it wasn't

an accident. Everything she had done was designed to manoeuvre him into solving her problems with James: his meanness, his unkindness, his impotence, and his will to dominate, which was stronger than hers. Kate needed the comfort that money brings; she needed love; she –

'Look out!' Kate shouted.

A Volvo estate loomed in front of them. Peter braked automatically. It was travelling more slowly than they were; and like themselves it was hemmed in the outer lane by the continuous stream of traffic on their left. Behind them the horn of the coach blared imperiously.

All he had to do was stamp his foot on the brake. Make a steel sandwich with a filling of flesh and blood. The alternative was perhaps forty years of silence, forty years of secrets: each of them suspecting too much about the other; and neither of them daring to admit it.

'Pull over, for Christ's sake!'

Kate had her head below the level of the dashboard. Like the last trump, the horn behind them sounded for the third time. Nothing had really changed, Peter thought with detachment: scratch an adult and you find the child; scratch the everyday world and Emor is revealed.

'Peter – *please!*'

Suddenly the middle lane was empty of traffic. The Volvo swung into it. Peter followed. The coach surged past.

'My God.' Kate sat up. 'I was terrified. I really thought we were going to have an accident.'

'I couldn't find a gap.'

Peter pulled into the inside lane and cut their speed

to a sedate fifty m.p.h. His shirt was drenched with sweat.

'Can't we get off the motorway?' Kate said. 'It's much more fun by ordinary roads, and much less dangerous too.'

'Okay. There's a roundabout coming up.'

'It's not as if we're in a hurry.'

No, we've got the rest of our lives together.

The Mercedes rolled up the exit ramp.

Kate wound down her window. 'Do you remember the first time we came to Abbotsfield? In grandpa's old Rover?'

He nodded.

'And how we stopped at Carinish Court before we got there?'

'Of course I do,' he said. 'I wish –'

Peter stopped because he had everything he had ever wanted, and therefore nothing left to wish for. And it was exactly like being Emperor of Emor and having a fortune in sesterces: the power was no more than the power to direct a private fantasy for seven days, and the money could only be spent in the casino.

Kate brushed his shoulder with her fingers. 'I love you, Peter. Remember that. I really do.'

If you enjoyed *The Raven on the Water* look out for:

The Barred Window

Andrew Taylor

It is 1993 and Thomas Penmarsh has lived in Finisterre, the house by the sea, all his life, sleeping each night in the room with the barred window. He's only 48 but has been an old man since one evening in 1967 when he lost everything he valued.

However now his controlling mother has died and he is master of the house. When Esmond, his cousin and childhood confidante, comes to live with him Thomas is overjoyed – Esmond always looks after him . . .

But is Esmond all that he seems? And why is he so concerned that Alice wants to come home too? Darling Alice, who neither Thomas or Esmond have seen since that fateful night 26 years ago . . .

'A heart-in-mouth chiller of great power and subtlety'
Mail on Sunday

(Available from Penguin at £6.99)

READ ON FOR A TASTER . . .

One

'Do you believe in magic?' Esmond once asked me.

Assumptions are a sort of magic: spells to make sense of life or at least to make it tolerable. For example, I assumed that after my mother's death and the return of Esmond I should live happily ever after like a prince in a fairy tale. One man's magic is another's rational assumption and a third man's wishful thinking.

I lived happily ever after from my mother's funeral in May, when Esmond came back, until the end of September when I had my first intimation that something might be going wrong. At the time I was listening to Esmond and Bronwen, who were talking in the sitting room.

When eavesdropping, I always took the precaution of putting something on the floor. On the afternoon in question I lifted my book, a selection of Lorca's poems, from the seat of the chair and laid it on the carpet. No one had ever come in while I was on my knees but one day someone might; you couldn't be too careful, not where my cousin Esmond was concerned.

'I've just dropped my book,' I would say. Or my glasses or my pencil. 'Silly old me.'

The chair was a barrier between me and the door. There was a twinge of pain in my left knee and I felt very dizzy. I remember thinking that I was getting too old for crawling around on floors. I was forty-eight, which I know isn't really old. Most people would call it middle age. But I think that there was a moment in 1967 when I leapfrogged from being a young man to being an old one. I am as old as I feel.

I rolled back the corner of the carpet to expose a triangular section of broad oak floorboards. Part of a floorboard had been replaced by a fifteen-inch length of unvarnished pine. The carpenter hadn't bothered to nail it on to the joists beneath.

I levered out the rectangle of wood with my finger-tips. A spider sprinted away from the light. The bottom of the hole beneath was lined with wood-shavings and fragments of plaster. Tendrils of dust stirred like the grey seaweed in Blackberry Water. The hole was my private place. No one else knew about it. I kept private things there. Also, of course, I used it for listening.

I had not imagined the murmur of voices below: the other two really were in the sitting room. As a general rule they used this room only in the evenings. Still on my knees, I bent forwards with my head to one side so that my right ear was in the gap between the joists. The draught brushed my cheek.

'Has Rumpy had his walk?' my cousin Esmond asked.

'Oh, for God's sake stop trying to change the subject,' Bronwen said.

'You're making too much of this. Trust me.'

A spoon clinked and scraped on china. I guessed that Bronwen was stirring sugar into her coffee. It was entirely typical that she used the spoon as a pestle and the cup as a mortar.

'Had you any idea this was going to happen?' she said. 'You must have done.'

'It was always a remote possibility. No more than that.'

'You should have warned me.'

'Why? What good would it have done?'

'I like to know what I'm getting into, that's why.' When Bronwen was really angry, as opposed to merely tetchy, her voice grated like a grindstone on the blade of a knife. 'If you really want to know, I think you've been bloody stupid.'

'Calm down. We've got plenty of options.'

'If you ask me, it's time for us to –'

'Oh, I wouldn't do anything rash,' Esmond interrupted. 'Not if I were you. Is there any more coffee?'

'What do you mean?'

'Oh, you know. Thomas and I used to have a motto when we were children.' Esmond raised his voice and chanted: '*All* for *one*, and *one* for *all*. United we *stand*, divided we *fall*.'

'You bastard.'

I smiled.

After a moment Esmond went on: 'As a matter of fact, I think we've been rather lucky.'

'Are you insane?'

'Think of it like this,' Esmond said patiently. 'It's not so much a problem as an opportunity. But you haven't answered my question. Has Rumpy had his walk?'

'It goes on and bloody on.'

Esmond ignored this. 'I fed him this morning,' he said. 'He's got a good appetite for his age, hasn't he? But he also needs exercise. It's good for him.'

'Woof,' Bronwen said. 'Woof bloody woof. He can't enjoy life, can he? We should have him put down.'

'Rumpy? Oh no . . . it wouldn't be the same without Rumpy. You know that as well as I do.'

'He won't last for ever,' returned Bronwen. 'In my opinion, he's getting senile practically by the minute.'

'Aren't we all?'

'And sometimes he smells.'

'Nobody's perfect, dearest,' Esmond said.

I replaced the board over the hole and the carpet over the board. A moment later I was sitting on the window-seat with the book open on my lap. The sky was lined with banks of grey cloud; but between the banks were shreds of pale blue. Perhaps the weather was clearing. There were two cats in the garden.

The first of them was a regular visitor to Finisterre – an old black-and-white tom with a torn ear and a limp. The second was a new one; she was a young tabby, about half the size of the tom and far more cautious. And she was beautiful. I hated her more than the tom because in the nature of things she had longer to live.

I rapped on the window. If the tom heard the sound, he ignored it. Like all old cats he had long since come to the conclusion that he was invincibly superior to the rest of animate creation. The tabby had the grace to stop and glance round: but when she failed to identify the source of the rapping, she too decided that it was safe to ignore it.

I stayed on the window-seat for nearly an hour. The cats made cautious forays across the lawn. As far as I could tell their base was in the shrubbery; they were ignorant of what lay beneath them. If there was one thing I missed from my old life, it was my ability to deal with the cats.

The sun came out for the first time in three days. It

streamed across the sea and up the garden. The stepping stones across Blackberry Water gleamed like tiny metal studs. The blues and greens were so vivid that they hurt the eyes. The sun threw the shadows of the window bars across the carpet.

I counted the shadows. There were six bars and therefore six shadows, just as there had always been for as long as I could remember.

At four-thirty, Bronwen came into my room empty-handed. I was expecting my cup of tea. She never knocked; but she never took me by surprise either, because she made so much noise as she approached.

I coughed and looked at her in what I hoped was a meaningful way. 'Oh, I thought it was teatime.'

'Esmond says you're to have it with him today,' Bronwen said. 'He wants you in the study.'

I blinked at her. She was a big woman with coarse, dark hair and firm, almost conical breasts. The hair came down to her shoulders and smelled faintly musty. She favoured tight jerseys and short skirts. In Welsh, Bronwen means 'white breast'; but I imagine hers were sallow-skinned and perhaps hairy round the nipples.

'In – in the study?'

'That's right. Come on, I haven't got all day.'

As usual, surprise made me dither and dithering made me panic. I couldn't remember where I had left my jacket; Bronwen found it on the back of the door. I wanted to comb my hair but my hand shook so much that I had to give up the unequal struggle to produce a straight parting. When I mentioned my need for a clean handkerchief, she grabbed my left arm just above the elbow and pulled me to the door.

'For Christ's sake,' she said. 'It's only Esmond.'

She led me across the landing and down the stairs. Her thumb and first two fingers dug into my skin between the muscle and bone of my upper arm. In the hall, there were Michaelmas daisies in white vases. At the foot of the stairs, Bronwen released my arm and prodded me gently on the shoulder, as though urging forward a reluctant child. Her capacity for unexpected gentleness always disconcerted me.

I crossed the hall slowly – almost with pleasure. The sunlight poured slantwise through the fanlight above the front door. Esmond had had the floorboards stripped and returned to their natural colour, and he had brought a pair of Turkish rugs from London. Together with the glaring white of the vases and the pinks and purples of the Michaelmas daisies, the place was full of colour. *Mine eyes dazzle*, I thought. An irritatingly familiar quotation from somewhere: for the moment I could not remember the rest of it, but suddenly I was no longer happy. I knocked on the study door, and Esmond told me to come in.

He was standing by the window. With the light behind him he looked half his age. He was tall, with broad shoulders and slim hips. His hair was as thick as when I had first met him, and the few grey streaks seemed a sign of distinction rather than age. When I was with Esmond I felt smaller, older and uglier than usual: he always had the power to make me feel that I belonged to an inferior species. As a boy, I had never minded. I think I was flattered that Esmond should condescend to associate with me.

'I want you to write a letter,' he said. 'Sit down. We'll have tea afterwards.'

He nodded towards the desk. I sat down behind it in the green leather armchair. The seat was warm from his body. A sheet of writing paper lay on the blotter. I uncapped my fountain pen, which by a lucky chance was in my jacket pocket, and tried it surreptitiously on the blotter. It still had ink in it. I glanced at Esmond to see if he had noticed.

His hands in his pockets, he was staring out of the window. I waited, rolling the pen between my thumb and forefinger. The paper had once been white but had yellowed with age particularly around the edges. I remembered my mother ordering a ream of this letter-head from a printer in Kinghampton. *Finisterre, Ulver-combe, North Cornwall.* No telephone number of course – the telephone had been one of Esmond's innovations.

At first I had no objection to waiting. I liked being with Esmond and I liked being in the study. It was a well-proportioned room and it was pleasant to see it freshly decorated and the furniture gleaming with polish. In the old days, before my mother stopped using the study, she did the household accounts once a month sitting in this chair at this desk.

I waited for so long that I began to wonder if Esmond had forgotten me. That was when I really did stop enjoying myself. When I was young I used to have nightmares about Esmond's forgetting me; I still did, though less often. There were several variations on the theme. Sometimes, in the dream, I would walk into a familiar room – the nursery, perhaps, or our classroom at Bicknor College – and he would be there. My heart would jump at the sight of him – an unpleasantly physical sensation, as though the heart were literally trying to tear itself out of my chest. But Esmond's face wouldn't light up with pleasure at the sight of me, or even with recognition. He would look puzzled and irritated by the interruption: that was all. It was as if I were a perfect stranger who had no right to be there.

Sometimes in the dream he wouldn't even notice me coming in. Sometimes he would be with someone else, a friend. He would laugh at me, as we children laughed at cripples and anyone with a physical disability. All the different versions amounted to the same thing. The point was that Esmond had forgotten that we were cousins and friends: that he saw me objectively, with the cool and unbiased eyes of a stranger.

'It's the 30th September,' he said.

I wrote down the date. Esmond turned away from the window. He wandered across the room to the cupboard that filled the lower half of the alcove on the left of the fireplace. There was a row of directories on the cupboard. He ran an index finger along their tops and examined the fingertip as if checking for dust.

'My dear Alice,' he went on, still staring at his finger.

I waited, pen poised. '*Alice?*'

'Yes.'

'*Our* Alice?' Somehow I could not bring myself to say 'my'.

He nodded. 'Trust me.'

I wrote.

'Thank you for your letter. I was sorry to hear about your marriage. Of course I'm not upset by your suggestion that we meet.'

'Could you slow down, please?' I asked. The nib scratched on the paper and my fingers ached.

'New paragraph,' he said after a decent pause. 'However, I am not in the best of health.' I glanced sharply at Esmond, who still wasn't looking at me. 'I live very quietly down here with my cousin Esmond and his wife Bronwen. My doctor advises me to avoid travel – and indeed any excitement. So, in the circumstances, I must decline your kind invitation to come up to London.'

After 'excitement', I stopped writing and murmured, ' "Decline your kind invitation . . . ?" '

'What's wrong with it?'

'Would I say that? It's a bit formal, isn't it? A bit pompous.'

'What do you suggest?'

'How about, "So I'm afraid my coming up to London is out of the question"?'

'All right. Well done.' He waited while I wrote the amended sentence, and then continued with the letter: 'But it would give me great pleasure if you could come here for a few days. It would give us all a chance to get to know each other.'

'No,' I said. 'Please, Esmond – I don't think I could bear it.'

He frowned at me. I wrote down what he had said.

'Esmond or I will phone you,' he went on, 'in a day or two. With best wishes . . .' He paused. 'Yours truly, Thomas Penmarsh. That's all. You'll find an envelope in the second drawer down on the right.'

I opened the drawer. 'I don't understand.'

'You don't need to understand.' Esmond strolled to the desk. He picked up the letter and glanced through its contents. 'Trust me, eh?'

I took out an envelope. Before I shut the drawer,

I noticed a bunch of small keys, some with rust-streaked labels. Almost certainly the cupboard key would be among them. Esmond dictated the name and address – a private hotel in Earl's Court.

'Not an address that inspires confidence,' he said as he sealed the envelope. 'Come on. We'll have our tea in the sitting room.'

I felt myself flushing. I was embarrassed, and a little angry. 'Do you think I might read her letter?'

'Better not. Leave it to me. I don't want you to worry about it.'

'She might not like what we've done here. Shouldn't we have asked her permission?'

Esmond squeezed my shoulder. 'You mustn't worry so much. I'll take care of everything. That's why I'm here, remember?'

He dropped the letter into a drawer and moved towards the door. I stood up. In my haste to follow, I jarred my thigh against the corner of the desk.

'If you must know,' Esmond said, 'I think she's a bit strapped for cash. She's not looking for love, she's looking for a nice fat cheque.'

'Did she actually –?'

'You could read it between the lines.' He opened the door and glanced over his shoulder. 'It's a hard world out there. Lucky you've got me to look after you.'

The sitting room was a large room with windows to the south-west and the north-west. The tea tray was waiting for us on the table behind the sofa. I noticed with pleasure that there was a big plate of biscuits; I have a sweet tooth. We used the Crown Derby service. Only two cups had been put out, which suited me very well. It was quite a treat for me to have Esmond to myself – almost like old times.

He was no longer in a talkative mood. Having poured the tea, he sat in the big wing-armchair and stared at the fire. The new central-heating system at Finisterre was very efficient; but it wasn't cold enough to use it during the day, and in any case Esmond liked a proper fire.

I wondered if I had offended my cousin. I bolted down three Bourbon biscuits and drank the first cup of tea while it was too hot. The changes in routine had unsettled me. That and the news of Alice.

'A penny for them,' Esmond said.

'What? Oh, nothing.'

'Tell me.'

I scratched my bald patch. I had always found it difficult to lie to Esmond. 'I – I was wondering what she was like,' I said.

'Alice? We know she's mercenary. That's all that matters.'

'Yes, of course. I do see that. It's just that I'm naturally curious about her.'

'Naturally?'

'She's my daughter.'

'You're not the only one who's curious,' he said. 'No doubt it runs in the family. If you must know, she asked a few questions in her letter.'

I noticed that there was a tiny chip on the rim of my cup. My mother would have been furious. I heard the distant whine of the chain saw: Bronwen was busy – sawing seemed to give her pleasure. Someone nasty in the woodshed. My head began to throb and hum. I wished Alice were dead, like all the others.

'Questions? What about?'

Esmond took his time over lighting a cigarette. 'She wanted to know all about her mother, her real mother, that is. I think she may have heard something.'

I put down my cup, and stared at the sleeve of my jacket. I had lost a button from the cuff. In places the tweed was shiny with age and grease. My headache was much worse.

'Don't worry so much,' Esmond said, and his voice sounded far away but full of irritation. 'I'll look after you. You're quite safe.'

I shrugged.

'What you need is a bit of fresh air to blow those blues away.' He smiled and clicked his tongue twice against the roof of his mouth. 'Come on, Rumpy,' he said to me. 'Walkies.'

He just wanted a decent book to read ...

Not too much to ask, is it? It was in 1935 when Allen Lane, Managing Director of Bodley Head Publishers, stood on a platform at Exeter railway station looking for something good to read on his journey back to London. His choice was limited to popular magazines and poor-quality paperbacks – the same choice faced every day by the vast majority of readers, few of whom could afford hardbacks. Lane's disappointment and subsequent anger at the range of books generally available led him to found a company – and change the world.

'We believed in the existence in this country of a vast reading public for intelligent books at a low price, and staked everything on it'
Sir Allen Lane, 1902–1970, founder of Penguin Books

The quality paperback had arrived – and not just in bookshops. Lane was adamant that his Penguins should appear in chain stores and tobacconists, and should cost no more than a packet of cigarettes.

Reading habits (and cigarette prices) have changed since 1935, but Penguin still believes in publishing the best books for everybody to enjoy. We still believe that good design costs no more than bad design, and we still believe that quality books published passionately and responsibly make the world a better place.

So wherever you see the little bird – whether it's on a piece of prize-winning literary fiction or a celebrity autobiography, political tour de force or historical masterpiece, a serial-killer thriller, reference book, world classic or a piece of pure escapism – you can bet that it represents the very best that the genre has to offer.

Whatever you like to read – trust Penguin.